Sons and Daughters of Ease and Plenty

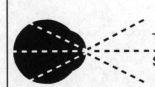

This Large Print Book carries the
Seal of Approval of N.A.V.H.

Sons and Daughters of Ease and Plenty

Ramona Ausubel

THORNDIKE PRESS
A part of Gale, Cengage Learning

GALE
CENGAGE Learning®

Farmington Hills, Mich • San Francisco • New York • Waterville, Maine
Meriden, Conn • Mason, Ohio • Chicago

GALE
CENGAGE Learning®

LIBRARY OF CONGRESS CATALOGING-IN-PUBLICATION DATA

Names: Ausubel, Ramona, author.
Title: Sons and daughters of ease and plenty / by Ramona Ausubel.
Description: Large print edition. | Waterville, Maine : Thorndike Press, 2016. |
    Series: Thorndike Press large print reviewers' choice
Identifiers: LCCN 2016028659| ISBN 9781410493835 (hardcover) | ISBN 1410493830
    (hardcover)
Subjects: LCSH: Upper class families—New England—Fiction. | Children of the
    rich—Fiction. | Social status—Fiction. | Large type books. | Domestic fiction.
Classification: LCC PS3601.U868 S66 2016b | DDC 813/.6—dc23
LC record available at https://lccn.loc.gov/2016028659

Published in 2016 by arrangement with Riverhead Books, an imprint of Penguin Publishing Group, a division of Penguin Random House LLC

Printed in Mexico
1 2 3 4 5 6 7 20 19 18 17 16

For Ned and Hank
I wish I had known you longer

1976

Summer fattened everybody up. The family buttered without reserve; pie seemed to be everywhere. They awoke and slept and awoke in the summerhouse on the island, ate all their meals on the porch while the sun moved across their sky. They looked out at the saltwater cove and watched the sailboats skim and tack across the blue towards the windward beach, littered with the outgrown shells of horseshoe crabs.

Picture the five of them, looking like a family. Fern was happy because they were together all the time. She baked. Not well, but muffins were muffins and they never went uneaten. Edgar wore the clothes he kept at the Vineyard house, which were stiff with salt and faded from sun. At dawn and dusk and six times between he rolled his pants up and stood at the surfline, his feet sinking a little deeper with each wave. Fern wore a kerchief and dug in the garden, trying to make the cucumbers come up. Cricket was always in a sundress with a rainbow on it, the twins in shorts and sailor shirts embroidered with the name of their grandparents' boat. Fern was a mother and a wife and herself all at once. Edgar rumpled his children's hair, kissed his wife on the temple, mended the sails and painted the hulls, sailed out in the Sound and bobbed there, pretending the shoreline away.

Edgar loved the eelgrass and the cold water and the thunderstorms so much it was unsayable. He thought that if a poor person told you he loved the eelgrass you would believe him immediately, and how unfair that was if you happened to be rich. As if his feelings were purchased and therefore not true, not a strum he could hear in his ears when he dove from the wet deck of his boat into the Sound, which was the precise cold it had been every summer, and the moon jellies brushed against his legs when he kicked and he held his breath and stayed under as long as he could, submerged in that perfect brine, memorizing for the thousandth time this feeling. That he had a hand-built wooden sailboat made him only able to talk about his swim, his ferocious love for this water, with other people who

8

also had wooden sailboats. Back home, taking his car in for an oil change, he would not be able to answer the question honestly: how was your summer? He would have to abridge, "Beautiful. Water and wind." He knew that the summerhouse, the sea view, belonged to him because he paid for them, yet it felt like his bloodstream pumped with this place, like the rocks and waves and salt-muck were in him, that he was of them. But money, old money, got all the press.

The children were brown with white, white behinds and they wore anklets of poison ivy blisters. For them the whole point of life was to be wet and dry eight times a day and never clean. As the children understood it, there were places where it was summer all year and they could not believe that their parents had chosen this northerly, four-season land. The parents did not have a good explanation. Only that their kind of people did not live in warm places. They could visit — Edgar's parents owned an island in the Caribbean — but then they had to go back to New England or Chicago or St. Louis or Kansas City, as if the particular ratio of city to country, winter to summer, brick to grass, was necessary for their species to survive.

In the evenings they rowed to a nearby beach for a supper picnic. Fern with a loaf of not very good homemade bread in a checkered cloth on her lap, the kids leaning over the lip of the rowboat hunting for jellyfish, and all of them in the music of Father's oars dipping, rising, dripping.

There was always sand in the bed and none of them wanted it to end.

August arrived despite their prayers that it would not. Each swim and sail meant more. At the county fair Will entered a small schooner he had carved and won first place, but Cricket's blueberry pie and James's bouquet of flowers went ribbon-less. They rode the Ferris wheel and admired the blue-ribbon piglets and watched the ox-pull. They begged the days to pass more slowly.

On the morning of Edgar's birthday, the phone rang. It was Fern's family's lawyer. She could picture him with his polished mustache and fat-collared jacket, his feet on the desk. She had talked to him once when her parents had died the winter before and he had told her that he was sorry for her loss and would call in some months when the affairs were in order. Now his voice was flatter. "Fern," he said. "I don't know how to tell you this."

"I'm already an orphan," she said, trying to make a joke. What other news was there?

"There's no more money."

There had been so much for so long, the kind of sums that seemed immune to depletion. "How can there be no more money?"

"It was spent. And your father seems to have made some very generous gifts in his last year."

"Do you mean *no* money?"

"The eventual sale of the house will pay the taxes."

Fern found Edgar on the beach scraping barnacles off an old mooring.

"There's no more money," she said to him through the wind. "The money is gone." It was like announcing a death. The long-ago earning of that money — slaves, cotton, rum — and the spending of it, were done. The money had lived its own life, like a relative.

"What do you mean?" Edgar asked.

"Apparently some of my mother's sculptures are worth something."

Edgar put the scraper down in the sand, got up and walked towards the water, dove in. He stayed under long enough that Fern thought he might not come back up. She called his name. She dove in too, wearing her dress, which dragged her down. She called him and called him. She spun in circles trying to find the ripples or bubbles that signaled his body. A moment later, Edgar's head appeared halfway across the cove. He ran his hands over his hair and eyes. He had swum the distance in one breath. Edgar turned and floated on his back, and Fern could hardly see him — his body was just a shadow between air and water.

Edgar remembered going in a limousine with his parents to a fancy holiday party at his father's downtown Chicago office when he was six. To get there they had to drive through the poorest neighborhoods and he had looked out at those falling-down apartment buildings and the dim lights inside and the trash on the street and at the children and there was Edgar, little Edgar with his tiny tuxedo and his shiny shoes and the small pocketwatch his father had clipped to his belt loop. He was on the inside of the car and the other people were on the outside. Edgar had reached over and rolled the window down a crack and the air that rushed at him was cold and smoky. His father had smacked his hand and reinstated the barrier. He had checked to be sure that the doors were locked. Edgar had felt the wet wool of guilt fall over him. He had

12

looked to his mother to explain fortune, but she had bowed her head and was staring hard at her feet.

Even now that he was grown he could smell the limousine and he could smell the city outside. His had been a wished-for life, something viewed by everyone else from a great distance, and to voice even one experience of difficulty, of loneliness, was not welcome. Being rich had felt to Edgar like treading alone for all of time in a beautiful, bottomless pool. So much, so blue, and nothing to push off from. No grit or sand, no sturdy earth, just his own constant movement to keep above the surface. It was easy to hate riches when they surrounded him, but Edgar did not know how to be any other kind of person. He did not know that in every life the work of want and survival was just as floorless, just as unstopping.

When he had come out of the water and dried off, Edgar kissed his wife who was sitting on the sand in her wet dress. He said, "We'll figure something out." Though he had no idea how to earn money, this almost felt like good news. His first novel would be out in a year and maybe he could make something of it. They would be just like everybody else. She tried to talk but he said,

"Let's not ruin my birthday. I'm going to get a Danish."

He drove to the little seaside market for coffee. A beautiful woman in line behind him said, "You look like someone who would appreciate a party." She was wearing cut-off jean shorts and white go-go boots. Her hair was uncombed and sandy and long and her wet bikini marked her shirt. She was his age or older, he thought, but she seemed sixteen.

"Not me. I'm not that kind of birthday boy," he said.

"Is it your birthday?"

"Thirty-two," he said.

"I know how it hurts you boys to grow up. It's not so bad, you'll see." She borrowed a pen from the cashier and wrote down an address. "A friend of mine is hosting. Nine o'clock tonight," she said. "It'll be fun, no assholes."

All afternoon Fern thought about the magic key they still held: Edgar could leave their Cambridge life, go back and take over the family steel company in Chicago, his birthright as the only child, and fortune would follow him. It was the very last thing he wanted to do. He would not be able to publish the novel he had spent ten years

14

writing because it was about the son of a steel baron who walks away from his father's money. But here were these three children and herself with all their various needs and desires, and she had not made this family alone. She looked out the kitchen window at the blue, green and blue again. This was an expensive ocean to love. While the children played cards, Fern went into the bedroom and, shaking, put her finger in the rotary phone's different circles, calling Edgar's mother.

That afternoon Fern and the children baked a chocolate cake that looked more homemade than they would have liked. The frosting melted and pooled on the plate. They boiled lobsters and clams and laid a whole bowl of drawn butter at each place setting. The table was clothed and decorated and everyone took showers. Edgar had been out on the water and when he came back his cheeks and eyes were red. Fern wanted to take him into the dark and say something that would make their good life continue.

Mid-meal, the phone rang again. "Fern, sweetheart," her father-in-law said. "I hear there is something to celebrate. Are you having a party?"

She tried for cheer. "Lobster and steamers and chocolate cake."

15

"Good girl. Mary's on too. Say hi, Mary."

"Hi, darling," Fern's mother-in-law said.

"Can you put Edgar on the extension? So we can all be here together?" Hugh asked.

When their voices were all joined by wires, Edgar's parents sang to him.

His father said, "Edgar, I want you to know how welcome you are here at Keating Steel. In every way."

His mother let out a little chuff, the sound of someone who always knew she would win. "You'll see," she said. "You'll see how rich we will make you."

"Maybe it wouldn't be so bad," Fern said, almost too softly to be heard.

Edgar could not see his wife but he could hear her unsteady breath. He understood: she was trying to sell him. He had known her for eleven years and had never hated her, but here was a flare. He squeezed his fists until his nails nearly cut. Fern was ready to transform him into the kind of man who stayed up late in the night working to make the margins between cost and profit wider. So that she could continue to live in a house much bigger than anyone needed, he would have to spend his weekends playing the more dignified seasonal sports with men who ran other companies and they would talk about bottom lines and taxes and

16

subsidies and overseas manufacturing and their tennis games. Fern would turn as vapid as the other wives, all manicure and hairdo and crisp pleats. They would host and attend, host and attend in a spiral of meaningless parties. Their children would go on to do the same thing, and their children after, the whole ancestry one long string of spent and earned, appearance maintained, standards adhered to and passed on and one never asking what any of it meant, whether any good had ever once been done.

Fern wanted to see Edgar's eyes. She wanted to yell and apologize and hide.

It snuck up on Fern, how hard and fast she began to cry.

"My," said Mary. "Fern, what bad hay fever you have."

The children insisted on singing "Happy Birthday" as soon as their parents were off the phone. "Make a wish," Cricket said, and Edgar blew out thirty-two tiny flames, plus one to grow on.

Edgar looked at Fern. They both had red eyes. He said, "What about my book?"

"You made two thousand dollars on it. I don't know what else to do," she said.

"I'm going out," he said. "I'll be back in a few hours."

■ ■ ■ ■

Edgar went down the grassy path to his dark green coupe and drove away from Fern. The night was warm and the air half salt. Fern was left with chocolate cake on plates and three children who had been waiting all day to celebrate. He was left with the feeling that his life was being carved out, that his expected contribution was a shell, not substance. Both Fern and Edgar remembered the same thing: seven months earlier and after almost ten years of work on his novel, Edgar had sent it off to an agent. Two weeks after that, with shaving cream still on half his face, he had come running down the stairs, beating Fern and Cricket to the phone. Edgar had said, "Hello?" and then, "Uh-huh yes okay wow thank you," like it was a single word.

"He has an offer," he had said to Fern and Cricket. "He has an offer for my novel." Cricket had been the one to cry first. Fern and Edgar had both knelt so that the three of them were the same height and they had put their heads together and wrapped their arms around each other. The twins had jumped aboard the huddle.

"It's not a ton of money," he said.

"Who cares about money," Fern had said. "Who fucking cares about money." The twins had looked at their mother in shock. "Sorry," she had said. "I'm just excited." Cricket had been more proud of both of her parents in that moment than any in her life: her mother knew how to swear and her father had written a book.

"Who fucking cares about money," Cricket had echoed, sensing that in this happy moment nothing she could do would get her in trouble.

On this night, the woman from the store looked happy — she had little cheeses on a plate, she had a double-tall glass of gin. She had on white bell-bottom jeans and a white tank top with thin straps and no bra and high platform shoes, which she should have, as a feminist, disagreed with, but there she was, inches above the heads of the men in the room. She looked superior. She was superior. She popped a cheese in her mouth. It was cheap and that did not seem to bother her. The room was full of grass smoke and cigarette smoke and fat with bodies and they were all wearing very little clothing because it was the season for it, and hot outside, hot inside and all the drinks would have been better with mint, if

19

they had had any. In a few hours everyone would strip and run down the path to the beach, throw their naked bodies into the slosh of the Atlantic Ocean.

For Glory, this party was like all the other summer parties that had ever been, except that Edgar showed up.

"You came," she said.

"Listen. I'm married."

"Obviously. Everyone is married by now." Glory was tall and had the ragged lips of someone who'd been kissing all night in a cold car, in winter.

They talked in the drone of the party. They did not mention jobs. Money was another thing they did not talk about.

A leather-vested man with sideburns to his jawbone and rose-colored sunglasses, booze-breathed and too close to Glory, said, "You look hip. I've got a stash in my van."

Glory sidestepped him and moved closer to Edgar. "I've got a stash in my bra. Oh, wait, no bra. Guess it must be somewhere else." She winked.

"You shouldn't drink. It's bad for the soul," the man said.

"Men could stand to be reinvented. Men are due for an update," she said. "But you seem okay," she told Edgar. "I like you." She looked him over — he was all sinew and blue eyes, his day in the sun made obvious by the color in his cheeks.

"Thank you," he said. She made him feel small in a way that he liked.

"Don't worry. I'm married too." Glory pointed out her husband who was sitting in the corner wearing a button-down shirt with a big collar, high-waist brown pants and loafers and smoking a long, thin cigarette. He looked like someone trying to sell something for less than it was worth. She half loved him for it. He was real, at least. Dumbish, and no way would he be there when a revolution swept them all away, but honest and fair. He was probably talking about human evolution, which was one of the topics Glory had approved for social situations. That and political corruption in southerly nations, or food. He was not allowed to discuss anything about Glory or her family, his family. Their wedding was unmentionable. Everyone knew that they were husband and wife and that this had been a decision made by other people and that Glory tolerated while John waited at the gates of her broad and lush paradise. It was obvious, to look at them.

At 11:00 p.m., drunk and stoned, Glory said, "Do you want to get some air?" and Edgar took Glory out to his sports car, which was either a brave or disgusting car for someone who had just claimed to believe in socialism. Glory admired the pale blond leather seats and the wooden gearshift.

"You've never had an affair, have you?" she said.

He said, "I'm sorry. I should go home."

She leaned over and kissed him well, like it was enough, not a short and irritating detour on the way to the good part. Edgar had never kissed someone he did not love.

He pulled his head back and closed his eyes.

Glory looked out the window at the party. Everyone inside was enjoying the trap they had set for themselves. They were in the process of making the exact mistakes they had hoped for. Edgar saw John's leg in the window, in the same chair he'd been in all night. There were people near him. Smoke swirled around him. "I worry about him like a mother," Glory said. "I always hope he's gotten enough to eat and made friends."

"My wife —" Edgar started, but she interrupted him.

"I shouldn't have brought up spouses again. Let's not." She reached out to his thigh. "You don't have to do anything you don't want to," she said, teasing him.

"I'm feeling very confused right now."

22

Then a knock, and Glory and Edgar looked out his side to see who it was. A woman with long pale hair that looked like it had been carefully matted and a headband. "Are you leaving? I can't find a place to park." It was too dark to see the woman's face, but Glory knew the voice immediately because it was her mother's. Her mother, double-parked in her comfortable luxury station wagon and clothes a few years out of date that even Glory was too old to wear. She looked like she was in a play. "Mother," Glory said. "Mother, mother, mother? You can't be here." Glory's mother edged away. The outfit was worse than Glory could have imagined: her midriff was exposed (and very perfect, which made it all the worse) and her skirt was a mere strip of denim. She had silver anklets and no shoes on, and hers were the scrubbed and painted feet of a princess.

Glory's mother recognized her daughter at the same instant and, without trying to defend her right to stay or offer an excuse, she began to run. She passed her own car, the lights still on and the door open, and she ran. Glory ran after her and Edgar ran after Glory. They rounded a corner, sprinted the straightaway. Glory's mother was surprisingly fast. She took another turn down a

23

dirt road and Glory let her go. She watched her little mother whip away like a rabbit and Glory collapsed onto someone's lawn and Edgar fell beside her. They panted. They started to laugh. They had each hated their parents but had forgotten the surprising pleasure of being embarrassed by them. It made Glory feel young. Like they were living on the inside and the grownups were on the outside, and she half wanted to thank her mother.

"This is already better than other affairs," Glory said.

Edgar thought of Fern in their bed with their children nearby. She would be reading a book and checking her watch. She would be waiting to talk about a future that had been suddenly upended. Maybe she would tell him that she was willing to give it all up, the houses and the cars and the comfort. Or maybe she was waiting to thank him for being the man he had always tried to keep from becoming. He felt like an impossibility — how could he do what was needed and continue to exist as himself? To Fern, Edgar silently said, "I don't know what I'm doing. I'm almost completely yours," and he leaned over and kissed Glory. She kissed him back, reached up and tried to take his glasses off.

"No," he said, grabbing them. "I'm too blind."

"Four eyes," she teased, but he did not give in. He only took his glasses off to sleep. He felt unmoored enough without being sightless too.

Eventually, they walked back. Edgar pulled his car out and Glory parked her mother's and turned it off. She put the keys under the seat and left it unlocked and then she got into his passenger seat and said, "I'm taking you home. I'm taking you home and I might not ever let you leave." Later, he would look back at the unraveling and see that this instant was the point of departure. Edgar decided: once. And just like that, he set his life aside. He set his husband-self, his father-self, his son-self, aside. He was all body, all sensation. His heart was a flapping wing. He was simultaneously jealous of himself for what he was about to do and scattershot with regret. They drove a mile to her house, grey shingles and a big porch, a thousand paperbacks on the shelves. The bedroom looked out at the windward side of the island where waves battered and crashed.

As Glory undressed him, Edgar felt like he had a new body. He appreciated her hip bones and shoulders because he was a man with good taste and these were beautiful prizes, but the stronger drug was the version of himself he was meeting. This woman had never in her whole life, in the history of everything she knew, run her hand up this chest. He was the entire westward migration, the whole untrodden prairie, the shaggy peaks, the snow, and the cold sloshing Pacific on the other end.

Glory knew what he was feeling because she had felt it before. She also knew it never lasted. Everyone became familiar. There was no time, pretty soon, to bother kissing the ankles, the knots of blooded veins underneath the wrist. It was neck, ears, lips. Even lovers got tired. They had families. They had nothing to wear for the big fundraiser. They had a million things to do before school started and husbands or wives to lie to and love, and the empty mouth of nighttime.

When they were done, Glory put two cigarettes in her mouth and lit them, handed one over. "Where do you live?" she asked.

"Cambridge."

"No shit. Me too. Then we can do this again sometime."

A beat of terror in Edgar's pulse. This woman would not vanish into the summertime haze.

"How do you deal with the guilt?" Edgar

asked. His heart was pumping it out all through his system. *Fern,* his heart seemed to say, *Fern, Fern.*

"Eh. I make it worth his while."

John came home later and slept on the couch without bothering to knock on the bedroom door first.

Edgar drove back to his summer family in the dawn, the twin highs of sex and grass wearing off together. A doe leapt out of the blackberry brush and stood in the middle of the road, looking at Edgar. Still as a photograph. She watched him, her eyes reflecting the headlights. It was too late for Edgar to go unseen, to slide back in without a mark.

He told his drowsing wife he loved her and it was true. Things were blooming outside that had not been blooming a week ago and other things died on the branch that had been luscious. Edgar grabbed Fern hard around her waist. She was his wife; their pleasures, their troubles, belonged to both of them. Edgar wanted to implicate her.

Fern lost her nightgown easily. Edgar was a hot wind and everything loose was swept up. Fern bent. She felt as if she was just meeting this man, that she was in bed with a foreigner. She pulled her head up like a person coming out of the water. "Edgar?" she asked, looking for magnetic north.

"It's me," he said. "Who else?" He glanced around the bed, because he'd felt it too, a new presence.

"No," she told him. "No one else. I got confused. Where were you all night?" she asked.

"Just a party."

"What party? I'm sorry that I called your mother. I'm sorry we need money to survive." But her eyes were not sorry. Her eyes said, *Time to grow up now. Time to earn and support.*

Edgar suddenly felt hungry, very hungry. "Do we have any blueberries? I could make pancakes." Edgar was putting on his pants. He did not have time for a shirt. "Let's squeeze orange juice," he said. "I'm in the mood for fresh." The sun came over the hill and sent a razor of light into the room.

"I don't think we have oranges."

"We don't?" As if this made no sense.

"It's not one of the things I buy."

"The *only* thing you don't buy," he scoffed. All around them was the evidence of her material desire: the fat headboard of the bed, holding her up; the rug from a faraway, sandy nation carried by camel and freighter; the pale butter-colored sofa with

28

thin, modern arms that Fern had had made for this particular spot, to fit the dimensions of the stained glass above it; the stained glass itself, three deer in tall green grass, their long necks bent towards sleep. The modern house, all glass and view, and outside, grass and water.

"Don't pretend you don't care about any of this," she said.

Edgar ignored her and went into the kitchen and assembled the ingredients, began to measure and pour, a mess accumulating quickly around him.

The children woke up to the sound, stood in the doorframe, their father in a sunlit stream filled with flour dust and their mother watching him with narrow eyes, as if he had arrived without invitation. Edgar said, "Pancakes!" and the twins were gleeful, but Cricket saw how angry her parents were, felt the treacherous space between their two poles and refused to enter the room or eat the breakfast. She sensed that something big had been upset.

They packed up a day early and the children cried all the way home, flat furious to be taken away. The ferry ride back to the mainland was pain itself, their beings and their bodies pulled in opposite directions.

29

"Promise that someday we'll stay on the Vineyard all year," the twins pleaded to their parents. "We'll go to the one-room school-house and we'll swim even when it's too cold to swim." Why didn't they? Fern wondered. There was no good reason not to, except that their house was made of wood and glass and they would have frozen by December. Edgar thought of the house, the sea, the island and the fact that he only got to love the place because he could afford to. If he became Keating Steel, they could come every summer of their lives and their children's children would grow up with the same salt-smell in their rooms as they fell asleep, the same blackberry stains on their fingers, the same memorized feeling of utter peace after having jumped into the cove and stayed under as long as their lungs would allow. And if he did not become Keating Steel? Edgar could not imagine selling the house, not only because it would have been devastating (to think of telling the children made his throat cinch) but because it seemed impossible — the place was not real estate but body part, heart part, something beyond ownership.

"Someday," Edgar said. How long before the magic of a quiet winter island in an uninsulated house wore off? The first snow?

30

What absurd indulgence, he suddenly realized, to build a beautiful house that was
only habitable half the year. If they walked
away from the money, sold their Cambridge
colonial and all their things and retreated to
the island, this house would make them im-
mensely happy from May to October and
then spend six months trying to kill them.
Love, Edgar thought, good old love.

"Someday," Fern repeated. The same
seagulls the children had fed from the ferry
happily in June now seemed predatory. The
children closed their cracker boxes tight.
"Shoo!" they said, flinging their arms.

1965

Edgar's father, Hugh Keating, had always stood in his office in front of big windows high above the fog-sketched city of Chicago, knowing that in every building were rods of steel with his name etched on the side, the skeleton tattooed with the name of its maker. From that vantage point, from that height, he told the story — to board members, visiting businessmen, friends — of his family's humble immigrant beginnings, of the new metal city rising out of the ashes of the old wooden one. He thought again: thank goodness for poverty. It's much easier to be rich when your people were once poor. Sleep too comes easier, the mind peaceful with all that balance: a pile of gold and the counterweight of past hunger. This comfort was earned.

The missus, Mary, had made an intricate study of how to belong. There were such things as lower-class flowers (geraniums, chrysanthemums, poinsettias) and upper-class flowers (rhododendrons, tiger lilies, amaryllis, columbine, clematis and roses, though never red ones). She learned that the slower one drove, the higher his class. Cocktail wise, sweet was always low. Scotch and water (not even soda) was the highest. When they went to parties, she ordered two and then slipped into the ladies' room to sweeten them with packets of sugar she kept in her handbag. She made sure her husband's shirts did not gap at the neck — a sure sign of misbelonging. She practiced, with index cards, renaming everything in her home: formalwear, footwear, leisurewear, stormwear, beachwear, neckwear, tableware, flatware, stemware, barware, glassware. Edgar's mother's nightmares did not involve being chased or drowned but of someone catching her trying to eat an artichoke with fork and knife, of wearing floor-length to an afternoon affair, of everyone knowing that class for this family was not bred-in but a choice, or worse, a purchase.

Mary bore a boy, as hoped, and she gave her husband, seated in a wooden chair at the side of her hospital bed, a short list of names: Edgar, John, Henry. "What about

Hugh?" he asked, liking the idea of a tribute to himself.

"Hugh was never King of England."

"Neither is our son." The boy squalled like a brief, violent summer storm, then fell asleep.

"There can't be anything bad about having the name of a monarch," she said.

"I seem to recall an Alfred," Hugh said, joking,

"Edgar then," she told him. "I don't need your help if you don't want to give it."

The idea was to have four children. Either two boys and two girls, or three boys and one girl. A big family was one of the socially acceptable indulgences and it justified a bigger house, more cars, a stable full of horses. Giving anything for one's children, even if that something was a Thoroughbred chestnut mare that cost as much as a small yacht, was an act of generosity and selflessness. Mary and Hugh both silently looked forward to the purchases they would be able to make in the name of good parenting. Neither of them cared whether the children would actually want horses or sailing lessons in the British Virgin Islands.

During her pregnancy, the veins in Mary's legs had swelled into thick, raised ropes. Her calves were less pale skin and more twisting strands of blue. The doctor instructed her to keep them elevated above her heart, to massage them with particular oils. She would spend the rest of her seaside summers with a towel over her legs, the rest of her sundress days in thick stockings. Mary had wept over these things. She felt as if she had aged seventy years in the space of nine months, like the growing baby had detonated something poisonous inside her.

The doctor joined Hugh and Mary in the hospital room. "We've named him Edgar," she announced.

"That's a fine name," the doctor said. "Stately and proud. He'll go on to great things." This seemed like an official pronouncement and Mary logged it as fact. "May I?" he asked, pulling the blanket down from her lap. Her legs were dark with bruises, the blood gathered in underskin pools. Her veins were high and fat. "I would feel worse about this if you'd just had a daughter," the doctor started, "but with such a beautiful son to carry on the family name, it's easier for me to tell you that you can't have any more. The risk of a blood clot is too great. You could die."

Edgar was asleep in his bassinet and both of his parents looked at him. Wrinkled little monkey-faced newborn, still looking halfway like a water creature. The ghost of the family they had intended to become, the fleet of them in matching Christmas outfits, matching tennis outfits, matching riding outfits, dwindled to a quiet three. Neither Hugh nor Mary cried while the doctor was still in the room, but for the first months of Edgar's life, as he slept less and looked around more, as he fattened up and learned to grab things in his dimpled fists, their eyes were red-rimmed and swollen.

Edgar had to live the childhoods of all his brothers and sisters who did not exist. He took fencing, tennis, rowing and ballroom dance lessons. He learned to jump horses, sail boats, speak French and Latin, and recognize the architectural features of each great era. At age ten, he was enrolled in a figure drawing class in which he sat with a herd of older women and rendered the slack necks and falling breasts of a variety of models. His mother wanted him to play an instrument but his father vetoed most of the options: violin (too screechy), saxophone (too black), piano (too feminine), flute (homosexual), until he was left with a clarinet, an instrument that none of them could even remember having heard. All through his school years Edgar was busy from seven in the morning until he fell asleep. There was no time for friendships and he found himself talking to peers only while they were all otherwise occupied with something that their parents hoped would make them better, rounder adults.

Edgar's father floated above the social pressure. He felt that they had earned their way and had nothing to apologize for. Which was what led him to the Mercedes-Benz dealership on a bright Saturday in summer where a flock of suited men lit and relit his cigar, poured him bourbon, slapped him hard on the back while they walked the perimeter of a jewel-bright coupe, blue as blue, like they were circling a high-mountain lake. "I won't say it'll change your life," one of the suits said, "but it'll change your day. How many times are you going to press your foot on a gas pedal? Thousands. This is the pedal you want to be pushing." Hugh handed over his old keys and a banknote and left with the windows down and the new leather warming against his back. He took his fedora off while he drove and let his hair tousle in the breeze. He pulled into the construction dust of the family's forthcoming country summerhouse in the middle of a hundred acres of prairie and forest, the horse paddock to his right, the place where the swimming pool would be to his left.

The car was like a blue mirage. Mary was standing with a man holding blueprints. Not recognizing the car, she thought someone was lost and did not feel like having to offer lemonade while they used her phone to get better directions. "Look," she said to the man with the blueprints, "I just need to know how many curves will make the driveway seem leisurely but not indulgent and that's how many curves I want." Every decision in the house was a danger: it had to look understated and modest while still making other women jealous. It had to be beautiful in a way that seemed effortless, as if it had simply sprouted out of the good earth like an imperfect, perfect flower. There could be no columns or mock Tudor. No leaded windows, yet there ought to be a lot of glass to show that one had servants to do the polishing. The house was to be built of blush-pink bricks freighted in from a particular mill on a particular sea-wracked cliff known for its gentle sunset shade of clay.

Mary swatted a mosquito on her arm and wiped away the star of blood and body left behind. The blue car stopped and turned up yet more dust and she hated whoever it was in the way she had been trained to hate him — here was a person who was showing off his money and enjoying it, both of which she knew to take as a personal offense. The air cleared as a man stepped out, and Mary saw that the man was her husband. He held the keys like she was a dog he wanted to trick into coming closer. Here puppy, here stupid dog, I've brought you a bloody marrowbone.

Mary's body offered her two choices: run at him, swinging her fists, or collapse on the ground. She chose the former. "Has anybody seen you?" she screamed, like he had shown up with a murder weapon.

"It's top-of-the-line," he said, repeating what the salesmen had told him and finding the words less meaningful this time around. "It's German engineered. You press the gas pedal thousands of times." Nothing was making sense.

"You bought this? You bought this without talking to me? Where is our old car?"

"I don't know what you have against a nice car."

"This is the car driven by African dictators and California dentists. You will ruin me. You will ruin both of us."

Still standing there was the man with the blueprints and Mary remembered him, a witness to the crime. She brushed her pale yellow dress off and walked calmly over. "If you could avoid mentioning this to anyone, I would very much appreciate it. My husband doesn't always think straight."

"It's a beauty," the man said. "I'd be thrilled if I was you. A car like that?"

"Yes," she said. "Well, it's not for us." The larger "us." His kind maybe, which was exactly her point.

By the time the sun went down she had taken them back to the dealer and picked out a beige Cadillac, three years old, slow and respectable. It was not even completely clean inside. Mary drove. Hugh picked someone else's dead cigarette out of the ashtray and threw it out the window into the blurring poplars. Mary drove the long way through the center of town so that they would have a better chance of being seen.

All through Edgar's high school years, his mother attended to the particulars of social success like a doctor to a dying child, and every year it seemed to exhaust her more. She monitored every aspect — hairdo (round with a small flip at the ends, sprayed stiff), sweater-set shade (pastel), charitable gift sizes (significant without being showy), length of vacation (husbands went for six days, wives and children could stay on for two weeks), books to be discussed in mixed company (anything French or British), proper density of driveway shrubbery (very), race and age of house staff (the paler the better, not older than forty).

Mary did not gain confidence as time went on. Instead, the more she learned of it, the more intricate the labyrinth became. Wallpaper and lighting were frequently torn out and replaced at great expense. The house, to Mary, was a series of landmines. If she was found to still have Queen Mary chairs six months after everyone had gone Arts and Crafts, her entire social existence might be blown up. And no matter how hard she tried, she could not find the right dish to serve at a dinner — the Old Moneys always served the same slab of grey beef with brown gravy and potatoes, and never enough of it, but Mary was far from established enough to pull that off. Many times Edgar came downstairs for a late-night snack after studying and found his mother asleep beside a stack of cookbooks. Beneath her head, a list of the pitfalls of each dish. Soufflé: falls. Lasagna: too Italian. Champagne and caviar: trying too hard. Lamb chops with mashed potatoes: fattening. Fish: the smell stays in the wallpaper for days.

41

Edgar woke his mother, draped her arm over his shoulder and put her to bed beside his snoring father. "Who cares what everybody thinks?" he whispered. "They're just old rich people. They didn't make the world."

"Thank you, love," she said. "But you're wrong, they did make the world and they still do."

The money in Fern's family was so old they only remembered the broad strokes of its origin (rum, cotton, slaves). This bloodstream, her parents felt, was not bought or earned. They were true Americans, men and women who had settled on this land before it had a name. Absent from their stories was even a mention of the people who had already populated the mountains and valleys when the early pilgrims had come ashore. As if, upon the arrival of men who considered themselves superior, the natives had quietly, obediently, evaporated into a cheery summer-camp fantasy — a young brave in a canoe with a tomahawk, a pretty topless squaw on shore wringing lake water from her hair.

Members of Fern's Old Money family had met George Washington, served as Senators and international Ambassadors, seeded the burgeoning lands with their sons and daughters and cotton crops, tended to those children and crops with slave labor, a fact that they had ceased to mention by the time Fern's generation had come along. The truest luxury of long-term wealth was that no one in the family thought about money anymore. As if comfort was joined with the Westwood cells. They had not earned anything new for a hundred years and no one went to college in order to get a job — instead they went to learn for the sake of learning, to deepen their reservoirs of language, culture, philosophy, art. They spent a significant amount of time giving money away.

Evelyn Westwood, Fern's mother, was an accomplished sculptor. Her father, Paul, when not suffering from crippling migraines four days a week, spent his time serving on the boards of deserving causes. They lived in an eight-bedroom Arts and Crafts house on fifty acres of prairie a mile from Lake Michigan. They had two maids, a cook, a chauffeur and four Thoroughbred mares. Fern and her brother, Ben, had been raised by Irish nannies. In the attic were giant steamer trunks that the family had used many times to travel to Europe to look at art and architecture, to eat, to walk in Paris in the spring and Italy in the summer.

From the outside, Fern's parents looked like the people Edgar's parents hoped to become. Money was relatively easy to earn; status took generations.

But from the inside? Imagine Evelyn before Fern, Evelyn before Ben, Evelyn even before Paul: she had short hair though shoulder length was the style and naked lips though the girls were all slicking on red. Instead of a knee-length dress cinched at the waist she wore a red silk robe that was given to her mother by a Chinese empress. Her parents had built Evelyn, showing promise, a sculpture studio when she was fourteen, out in the prairie behind the family estate. Her parents were proud of her. Sculpture seemed perfectly safe — she made fawns, geese, children with watering cans — and the hobby seemed a nice complement to the rest of her grooming.

While all the parents thought about the Allies fighting Germany and Japan, Evelyn's friends spent whole evenings in Lolly Roitfield's fourth-floor turret parsing the football roster, taking the boys' bodies apart in their minds like doll bits and restacking them into a perfect configuration — Chip's chest, Edward's height, Albert's legs, Theodore's hair and the beatific face of Crosly

Marsh. They dressed this perfect man in a leather football helmet sometimes, then a suit and fedora, then, if they were feeling brave, a pair of swimming shorts with a backdrop of Lake Michigan in full heat, a gingham picnic blanket and all the girls in two-piece swimsuits despite their mothers' best efforts to force them into the woolen bathing dresses of their youth. But while the other girls constructed boys, Evelyn sat to the side, not because she was shy or unwanted, not because she did not think about boys, but because she liked the angle. She had a sketchpad out and she too was creating bodies. The group of girls on Evelyn's page were both fluid and precise.

By graduation, a few girls already wore little sparklers on their ring fingers. They had been debuted in white charmeuse and shantung silk, bent into deep curtseys while the gentlemen of society had scanned the line. The girls who would go to college went because that was where they would meet the right men. There they would stay up late talking about which courses attracted which boys. Evelyn applied to all the same colleges but she also applied to the Art Institute. Her parents debated whether to let her go — she was not pretty enough to coast on looks — but in the end it was their status that gave them confidence. Theirs was one of the oldest families in Chicago. Their house, built by Evelyn's grandfather, was pictured in more than a dozen books on architecture. Their rosebushes were so old that some of the branches were as big as ankles and when they bloomed they were just imperfect enough, as if someone had come out at dawn and carefully ruffled them. This was a family of such polish that Evelyn was desirable even if she showed some talent.

At school she was twice as good as all the men. The teachers always looked at her work with bright eyes, then at her. They squinted like they were trying to bring her into focus — was she really a girl? Too bad.

The only teacher who took her as seriously as she deserved to be taken, who lent her rare and expensive books on sixteenth-century sculpture, who stayed with her after class, the room still earthy with wet clay, the grey chalk of it in their nailbeds, talked about a carved medusa he had seen in Istanbul and how it reminded him of her. She thought he meant her work, but no.

"You have that same fire," he said. "Wrong hair, though." She touched her flat locks, short against her skull. She changed the subject to the magic trick of sculpting eyes.

"You have to think of the eyes as gesture more than organ," he said, flicking his wrist. And then, without wondering if he had earned permission, he leaned in and kissed her with his whole wet mouth and all the compliments he had ever given her on her clay, the way she had summoned the reclining nude, how he had almost been able to feel her deer breathing, all of that was snuffed out. It was gesture. She was a woman and that fact would always matter more than talent. *She* would always matter less.

Evelyn had to get married if she wanted to keep working. It was 1944 and there was no place in the world for a single woman artist, at least not in her world. She had plenty of suitors and her parents pushed for a van der Rohe, a Tisch or a Kensington, as if they were all choosing a new accessory rather than a human with whom their daughter would spend all her remaining nights and days. Evelyn searched the men for the most benign, the least likely to pay attention. Paul had a firm jawline, the family stock was decent, the house a little new but not embarrassingly so, but her parents had eliminated him because he was crippled with frequent and debilitating migraines, headaches that made him blind, unable to

47

speak. Evelyn felt sorry for him, suffering so, but it was the migraines that made her pluck him out of the reject pile — on the days when he had headaches she would be nearly husbandless, nearly alone. Indeed, for all their years together, when Paul noticed the first glimmer at the outer edge of his vision, Evelyn made him a cup of strong tea, settled her husband in the bedroom with a cold cloth and drew the velvet drapes. Then she walked out to her prairie studio and fell into the clay as if she was nothing but a glorious pair of hands.

She wanted only to work, but Evelyn's body still had ways in which to betray her. It held the bundles of tiny eggs, the little stirrings of life, and soon one of them was brightened with a mate, divided, divided, lodged and began to grow. Evelyn felt convulsed with sickness, immediately forsaken for the parasite. Though she had not expected to get out of motherhood altogether, she had meant to put it off.

Paul was happy for the news. He looked forward to a person in the house more helpless than himself. He was, so often, an abstraction. Half the time he lay alone, brain scrambled and so deep in ache and confusion that he truly was not part of the world. The days when he was well were spent waiting to be unwell again. He made just the gentlest motions towards living — ate meals, read about the tightening of the Iron Curtain, dressed himself, walked in the prairie and along the lakeshore, voted on one or another board's agenda, went to the club to which all the men belonged, oaken and ancient, a place where money was like atmosphere: vital to every breath the membership took but completely invisible to them.

Evelyn said, "We're going to hire help. Don't think I'm suddenly going to turn into a mother with a stuffed pork shoulder in the oven." In twenty years, when women burned their bras and quit getting married and slept with bearded men in parks, in communes, in apartments with full ashtrays and empty refrigerators, Evelyn would understand perfectly. If only she had been born a half-century later, she would have been the first one to set the world alight.

"Hire whoever you want," Paul said. He knew that he would be little help, rendered useless by his own brain.

Evelyn got bigger and bigger, swelled past the point that made sense. The doctor felt her belly and declared with glee "Twins!" Her body, her own ever-inventive ruin. Paul celebrated with chocolate cake and red wine

49

even though he knew they were both head-ache triggers, knew that he would spend the next day in a cave of delusion and pain. He figured he might have anyway, and some-times he needed a good thing, sometimes pleasure was worth it. Evelyn took a nap while the babies inside her roiled like they were their own storm.

By the time she went into labor she was so huge and uncomfortable that she could hardly walk, much less sit or stand to work. Her hands were nervy without their clay. Their driver took them to the hospital where Paul was as clear-headed as he could ever remember having been, where he paced the waiting room like a chained dog while the other husbands smoked and drank coffee.

To Evelyn, the doctor yelled, "A boy!" first, and she felt relief like a punch in the face. "Thank God," she said. But then, a moment later, "A girl!" and Evelyn said, "Shit." Paul was there then — had he always been there? — and he was holding the first baby, the boy, while the doctor had given the girl to Evelyn. In the girl's scrunched face Evelyn saw the entire path: pigtails, dollhouse, riding lessons, foxtrot, engage-ment, white dress, all in service of the repetition of this very same moment. An-other perfectly wasted life. Maybe the girl would care about something along the way — art or history — but it would be pressed out of her slowly until she was nothing but a woman, nothing but a mother. "I want to trade," she said to Paul. He was happy to because he wanted to examine all of his treasure, these two pinkened elves that had suddenly fallen into his life. He looked forward to everything about them. The only thought he needed to banish was the fact that he would miss half their lives, locked alone in the dark while the children splashed in the rain, learned the Greek myths, fell in love.

The nannies were Irish girls who would stay on until it was time for them to get married, and Evelyn had chosen the least beautiful applicants in hopes that they would take longer to find suitable mates. After the birth, Evelyn stayed in bed as long as directed by her doctor and then handed the little pink and blue bundles of Fern and Ben to the nanny and went back to her clay. Evelyn had wriggled out of wifedom by marrying a cripple and now she wriggled out of motherhood by paying other people to do the work for her, but she could not wriggle out of being a woman. Her sculptures were purchased all the time but she was never paid well. She knew, and she was right, that if she were male her work would have been collected in museums, but because she was female it all ended up in cemeteries.

The Cold War began, the first monkey astronaut was shot into space and the President ended segregation in the United States military. That was all peripheral, reported on the news. Meanwhile Evelyn marched through her universe's particular vision of womanhood: luncheons in fine homes, fundraiser galas, horse shows, thank-you notes, condolence letters, garden tours. Much later she would wonder why she had not skipped all of it and become a recluse, going outside only to walk between studio and house. It was not a sense of duty that had made her go to the events but her abiding fury. To see the other women, the little wives, shuttling across the house like game pieces, everything from waistline to finger-bowls to rose varieties suffered over, made Evelyn's own prison seem a little bigger. Her social life was like entering a zoo; leaving it made her feel, at least for a moment, almost free.

The babies turned into children. Evelyn paid minimal attention to Fern, who seemed sweet but ordinary. She played with dolls like all girls played with dolls. She also ran and climbed trees when no one was looking, not realizing her mother would have been relieved to see her attempt something dangerous, something dirty. Ben, no matter how hard Evelyn tried to see him as strong or quick, the picture of masculine ease, remained a vague smudge of a boy, someone passed by and passed over. He was hugely tall and it was as if he did not have enough self to fill that whole body. He was quiet and so pale as to look out of focus. As time wore on, Evelyn slowly gave up on him. She had hoped that because he was a boy he would not have to suffer or fight, that his voice would be easily heard in a room. Not Ben.

And what about from the inside? He wanted just like every person wants; he had an encyclopedic knowledge of predators and prey. He imagined exploring caves and caverns in faraway continents where the click of the bats and the echo of water dripping were the only sounds. He liked the idea of being sealed off. It was a relief to think of being intentionally alone.

Even though he was big, Ben had a way of blending into the background. Fern sometimes felt as if she hadn't seen Ben in days, though he had been right there all along, his huge frame seated at the kitchen table, silently reassembling with tweezers and glue the skeleton of a dead sparrow he had found and dissected. Still, Fern counted on Ben. His vagueness made her look and feel specific, normal. Her father was sick and her mother did not like to look at Fern, the girl of her. The siblings watched the family's color television where news of the world filtered in between cartoons. Segregation was ruled illegal, a black woman refused to give up her seat on the bus, a pretty actor died in his car. All of it felt far away. The place in which they lived was an unrippled surface. Fern felt safe, yet even as a girl she sensed that safety was a lie. Everything else was also true.

Fern and Ben shared a bed, and in sleep their twin bodies did not recognize their separateness. For Ben it was the kindest the world ever felt. Fern liked it too — lying beside him was the only place where the searching hum of the world went quiet.

They went on this way, Fern ahead and Ben a few feet behind, a quiet shadow. They were silently together in grammar school as the pen of obedience was slowly built around them, silently together in the wring and wrench of middle school, silently together as they walked their new bodies through the high school halls, little adults, little pretenders. Alone at home, Fern sat close to Ben, talked to him about his latest interest — the migration of the monarch butterfly, the boneless structure of the shark. Again they sat in the blue light of the television and the anchors reported the facts of all the elsewheres: in Berlin, a wall was built between East and West; for thirteen days, everyone believed that the Soviets might launch an atomic missile from Cuba; the president was killed. Fern confessed that she felt tangled inside, not realizing that everyone did, that there was no person free of this. Ben listened and nodded and she knew he understood.

Fern grew stickier with a certain group of especially rich, especially pretty girls and she started to ignore her brother even at home, left him to coast in her wake. Because Ben was almost part of her, because their bodies had invented themselves together and they could never be completely prized apart, Fern thought she could afford a little meanness. She would never have risked it if she had known she could lose Ben.

Then, when she was seventeen, came Edgar, Yale senior, thick glasses, whippet arms and storm of ideas, and there went Fern: any retaining walls that had been built around or inside her burst open. She was all shatter and splinter, all grateful wreckage. Through the summer it was Edgar at her side with no place behind her for Ben. Ben spun in the eddy while Fern went downstream fast.

Ben's circuitry fizzled at the ends. He felt amputated. It was all right to be less than whole when his twin could stand in for the rest, but without her, all the missing pieces turned bright and burned. He tried to steady himself in his old books: butterflies, bats, stories of sailors and treasure and islands where the only drinking water was a brackish spring. Evelyn and Paul did not notice that Ben was a flickering bulb. Out of habit, Evelyn continued her blind attempt to make a man of him and signed Ben up for the crew team. He was never put in a boat because his oars always bit the water too early or too late, so while his sister spent the summer falling in love, he spent it sitting on the lakeshore beach littered with dead herring while he listened to the other boys work their bodies back and forth as one. Ben lay his huge body back on the sand, smelled the fishrot, while the coxswain's voice blew over the water. "Catch! Drive! Finish! Recover!"

Meanwhile Fern and Edgar were driven

the hour to downtown Chicago by her parents' chauffeur where they sat in the park with a picnic of cold grapes and cucumber sandwiches and watched a play (parents felt entirely safe sending their teenaged children into the city alone if Shakespeare was involved). It was humid and hot and there was no shade and all around the park were glass skyscrapers reflecting the sun, but they noticed none of these discomforts. Neither did they remember the play or even really see it. What occurred for Fern and Edgar was this: they held hands. Sometimes they entwined their fingers, sometimes they rubbed the other hand softly with a thumb, and to the two of them it felt as if their entire lives, the history of every civilization, the smack of the universe being born, were all together in that hold. Their palms sweat and every once in a while they would break to wipe them on their thighs, laugh, then quickly rejoin. Until now, the fact that Fern was a girl had rendered her purposeless. Suddenly there was a reason for her. She knew that she was standing at the entrance to the express path that her mother so hated but to Fern it felt like she was about to be born. Love might make her, finally, visible.

Fern tried to talk to her parents about Edgar at dinner one night. She wanted to tell them that she was in love, that she could not contain the feeling within the bounds of her body. It was harder than expected to explain. "Edgar is amazing," she said. Paul smiled at her. He was all the way at the head of the table, too far to put his hand on hers, which was what he would have liked to do.

"I'm happy for you," Ben said. He was. But also endlessly sorry for himself. He was being replaced, and Fern, though she knew this too, could see her brother receding in the distance, yet was so happy that she couldn't help but leave him behind.

Evelyn did not want to be cruel. Fern was so earnest at her seat, napkin in her lap, ankles crossed, cutting a green bean into bite-size thirds with a knife and fork, dabbing at the corners of her mouth — a lady. She was falling into the domestic void as happily as if it were a warm bath. Evelyn could see love like sweat on Fern's skin. See? It was better that no one had expected Fern to do or know something — the flood of love would have washed it all away no matter what. "I don't like his parents," Evelyn said. It was the nicest statement she could muster.

"What's wrong with his parents?" Fern asked.

To Evelyn it was obvious: they were a new

58

family with new money and a new house and every movement they made was filled with effort. It hurt to watch all that trying — the endeavor was belonging yet every movement made them more obvious as outsiders. If his family stayed for three generations they might pick up the scent of the place, start to seem less like foreign animals. Evelyn did not have another nice thing to say and she knew the rule. "Pass the salt, would you, Fern?"

Ben harbored a selfish hope that his mother's cruelty would puncture the balloon of love that was carrying his sister away. He would catch her if she fell.

Paul attempted to raft them out of the muck with a conversation about *War and Peace,* which he had been trying to read for months, but the women refused to be saved.

Fern and Edgar went for horseback rides in the prairie and walks by the lakeshore. They listened to the Beatles. They celebrated with root beer floats when the Civil Rights Act was passed. The war in Vietnam began, escalated. Fern and Edgar tried to articulate the feelings they had: like a quiet fusion, he said; like a meeting of two breezes or streams, she tried. Both agreed it was inevitable.

Then, a cut in the form of a letter. It was addressed to Ben. He had been drafted.

For people like these, people who lived aside from the scramble and burn of work and the city, it was easy to think of current events as happenings restricted to the news. These were stories, not real events, not real boys in a real war. At least not their boys.

But President Johnson had announced that he would double the monthly draft calls to thirty-five thousand. The war's arms were getting longer, the fingers greedier. Young men departed for Vietnam and came home weeks later, sometimes days later, in body bags. The ones who survived described an invisible enemy — the people they were supposedly there to protect looked identical to the ones they were meant to kill. There were boys who believed they were helping. There were boys who did not trust the mission or the President but soon it didn't matter anymore what they thought. They were all boys who slept in swamps, watched their wounds rot, dragged their maimed friends to reed beds where another teenager tried to sew closed whatever part had been ripped open. They were all boys who killed or watched while someone else killed. They were all boys who looked up while a helicopter reeled in the bodies of guys who had been alive the day before, guys who had love letters in their pockets and bullets in their stomachs. They were all boys who remembered home.

Evelyn and Paul had sat in their living room and watched while US Marines set fire to the grass roofs of a village and women and children wept at the edge of a rice paddy. They had watched while bodies were hit and fell. In cities across the country boys burned their draft cards and were arrested. Protesters gathered in Washington, New York, Chicago, and at the edges of these protests were people yelling at the ungrateful kids, people who believed that America was doing the right thing and hated these indulgent teenagers who were trying to take a flame to the needs of their great country.

Evelyn held her son's draft card in her hand. She understood that so, so many young men were dead, but she had another thought, unbidden: *Manhood, inevitable in war.* Paul thought: *I hope, I worry, I hope.* Fern woke back up to the truth of her brother, thought: *No.* She told her mother that it was a mistake, that he would never make it out alive, even in the best of circumstances. "They'll devour him," she said.

61

"He'll be fine," her mother told her. "People from here don't get sent to the frontlines. He'll sit in an office someplace. He's big and he's smart." Even in Evelyn, least mothering of all mothers, there were twin knots of concern and kindness. She thought that a man who acted like a man could do anything he wanted, that his whole life would be easeful, and she wished this for her son. She wished for him a world of unlocked doors. With the armor of money and stature there to protect him from being sent overseas, maybe the war would be a favor to Ben. A means for him to grow up.

Fern said, "Have you ever watched him in a room full of people he doesn't know? He disappears. He'll be trampled."

"How can he disappear? He's enormous," Evelyn said. "Anyway, it's not a choice, he's been drafted. What am I supposed to do, send him away to San Francisco to be babysat by those hippies?"

Over the last few weeks of summer, Ben's fuses all shorted out. He came downstairs on the day he was to be driven away wearing dress pants with his undershirt and a pair of slippers and a straw hat from the attic. He stood at the door and tapped his fingers on his heart in counts of sixty, over and over. "Ben. What are you wearing?"

Fern asked. She brought him a real shirt and buttoned it, tied his shoes. She brought the suitcase she had packed for him. She had tried to calculate the books that would be least likely to get him beaten up (nothing about birds). She had written down a story he could tell about a girlfriend and sealed this in an envelope. In a second envelope she included evidence of this invented love: two letters written by the unreal girl, a locket engraved with her name on the back. And inside? A week before, Fern had disguised herself with a wig and makeup, slipped out of her clothes, taken a grainy photograph in half light. Sex might offer some protection, even if it was fictional. A sister would have been no armor at all.

Ben had no clear thoughts in his head. Without his sister and his home he felt that he might simply cease to exist. And that did not even take into account the air raids, the helicopters, the guns. He tapped his heart. His eyes darted.

"Stop being theatrical," Evelyn said. "You are going to be no less safe than you would right here at home." She knew she was cold. She tried to say she loved her son because she did — she had practiced saying it in her head but now her mouth was unmoved.

Paul stood by, still circling a headache, trying to comprehend what was real.

Fern hugged Ben. She felt the body that had once been her counterpart, such a different body from the one she had lately been snuggling into. Ben smelled like he had not showered in too long. "You just have to go unnoticed," she whispered. It seemed like his best hope — so far, he had done this without trying. "Call me and I'll come rescue you anytime. We'll all run away to Italy." His eyes looked foggy.

Ben started to laugh and could not stop. At first they all laughed with him, his parents in their summer linens, his sister in a sundress, none of them knowing what the joke had been, all of them trying to survive an unsurvivable moment, but then they stopped laughing and Ben kept going and going. He laughed while they hugged him and put him in the car. He was still laughing when the door closed and sealed him into the chamber, still laughing when Evelyn tapped on the trunk to tell the chauffeur, *Okay, all set. Take him away.*

Fern called Edgar from the phone in the hallway. He did not ask her to explain anything, just listened while she wept.

Edgar went back to college in the fall and

they wrote letters while Fern took Home Economics with the blue-haired Mrs. Sparrow and Edgar studied Greek History and Sociology, subjects his parents would never have approved of. It was 1965. Most of the students looked the way they had for ten years: smooth hair, neat dresses and pants. A cigarette if they were feeling rebellious. Maybe they drank beer. There were a few boys who grew their hair long. Jack Kerouac was on certain bookshelves. There was a new thing to smoke. On the weekends, a new kind of girl showed up from other campuses, from the city, wearing jeans and cropped shirts, pale bellies exposed to the sun. Edgar stood at the outskirts of the tame anti-war protests on campus and once went to New York for a bigger one, but like most of the students he also went to class on time and studied in the library, some because they were good kids on their way to good lives and others because college was their pass out of the draft. Edgar read Marx and he also read William Butler Yeats. He listened to folk music while he studied sine, cosine, tangent. He tacked up a picture of Malcolm X on his dorm wall and then he put his head down and wrote his papers and passed his tests.

Edgar and Fern confessed the things that

young lovers do: *my parents are horrid; it feels as if there's a hole in me that needs filling; I worry about the way I look; I worry about dying and other times I wonder if dying is the answer; I want a different kind of life, a bigger life; the world is terrifying and unjust and we have to change it.* They wrote the names of big cities as shorthand for *A place where no one is watching:* New York, San Francisco, Paris. *I've never met anyone like you,* Edgar wrote. How was it that out of the perfectly tended soil these two weeds had been allowed to grow?

They wanted to travel but not in the luxury their parents did: they imagined riding the mail boat through Polynesian islands, a rickety train filled with the smoke of a coal-powered samovar across the USSR. Fern said she wanted to be an archaeologist. Edgar did not know what he wanted to be but not because he was stagnant. He was a typhoon inside, a fast-moving storm, the whole brunt of which blew *against.* He did not want to own or be president of a steel company. He did not want to send lesser men into the mines to breathe the black air. He did not want to know the names of cigars or scotches or sit in endless conversation about which of the obviously crooked politicians would best

66

protect his business interests. Edgar said all of this to Fern and Fern wrote back that she understood, that there were much more important things than money, that art mattered and education, justice. Knowledge, philosophy, poetry. Fern talked to Edgar about Ben who sent letters of quiet desperation. *I have a black eye but it's healing up. The guy in the bunk above me spits on me in my sleep. I keep my shoes shined. I miss you, I miss you, I miss you.*

To Edgar she said, "If only my brother was a girl. They don't send girls to war and my parents wouldn't have cared what he turned out to be."

"We could try to hide him. People are going to Canada."

"Thank you for not telling me it's going to be okay," she said. They stayed on the phone all night talking about the ways they could save Ben and save the world and save each other. Fern's window turned dawn-blue. She woke up still holding the phone to her ear. "Edgar?" she said into it but he did not answer. Then she listened again and heard his steady breathing, sure as sure.

Before Halloween, Edgar told his mother that he wanted to have Fern's family over for Christmas dinner. Mary saw in her mind the effort and peril of a white-linen table-cloth and a roast goose, a hundred side dishes, each of which could be ruined a hundred different ways. "You had better really like this girl," she said. Nothing would secure their stead better than a marriage into such an old family, Mary knew. She also knew that she would have to be the one to prove their worth again and again to these Old Moneys. For the next six weeks she thought of nothing but Christmas Eve. She had the cook practice each dish six times. She tried twelve different floral arrangements. She opened every drawer in the house every day, sure that on the night of the party someone would go snooping and find a mouse nest in the one place she had forgotten to check. Mary was a woman at war.

On the first of December when the light displays started to go up, Mary drove to the suburbs with a notebook and drew sketches of each façade. No one had colored lights — the houses were all haloed in white like rows and rows of humble angels. Eaves were always decorated and it was acceptable to entwine a well-sculpted hedge. There was always, always a wreath with a red bow on the door. The oldest mansions were lit with reservation and the newer colonials were overdone. Mary aimed at a mid-mark. It was hardly their first light display but Fern's family would be the highest-ranking dinner guests they had ever had and behavior over the holidays was the basis of the social rankings for the following season. Mary knew that her invitation to exhibit a bouquet in Champion Bancroft's spring flower show depended on her performance now. She knew that she would either be invited back to Fluffy Turner's book club or told it was going on hiatus, though of course there would always be six cars parked in the drive on Tuesday evenings.

Edgar came home two weeks later reading the Communist Manifesto. He and Mary sat together at the big dining table while she polished the four-hundred-piece set of silver and he read aloud. "Constant revolutionizing of production, uninterrupted disturbances of all social conditions, everlasting uncertainty and agitation distinguish the bourgeois epoch from all earlier ones," he read.

"Edgar, I have no idea what any of that means."

"Here's where it gets good," he said, starting again. "All that is solid melts into air, all that is holy is profaned, and man is at last compelled to face with sober senses his real conditions of life."

"Which are?"

"Which are that the proletariat is forced to fight for decent pay and rights. It's class war, Mother."

"You do know where you grew up?" she said. "You do know whom you have invited for Christmas Eve dinner?"

"Fern's different," Edgar said. "We're both different." He left the table with his book. He tried sitting in his room, but it was the room of a rich kid. He tried sitting in the living room, but the walls of leather-bound books in mahogany shelves could not be described as proletariat. He tried sitting on the porch, but it was twenty-five degrees outside. Finally, Edgar settled in the barn. He had to overlook the horse tack and the fact that it was heated (he was sure Russian horses did not need heated stalls), but at least it smelled like animal shit. At least the ground was covered in hay.

Christmas Eve arrived with Fern in a red velvet dress with a wide skirt, her hair pinned in a neat twist and her mother in the usual black, her hair short, her lips red. Mary hugged the girl and Fern hugged her back. She was warm and pretty and complimented the light display. "You are very sweet," Mary said. Edgar took Fern to the parlor window to look at the snowfort he had built behind the house. It was bluish in the dark and almost glowing. "Will you move in with me?" he teased.

"How many bathrooms?" They both laughed.

"I can't believe they wouldn't send Ben home for Christmas," he said.

"I dreamed that he was drowning and my dress was too heavy to save him."

In the window were their reflected ghosts. They took hands and looked at the image of themselves. How very much this joined pair comforted them.

The fathers drank their drinks and talked over the particulars of a horse race they had both heard about but had not seen. Paul felt surprisingly good. It could shift at any moment, he knew, but for now he was enjoying the clear-headedness. Hugh asked after Ben. "He's on a base in Indiana," Paul said. "He seems all right so far. Probably no different than a college dorm." The statement sounded like a question.

"I expect you worry about him," Hugh said, having seen Ben at the library a few months before, his big body hunched over a book about lilies. He corrected himself, knowing his wife would cut his tongue out

71

if he ruined this night. "Just as we all do. Worry about our children, I mean. I'm sure he's going to be just fine."

The mothers took a tour of the house and Evelyn politely noticed the pleasing shade of white of the crown molding in the sitting room. Mary thanked her but the comment sent a shot of rage down her spine. To compliment a shade of white was to insult everything else.

"Yes, I'm very careful about whites," Mary said.

"One must be," said Evelyn. "The wrong white can ruin a room."

The goose came out hot and glistening and the mashed, stewed, baked and broiled sides were all pristine. Mary said quiet prayers of thanks. If she could have, she would have gone upstairs for the rest of the evening to cry tears of relief. Conversation was pleasant, wine was poured at the correct rate, the children looked at one another across the table in a way that made the adults nostalgic for their youth. It was the Christmas Eve they had all been hoping for, until Fern's father turned to Edgar and asked him about his studies. "I'm studying Marx," Edgar said. "And I'm finding it very interesting."

Fern's father was quiet, as one ought to

be if one wants the dinner to proceed without incident, but Hugh could not leave the statement alone.

"You give your child everything and he comes home from Yale a communist. Aren't we busy fighting a war over this?"

Edgar muttered something about the war being criminal and the family being a bourgeois institution.

Fern had no map for getting her beloved out of this tangle.

"Edgar took a Greek History class," Fern said. "I would love to visit Greece."

"It's sweet of you to try to rescue me," Edgar said to Fern, "but I don't need rescuing. My father should know that I disagree with everything he stands for."

Fern's mother excused herself and went to the powder room. Hating the world was plenty familiar but saying so in better company was unacceptable. Paul sat very quietly, arranging butter on his bread. Edgar said things about private property and the capitalist agenda and heavy progressive graduated income tax and his father said, "You are a spoiled shit," and his mother, whose hands were pink and shaking said, "What did I do to deserve you for my only child?" When Evelyn returned they all went quiet for a moment, remembering their manners. Fern wished hard for her brother, a person whose eyes could always settle her. The absence of Ben was thunderous, much louder than the boy himself had ever been.

Edgar stood up. "I'm sorry. I apologize. I shouldn't have brought up such topics on a holiday." He looked at the faces of his parents, his sweetheart, her parents. "I asked for this evening for a reason," he said. His voice started to crack and he wrung his napkin. "I wanted to ask Fern . . . Fern," he said, turning to her. "I wanted to ask you to marry me."

Before her father wondered whether *his* was the approval the boy should have sought first, Fern stood to meet him and took both of his hands. "Of course I will," she said.

"I thought you just said family was a bourgeois institution," Hugh tried to say.

"Shut up," Mary told him. "Shut up right now."

The boy and girl did not hear his parents fighting and they did not hear her parents try to find enough air in the room. *There she goes,* thought Evelyn, *just as I expected. Next she'll call to say she's pregnant.* Paul felt a needle-stab of pain. No one had ever looked at him the way the young couple was looking at each other.

In front of everyone, Fern and Edgar

leaned close and kissed.

Mary was up all night and the words that banged in her head were *Fuck it.* Fuck the roast goose and the four hundred pieces of silver. Fuck the book club and the flower show and the appropriate light display. She went into Edgar's room and found him reading by candlelight.

"You're right," she said. "It's all bullshit. The entire thing is bullshit."

He kissed her on the forehead, the second most important kiss of his life and both in the same night. But she would not relinquish her worldly possessions and join the movement to unionize the workers. She was not going to rage against private property or call for socialized medicine. By morning, by the time the Christmas sun rose over the pale pink bricks of their home, Mary had made a different kind of upending.

There was French toast on the table and Edgar and Hugh each had an envelope on his plate. They sat down, poured orange juice. "Open them," Mary said. "Those are your presents from me."

Hugh went first. In his envelope was a hand-drawn map of an island with little palm trees and arrows pointing to various features including a mermaid lagoon and a

75

harbor. "We still have to work out the details," Mary said.

"A map?" he asked.

"It's an island. It's in the Caribbean. I'm buying it for you. For Christmas." Mary's voice was flash-bright.

"This is not real."

"I don't care anymore," she said. "I don't care what all these people think. We have so much money. We should be having fun. From now on, fun."

Hugh could not get to his wife fast enough. He picked her up in his arms and kissed her hard on the neck. "What else will we buy?" he asked.

"Cars," she said. "Boats. A plane. We can go anywhere we want."

"An island?" Edgar was disgusted. "Have you thought about the people who already live there?"

But no one was listening to him. His parents were kissing in a way he had never seen them kiss. In a way that made him feel extra, unwanted, in the way. Quietly he opened his own envelope. In it was a piece of paper that read *Ticket* at the top. Below it said: *Your Freedom. Go be a communist. Travel to Africa. Learn to play the flute. No questions asked.*

"What is this?" Edgar asked.

Mary broke from her embrace, her face pink and full. "When you're ready, you can come back and earn a living with us. I'll put enough in your account to hold you and Fern for a few years. You don't have to keep the money if you don't want to. Give it to the natives. Or you can keep it but believe it's evil. I don't care. Do whatever you want."

"What if I don't come back?"

"You'll come back. You'll see."

The room sounded different. The whole house. They ate too much for breakfast and too much for lunch too. It was a good day to be a family, freedom sudden as a drug in their veins. They walked outside and admired the dry, solemn tendrils of a weeping willow and the steady green of a pine.

"I can't wait for tomorrow," Hugh said. "Tomorrow, we shop."

"You know I really disagree with what you're about to do," Edgar said.

"I know you do, sweetheart. And we think your ideas are nonsense."

None of them could remember having been happier.

1976

Fresh school supplies were a small consolation for Cricket, but neither of her brothers was comforted by a bouquet of sharp pencils. On the last day of summer, the lurk of school at their doorstep, Cricket and the boys put their bathing suits on and spread towels all over the yard. The Boston heat was a blanket over everything. They brought magazines outside. Cricket had her first beauty magazine, found on the beach on the island. Everything she had not known to worry about yet was contained within — pimples and periods and hand-holding and a flatter tummy and shaving and dancing with boys. Her body was still little-girl and would be for several years — she was nine — but she could feel the presence of that cliff in the distance. The twins at six were still deep in childhood's safe hold.

She studied the shapes of the teenagers in the pages and the spread of five girls in bikinis. How could she ever make that transformation? The magazine was not a map or a comfort — only a catalogue of concerns. When she opened it each time it was with anticipation, but by the time she closed it the only feeling left was shame.

The twins dog-eared a catalogue of baseball cards with nothing but delight and hope in their voices. "The Hank Aaron in pristine condition is worth like eighty dollars," Will said. "Just think what we could buy. Pogo sticks, new bikes, a model ship." James looked at Cricket's page, which was a color wheel used to decide one's clothing palette. He didn't get it. Being a girl seemed like a choice Cricket could make or unmake. Why not always build and dig and explode and collect? Cricket pulled her long braid around and studied the color of her hair in the sun. It was dirty blond but in the light there was red. She looked at the color wheel. She was in the blues and greys, never the greens or reds.

The boys suggested they play in the hose, but Cricket shushed them. "We don't need the hose. We're pretending we're at the beach."

"But," they said.

"Like it or lump it," she told them, repeating her mother. When the twins went to the yard's edge to pluck ladybugs from the tiger lilies, Cricket told them to watch out for jellyfish. The boys dug up dirt and tried to build a sandcastle. It was full of threads of roots and earthworms. They hung towels from the laundry line and pretended they were the sails of a ship with which to tack and jibe against the wind. Eventually they all fell asleep in the sun and their backs turned pink, which they secretly loved. That night, in the bathroom, they would brush and wash and then sit on the floor, pressing a finger into the burn of a shoulder to watch the white print turn red. They would take their sunburns to school with them, and their skin would hurt under the blue and white uniforms. At least there was that, at least there was proof that they had once been free.

Since they had come home from the island the day before, Edgar had not wanted to look Fern in the eye. He had gone out early and come back late. Then he had called from his writing studio to tell Fern that he had made a dinner date for them with another couple. "A double date?" she had asked, and it sounded like high school.

"Sort of," he had said. "Wear something nice." He had told her he would pick her up at seven o'clock.

She dressed and redressed: wide-leg red pants and matching vest, a long daisy-print dress, a jumpsuit she had never figured out how to wear and the pale blue dress, now so old-fashioned-looking, she had been wearing when she first danced with her husband when she was seventeen. She remembered the feeling of floating inside her own body. She had been the sea and the swimmer both, and the water was salt-soft and in it she was buoyant.

At Fern's feet, the dog searched around for anything dropped to eat. She bent her front paws and muzzled under the dresser.

"Stupid dog," Fern said, "there's nothing for you here." Fern felt unfastened. She was getting dressed for a man who had suddenly taken the place of her husband and all her resources were scarce. Everything around her — the house, the furniture, the manner of life — was poised to evaporate. She was a soft body trying to prepare herself for the unknowable future.

Fern looked out the window at her brood, three bathing-suit nappers in the yard. She could almost feel their sunwarm skin on her palm. The sweat on their scalps. Fern could see Cricket's magazine, could almost hear the clink of a lock as her girl entered the

81

room of self-doubt. She wished hard that there was a world in which Cricket would not have to pass through this stage, or ever enter the next.

Fern knew that the children would stumble in soon, slow and happy, looking for something to eat. She should scold them for being uncareful about the sun, but the school year would start in the morning and that seemed like punishment enough.

The dog fell asleep for a moment. She twitched in a dream almost immediately. Fern had been trained to distrust a faulty body. She had been kept at a distance from her grandparents the moment they showed their age, as if it was contagious. And when Evelyn had started to shake slightly — for each intended movement, dozens of tiny stowaway movements jangled in her body — she had begun to decline the invitations to parties as a courtesy to the other guests whose dinners she imagined her mortal body would ruin. She was fifty-eight. Not old, not sick. But her mother's body had betrayed her, and she was sure that no one wanted a decrepit woman for a wife or a friend. And then Evelyn had called two years before, so happy, to report that her doctor had suggested she have pills that would end her life before her body gave way.

82

"Your doctor suggested this?" Fern had asked.

"This is good news, Fern. I wanted to tell you so that you knew it was a possibility for you too, down the line."

"You aren't going to do it, though," Fern had said.

"When it's time. It's not suicide if it's time."

Her mother had had the pills for a year before Fern had received the call from her parents' maid saying that both mother and father were tucked in bed and neither of them was alive. "Father too," Fern said, coming to understand.

The maid had been hysterical. She thought it must either have been a divine act or a murder, but Fern knew that it was a little bit of both: her mother's attempt to save them both with a benevolent boost into a lighter kingdom, and a killing. These deaths had taken place six months ago, at the coldest point in winter yet only weeks before crocuses split the earth. Fern remembered standing at the phone that day, the house still morning-cold, and saying out loud to the maid on the other end of the line, "I am an orphan."

Today Fern understood her mother's distrust of her own body better — she felt like the shell-less hermit crab Cricket had brought to her on the beach during the summer, the little pink spiral of a creature in the girl's hand, the gulls already circling. She was young still but without the protection of wealth, she felt exposed, perched. The dog looked up with milky, cataract eyes and seemed not to recognize her own life. Maggie had shown up on their doorstep three years before and they did not know how old she was. Older than they thought, maybe. To Fern she looked like an animal that was about to fall apart.

Here Fern was, a small person in a big house, quite alone. There were decades of need ahead of her and three children and she was just a woman with no money. Edgar could save them or he could let them starve — she did not get to decide. The dog looked up, pan-eyed. There were grey patches in her fur and her back paws twitched under her efforts. She seemed very old suddenly, helpless and sad, and Fern was a woman with nothing extra. Fern checked her watch to see that she had time for an errand before the dinner. Still wearing the first-date dress, she scooped the animal up into her arms and carried her out of the room, down the stairs, through the hall, out the front door and down the steps and into the brown station wagon. Maggie whined all the way to the vet.

In the orange-walled office smelling of animal pee, Fern put Maggie up on the stainless table. She had dinner-party makeup on and wished for a way to hide. Her hands in the animal's fur were disorganized. She could see that the vet was as worried about the woman as the dog. "I think she's suffering. Is she suffering?" Fern said.

The vet listened to the dog's heart and felt her soft belly. He shined a light into her eyes and ears. "She's definitely aging," he said. "Everyone has a different tolerance for decline." He had bread crumbs in his thick blond mustache — he was not the person to ask about saving oneself from the small humiliations.

"Is it awful for her? Look at her. Maybe it would be kinder to let her go." Fern fought the need to cry. It seemed terribly dangerous to be a living creature, a body in need of nourishment and love for the duration of its existence.

"She's slowing down. Tired. Possibly sore in the joints. She probably has more time, though, if you aren't ready to let her go." Maggie looked confused and sad to Fern. Or maybe it was only her own reflection in the animal's eyes.

"Will you keep her overnight for observation? I don't know what to do."

The vet agreed to watch the animal for twenty-four hours and had Fern fill out the intake forms. Maggie was crated in the back with the barkers and whiners and sleepers and Fern bent down to reassure her. "Let's just see what happens, okay?" she said, touching the dog's wet nose through the grate. "You're a good dog. A good girl. A sweet and good girl."

On the way home, the car was silent. The city slipped by. Fern drove along the Charles where a dozen white triangles of sails tried to find wind. Fern tried to believe in generosity. She tried to believe in reprieve.

Fern stood on the curb feeling too old to stand on curbs. Edgar finally pulled up from his day in his dark green sports car and she straightened up to greet him. She put her thumb up but he did not smile at the joke.

"You can't wear that," he said. Discomfort ticked in his eyes.

"I couldn't decide." She already regretted the reminder of their beginning. Their young selves joined them in the car but they were not entirely welcome. Too much was not the same. It seemed unfair, to love that hard with your heartmuscle still so wet and new.

They had a little time, Edgar said, patting her knee. The sound of their takeoff rattled up Fern's spine to her brainstem. She put her head back against the headrest and closed her eyes.

"I'm sorry that my father gave everything away. I never wanted you to have to do something you hate."

"Clearly money will find me and trap me no matter what I do," he said. Edgar did not feel like less of a stranger than he had the past four days, to himself or to Fern.

He parked near Harvard Square where everyone was young and unpressed and lovely and encumbered with books. Inside the shop, a girl put dresses in a line. Edgar said, "Let's see you get beautiful." He was a different person than she was used to. He had opened his top button and deepened the part in his hair and wore his low brown boots and jeans and he hadn't shaved in four days. He was twitchy and nervous.

Fern had to be zipped and unzipped every time so that even the unflattering dresses were seen by the girl. "No, no, no," the girl said about one. "Don't let him see you in that." And then, "This one does a lot for you."

Each time Fern did the walk from the silk-draped dressing room to the center of the store where Edgar was sitting on a sofa. He gave a thumbs-up or -down. He asked her to turn around so he could see the back. Sometimes she saw in his face a jag of pleasure, sometimes she was a question he did not have the answer for.

"Just tell me which one you want me to wear," Fern said. She did not want to keep trying, to keep being naked in front of this young maiden who tugged at the seams, trying to get them to lay flat against a too-deep curve.

"The long red one," he said. "She'll wear it out." It had a plunging V, draped over her shoulders, shushed across the carpet.

After they paid and left, the shopgirl ran outside after them. She came up close to Fern and Fern thought she was about to be kissed. The girl's breath was mintsweet; she had thought of every single manipulation of her little body. Out of her hand came a small tube, and she said, "Open your lips," and in three sweeps, she lipsticked Fern. Top, top, bottom. "Now," she said, "press."

The house was a tall Victorian, dinner was pork chops, conversation was weather, American apathy and political unrest in

Guatemala where Glory and John Jefferson had recently been. Why were they in this particular house with this particular couple? Fern wondered. Nothing good came of a dinner party, she thought. She wanted to be alone with her husband, to talk about Chicago and money and all the years they had ahead. Edgar was too happy to be here. Manic. The hostess had the big, frilled hair that everyone wanted and her eyelashes were long and she wore, to great effect, a jumpsuit like the one Fern had been unable to figure out. Fern asked after the washroom and John Jefferson walked her there, down a hallway that seemed very long. Instead of gesturing to the end and letting her make the journey alone, he was behind her the whole way.

"We redid this place when we bought," he said. "You should have seen the roof. You should have seen the foundation."

"It looks nice now," Fern said, wishing for a light switch. The walls were papered in avocado green. The runner was patterned with oversize orange and red flowers.

"*You* look nice," he said.

Finally, a door.

"Here we are," John said, proud. He turned the knob, flipped the light on, smelled the room. "Clean and fresh." He smiled.

"Thank you, John. Thanks. All right."

The man waited for Fern to enter and then he closed the door for her. She listened for the sound of his retreating footsteps, but heard none. He could not possibly be waiting for her. Everything was orange — the tile, the sink, the toilet — except the towels, which were white with rainbows arcing across their corners. Fern used up time looking in the mirror. Her hair was old-fashioned, too neat. The red dress was unconvincing on her. There was a photograph on the wall of Glory wearing a wreath of flowers and standing between two bare-chested Polynesian women.

Fern pulled up her dress but could not pee.

She went to the door, put her ear against the cool wood and listened for John's breathing. Maybe he was pressed there too, trying to find her sounds in the small room.

Fern flushed for no reason. Washed her hands. She did not have the shopgirl's red lipstick, but she applied a coat of the old pink that was always in the bottom of her purse.

John was halfway down the hall, holding a framed photograph of his sister as a baby.

"God," he said, "I remember exactly what she felt like in my arms at this age." He hung it back up, then, with his big, warm fingers, he straightened Fern's dress strap. "Where would you like to go?"

"I was going to finish my dinner," she said.

"Well," John said. "I thought . . . I was told. You and I were supposed to . . . I thought that was the idea. Glory told me. Your dress," he said gesturing at the evidence. He looked distraught. Not threatening but punctured.

"Are you crying?" Fern asked. John could not seem to find a place to put his hands. Fern felt sorry for him and sorry for herself but was afraid to risk touching him. She went back to the bathroom and got a length of toilet paper, which she brought to John. She put one finger on his shoulder, the smallest touch she could think of, while he wiped his eyes and blew his nose. He found his cigarettes in his back pocket and lit one.

"I'm so embarrassed," he said.

"It's already forgotten. Come on," she told him. The rest of the house began to lend its light.

What she saw was one body and not two, at first. It was just Edgar's back until it was not anymore, until Glory's hands were also there, wrapped around him. Ten red gashes of fingernail polish. "Oh," she said out loud, and the attempted kiss in the hall made a different kind of sense. *He's trying to give me away,* she thought.

Fern knew that her husband had felt worried and helpless. She had been trying to be good enough to carry him through — his patient wife, loving him in the circumstances. Now she understood that she was stupid, that he was lost, that they were, for the first time, not each other's immediate salve. Edgar and Glory Jefferson looked familiar with one another and Fern watched because she had to. Fern had wondered what Edgar would do to survive this part of life, to survive his family's needs, now unmet. The answer was here in a stranger's dining room, between soup and entrée, the centerpiece an autumnal bouquet surrounded by small pumpkins, the smell of scarred pig flesh in the air. Fern had never seen her husband kiss before. He moved jerkily. From behind, he looked like a bird, pecking at garbage in the grass.

The woman was liquid in his arms. Slipping and grabbing and looking very warmed up. Fern could practically hear the race their heartbeats were in.

"Sweetheart," John said. He stubbed his cigarette out in a red ashtray already half full of butts.

His wife turned around. She looked frustrated more than sorry, like she had been woken up before she needed to be. "I thought you'd gone," she said.

"Fern," Edgar said. He inspected his wife for signs of rumple or muss. He looked deeply sad.

"We're all done," Fern told them. "We're all finished."

"Yes." Mrs. Jefferson smiled. "Of course." Her husband received the volley of contempt she tossed his way: ten or fifteen years of marriage, two or three minutes each time, and then he was ready for something sweet and sleep.

Edgar came over to his wife and squeezed her hand and she could not tell if it was with sorrow or pride or terror or regret. He leaned towards her and he smelled tinny with spit. She jerked away. "We are not even," she said.

"Well, then, I expect you're hungry," Glory said to the group. "Shall we have our pork chops?"

"I'll be in the car," Fern said. "Eat if you want, but I'll be in the car."

Edgar followed Fern out and they both got into the car and he backed out of the driveway onto the night street. Fern wanted the dress off. She wanted a door to slam and hide behind, but she did not want to drive home because that felt too much like an act of forgiveness. She told him to pull over, shut the engine. She slapped the dashboard.

"When did this start?" she shouted.

"Tonight. This is all that's happened," he lied.

"Was this Glory Jefferson's bright idea?" Fern had read about swingers and key parties and some magazine article was always proclaiming the end of monogamy, but none of it had seemed real or possible in her world.

Edgar felt so much and yet none of it was enough. "I don't want to retract my novel," he said, "and I don't fucking want to be a steel man."

"Are you going to live on her money instead?"

"My life walked out on me and then she showed up. I guess I just wanted to look away." He realized that in the fog of his head it seemed almost as if the question of what they were willing to sell in order to survive — Edgar or everything else — could be overpowered with the noise of a shared affair. When Glory had called him in the morning and made the invitation, she had sounded so clear-headed, so sure that what Edgar had done in column A could be easily balanced by what Fern could do in column B. She had said, "If everyone's kissing then kissing's not a problem."

"I don't know what to do. I do not know. I do not." She was yelling by the end.

They sat there on the side of the road, houses dinner-lit, silent beyond silent. Edgar polished his glasses and put them back on, blinked at the seen world.

Edgar thought of the first thing he had had published, an excerpt from his novel in a glossy magazine. Fern, proud, relieved, had gone to the store and bought every celebratory food she could find: caviar, cake, champagne, lobster, but when she had come home Edgar had said, "What I really want is to go out for pizza." She might have been hurt on another day, felt stupid because she should have known, but that day happiness could not be undone. Fern had put the expensives in the refrigerator, scrubbed the children's yard-scummy cheeks and said, "Pizza it is." The adults had drunk beer and the kids had sipped Shirley Temples and then they all had ice cream dessert. "To the author," they had said, clinking. There had been other celebrations to come but this one had been the purest. Edgar had worked at his book for years and he had finally been able to call himself a writer. It had felt like coloring in the last years of his life — yes, those were real. Yes, it had counted.

Fern now sat beside him, willing to erase everything. She said as much.

"At the risk of sending you into her arms, you are not welcome at our house tonight."

"Where am I supposed to go?"

"Walk to a hotel. I don't know. That is your problem to solve."

Fern stepped into the house and there were the children, mounded up on the floor like left laundry, asleep. The children always fought sleep with all their strength but once they were down they went so deep that they could remain unconscious through hurricanes, fights.

"Where is the sitter?" Fern asked, trying to rouse them. "Sweethearts? Wake up and go to bed." She knelt beside her bunch, began to untangle them. There were so many arms and legs. The bodies grumbled and snuffed. "Mother?" Cricket said. "Where is Father?" The boys opened their eyes and Fern wanted to hug them all but her arms were insufficient. She was well outnumbered.

Fern tried to replay the day, tried to find the memory of calling Miss Audrey to babysit. She had meant to, she had thought about it, but she could not remember hearing the woman's voice over the telephone.

"Where is Maggie?" Cricket asked. "We lost Maggie."

"Yes, we lost her and we need her," said the twins.

"I'm sure she's fine, my loves."

What Fern had thought of as a gift to the animal early in the evening had turned into something that she could not utter to her children. She did not try to explain aging or love and how much harder it was to keep trusting beauty the later it got. How, though she was only twenty-eight years old, she seemed to have passed into the long slide during which time a woman became less and less valuable, and to keep her around became an act of charity rather than pleasure. Fern turned on a lamp, unearthed the markers and paper and laid them out on the living room floor for her flock. She said, "Let's make some signs and hang them up in the neighborhood tomorrow." *Lost Dog, Reward.*

"How much reward?" Will asked. Fern, knowing exactly where the dog was, could be generous.

"Five hundred dollars," she said. "No, a thousand." Everyone was cheered. Such a good mother, so devoted.

"Where is Father?" Will asked.

"He'll be home later," she said, arranging them at the kitchen table.

Beloved, they wrote. *Maggie, Maggie, Maggie.* There was a stone of something in Fern's chest so heavy it felt like it might fall through her, tearing everything soft on its way down. Hatred. For Glory, for Edgar, for the fact of the kiss, the fact that he had wished to lend her to John Jefferson, the fact that she did not have a good or fair solution to their survival either, the fact of everything they stood to lose.

Cricket said, "Couldn't we put them up now? The sooner the better?" It felt good to Fern to be taking care of someone. It felt good to be acting out the saving of a lost love. It felt good to be part of a mission that did not involve Edgar. She hoped he was sitting on the edge of a sagging hotel bed, stale smoke in the drapes and a sad glass of beer on the table. She hoped he was wrung out. Fern found and distributed sweaters and flashlights and walked with her flock up the neighborhood streets, down the neighborhood streets, all the station wagons parked in a line, and they tacked a sign to each lamppost. Inside the houses, people were cleaning up from their day, drinking a nightcap, rubbing their eyes, bidding good-night. The children called and called. *Maaa-ggieee!* The name stretched out and turned musical. It was a whole song. Fern sang it too. She sang and she believed it. She tried to trust what she had done. Maggie would always be young enough now. No one would remember her stalking away from a mess on the floor, too weak to lift her back legs completely. *Maaa-ggieee!* went the song. She could be — she was — anywhere.

1966

After they were married, Fern and Edgar had driven to Kentucky and rented a little house for the summer. He was twenty-two and she was eighteen. Other young people were going to San Francisco and New York, sloughing off the idea of marriage like it was a pair of handcuffs. These were the same people whom Edgar had seen at protests and who had showed up on the news. At twenty-two, Edgar already felt too old to join them. It was almost as if he was not part of that generation. He was married now, an adult, and it was too late to move into an apartment in California with ten other people, smoke joints and stay up until dawn. Fern and Edgar agreed with the values, the politics, but they were relieved to feel these feelings in a warm house. And they were just as happy not to share one another.

Anyway, the hippies seemed indulgent. It

was all hedonism and music and too much sunshine. Edgar and Fern were seeking something much more real. To them, it felt good to cultivate discomfort, to live in coal country with people who had no luxuries, to push their young bodies and minds up against the grit and truth of danger and hardship, heat and sweat. Edgar had pictured miners with soot-faces and wrecked hands. He had decided that he wanted to write about their lives, the deep earthen dives they made for the sake of carbon, for the sake of fire, for the sake of metal. He imagined himself telling their story, the newspapers printing the truth, shaming the owners, his father declaring the miners heroes. He knew this was idealistic and stupid, but he thought: maybe. Weren't good works always completed against the odds?

It was not only saving that Edgar wanted to do. He saw in the workaday lives a kind of relief and salvation. The daily job, the weekly pay, beans in the pot and freshly picked blackberries in the bowl, hands scabbed from the thorns. There was honor in this. Honor he envied.

Fern wanted to play house with her new husband. She wanted the little cottage with just enough windows for which to sew curtains. Just enough space in the kitchen to make an omelet. She'd knit something. She and Edgar would sit at the table and read aloud to each other. Marriage was a jailbreak. Fern was free from the slow and steady drip of dislike that was her parents' experience of the world.

Ben, though. Fern thought about him all the time, how they had built a fort in the skirt of a pine tree in the prairie when they were ten where he had asked her to promise that they would die at the same time. He explained that it seemed like an important detail — they had entered as a pair and lived as a pair. She had said yes and meant it, but how quickly she had abandoned him when love sparked a few years later. She told herself that she was a good sister — she was doing what women did. Even twins were meant to go their separate ways. She sent care packages with cookies and candies and each time she enclosed a letter from the invented girlfriend, though Ben never told her if he used this story.

In the central highlands of Vietnam, American B-52s dropped seventy-six bombs. They counted more than a thousand Vietnamese bodies in the jungle after the battle. The news crew sent footage home, the reporter in his helmet crouched behind a tree, yelling over the chop of a helicopter,

102

and right then, something exploded and the boy to his right, so dirty that it didn't matter if he was blond or dark, flew off camera, and the reporter looked into the lens and his face was shock-flat, and he just sat there because he was not allowed to intervene. He was only there to observe.

And in Indiana, on an Army base that had trained and lost 59 Benjamins, 314 Johns, 211 Davids and enough other boys that they had ceased to track them by name, Ben sat on the edge of his bunk bed and watched a bird that had flown inside. He knew that he could not catch it so he waited for it to fly against the window hard enough that it fell to the ground. Maybe the bird would still be alive, he hoped, only stunned, and then he could carry it outside. He should have been in the mess hall. He would get in trouble but he didn't care. Ben was suffering his own stun. That morning he had received his assignment: he was to be trained as a motion picture photographer, part of a four-man team that would film the war for military archives. Not an office job. Not safe. He would be deployed in four weeks, but instead of a gun, Ben would stand in front of the war holding nothing but a camera.

The bird fell. It was still breathing when

Ben brought it outside and set it at the base of a fall-bright maple tree, encouraged it gently with a red, red leaf.

Ben did not tell Fern about his assignment. Shame and fear had knitted everything in him shut. He wrote to Fern and called once a week but all he reported were the meals, the exercises, the weather. He sounded farther away than he really was. His voice was mostly air, just a whisper. Each week she wished the same wish, "Just try to go unnoticed." And then he went back to learning how to film without flinching and she went back to the game of husband and wife in the little house with the little pots and pans and a table just the size for two.

Fern and Edgar went to the market together and chose jam and bread, which they ate in bed, naked and too hot for sheets. They went dancing at the hotel ballroom on a Friday night, all the men clean-shaven and the women in gingham dresses. Fern's blond hair was teased and set and she had on a short, straight dress and white pumps. She was delighted by the banjo and mandolin, instruments her parents would not have been able to name. There were two fast songs and then a slow one, the music growing soft enough that the overwhelming sound was of feet shuffling over wooden planks. Sliding together, landing together, everyone's arms around a neck or a waist, each a scented pair: aftershave and rose.

There was pleasure in pleasure and Fern and Edgar had plenty of that, newlyweds that they were. There was also pleasure in bearing witness to the life of this unknown place. The miners really did come up from below with their faces black. Edgar felt validated in both his belief in good, regular work — these people were grateful, honest — and also his belief that what his father did for a living was possible because of the suffering of poorer people. All summer, Edgar picked the scab of guilt. It felt good to feel bad. Someone in the family had to.

Ben stopped sending letters but he still called on the phone. He was quiet while Fern skimmed over her everydays, not wanting to say too much about how happy she was, despite missing him. Ben said, "I don't want to talk, Fern, but don't hang up. Just hold the line." She leaned against the wall until her knees ached and then she slid down and sat on the floor. She knew he was there from his breathing. More than an hour later Ben said, "Thank you. I have to go." She heard his end of the phone find its cradle and then the line went quiet. She imagined him taking a deep breath before straightening his body into a pole, looking at the far horizon and saluting. This was a season of worry and joy living side by side in Fern. They did not cancel each other out or blend to create a soft grey. Love could not temper fear and fear could not temper love.

Fern and Edgar became friends with a black miner and his wife. They did not say aloud that they were proud of this fact, yet they were. They wanted to transcend the legacy, to be the generation that made it right. The couple, in their fifties with children already grown and gone, invited them over for hamburgers and beer. They talked about summer and weather and winter and parents and food and it seemed like skin was just skin. They got a little drunk. The men stood on the porch smoking and the stars were just beginning to pop and a few fireflies drew lines in the dusk and there was no moon and it was perfect, a perfect night.

The man said, "I wonder if I could ask you for a favor." He admitted to Edgar that he was illiterate and asked for help writing a letter to his family at home.

The man produced an oily piece of paper

from his pocket and Edgar understood how much it cost the man to make this admission, to hand the blank sheet over. The paper was slightly wobbly in front of Edgar and he wanted to go home with his wife and drink water and bite her neck and sleep. He rubbed his eyes and used the railing as a hard surface on which to write.

He wanted Edgar to describe a particular lake with a rope swing. He wanted to say how much he missed his mother.

Fern and the miner's wife walked outside with a plate of cookies. Fern said, "You might have to take me home now, my love." It was very dark by then, all stars. The miner and his wife drew close together and he kissed her on the top of her head.

"We forgot a flashlight," Edgar said.

"No trouble," the miner told him and sent his wife inside. She returned with a laundry basket full of headlights, flashlights and lanterns, a man well prepared to move through unlit places. He insisted that Fern and Edgar each have their own. "Better to have too much light," he said.

"Wait. We have to finish your letter," Edgar said.

"Don't worry," the man said, "I can sign my own name." It was a joke; it was not a joke.

Fern chose an old-fashioned kerosene lantern and Edgar took a flashlight with batteries. They went out into the rich blackness, making halos of yellow and white. Fern pressed away a thought of boys like her brother in a night yet darker than this, the only bright spots explosions that might kill them. She took Edgar's hand. With less vision they noticed sound: their feet on the grass, mosquitos, the pop of a firecracker a few miles away.

They stayed on into winter. Edgar kept writing letters for the black miner. They went to the Friday dances and ate pancakes on Sundays at the diner. They adopted a stray tabby cat. Edgar's parents kept asking if they were finished yet, ready to come back to the regular world, and Fern and Edgar kept trying to tell them that they had it wrong: *this* was real. The other life was the one full of falseness. Fern's parents had no such question. Fern and her father talked only about Ben, though there was little to say. She and her mother talked only about the cherry tree in the house orchard that had been overpruned and the gardener who now had to be fired.

It was already cold outside by November. "Gin and tonic?" Edgar asked and she smiled for him. She heard the tink of the ice but not its hiss. He hummed to himself while he poured.

"You know where I'd like to go is Egypt," she said.

"Because it's warm there?"

"Because of all the old things they have. And because it's warm."

The snow had fallen for the last week. It had rounded out the corners on everything — the tables, the wooden chair Fern knew she ought to have brought in. She came from people who thought they were too good to run from the cold, too hearty, too real. Fern allowed herself only short dreams of summer, properly earned summer, after winter and after spring.

"Add another log to the fire, would you?" she asked. This was a beloved job of his. If he tended his fire as completely as he would have liked, they would have gone through their season's supply of wood in a few days.

"I'll wait a few more minutes."

"We can get more wood," she said.

"This is a winter's worth," he said, gesturing to the pile under the eaves. "This is enough for everybody else."

Whether to buy their way out would be a constant question. To be like everyone, to be regular, a constant dream. For him it tasted sour because he failed at it and for her it tasted sweet because occasionally she succeeded.

Edgar whittled, turning something rough over in his hands, imagining a way to smooth it. Reflected in his thick glasses: the bald trees outside, grey-gold. A siren sounded.

Fern untangled a length of yarn, which was orange and scratchy. The cat was at the other end. For the cat, this ball was its own celebration. Fern carried the one end carefully through each knot, loosening as she went.

Another siren and another. "I wonder what's going on," Edgar said.

Edgar turned on the radio but it wasn't music that came out. A man's deep voice said the second half of a sentence, ". . . no known survivors."

The cat, at that exact instant, choked on the orange string. Fern dragged it, wet, from the cat's throat.

They turned the radio up, listened until they had heard the whole story. The mine had collapsed with twenty-nine men inside. There was a fire. No one could go down to search, and it was unlikely they would find anything but bodies if they did.

Edgar called the wife of the miner but the

line was busy. Everyone's lines were. He called his father. "Turn on the news," Edgar said.

"It's on. They're talking about the hippies."

"Your mine just killed twenty-nine people."

"I don't have a mine, Edgar. I have a steel factory and we have an excellent safety record. And if you're still spending that money then it's your factory too."

The line was quiet. "Edgar," his father said. "I should tell you. There's a letter here for you."

"Don't you feel responsible at all?"

"Edgar. It's the draft."

The room stilled. Edgar looked at the scratched wood of the table, at the seam between floorboards and wall, at his wife, his beauty, their marriage still so new. "The war?" he asked, and Fern — who had watched the fall of her husband's face had asked, "What? What happened? Is everyone all right?" — understood.

"But we're married," she said. "They're not drafting married men." Love saves us, she thought. What better reason could there be?

Edgar hung up the phone without saying goodbye. Fern sat on his lap and smelled his scalp and made cuffs around his wrists with her hands. Their lives were promised to each other, legally bound, but they still felt another body in the room.

They drove that night through the town. In one house there was a solemn gathering, everyone in the lamplight in a circle around the blue flicker of the television. Fern and Edgar had lost no father, no husband, no son. They were tourists, observing the everyday marvel of working-class lives, black lives. Edgar wanted to apologize for his very existence. He had spent his father's money to rent the little cottage, to buy the diner pancakes on Sunday morning, the Friday night steaks, the stamps he had given to the miner.

Edgar slowed the car in front of the house where the black couple lived hoping to be surprised to find the big man's frame at the table, safe. "Maybe he had the day off," Fern said. But the curtains were drawn and there was only one silhouette behind them, one small female shadow. The miner's grandfather might have been owned by Fern's great-grandfather; the miner's father might have died fighting to be free; the miner had died because he was poor. Edgar took his wallet out of his back pocket and emptied the bills. He did not count them but Fern saw a hundred-dollar note in the pile and a book of stamps. He got out of the car and put them in the mailbox. Edgar thought of the word *fortune,* both accumulation and luck. Inside was a woman on the wrong side of both, while his own numbers ticked steadily upward. He drove home holding Fern's hand, coasted the last mile with his lights off. The emptiness of night, the darkness, seemed like the only honest thing.

Edgar said, "We could go to Canada. We could go to Mexico."

"We don't have to run away. You just tell them you're married and you don't have to go." She would not have been ready to flee even if she had to. She was eighteen years old. She was, for the first time in her life, cooking her own meals. She was learning to drive a car. She was imagining going to college someday and having pretty little babies who grew into pretty boys and girls whom she would raise and admire with the man she loved. She wanted a home, her own home.

Edgar stopped the car in front of their house. He looked at his wife. He understood in her face that she was afraid, that she knew there existed the possibility of losing him. They watched three bats disappear behind the house and come back, disappear and come back.

"I'm scared too," he said.

Edgar thought of the miners, still under the ground. The wrongs in the past, the wrongs in the present. He thought of the miners' wives and daughters, their mothers.

Edgar squeezed hard on the gearshift. "Everyone else in the world has to do what they have to do to survive."

"Are you saying you'd rather kill and maybe die than get out of it for a legitimate reason?"

"I'm saying the world isn't fair. Why do I deserve safety when someone else doesn't?"

All night, Edgar dreamed of being buried. At daybreak he pressed his body against Fern's back and said, "I'm going to go where they tell me. Love doesn't save everyone else. Money doesn't save everyone else."

"You're half blind. What about that? Isn't that an excuse?"

"I'll leave that up to them. I'm sure they'll give me an appropriate post."

Fern felt a pain in her gut so sharp she put her hand there to feel for a cut. She said, "You have to come back." She turned to him. She wanted to slap him hard across the cheek, to burn herself onto him. "You have to fucking swear that you will come back."

The first weeks on base in Tennessee before Edgar left for the war were sweet, which surprised both him and Fern. He stood behind her while she cooked, imprinted the curve of her hipbone on his palm. She made him pork chops and buttered peas and they stayed up too late playing cards and drinking gin. He trained with other boys and his muscles changed shape, sharpened. She undid his buttons to find a new version of her husband, made it her work to leave all his muscles weakened and tired. They were a young couple in a house the same size as all the other young couples' houses; his income was earned. Their bed was always warm.

They saw hippies on television and one morning a carful of them pulled up to the pump beside Fern and Edgar at the filling station. Edgar felt a vague tug, sure that he would have been at home in their conversations, much more than he was with the other Army boys. Three girls spilled out of the backseat in jeans and cropped shirts. Fern felt suddenly as if she was wearing her mother's clothes. She touched her hair, which she had dried and sprayed. How had these girls managed to grow their hair so long already? Even if Fern had been brave enough to join them on their westward migration it would have taken years before she could look the part.

Edgar, dressed in the giveaway green, washed his windshield and kept his head down. One of the hippies passed him and said, with distaste, "Morning, man." A few years later people like him would spit on anyone in a military uniform, but it was early still and hatred for the war was a source of heat but not yet fire.

"Morning," Edgar said, trying to mimic the hippy's distaste, "man." The guys came out of the filling station a few minutes later with chocolate candy and sodas. The girls came out with cigarettes and matches. Fern and Edgar sat in their station wagon and watched the van pull away, pause at the street and turn right, heading west.

In the evening, the phone rang and Fern picked up. "It's Ben," her mother said. The kitchen lost its air. Her voice sounded like a rattle; this could only be an ending. Fern sat down on the floor.

"What happened?" she asked. Ben had not been deployed yet. He should have been safe.

"He's not dead," her mother said. "He's all right. They say he's going to be fine."

Fern imagined lost limbs, severed arteries, blood lost. In a single second she had pictured a hundred accidents: a misfired gun, a grenade that was supposed to have been fake, a car crash, a fight. "Tell me what's happening," she said.

"I don't know exactly. They just said they're sending him to a hospital. He's seeing things. He tried to fly away."

In the morning Fern took the train to Indiana and stood in the hospital room with the pale yellow walls where her brother lay in bed, his arms and legs encased and strung up from the ceiling. She asked him what happened and he told her that he had only meant to fly a short distance, just to the grassy place outside his room. He said, "I really thought I could do it. I never meant to hurt myself."

The nurse came with fish sticks and a pool of corn pudding and a slice of white bread. Ben, broken Ben, was so calm. He ate and they turned on the television and he laughed at places where a person was meant to laugh. Fern understood that he had indeed flown himself away. He had broken six bones to do it, but tonight Ben was not going to sleep in the Army barracks where he would be spit on from the upper bunk. He was not going to wake up to a hundred push-ups or the names, over breakfast, of the soldiers who had died in the war the day before. Fern was proud of her brother. Before she left she found a marker and drew a cluster of stars in the crook of his elbow.

On the day Edgar was to leave, Fern put on the green sheath dress she wanted him to remember her in and she melted the last-day-butter in the last-day-pan, and flipped his eggs without breaking them.

He said, "My girl, what a girl I have."

Fern said, "I'm about to get a lot better in your mind," and smiled. "When you come home, you might be disappointed." She did not want to say everything — she did not want it to be complete so that some god would think they had said goodbye so well that when someone needed to die, he would direct the bullet or the mortar in Edgar's direction.

"No matter what happens —" Edgar started, but Fern cut him off.

"You're going on a journey, an adventure. Your whole regular life will be here when you return. It'll be just as plain as ever."

Fern wanted to sit on his lap and kiss him all over his tanned face and give him the store of good-luck charms she had been gathering — the red-to-grey feather from a cardinal, her father's watch, a lock of her hair, a square of satin from her wedding dress. Instead, she let the silence settle in. She let Edgar mop the yolks and drink his coffee.

As they waited on the platform, a higher-up approached Edgar and said, "Change of plans, son," and handed him a folded piece of paper. "When you get to St. Louis, you'll be taken to the airport." Edgar looked at the typewritten page.

"Alaska?" he asked. "What do they need me to do in Alaska?" He looked at the paper again. "Because of my eyes? They didn't seem worried about that before."

Edgar looked like something shaken out, wet fabric in the wind. Fern stared at the ground. She did not explain that she had called his father after Edgar had gone to sleep the night before and asked for help. That she had begged him to find someone who knew someone.

"Oh, sugar," Hugh had said, "I already have."

It had been easier even than Fern could have dreamed. Edgar's father had had to make only one phone call to a college buddy, a General, and in his conversation

he had not even had to ask for the favor —
just in mentioning that his son was bound
for the central highlands of Vietnam, Edgar
had been rescued. The two men had spent
the rest of the conversation talking about
football, and within an hour, Edgar's assignment had been changed from the frontlines in the jungle to a post in the icy north
where the only threat was an impossibly
unlikely attempt by the Russians to cross
the frozen churn of the Bering Strait.

"Thank you," Fern had whispered into the
phone.

"Don't worry — I'll never tell him that
you called."

When Fern had woken up in the morning
and there had been no messenger at the
door to tell Edgar that his post had changed,
she had thought they had forgotten or that
the message would be too late to save him
or that she had dreamed the whole thing.

"Did you do this?" he asked. Was he
angry? His face was red.

Here was money, rafting Edgar northward,
alone again.

The base was a tatter of lonely women. The
black women must have gathered in a different house because the luncheons Fern
was invited to were populated with girls as

pale as her. When they gathered, the sound of them was shrill and made Fern nervous. It was as if they had all grown up together in the same house, were all sisters.

"What would you like to drink, Fern?"

"Water? Please," Fern said. The next person wanted punch, and the person after her.

"Sure, punch would be nice."

"I'd love punch, if you have it."

"Punch, punch, punch," they all said with the same cheerful smile.

A tray came out of the kitchen with twelve glasses of bright red and one clear. Fern lowered her head. She had no problem with being just like everyone, but here she wasn't.

One of the girls asked Fern where she was from.

"Chicago," she said.

"Me too! Whereabouts?"

"North Shore," she said.

"Oh, fancy," the girl said. "What are you doing here? I thought people like you got out of situations like this." Indeed they did — all of Fern's and Edgar's classmates were in medical school, working towards PhDs in Russian Literature or already employed by law firms. They were secure in the idea that they were more valuable at home than in the jungle. Fern did not mention that while all the girls from the city, the girls from the town and farms had boyfriends and husbands who had been deployed to the jungle, her love was in Alaska. She was on an unknown planet, the only one of her kind. Fern wished for her brother. She was a person who had a match in the world — someone who had been born beside her, grown up beside her, who knew the particular nick and burn of their family and home.

The girl pressed for more details. Town, street. She kept knowing the places Fern described right down to the fence, the meandering drive at the end of which was a perfectly calculated view of a big house. "It's white with blue shutters, right? Aren't there some kind of pink flowers in window boxes?"

"Geraniums," Fern said. She felt as if someone had removed her skin.

"We used to go for Sunday drives up there. Papa liked to look at the big houses and pretend we were going to buy one." She turned to the group. "We should be nice to Fern," she said. "She lives in a mansion."

"It's not a mansion," Fern said.

"You should be happy. Aren't you happy? Don't you wake up every morning and think how lucky you are?"

When Fern got home, there was something in her mailbox. It said only, *Miss you.* He did not sign his name but she knew the writing: Ben. She called the rehabilitation facility and asked for his room.

"Am I crazy?" Ben asked.

"You are you. The world is what's crazy."

Edgar, in Alaska, was a misplaced toy soldier. He had been flown to Fairbanks then Nome and then driven in a jeep by a logger with a black beard and no eyebrows to an expanse of white tundra that seemed to be edgeless. There were no roads, just snow and snow and snow, and in the middle, a tiny log cabin with a curl of smoke coming from its chimney. Edgar could not have conjured a scene less reminiscent of war. The jeep stopped and the driver said, "Welcome home, soldier." He threw Edgar's rucksack on the snow and drove away. Edgar stood there and the wind kicked snow onto his face. He was wearing the same clothes that the boys going to the hot jungle wore. He had no hat, no coat, no gloves. His boots, as he walked to the little cabin, began to soak through.

Inside: a single room with four bunk beds along one wall, a metal table and chairs, a sink, hooks with parkas and snowboots below. A young man, fat and pale, was sitting in front of the fire with a sketchpad. Edgar could see the drawing — a naked girl lying on her side, a kitten curled up in front of her. "Nice," Edgar said, gesturing towards the drawing. The man looked up at him and said, "Welcome to nowhere."

Another man came in later, spit blood into a cup, his lungs wracked from running for hours in the cold. He did three hundred push-ups, four hundred sit-ups, then went outside naked and stood there in the arctic evening, the sunlight hardly more than a grey fog. Edgar, from the window, looked at the man's body, imagined his sweat turning to a crust of ice. It got dark and Edgar checked his watch: 4:00 p.m.

"We call him Runner," the fat kid said. "By 'we' I mean 'I.' "

"Is there anyone else here?"

"Nope."

"What are we supposed to be doing?"

"Fuck if I know, brother. I'm drawing fucking kittens. Best job in the Army. Better than getting my legs blown off."

They had a radio, which Runner knew how to use, but no one ever called them on it. Runner ran every day and hardly spoke. The other boy, who Runner called Fatty, kept a series of jam jars filled with urine under his bunk. They had rations in crates in the corner. The sink didn't run so they melted snow in a pot over the fire. There was a pit latrine out back and Runner had built a wooden platform on which to stand while he poured a pot of boiled snowmelt over his head.

Edgar figured that both of the others were also rich, that they had the kind of fathers who knew whom to call to move the game pieces of their children into safe territory. He hung on to the thread of anger at Fern for rendering him so useless at the very same time that he was eaten up by gratitude for not being imminently dead in a rice paddy. Next he hated himself for ever having thought he might serve a purpose in the world, that he might ever have been anything but a rich kid. Edgar wrote to Fern and described the whiteness, described the silence. For three weeks no one came or went.

Then, across the ice came a sled pulled by dogs. Runner was out but Edgar and Fatty sat at the window, watching the approach. "Who the fuck is that?" Fatty whispered. He seemed terrified. He was sweating. They had their guns at their sides.

The sled stopped and a person stepped off, yelled at the dogs, which all lay down in the snow. The person, almost child-size, was wearing a fur coat and fur boots and carried a leather bag. The voice at the door was high and then whoever it was came inside, and Fatty pointed his gun until the hood came off and it was a girl, dark-haired, pretty, her cheeks red with cold.

"Put those things away," she said. "And make me some coffee."

The two men scurried like mice. The girl sat down on the floor by the fire, opened her bag and took out a stack of newspapers, magazines and books. She worked for the library, she explained, and had the assignment of bringing materials to the far-flung villages, mines and outposts. She drank her coffee and said, "Here's your fucked-up war," and shoved the newspapers towards Edgar.

"Are you an Eskimo?" Fatty asked, as if he had encountered a unicorn. Edgar could see him imagining undressing this girl in an igloo carpeted with otter pelts.

"I'm Inupiat," she said. "But I'm also American. I'm here to make you feel guilty about your job." She drank her coffee, left the cup and shut the door hard. Edgar

126

jumped up, got the letters out from under his pillow and chased the girl. It had started to snow.

"Will you mail these for me?" He explained that they were for his wife, because having such a person made him feel credible, worth saving.

"Are you grateful or angry?" the girl asked.

"Angry," he admitted. "And grateful." He thought of Fern. Her absence was a bee sting that had suddenly ceased to be numb. He could have scratched his skin off with want for her.

"You should be," she said and took the letters.

The other boys went to bed and Edgar stayed up. He had read the papers before he left but now, in this quiet, the stories hit him. There was a sound outside the cabin and Edgar sat up. He took a flashlight and cracked the door. Two reindeer pawed at the ground. They looked up at Edgar's light, their eyes bright marbles, and then they turned and ran.

After Edgar had been in Alaska for six weeks, the jeep returned with more food and also a box of stationery and three typewriters. "The guys down in Nome sent these," the logger said.

"They couldn't be bothered to come themselves?"

"I'm the only one who knows how to get here."

There was a list of names and no one had to tell the boys that this was a catalogue of the dead. Just to see them laid out like that — all men, their rank, two dates. The driver said, "Guess they need more letter-writers." There were mothers upon mothers upon mothers who needed to be told that their sons were dead.

The man said he would be back every day. Right now, today, there were thousands of living bodies in the war but everyone knew that a certain number of them would die by nightfall, by morning. The question was which ones.

The three men put matches to the wicks of their kerosene lanterns that night and began to type.

Dear Mr. and Mrs. Kingsly,

Please let me be the first to tell you how bravely Private First Class Kingsly fought and how respected he was. He died the way he lived. You should be proud. We thank you for your service and patriotism and offer our sincere condolences.

Dear Dr. and Mrs. Thomas Abbot,

I cannot imagine the loss you feel at this time. First Sergeant Abbot was a generous fighter and a good friend. He was one of the finest men we had. Our hearts go out to you.

Edgar tried to make each letter unique even though he knew nothing of the boys he was writing about. These were whole lives, or had been. He tried to say the same thing a new way dozens of times a day. Later there would be a handwritten note stapled to the newest list: *Lieutenants, Just follow the script. Please and thank you.*

At night Edgar used the typewriter to write to Fern. He told her that he had started to write a novel. He described a plot: a young man with money that he didn't earn or necessarily want, a father who did nothing but acquire, a question of how to create a meaningful life of one's own. In the letter, Edgar wrote that he was working on a few pages a day, between work orders. *It's really cold. There's nothing else to do.* He tried to describe the place where he was, the way ice gave way to ice and how the line between sky and land was just a smudge. That was it. There was nothing else to look at or see. Just white and white and white. Privilege was a kind of nothingness, suspending him outside of the lived world. Not even color joined him there.

Fern did not ask where the character of the wife was in this novel. Instead of asking, she wrote, *I wish you were here.*

And then: *Edgar, my love, I'm pregnant. We're going to be parents. We are going to be a family.*

1976

The night after the dinner party at which he had failed to pair his wife with John Jefferson and thereby even out all wrongs, Edgar stood with Glory at the milks in the health food store, looking for her brand and fat percentage. She liked the farmed stuff, something that still had a faint cow scent. Edgar never shopped with Fern. He was used to the items in their cupboard. He thought of them as the foods that were available to the American family — he had not ever considered Fern as a choice-maker, rumbling down the aisles, editing what her family would be made of. Glory, holding the basket against her bright, smooth legs, had a different list: dark bread, black grapes, yogurt and a shining ham for her husband. While they walked the sugars, the cereals, she played with the hair on the back of Edgar's neck, which he had meant to trim but now felt grateful that he hadn't.

The night before, he had begun to walk towards Harvard Square where there was a hotel, but Glory had run after him. "She's going to forgive you," she had said. "Yours is a good marriage and it'll survive this. But in the meantime there's no sense in being alone." Edgar had slept in the guest room that night while John's snores had rattled the walls. Edgar had felt displaced, distant. He had thought about the day they had received the keys to their new house in Cambridge. How he, Fern and Cricket had sat on the polished floor of the big empty living room, the bay windows a clean view into the thick green of a summer maple. It had smelled like fresh paint. Cricket had said, "Can this be my room?" and Edgar had laughed and said, "Maybe." They had walked through the house: the kitchen with its views of the roses in the backyard and the lawn, the long creaky stairway to the huge basement, the winding staircase up one, two, three stories, with bedrooms everywhere. The bathrooms with their claw-foot tubs and leaded windows that made the leaves outside go slightly out of focus. Cricket had said, "Do we really get to live here?" She had only known the Army base. She had not realized that she was a child of privilege, that houses like this for people like her were supposed to be perfectly normal.

Edgar had known his daughter would adapt and come to think of this as regular. He had seen that they stood at a junction and a part of him had wanted to put the house back on the market and move into an apartment, but there were his girls at the window, and everything outside had been bright, bright green. "We do really get to live here," he had said. Fern had kissed him on the back of the neck and laughed when the short hairs had pricked her lips. What would it be like not to fight against himself? Edgar had wondered. What would it be like to say yes instead of no? He had tried, he told himself. See?

Glory had come in in the middle of the night wearing a sheer mint-green nighty and undressed Edgar without asking first. She did what she wanted with him and then lay there smoking. It felt less than half as good as it had on the island. He knew Fern deserved to be angry, but here he stood in a doorway that she herself had cracked. From the slushes of his mind had sprung a question: Where else am I supposed to go? What other choice do I have?

In the grocery store Glory chose a box of black licorice. She said, "Have you thought about my idea? I really think we should go away. We won't be able to enjoy each other properly if we stay home. This," she said, sweeping her arm over the foodstuffs gathering in her cart, "is a waste of a good affair." Love was not her ambition, escape was.

She had pitched this idea in the same hushed telephone conversation as the dinner party.

"Where?" he had asked.

"Mexico. Sunshine and revolution. Alcohol at sunset. You know how to sail, don't you? We'll sail." Edgar had only had to hear that word. He had thought about the possibility of a storm or the chance that he was unprepared to travel all that way. He had thought about his wife and the damage those weeks could do. He knew he would miss his children. Then he had thought of the slice Chicago and duty were about to cut across his life. He was in the last weeks of his own time. The pretty girl was fine but he was in it for the saltwater, for the wind. In the health food store, the whole big room smelling like turmeric and curry powder and tea, he said yes to Glory as if this fact — his ambition sea more than sex — would protect him against the resulting damage.

"I knew you would come around," she said.

Glory wheeled them to the flowers, which were cheap and themed for the season. Everywhere they looked, the men and women of retail had turned things orange, brown and yellow. She chose two bouquets, opened them and tore out the carnations. She said, "You have to be kind if you want her to be here when you get back."

The first day of school was a tightening for Cricket and the twins. Uniforms — navy and white, pleats — were new and stiff. The boys had neckties and the girls had headbands that pressed on their skullbones. Summer's spaciousness, the salt of it, evaporated so fast. The children stood outside school kicking dirt for five more minutes before someone shooed them in. They tried to ruin their shiny shoes. They asked who was in which class and chewed the teacher's names like unripe fruit. Mrs. Brown, Mrs. Lumpkins, Miss Studenberger, Miss Nolan. Escape was on everyone's minds, though Cricket did take pleasure in her new backpack filled with sharp pencils, the perfect square of an eraser, unscratched paper. Her lunchbox, which did not yet smell like old peanut butter.

Cricket walked her brothers to their classroom and helped them find their cubbies. She knelt and said, "I'm just upstairs. Be good. Eat your lunch. Be nice to each other." Their little desks made her sorry. All summer, they had been moat-diggers, clam-gatherers, sailors, tree-climbers. Now she watched the boys tuck themselves into the chairs, look ahead at the big blackboard. They would learn to read. They would learn to add small numbers together. Reprieve was a short break in the middle of the day to blast from one end of the playground to the other, a scummy orange ball in front of them.

Cricket, like all the fourth graders, was given a social studies textbook: *The Building of America: Class, Race and Society.* None of the children knew what that meant. Miss Nolan, wearing plaid pants and a sweater vest, her long black hair parted in the center, said, "This is high school level but by Christmas you'll be ready. Our first unit is on Indians." She looked around the room. "You will learn to become Americans this year. What does that mean to you?"

Hands shot up. "Fireworks. Freedom. The best country in the world. Number one in baseball."

"Sure," Miss Nolan said. "Pie is also good. But have you thought about the gas crisis or the recession? Have you thought about the Black Panthers or the Civil Rights Movement or the Vietnam War? Have you thought about the Gold Rush or the Robber Barons? Have you thought about the Navajo? Have you thought about the Conquistadors or the Front Range mountains or the Great Plains?" Cricket had not. The less studious among the children began to worry about their upcoming homework. Cricket felt her temples warm up. She wanted to know all of this.

On the big table by the window there were art supplies. Miss Nolan walked over to them like they were treasure.

"When the first white men arrived in America," she said, "they got sick and died because of Indian germs and the Indians got sick from the white men's germs." Cricket looked up at her, waiting to understand. "The Indians were sometimes kind and generous, and other times they weren't. They did something called scalping, which is when you cut the skin off someone's head. But the white men were cruel too. They killed many Indians and stole their wives. They forced the Indians to believe in God."

The teacher handed out feathers and clothespins. She handed out scissors and glue. She stood in front of the room, which smelled like art projects come and gone — clay and paper and paint and paste. The school floors, no matter how hard or how often they were cleaned, were always speckled with tiny flecks of cut construction paper.

"Imagine that," Miss Nolan said. "You are foreigners in a strange land. It's vast and beautiful and you do not ever, ever want to go home." Cricket was quiet; she was attentive and she was somewhat afraid. These were good kids, obedient kids. They had rules at home and they followed them. These children lived in fear of having a note sent home from the principal. The teacher looked at their idle hands, the supplies untouched.

"Are we supposed to be the Indians or the white men?" a fat boy asked.

"Both. The truth lies in between. Now make art," she said. She picked up a piece of orange paper and scissors, cut it into the shape of an indistinguishable animal. "Art," she proclaimed. She must have seen the questions in the children's faces because her neck reddened. "Anything is art," she said. "Don't you get it? Everything in the world is art."

Cricket picked up a piece of paper and held the scissors to its edge. Miss Nolan

138

walked over to a record player on her desk and laid the needle down. Relentless harpsichord music filled the room. For an hour, the teacher stood above her pupils silently, while they tried their very best to make art. They were afraid. They cut and glued and pressed and glued again. They did not understand what they were making, or why. It was not the paper-plate turkeys they were used to, the holiday cards, the steps one through four. Cricket was just as confused but she loved the feeling, her fingers tacky and feather-stuck. The children ended up with crazed messes: a clothespin covered in pink fabric, a rat's nest of construction paper, everything glue-soaked. At the end of the hour, the children let go of the breath they had all been holding. The teacher lifted the needle and the room fell silent. She laid the messes out in a line with a sign that said, "Pilgrims, Indians."

"See," she said. "You actually made something. You." She pointed to Jack Bishop, who was good at football. She turned to Birdie Breyer who was small for her age, whose front teeth were bigger than her eyes, who must have weighed hardly more than a fawn, and Miss Nolan picked her up and brought her to her own briny face. "Even you, little girl. Art." Cricket was in love.

■ ■ ■ ■

One of the neighbors, Louise, had called Fern in the morning with a request. "I need a bride. Today," she said. She explained that she volunteered at the old folks' home where the Alzheimer's patients had forgotten almost everything. They no longer remembered the faces of their own children and everyone had given up trying to make them happy. So, Louise said, she had had an idea: a wedding. White dress, tuxedo, half the room for the bride's side and half for the groom. An altar. It would not matter that no one in the congregation knew these people; they did not know anyone. They would feel good, and maybe they would even see something familiar in the bride or groom, maybe they would have the sensation of being in a room full of family. No one invited them anywhere anymore because they might wander off, might walk into traffic, might say something unfortunate. Yet Louise felt that they deserved a celebration, deserved to go to bed with feet sore from dancing. Fiction, in this case, made it possible. "My original bride got the stomach flu," she said. "It's at one o'clock today. You'll be done before your kids are out of school. Can you do it?"

"Edgar isn't in town," Fern said, not ready to admit what was happening.

"No, no, not Edgar. I have a different groom. Someone cheerier."

The instructions were: attain a cheap dress (the other bride was three sizes smaller than Fern), whatever hair and makeup she could manage in time. After last night, Fern was glad to seek out this small revenge. Edgar had been the one to kiss another woman but now she was the one to be someone else's bride. Fern looked in the phone book for dress shops and it was a young feeling to run her finger down the listings, to dial, to say, "I need a wedding dress right away. Do you have any sample sizes available now?" At the dress shop she tried on the options, chose the most expensive. It had long sleeves and a high neck, a ruffle around the collar. The silk was heavy and cool on her body. Fern wrote a check so that Edgar would see what she had done. She wanted to punish him by spending everything that was left.

Fern went to the beauty parlor and had her girl curl her hair into big feathery layers, Glory Jefferson layers. She sat in the chair watching her head turn prettier, thumbing a fashion magazine two seasons out of date. Fern had not said she was getting fake-married and she did not mention what her real husband had done or the fact that she might be poor.

Fern thought of her real wedding, which had been covered in the local paper and reported, as all weddings joining two good families, as perfectly charming. In the pictures: the older ladies in wide skirts puffed with tulle, beehives and cat-eye glasses. The younger ladies in shift dresses and pumps and heavy black eyeliner. It had seemed peculiar to Fern that the grown-ups all condoned this event, which would mean the end of their ownership of her and Edgar. It seemed like they ought to have put up more of a fight to keep the children whom they had birthed and raised. Just like that? Married and gone? But everyone had seemed so pleased.

It had been warm in the sun. The guests were all parent-friends, not Fern's or Edgar's. To Fern's parents the guests had said, *Congratulations* and *Good match* and *Such a beautiful day.* To the bartender they had said, *Gin and plenty of lime.* To each other they had said, *Tell me more about that gorgeous pheasant-shaped brooch you're wearing,* and, *Where are you having Bill's trousers hemmed now that Henning's is closed?* and *I*

142

should think that the coloreds would rather join a country club of their own making. Glasses had been drained, noses had been powdered, the day had grown a little hotter.

To the music, Fern, in a dress with an empire waist and a huge skirt, white gloves up to her elbows, her hair frozen in place and a bouquet of primroses, had walked with her father down the grass aisle. Everyone had smiled at her, predicting her future: four children, a lifetime of parties, the yearly vacation, a long retirement and a quiet death, announced in the same newspaper as the wedding would be (a good woman saw her name in the paper three times: when she was born, when she was married and when she died; she should otherwise make no news). All according to plan, the guests' smiles had said. Fern had felt something turn in her stomach. She had wanted those things, most likely. She had wanted Edgar and babies and the feeling of summer returning each year, the smell, and setting up the hose for the children to spray each other, and then autumn and the trees turning riotous and orange and she would bake something for everyone to have after supper. The rotations, everything returning again and again, each time just enough the same to feel like coming home, but so dif-

143

ferent too.

There Edgar had stood, waiting for her, his posture his own and his thick glasses clean and reflecting light. Promises had been promised, dances danced, toasts sealed with clinking flutes. Every time Fern had seen Edgar's parents, they had been laughing. Her own mother smiled, but Fern knew she was disappointed — wifedom was not something Evelyn held in regard. Paul had seemed truly happy, but he had gone inside with a migraine before the ceremony was over.

To Fern, Edgar had said, "Now that we're married we never have to go to a party like this again."

The bride and groom had been released finally into their life. His parents had rented a car for them to drive away in, a white convertible Rolls-Royce with a huge chrome grill and whitewall tires and white leather seats. The car had been packed, the chauffeur was at the ready, the hotel had been paid for by one father or another, and the couple had kept looking at each other but then looking away again. They had held hands in the backseat as they were driven out into their future. Fern had felt the very specific warmth of Edgar's skin, different from anyone else's. Suddenly, the car had slowed and they had both jolted forward. The road ahead of them had turned all silver, shimmering and slippery, like mercury had spilled over it. It had smelled like the sea.

"What is it?" Edgar had asked. The driver had stepped out and walked towards the strange flood. He had bent down and continued walking until he had come around the curve where a fish truck sat. Edgar had stepped out too.

"Careful," Fern remembered saying. Her first wifely worry, and it had made her throat feel warm.

When he returned to the car, Edgar had said, "Herring. Hundreds of thousands of herring." Once she had known what they were, she could not see them any other way. Fern had gotten out too, and they had stood there watching the creatures slip and settle. The fish were dead, but their round eyes had looked afraid.

Fern and Edgar had stood together in the silver sea. They had felt as if they were walking on water. As if all the fish in the depths had swum upwards in order to lift these lovers. As if to deliver them ashore.

Fern checked her watch. She peed. She took the dress out of the closet and stripped to nothing, starting again in all white lace. The dress had a string of tiny silk buttons down the back, meant for a sister or best friend to fasten. Fern, alone, struggled a few closed. She would have to wait for Louise to help. She looked at herself in the mirror. Her big waves of dark blond hair, her lashes fat with black mascara, all that white fabric. She was too old for this, but with the hair and makeup she looked almost right.

Fern the fake bride was in the kitchen drinking water when Edgar came in the front door. He had flowers.

"What?" he said.

She chose not to explain.

He looked her up and down.

"Button me," she said, relieving none of his questions. She wanted to push him to the ground, to break him, and she also wanted his familiar hands on her skin and for his touch to be what it once was: a reassurance.

Edgar put the flowers down on the counter and tried to take his wife's hands. Fern felt the prickles of being caught at something stupid start at the back of her eyes. Edgar did not say, "Let it fall off," and devour her. He did not press for an explanation for the outfit. He did not ask her about money spent. She refused his hands. He turned her

146

around and, button by button, closed her up. The dress was tight and hard to breathe in. He did not tell her how sorry he was or what she meant to him. He said, "You look nice."

She said, "Screw you." At least she could wield the small weapon of confusion.

Fern took the flowers — one thing she had not prepared for her costume — and walked out of the house with hot, dry eyes. She drove to the sad, avocado-green-walled community center, waited for the organ music and walked down the aisle surrounded by withered but happy forgetters. Under the fake-flower arbor, an actual giant. He reminded her of Ben. His pants were polyester, brown, a little too short and he had a red carnation in his lapel. His huge face. His hair was dark and straight, deeply parted, his sideburns long. Her brother had been gone for eight years. What would Ben have looked like now? His death was not all absence — it sometimes felt to Fern that her twin brother's body had merged with her own. As if they were never meant to have divided in the first place. When she approached the altar, the giant took her hands, her little pale hands, into his big calloused ones and smiled at her, wide and true.

147

There was also a man dressed as a priest — surely he could not have been a real priest? — who asked all the usual questions. Fern and the giant said yes to them. They promised. Fern pictured Edgar in the back of the room. Imagined that he had followed her and now looked on while she married someone else. And when it was time for the last part, she reached her hand around the giant's huge neck, bent him towards her and she kissed him as hard as she could. He tasted like ash. He was generating so much heat.

The forgetters grew misty for the newly-weds, reached into their pockets for hankies, clapped and whooped when the pair walked back down that aisle, big hand, small hand. Fern could not tell in their faces if they truly thought that two people had been married that day or if they were simply enjoying the theater. They seemed happy, sincerely happy, and their faces were bright.

Only after the two had opened the door to the world, reentered the day, did they realize how dark it had been inside. They stood in the courtyard where the grass was green and the fountain was dry. They squinted against the light, against the summer's end. It was as if the sun was emptying itself out now before winter. Above them were white streamers and little plastic silver bells.

"It'll pass," the giant said. Fern could feel her lipstick drying. She wet it with her tongue.

"What?" she asked.

"You wouldn't have kissed me if you had had a better day." His voice was deep and slightly electronic sounding. Like it had been prerecorded. She had to bend her head back to see his face.

It was too bright. Here she was in a wedding dress with a huge groom in the middle of a real day, in the middle of her very own city surrounded by a hundred people she had never seen before who all thought they cared about her. All that money she had spent. "You are not my husband, but I do have a husband," she said.

"Of course you do."

Louise was wrangling. She could have used a lasso. Grey-haireds spiraled off like wind-caught dust, going eastward, westward, purposeless and searching. They drifted towards Fern and the giant and offered their congratulations.

"Your mother must be so proud," they said and Fern thought of her mother's little body, gone from the world. She had no idea

149

if her mother had ever been proud of her.

"The most beautiful bride I've ever seen," they said, and they seemed to believe it.

"You make a fine couple."

"The last time I saw you, you were this big." A hand flattened at hip-level, a head shaking in disbelief. "I hardly recognize you." Fern gave a kiss to this woman, on the cheek, and told her that she looked beautiful and thanks for coming, it means so much. "To have someone who's known me all my life," she added. This lie was an easy gift to give.

Each of the forgetters had a plastic champagne glass with fizzy that was too gold to be the real thing. There was a terrible cake, a foot tall and bright white with blobs that were meant to be flowers along the seams. The couple on top had the wrong plastic hair color and neither of them was a giant. Fern and her groom took hold, together, of the plastic knife and, with it, split the white mountain. Inside there was yet more frosting. Just looking at it made Fern's teeth hurt. Fern and the giant each gathered a forkful, reached across to the other's mouth and placed, as if it were a sealant for this new endeavor, a glob of white on the opposite tongue.

An old man came up nose-hair close and

breathed on Fern for a moment while he mustered the energy to speak. "Never," he wheezed, "fight with clothes on. My advice."

Fern felt slightly sick. She looked at her two feet on the ground, the new white shoes already scuffed. She looked out at the sea of guests. The forgetters were, as a rule, short. Their spines must have compacted throughout all their years on an earth ruled by gravity. Their fingers were thin but fat-knuckled, holding cake plates and enjoying the white slop. Most likely they had been advised by their doctors to cut fat and cholesterol, to make smart choices about nutrition in these, their late years. But they did not keep track of this information any more than they kept track of anything anymore. What was in front of them was all that mattered. There would be grey string beans on their plates later, and for the ones with no teeth, grey string bean puree. The cake was a treat: creamed fat and sugar, spread thick. Fern went for a piece herself, wanting to feel the celebration.

Edgar, the fact of Edgar, the idea of what he had done, stood beside Fern like a shadow. She tried to imagine him after she had left in her white dress. Did he sit down on the sofa? Turn on the television? Did he cry or scream or fall asleep on her side of

151

the bed or call his mother or look for the dog or fix the dripping sink or root around in the basement freezer for an ice cream sandwich or order something from a catalogue, or did he simply sit on the floor with a glass of cold white wine and listen to the emptiness he had begun to create there?

Fern had never considered losing Edgar any other way except a heart attack. That was how it was meant to happen: struck while playing tennis, while walking in the sudden fire of fall leaves. They were bound together, magnets that were just rocks without the other. The idea that the marriage could fail had not been in consideration.

The giant had a circle of old ladies laughing. His big face was lit by the story, whatever it was. Fern heard the word *shoemaker,* the word *rustic* and the word *Chevrolet.* The women cracked up. Who knew if they could even hear what he was saying. One of them had frosting on her cheek, and this fact nicked at the nerve endings in Fern's chest. She looked away.

Louise came around, insisting they needed to stick to her schedule. These folks were born in the olden days and they had an early bedtime. After cake, the bouquet.

The women gathered on command, their

152

short hairdos dyed or white. They wore plastic beaded necklaces strung by grandchildren who were at least a little bit afraid to come visit. They wore lavender, petal-pink, dove grey. Maybe they did not remember that they were old and empty of mind. Maybe they felt light and full of perhaps. Maybe they were humoring this younger woman, thick with good intention. It should have cheered Fern to see these happy elders enjoying a few good hours, but all she could think about was them later in dark rooms, a lone body in each one, a sad photograph in a frame, everything good already passed. *Here it is,* Fern thought. *Here is the worst case.* Perhaps her mother had been right to leave early.

Fern turned her back. These were her flowers, she remembered. Edgar's gift. She considered not throwing them, considered running away. She imagined the flowers in her dining room, in her car, in her trash and found no surface on which they made sense.

Fern gave a hard toss and Edgar's flowers were in the air. There was a shuffling sound and then a tiny woman emerged with her prize in the air. She could not have been more than four feet tall. She was joyous, frenzied.

Throwing, Fern found, was the very thing

she wanted to do. She would have liked to throw the cake, the plates, the champagne flutes.

The giant came over and he picked Fern up in his arms. The crowd went wild. He lowered his big head and his lips were fat and warm.

"Consider where else you could go," he told her. "Consider the mountains. How tall they are, and full of caves. Or out West, where some places it never snows."

"We're broke. The dog is old. My husband might be having an affair. It feels like I have so many children. I'm very tired."

"They'll be fine for a few weeks. Come with me. I'm leaving this afternoon. There are roads from here to everywhere else," he said. "Paved roads, and food along the way."

The children walked home at the end of the day as usual. They kicked the newness off their shoes and said, "Fine," and "Boring," and "Slow," about school and then, wistfully, "Sand," and "Water," and "Sleep," about summer.

Mother was nowhere to be found. Her reading glasses were on the table and the newspaper was open to the funnies. There were two cans of soup on the counter, unopened. Father was never home at this time so his absence caused no alarm. Cricket told her brothers to do their homework. "No homework in kindergarten," they told her. "Well, then learn something about the American West. Do you even know where that is? Do you even know anything?" Cricket was annoyed that she could not make her voice sound older, more Miss Nolan. To grow up to be anyone else seemed like a waste of time. Her brothers looked up at her with their big brown eyes. They were sweet boys but boys and so necessarily less smart, but Cricket would do what she could to teach them. She found a can of beans in the cupboard and a bag of frozen corn and explained that these were the main foods of the natives. "Also meat," she said. "But you have to hunt it if you want any. Berries in summer, and squash." The boys said, "Okay," and "Wow," and "I see." Then they wanted to know if it was all right to watch television. "No TV," said Cricket. "No TV until you understand our country's history."

All three children had hoped Maggie would greet them, at least. Welcome them home with her cheer and chuff, to make them kids again. But she too was absent, so the children went looking. They tossed her name out and out and out. They looked over the neighbors' fences and in the shade of the maples; they looked in their own yard and in their bedrooms and under the kitchen sink. "Where is that hound?" they said. "Where has she gotten off to?"

Neither parents nor dog came home for the second night in a row. Last night they had gone to sleep watching television but tonight, because Cricket wanted her parents, when they returned, to see how capable she was, how very worth caring for, she put the boys to sleep in their beds and then read under her blankets with a flashlight even though no one was there to scold her. She dreamed about math, though she tried, even in sleep, to will her brain to conjure a cartoon-flat mesa, a herd of elk and her arms pulling taut the spring of a bow and arrow.

1967

The December after Edgar left for his post in the great north, Fern was much too pregnant. She stood in the shower watching the water roll over her belly. The baby pressed a heel out, deformed her further. No one ever had said anything to her about how strange pregnancy would be, how aggressively strange. None of the mothers she had grown up around had talked about it. All the questions she asked her doctor ended with the same answer: if your mother was very late giving birth, you could be too; if your mother gained a lot of weight, you might too; the length of your mother's labor is the best indicator for the length of your own. But Fern called and her mother claimed she had no memory of what her pregnancy was like, what her birth was like. She preferred to create children out of clay.

All during her childhood Fern had thought about the time when she would be a mother and how generous she would be to her children, and how she would play with them all the time and run with them and imagine monsters and fairies and winged horses with them and buy them giant stuffed toys. Now that she was on the threshold of mother-hood, the feeling Fern had was of being eaten alive from the inside, this creature taking the food and water, taking the blood to grow her own bones, her own skin, her own nails and hair and eyeballs and intestines and lungs and the meat of a heart.

Fern's mother called to tell her that Ben was still exhibiting signs of insanity, that was the word she used, but they had spoken to his doctor who had a new solution to offer. They could put him into a new facility and start a heavy regimen of electric shock treatments. The doctor, Evelyn said, proposed the idea and the start date at the same time, having already taken the liberty of penciling Ben in, seeing so much promise in the therapy. "I can't offer this to everyone. The procedure is expensive," the doctor had told Fern's parents. "We want to be very aggressive."

Evelyn did not have the instincts other mothers did and she was aware of that, but the idea that one should do everything they could for their children seemed obvious. Here they were, lucky in wealth, with a doctor who considered himself an expert and a son who thought he could fly, a son who needed help. It would be a shame to do nothing when a person had the means to do something.

Fern's parents were not asking her opinion on the treatment. "We have to try everything," her father said. They were not able to answer her questions and neither of them wanted to talk about how uncertain Fern was.

Ben sent Fern a letter afterward.

Dear Fern,

I saw *The Sound of Music.* Yesterday we had Chicken Marengo. They are going to fix me with electricity. I miss you.

Ben

Her parents had decided to alter Ben. Nothing was more terrifying than what families could do to each other. Fern found the place on the map, bought a basketful of treats — marshmallows, chocolates, gummies — and drove the distance to her twin, listening to the radio. Blacks were marching in Chicago, in Mississippi. Whites were burning their draft cards. Hours later she parked in front of a huge ivied building. *Brookridge Home,* read the ironwork over the door. It was a mental hospital, she realized. An institution.

She found Ben sitting alone at a table, dealing three hands of bridge. Beside him she saw six cans of soda and an empty bowl with pink milk at the bottom and there was a moment where Ben looked at her and neither of them was familiar to the other.

"Look at you," he said. His voice was thin.

She put her hands on her huge round belly. "I know. I'm enormous." She had imagined keeping the tears away until after. She had pictured herself collapsing in the car, but here she was, crying immediately. It was all a story — doctors and currents and promises — until she saw Ben, and his light was dim.

On a stand, a television showed a helicopter hovering above a thick pelt of green, all the leaves blown aside, a body being raised up. Ben said, "I was supposed to die that way," and Fern said, "No, not you. You are safe." She touched Ben's forehead.

"It's spaghetti night. Did we use to have an angel?" He said this without emotion. His voice was murky water.

"I don't know. Did we?"

"In the prairie."

"We had a statue of the archangel Michael."

When Fern and Ben were in ninth grade, the family had gone to Europe for the summer. It was Fern who had discovered the statue of the angel in a huge antiques store. That night she had dreamed that the angel flew in her window and lifted her up, pulled her nightdress off and kissed her hard all over her body. She had woken up sweating, and had begged her father to buy her the statue. He had assumed, as she knew he would, that her interest was in the artistry, the story of the angel's protection of children, his defeat of Satan.

The statue had been purchased for a large sum and sent home by crate. Weeks after she had first fallen in love with him and on the other side of the ocean, Fern had pried the nails out and found her angel in twenty-nine pieces. Dust was everywhere. His body had crumbled on his journey to her. It was the first time she had felt defeated by love.

"Is that the angel you mean?" Fern asked Ben.

"People say they aren't real."

"Oh, I see." She saw no reason for a sharp point. "This one was real."

Fern stayed and watched the rest of a show about crocodiles, offered sweets every five minutes. In the flash of the television she looked at Ben's living body. His old skin and eyes and the flush in his neck. The shell had not changed, except for a long scar across his scalp, marking his loss.

"Ben," Fern said to the silent shape of her brother. "I feel lost. I don't know what I'm becoming." She put her hands on her belly. He looked at her. He gave a half-smile, like he had caught sight of something and then lost it again. It was hard to tell what was missing from him, if it was cognition or feeling. Whatever was left felt like all she had. "I was in high school and then I was a wife. I'm still a wife but without a husband to take care of. And I'm about to be a mother but I have no idea what that means. I am completely alone and I feel like I am waiting to die."

Fern thought of the people who were supposed to be the ones to love her. Her husband was far away. She had called her parents and they had flooded the conversation, flushed her voice out with news of the house's rotting foundation, the charity ball, the cast her mother had made of a dead fawn she had found in the prairie. Evelyn had said, "I assume you don't want me to come for the birth." The last word was spit out as if it were something rotten. Fern

162

certainly would have wanted a different mother to be there since her husband was not, but no, Fern did not want Evelyn. "Don't trouble yourself," Fern had said. "I'll be in good hands."

Fern had called Edgar's mother and admitted more than she wanted to about how carrying the child of someone absent made her angry. How she missed Edgar so hard she was a bruise, but Mary had not offered to come. Two days later a box had arrived filled with silk stockings, a nightgown with an intricate lace bodice and a jewelry box containing a sapphire pendant as big as Fern's thumbnail. The note had said, *Chin up!* and had her mother-in-law's perfect signature. The necklace had been cold on Fern's chest. It had felt half alive.

Ben knelt down on the floor in front of his sister. It looked like he was going to ask her to marry him. "Benny," she said, trying to save him from embarrassment. But he stayed and took her foot out of her patent leather pump. Ben gave her toes a squeeze and then sat back in his chair. He picked up his napkin and spit on it and began to polish Fern's shoe. "Here," said Ben. "See?" And there, in the black shine, was his proof that she was alive: the pink smudge of her face, reflected.

■ ■ ■ ■

Fern grew larger, hid behind her clothes and kept her head low. It seemed inappropriate to go out in her condition, to be seen in such a physically exaggerated form, and with her husband away too. Much more intimate than being naked in public was to be pregnant in public. It was as if her whole life was visible — sex and fear and hope and the coming unknown. Everywhere she went people warned her that the next part would be so hard. "Enjoy this time," an old woman in the bakery said. "When the baby comes, you'll never be the same again."

She said, "I'm already not the same. Look at me." The old woman smiled back, deaf and happy.

"My name is a good name," the woman said. "Ruth. You should use it if it's a girl." The woman was wire-thin, her collarbone a sharp edge beneath an old dress. It was the woman's turn to order bread and she asked a question about each loaf, pointing her bony finger, bidding the baker to turn it over so she could inspect the underside. "Looks a little overdone, that one," the woman said. Fern could feel the blood pooling in her ankles and fattening them. She knew when she got home that they would be thick and sore.

Finally, the baker took out the pumpernickel, which was already overbrown and could not be faulted for such a color. The old woman seemed unsure. The risk seemed to weigh on her, the whole week counting on this bread for sustenance and comfort. Fern softened for her. She said to the baker, "Would you throw some scones in her bag, from me?" The woman did not notice the gift as she counted, in coins, her total. Her fingertips were stained with nicotine.

The next time at the bakery, the same old woman was there. She was wearing the same dress and the same shoes. "Did you enjoy the scones?" Fern asked.

"I threw them away. People don't give you things for free unless they are poisoned or spoiled." She studied Fern's protrusion. "You should have that baby. There's no sense in keeping it in." Around the woman's neck was a small gold Star of David. It made Fern feel charitable. Poor old thing.

Fern looked at the woman's wiry eyebrows and considered reaching out and plucking one out. Would it be so terrible to run into someone kind? "Waiting is hard," she said.

"You think waiting for life is hard, try

waiting for death. Any day now," the woman said and she checked her watch.

Again, she had the baker show her the underbelly of each loaf, asked what time they came out of the oven. She chose a rye this time. "Just give me half, in case I don't make it past Thursday."

Fern said the same thing to the baker, taking the remainder of the woman's loaf.

It was the old woman who moved on first. The Sunday loaves were out, studded with raisins, and Fern waited outside smelling the bread, planning her order. She waited fifteen minutes, thirty, her feet fat and the ligaments in her hips pulling. Fern said a little prayer for the old woman and wished her good rest. *Ruth,* she said to herself, *good luck wherever you are, Ruth.*

Edgar had no other job but to administrate the deaths of his generation, sign the thousands of condolence letters. *So sorry for your loss, your loss, your loss too.* These letters were not addressed to people where he grew up — they went to Bakersfield, Omaha, Tampa.

Edgar had written to these mothers each day, over and over to say that he was sorry because the dead were not strangers. The dead were theirs. Edgar knew that the let-

166

ters would arrive with some artifact of the absent — shoes, a watch, the green shirt. He did not know whether these artifacts had actually belonged to the ones they were said to have belonged to. That jungle. The ants and snakes and vines. What if nothing was saved? But you could not tell a woman her son was gone and not give her fingers something to hold on to.

He longed for any number of unremarkable mornings. He thought about the novel he had started and the few good pages were a tiny, hopeful island but not enough to soften the bite of missing his wife's pregnancy, of not being there to cup her swollen feet at the end of the day, to put his ear to the doctor's fetoscope and hear that new heart. At night he lay on his back and he could feel his entire skeleton. The hard parts that would remain after the soft parts had gone.

Edgar awoke one morning to find Runner sitting on the floor with a steaming cup. He was wearing his parka and boots. "Are you going someplace?" Edgar asked. As if there was someplace to go. As if they would ever leave this sheet of ice.

"I can't do it anymore, man," Runner said. "I can't be part of this fucked-up machine." It was the most he had talked since Edgar had arrived.

Edgar sat up in bed. "And?"

"I'm leaving."

"There's no place to go."

"They'll assume I'm dead."

They would, because how else would it end? A single man in the sharp cold, wind and ice, a roadless expanse.

"The sled tracks from yesterday are still visible. I'll either die or I'll live. I can accept both possibilities." Runner stuffed his pockets with food rations. He said, "You want to come?"

Edgar wanted to say yes to escape, but what he really wanted was home and he would not be allowed back if he ran.

Runner knew that Fern was pregnant. He knew Edgar had ties connecting him to a world he could not walk away from. He shook Edgar's hand and said, "Tell Fatty I said goodbye and good luck." Edgar wrote his home address down and stuffed it in Runner's pocket. "If you ever need help . . ." he said. And then Runner opened the door and started walking. The dawn was a shell, opening. Edgar watched the figure recede along thin sled tracks. He watched until Runner was a dot, then nothing, gone beyond the curvature of the earth.

■ ■ ■ ■

On the day that Fern went into labor, she circled her house for hours. She drank cold water through a straw and she paced.

Fern remembered a day: she and Ben had been running, racing, sprinting. It was not lunchtime yet but they were ravenous. They picked blackberries in the garden and shared a fleshy, sunwarm tomato. The kitchen seemed terribly far away, and the province of grown-ups, and they did not want to break the seal. All afternoon they played and picked what was growing: rhubarb stalks, currants, raspberries, unripe pears.

Fern's mother walked through the garden from her sculpture studio at dusk and found the two lying on their backs under the apple tree, counting its coming fruit.

"We could live a week, at least," Ben said.

"A week's not long," said Fern.

Her mother looked at the fruit cores, the discarded stalks. "My god," she said, "Fern, you do nothing but *eat*." No mention of Ben whose boy-body deserved the nourishment, needed the fuel. That night at dinner, Fern served herself the smallest of portions. A spoonful of peas, one small potato, two

169

bites of fish. She wanted to show her mother that she was not an animal. That she was a lady, and in so being, could survive on hardly anything at all.

There came a moment where the laboring Fern took her clothes off and turned on the hose, drank from it. Stars shot and fizzled, her body was hot with pain and then at rest. Then red and white lights spun on the leaf backs and she looked up to see her neighbor peering over the fence and an ambulance in the driveway. She tried to explain that she was fine, she was good, she was doing the work, but the men's arms were strong around her back, and they carried her, naked and enormously round, into the back of the van like a wild animal that had wandered into the neighborhood and threatened to disturb the peace. They covered her in a scratchy blanket. *Hush up, little woman,* their arms seemed to say, *we're here to contain you.*

Fern studied her newborn, fresh and ripe. "She has your eyes," the nurse said, but Fern thought the girl looked just like Edgar, as if she were a container for the overflow of his person. She had planned on another name — Edgar's grandmother's — but when the nurse brought the birth certificate for her to fill out, she thought of that old woman in the bakery who had come into her life at the end, as they each prepared to cross the border. Fern said a small prayer that the woman had gotten the bread just right, eaten the last piece on the day she died, had nothing left over that needed to be thrown out. She wrote the name down: *Ruth.*

Fern stood in front of the big mirror, and though her belly was still soft and misshapen, she felt lightened. There she was — her same hair and her same legs, her same face. Out loud to her reflection she said, "I'm still here," and she knelt on the floor and wept.

The first morning at home, the phone rang. "Fern," said a voice.

"Edgar." She thought it couldn't be. Her breath was warm against the plastic telephone. "How are you calling me?" He told her that he had walked for seven hours and hitchhiked for four to get to a phone where he could make the long-distance call. He did not waste their few minutes describing the way his legs felt after walking that long in the snow, how he had nearly lost the sled tracks and been sure he would die, that his body would only be found in summer. He did not tell her how strange it felt to be in a place where there were other humans, where things were for sale, about the chocolate bar softening in his pocket. The connection was heavy with static. "Did you have the baby?" Edgar asked. "I had a dream last night that you had." That he did not know if his baby existed on earth yet, that he did not know that it was a girl made Fern feel like she had been caught in a lie. She had gone on ahead without him. "It's a girl. She looks just like you, Edgar," she said. The fuzz between them thickened. "Can you hear me? Are you there?" she asked. "I named her Ruth." She was embarrassed by the name. By the decision made on her own without good reason.

"Ruth?" he repeated back. "Are you okay? Fern, are you okay?"

"You're alive," Fern said out loud. She had been holding a place for death, for disappearance.

"I'm alive," he said.

"I really need you." She wanted to swat the static away. She wanted a clear connection to her husband more than she wanted anything.

"I know. So many people are dead. All there is is nothing here. Whiteness. I know I've told you before but it's so cold and so dark. I can't believe you gave birth. I can't believe I missed it." Not knowing if she could hear everything he said, he repeated the most important thing. "Fern, I love you. I love you. Hello?"

"I'm here. I know it sounds stupid to say but I was shocked by how much labor hurt."

Edgar, on the far end of the line, was envious of a body that could feel unrivaled pain and produce an unrivaled prize. He wanted to ask what the baby looked like, what she felt like to hold, how she smelled. "She's delicate," Fern said. "She's tiny. I don't know what I'm doing." It was hard not to imagine the path this poor creature would have to walk, the world so tumbled with pain.

"I wish I could be there," he said.

She said, "I don't belong here without you."

He wanted to say *Thank you* but the words seemed much too small for what she had done.

Edgar stood at the phone and ate his chocolate bar. The sugar hit his tongue hard. His back was sweaty. He said his parents' number to the operator.

The next voice was his father's: "Yes?"

"It's me, Edgar. I just wanted to tell you
—"

"Edgar, Edgar! Where are you? Mary! Edgar's on the phone. Edgar? Are you there? Are you all right?"

"Dad. I'm fine. I wanted to tell you that you're a grandfather."

"Yes, Fern called yesterday. Congratulations, my boy." It was this that hurt: he had not been the first to know. His parents had already celebrated, had already lived a whole day knowing that the baby had been born. He answered their questions about his safety, promised that he was fine, but he could hear pain in his mother's voice. There was too much to say so they said little and hung up, all of them missing each other more than they had before they had spoken.

Edgar bought a can of condensed milk and a box of crackers and sat on the bench out front drinking and eating and saying to himself: *I have a daughter. I have a baby girl. I am somebody's father.* The road in town was mud and rock. A stray dog nipped at a dead bird. That night Edgar slept in a boarding house where he ate a giant steak, took three showers and two baths before beginning the journey back to nowhere.

In Tennessee, Fern ate steamed green beans and nursed the baby. In Chicago,

Edgar's father called the same General who had saved Edgar once and said, "Edgar's a father now," and his attempts to keep his voice calm were thin. Mary was beside him, trying to listen in on the conversation. "Congratulations," the General said, and then to clarify, "Doesn't it seem to you that families as nice as yours should be together?"

"Yes," Hugh said. "Yes, yes." He managed to keep his breathing steady until he had hung up.

It was two weeks before Fern made it to the bakery again. And when she walked in, there, inspecting the crumb on a loaf of wheat, was the old woman.

"Oh!" Fern said. "You're alive!" She was relieved and she was strangely annoyed. She had prayed for the old woman in heaven, she had mourned her. Now she would have to return to the state of waiting and do it all again.

"Do I know you?" the woman asked. On two of her fingers were giant, fire-bright diamonds, unmistakably real. Fern looked at her to make sure it was the same person. She had always assumed the woman was poor.

"I was pregnant last time we met."

The woman studied her and seemed not to find anyone she had ever seen.

"This may seem peculiar but I actually named my baby after you," Fern said. "Ruth." She wanted delight. She wanted thanks. She had given a dead woman an eternal gift, except that the woman was alive again.

"I'm not Ruth. I've never been Ruth."

"What?"

The woman turned away from Fern, asked to see the bread bellies and found nothing to her liking. She said, "If I'm going to die with something uneaten, it should at least be top quality." She looked at Fern. "I once knew a Ruth. She lived in sin in the state of California."

The bell rung her out.

1976

The diner waitress seemed to know and love the giant the moment he appeared at her table. She was short and wore a little fabric cap and frilled apron and Fern figured she would have been a pretty girl before the bacon and patty melts had started to add up. The waitress tousled his hair when he ordered dinner off the all-day breakfast menu: six eggs scrambled well and dry. She nicked his ear between thumb and forefinger when he asked for a coffee warm-up. Little Fern had vanished in his shadow. Her hamburger order was written down without eye contact, without a smile.

The giant had told Fern that his name was Malachy, Mac for short, but she still thought of him as "the giant" because no name seemed name enough for such a person.

"You've been here before?" she asked him. He had not and he did not see why she was asking. She was afraid to ask him what it was that made the waitress so nice — terror or nervousness or feeling sorry or the thrill of a man who made the woman feel tiny, a man who could pick a little lady up like a leaf.

She wanted a map to spread across the Formica table. She wanted to trace a route like her father would have done, bent over with his strong reading glasses. They had threaded their way out of Boston, through the dense treescape of western Massachusetts.

"Onward," said the giant. "Westward, ho."

They were still within the magnetic pull of home, still on recognizable highways, the usual greenery. She could have gotten on a big chrome bus and been back at her own doorstep in time to sleep near her family. In those few hours she knew she could justify forgiveness, construct a self that believed more in her marriage than in the specifics of faithfulness, honor her children's need for an intact home, begin the discussion with Edgar about what each of them was willing to give up.

"Don't think about going home," the giant said. "You have to punish him more. You have to have your own journey. Missing you will be good for him. It'll make him realize what he has." If the marriage ended

Fern knew it would not matter what the lawyers drew up: Edgar would get out with dignity, she would get out with children. That's how it broke down for men and women. She wanted to throw everything in sight, to break things, to cause pain.

"Let him miss me," she said. "I think I'll feel better when we cross some state lines, Malachy. Mac."

The frizz-haired waitress came by with a plate. "On the house," she said, sliding a piece of chocolate cream pie in front of the giant. "Come back at breakfast and you can have another," she said.

"She likes you," Fern said.

The giant cut a bite.

"Pie is my favorite," he said. Fern still was not used to the depth of his voice. She still was not used to the amount of space he took up, his big head always far above hers.

"How would she know?"

He shrugged. "She's good at her job." Fern wondered what it would be like to proceed through a world where someone already knew what made your heart beat faster.

"By the way, I don't expect you to have sex with me," he said.

Fern poured the last of the cream into her coffee. She was surprised by the flicker of disappointment she felt. She had thought of sex as something she could store up. Not because she wanted it herself, not because it was warm and sweet, but because it was desirable to others and she was the one who possessed it. It was easier, more comfortable, to be a person in possession of something. It was also a way to hurt her husband. In the thick hours of her escape she had wondered if and when. She was afraid of his size. She had pictured succumbing, as in a flood. But it was Edgar she had hoped would suffocate if she had had sex with the giant. Thinking of Edgar kissing that woman made her want to do it now, to throw the giant on the table and climb on and end up in the paper and get arrested for it and be marked, for her marriage to Edgar to be marked forever by something she had done.

"I hadn't even thought about it," Fern said. She helped herself to the pie. The sugar was smooth on her tongue. She pictured the children in Edgar's care. Fern took pleasure in the thought that he would screw things up, that a note would be sent home from school reminding him of whatever he had neglected. The children would be fine, though, she told herself. They were not babies anymore and could ask for what they needed. Edgar's mistakes would not be deadly. He could figure out how to make the lunches, the dinners. Anyone could survive a few weeks without a mother.

After the wedding, Fern and the giant had driven to her house, empty and quiet, and she had run inside, changed out of her wedding gown and gathered some clothes and creams, made up her children's beds. She had also found herself taking some clothes from each of the children's drawers, a shirt from Edgar's. It was not habit that had made her pack for the family she was leaving behind but it felt more practical than nostalgic. To mend the tear, she would need both pieces of torn cloth. Fern had written a note. *Edgar, I have to go away for a few weeks. Whatever else you're doing, I need you to take care of the children. The boys like peanut butter for lunch and Cricket likes tuna fish. Please get everyone to bed on time. I hate you right now. Love,* she wrote. Fern did not leave this note on the refrigerator or the kitchen table or the bed, or any of the other places her children might have found it. She was not leaving it for them, after all. She left it under the lip of Edgar's box of watches, on his high dresser, well out of reach of small hands.

But Edgar had not seen the note because

he had left just after Fern in her white dress and he had not written his own note to say that he was going away because the whole purpose of a mother was that she was always there without having been asked. Because Edgar could not imagine the absence of Fern. He had driven the now familiar route, knocked on Glory's door and she had let him in and asked him how it had gone with Fern, with the flowers and the news that he was going away for a while. "I gave her the flowers," he had said.

"Did you tell her you were leaving?"

"Not exactly. She was wearing a wedding dress."

"A wedding dress?"

"I don't know."

"You have to tell her. You can't help that she'll be angry, but you can keep her from worrying. Call right now." Edgar had tried but Fern had not answered. He had lied to Glory and said she had, sensing that Glory, in order to set out on this journey, needed to hear that he had done at least this small thing. Whenever doubt tickled at the back of Edgar's throat, which it did every fifteen or twenty minutes, he reminded himself that his wife had easily chosen comfort over love, objects over him. He could not imagine his future without Fern, but she was going to have to be willing to sacrifice. A few weeks apart would make clear how much he was worth to her.

And the children? Edgar remembered a day on the island, sailing with them across the cove to the harbor where they ate half-shelled clams with cocktail sauce on the dock while they watched the old rusted fishing boats unload crate after crate of lobsters. Cricket slurped raw clams and Will wished for a lobster pot so they could feast every night and James said, "Maybe we should buy a boat big enough to live on forever." They were such brave and wild and perfect little people. He wished they could have been with him, though he knew this made no sense. Wasn't he trying to run away?

The giant and Fern drove in silence. She looked into the backseat of Mac's big brick-red station wagon to check on her children and the backseat kept being empty. She knew they were not there but the timer in her body still went off — Cricket must be hungry, Will must be thirsty, James is getting tired. She had never left them for more than a few hours and the thrill of it would carry her for a while, the sheer idea of a single body, responsible for only itself. But already she could tell that this idea was a

183

lie. Their little ghosts had followed her and always would. They had been born into the bigger world yet here, still in their mother's body, was the shadow of each. Fern understood only hours into her journey that no matter how far she traveled she would never be alone again. It was half comfort and half terror.

Fern looked over at the giant, his huge hand on the steering wheel, the air conditioning blowing his hair. She wished he was Ben but he was not. She resented him for it.

Fern said, "Who are you anyway? What do you do?"

"I work as a security guard at a bank. Basically I just read novels all day and chat with the tellers and eat snacks. It's a good job."

He sounded sincere but Fern still felt sorry for him. She had been bred to believe that menial work was meant only for those who were not smart or fortunate enough to do better. "Has anyone ever tried to rob the bank?"

"Never. We're a small bank and I'm a big man. My hope is that between those two things we will avoid it."

It got dark. Mac said, "Would you mind getting us a room?" and handed her cash.

Inside the motel room the giant sat down

184

on the king-size bed — the motel had had only one room left — which sank beneath him. There were actual rats in the walls. The rats sounded as if they were carrying out a great overturning of their society, a revolution of claw and tooth. Fern had almost always stayed in real hotels with bellhops and concierges there to offer a suggestion for good steak, good booze. If Edgar refused the job, refused Chicago, this would be their life. She had done the calculations while driving: they could sell the house and buy something tiny, use the difference to pay for the basics. At least she thought this seemed possible. Fern had never had to keep track of money and she had no sense of what they spent and when, no sense of the difference between what was needed and what was only desired. Maybe, ten years from now, she would come to think of a room like this as a great luxury. Or else Edgar would give in and they would buy their own island, their own jet. That those were the two most likely scenarios made her life seem unreal.

Fern opened the well-worn leather suitcase monogrammed with her mother's initials. The gathering had been rushed and she wanted to neaten. The ironing board was tucked into the wall and Fern unfolded it and heated the iron. She set it to steam and listened for the bubbles. No part of her body felt true or real, no part of her head. She called her own house and the phone rang and rang. She imagined her family out for pizza, Edgar trying to disguise her absence with food and soda. She hoped Cricket had done her homework. She wished she had included a reminder about the special soap Will needed to use to clear the rash on his back and the old freedom songs James had recently begun to love.

Mac turned the little silver knob on the television and the thing came to life. He lay down, put his shoe-feet on the bed, the volume on too high. The newsman, his hair pasted to his head, his mustache thick, said, "One wonders — could such a crime have been prevented, if only someone had spoken up?" Fern could not see the screen, but she knew there was a picture of a little girl who had washed up on the bank of the Charles. She had seen the news already. The girl's hair would have been full of crabs, her skin grey, but all they showed was the yellow tape.

Fern gave herself the time it took to pee and wash her hands to cry.

The mother of the dead girl came on screen and said, "She was going to be a fairy for Halloween," and her whole body col-

186

lapsed, as if everything within it had been liquefied. Fern thought of the long list of things she knew would undo this woman: favorite doll, too-small bathing suit, baby shoes, stack of thumb-worn books, hair in the shower drain, hair in the bed, hair twisted in the weave of the rug.

Fern had lost all her babies too. They were not dead, not sick, not kidnapped, yet each was gone. The crawler, the just-upright teetler, the question-asker, the new reader, the daring ocean-swimmers, the shark enthusiast, the midnight bed-crawler. At each stage Fern had been invested entirely in this person, their universe of games and questions and fits and laughter swelling to replace everything else. Then that stage had gone, completely. The children did not even remember huge swaths of the time she spent with them while Edgar was writing — songs they had sung five hundred times, stories Fern had told at bedtime, bodies of water in which they had splashed. Fern was the lonely keeper of these memories, and it made her feel almost crazy, insisting all the time on moments recollected by no one else.

Fern remembered being pregnant, then holding those little imps. In what seemed like a moment, they were climbing trees. James punched someone at school. Cricket asked what dying felt like. Will broke his leg. For a whole year the twins had gotten up for the day at 4:30 in the morning and Fern would have done anything to change the habit but then the phase had ended and Fern had remembered those early hours like a dream — she and her boys on the sofa with tea and a stack of books, the night still dark around them, a fire if it was cold. Fern had lost something every day as a parent.

Maybe, she thought now, her flight would make her children more grateful, slow their growing a little.

Fern lay down on the bed next to the giant and felt the heat of his big body. She was not touching him, and still, the heat. The bed was big enough for both of them but he weighed so much more that she had to work to keep from rolling towards him. The bedspread was scratchy and cheap. The ceiling was stained. She listened to the rats in the wall. The sensation of lying on the same surface as a man who was not her husband was a tingle in Fern's feet. She had not done anything wrong, yet she was certainly out beyond the territory of a good wife.

"Where are we going?" she asked, realizing that they might have a destination and not just a point of departure.

"All the way across," he told her.

They gassed up before starting their next day's journey. He pumped, she paid.

"Where y'all coming from?" asked the woman at the register. The room was filled with smoke. Her eyeshadow matched the coffee stain on her paisley dress. She used the butt of her current cigarette to light the next one.

"East," said Fern.

"And you're going west." That was not a question. You had to be going the opposite way as you were coming from. Only one road, and that's the direction it went.

"When you get to Clayton," the woman said, "stop for potpies. They're better than the ones here, and you won't want to wait for Stonesville."

While Mac wet and cleaned the windshield, Fern tied a scarf around her hair and felt like her mother who had had a driving outfit. Evelyn had worn special moccasins and calfskin gloves that Fern had always wanted her mother to touch her with. Fern used to take her mother's gloved hands and press them to her own cheeks. Her mother's real heat through another animal's skin.

Driving again, she told her companion this story. It had been years since she would

189

have bothered Edgar with such a small memory, especially about her mother, whom he did not like. Mac asked the color of the gloves. "Green," Fern said. "They were very light green. Sort of key lime."

"That's a good pie," he said. "That is one of the best pies."

They were driving fast and the oaks had softened into maples. It began to smell like manure.

"Apparently we are supposed to stop for potpies in Clayton," she said.

"That's a good goal. Let's make that our goal."

The earth was flat around them, tamed by prehistoric glaciers. There was land and there was sky, both nearly featureless. Things made by people — houses, barns, roads, crops — were the only features to rise up.

All along the road out of town there were signs congratulating the 1976 high school class on their graduation. The signs were plastic, made to last, and months out of date. As if such an achievement deserved permanent recognition.

Dilapidated houses ran along the edge, tracks and stations, ice cold beer, dirt lots with the swirl of tire tracks, that giveaway sign of teenagers, late at night, building speed, spinning out, hiding in a momentary dust storm of their own making. Fern was sure that there existed here the girl who cut everything at home: coupons, bangs, jean shorts. Her boyfriend would have a good arm and bad skin. Maybe they would even stay together a few years, despite her mother, who had aged poorly, dryly, her hair a crackle of overdyed frizz, her skin undone and beginning to drape. Girls like that loved their mothers and did not think to hide them from their boyfriends. They themselves would look better at fifty, surely. Someone by then would have invented a cream, an elixir. The girls counted on this — basked sunnyside up at the pool with nothing between them and the heat but a slick of baby oil and a cloud of cigarette smoke.

Mac rolled his window down, just to remember real air, and in a second, the whole cab was hot and dusty. "Thanks for coming along," he said. "I should have said that already. It's nice to have company."

"Would you be doing this if not for me?"

"I've got business in California. Someone I need to see."

"Business business or personal business?"

He seemed reluctant to say. He smoothed his hair, curls that had been gelled downwards. He ran the windshield wipers, flicked the lights on and off, licked his thumb and cleaned a spot off the lacquered wooden steering wheel. "I have a son," he finally said. "But I haven't seen him since he was a baby."

"Does he know you're coming?"

"Yes. I'm going to pick him up and bring him home. It's finally my turn."

Fern pretended that it was reasonable to be driving at high speed away from her family. Motherhood, money, marriage — these were all suspended behind her. And with each mile they crossed they drew closer to the giant's son. One family stretching apart and one pulling together. Fern was still fooled by her own story of escape.

Clayton came along. Fern and Mac were hungry, having waited all afternoon. The sign for the town told them that there were eight hundred souls present, but everything was closed up. The gas station advertised old-fashioned prices and had no pumps. There was a real estate office that looked like it had been closed for years. Sidewalk weeds were thick. The giant pulled into a lot and parked, and their footfalls were the only sound. Fern looked for evidence of a fire, a flood. "Let's go," she said.

"We just got here. I want my potpie."

192

"There is no potpie. There is nothing."

The giant had already set off. He made big prints on the dirty sidewalk. In the beauty parlor window, two brown wigs, styled for the previous decade, had wilted and a pair of scissors was set out on the table in preparation for a haircut that might never be. There was a newspaper on the counter, more than a year out of date: *CEASE FIRE: All GIs Out of Viet in 60 Days.*

The coffee shop had a few forks out and the ashtrays were all full. The hardware store was still getting ready for another year's Thanksgiving.

"I'm starving," the giant said.

Which is when a woman appeared. She might have been eighty or a hundred or she might have been a deadwoman up from below. Everything she wore was brown and she walked with two canes. "Hungry?" she said. "I have potpie. Follow me."

Fern would have walked the other way, leaving a polite refusal behind her. Mac followed the specter of a woman as easily as if she had been his own mother.

"You're tall," she said to him.

"I'm actually a giant," he said.

"Good for you."

Her house was purple with purple everything and there was a black motorcycle out

193

front. She sat them at a table and brought, hot out of a gold-colored oven, two deep pies and two forks and an ashtray with a picture of an ace of hearts on the bottom.

"You smoke?" the woman asked.

"Only on special occasions," Mac told her. She poured a red drink into their lavender glasses, placed a pack of cigarettes on the table and then the woman, who did not say her name and did not ask theirs, began to climb upstairs. The giant dug into his pie. Fern peeled the crust back and looked for obvious signs of mice.

"They were right about Clayton," Mac said.

"That cashier can't possibly have meant to send us here."

"Where else? This is Clayton. This is where the potpie is. You're not eating yours?"

This felt like a test. You want an adventure, little woman? She was starving and the giant was showing no obvious signs of having been poisoned so she took a bite. It was silken and delicious. She could taste fresh thyme.

The woman did not reemerge. They sat awhile, waiting. Mac called up to her, "Great pie!" and there was no answer. He stood at the bottom of the stairs and tried again, climbed until he had ascended out of Fern's sight. She heard his footsteps above her. A house this old was not meant to hold a man that size. She heard the creak of doors.

"She's not here," he said, coming back down. "I can't find her anywhere."

"How can that be? Should we call someone?"

"There's no one to call." The empty town, the empty businesses.

Before they left, the giant slopped up the last juice off his plate with his thumb. They found a pencil and a notepad with the logo of a bank and offered their thanks. Fern looked in her wallet and found only a stack of hundred-dollar bills taken from the emergency envelope in the kitchen. She took one out.

"What are you doing?"

"I feel guilty not leaving something."

He smiled at Fern. If Edgar had been there, Fern knew the two of them would have debated whether the money would have made the woman feel cheap, condescended to, or if it would have struck her as terrifically kind. They would have suffered over it, no matter what their decision. Mac only smiled. "That's a big tip for someone that might turn out to have been a ghost," he teased.

No matter how hard Fern slammed, the latch on the door would not hold.

They drove on. The road had its own rhythm — meals, filling stations, whatever town came next when they got tired was the town they slept in. It was soothing, the non-event, the repetition, the open space ahead. The hope that her journey would cause Edgar pain made Mac into an accomplice. It made him Fern's friend.

Mac had little short hairs growing out of his earlobe that Fern had the urge to pluck. She could almost forgive him for not being her brother now. Ben, she thought, who had never had a chance to grow into himself. He had jumped out the window when he was eighteen years old and the doctors had begun their work on him just after. Who knows what kind of adult Ben would have been, who he would have loved. Maybe he would have been like Mac — unusual and happy, comfortable in his own form. She was glad there was such a person. "We have so much time," Fern said. "Tell me everything, from the beginning." The country was generous ahead of them — a seemingly endless stretch of land, of space.

"In the beginning," the giant started, and

196

then paused. "I was born premature, six weeks, and in those days they did not expect the best."

He told the story of his mother who decided not to send birth announcements until she could send the bad news along with. Her husband had left her when she was six months pregnant so she had already gotten used to being a source of collective sadness and discomfort. Now she would spread a new set of bad news: a baby was born, but. The giant's own mother had been one of six, only three of whom had made it. People used to be better at death.

Priests and nuns stopped in to dispense a little easy charity, performed baptisms without celebration. Here, tiny angels, sinless and suffering, just probable days or weeks until they returned to God's blue kingdom.

But Mac did not die. He began to gain weight — several ounces a day — passing the full-term babies, swelling into clothes for toddlers. When his mother was packing the miniature diaper the boy had worn when he was first born, doll-size, she discovered a note in its white folds.

Dear God,

It's Father O'Brien. Please, I want to believe in you so terribly. I hope this note finds you soon. Please send a sign.

This was the sign, she thought. My child, grown like a sudden weed, is God's sign. The giant's mother spent good money to have the note framed. She hung it above a small bronze cross that her own mother had worn around her delicate neck, the chain much too short for any woman who was eating sufficiently. The note, to her, was proof.

Mac grew. He was mistaken for a six-year-old at three, an adolescent at six.

His mother had vowed to find Father O'Brien and show him the good news. But there were so many, all over Boston, and every Sunday for years, Mac and his mother went on Father O'Brien missions, attending Mass and then approaching the priest after with the framed note. Each time, the man would apologize for not recognizing the note and offer his uneasy congratulations on the healthy boy — they always used the word "healthy" after struggling to describe him.

Leaving, the young giant's hair smelled of incense. Pigeons bothered the stone steps, their neck feathers puffing and flattening in the search for food. His mother kicked one hard enough that it flipped over on its side for a moment and struggled its little orange legs before getting right.

"Beggars," she said. "Beggars are beggars."

Every part of the giant's story was exotic to Fern. There were people in her world who believed in God — Protestants and Quakers — but they did so quietly. The incense-rich sanctuaries, the spindly woman marching her huge son from church to church as if she could prove, with one oily little piece of paper, the existence of the higher power.

"Did you think you were a miracle?" she asked.

"I just wanted to be a kid. God seemed a little overzealous."

"And now?"

"And now I think that the genetic lottery is complicated. But I still pray sometimes even though I doubt there's anyone listening."

The waitress at the next place brought a slice of banana cream and said, "This is the last piece and no one likes an orphan. Can I interest you? No charge." The pie had fallen in the middle as if in defeat. The giant cut the point off. "Wishing bite," he said. When they had finished the rest, they came back to this little triangle; each took some onto their fork and hoped, eyes closed, while the custard gave way to their hot mouth.

Miss Nolan said, "Journals out," and all the students reached into their backpacks and waited to be told what to do. Direct instruction was the format of childhood: add or subtract; write the letter A sixteen times, then write the letter B sixteen times; name three US Presidents; name the order, genus, species. The children waited, pencils ready, for their assignment. Miss Nolan looked at them. "Well," she said, "start writing."

"What should we write?" a scrawny boy asked.

"Write what you want to write. The point of writing is to say something, so say it."

The children were displeased or elated or terrified. It was quiet and pencils tapped. Cricket made a title page. "An Index of My Life." She wrote down the names of her childhood dogs and the ways in which they died. Car, mystery disappearance, rabies. No dog had survived more than a few years in their house. Something terrible always got to it.

Cricket thought about Maggie. Her breath

was always buttery. In the summer evenings on the island, once the light had loosened up, they had all gone outside to love her. A big heap of boys and girl and dog in the grass. "Let's say Maggie is our mother," one had said.

"Let's say Maggie can talk."

"Let's say Maggie can lead us to the treasure." They had tied scarves around their heads and then they were pirates and the island was fringy with palms and the cove was full of mermaids who had sharp fangs and hated all humans except these three littles and their dog whose fur they combed with fishbones. It had been safe because Maggie was there. Maggie the protector, Maggie the kindhearted leader and follower.

Cricket remembered months earlier on a night on the island when their mother had seemed too tired to say no to anything and they had begged, "Please, can we sleep outside with Maggie? Pretty, pretty please?" They had dragged blankets out, made a big mat over the grass and then slept in a heap in one corner, kids and dog breathing the same night in and out, and the stars fizzy above them, and the soft ears and warm black legs of their pet. They had hardly slept, it was that good. If only they could always live like this, they thought. They had schemed dragging one of the family's old steamer trunks outside and filling it with supplies, maybe planting a garden, harvesting fruit from the long snarl of raspberry bushes. Cricket knew how to sew, which had seemed important. The boys had a compass, though they had no plans to leave the yard.

Cricket looked around her classroom at the boys and girls scratching pencils on heads through bowl cuts and long bangs. That neither parent nor the dog had come home the night before made the memory greyer. That Cricket had been the one to make sure her brothers were dressed for this school day, their lunches packed, their hair combed, her own bookbag repacked with homework. It was as if the wish for orphandom that they had made at another time had just now come true. Cricket did not write that down in her journal. She moved on.

She listed the names of her teachers up until then and put a star next to Miss Nolan's name, knowing already that she was and would forever be the favorite. She wrote down people's birthdays and the years in which she learned what: the Greeks, the Romans, the Norse. She wrote down alternate names for her brothers: Boris, Stuart,

Nighthawk, Mark. She made a list of good jobs (pilot, copilot, horsewrangler, queen) and bad jobs (ambulance driver, mortician, housewife). Too soon, Miss Nolan said, "Close your notebooks." But then she went to the windows and drew the curtains. She told the children to circle up on the floor.

She took out a satchel and went around to each student, tied a strip of leather around their heads. She said nothing. The children hardly breathed. Miss Nolan passed out watercolor paint and brushes and instructed them to pair up and paint a stripe of color under their partner's eye. The wet brush was cold and soft. She set up a fake campfire made of crumpled red cellophane.

She said, "This is part of America." She said, "Imagine we are Indians. Imagine we're on the plains. We hunt for our food, which is rabbit, buffalo and deer, skinned with a piece of flint and hung up by their legs to dry. The women pick berries and gather herbs and leaves for medicinal purposes. The children," she whispered, "are given the bones to play with.

"Imagine that there are sandy mesas farther to the south and peaks to the north and that there is so much grass that it looks never-ending. We Indians are good at choosing where to set up our teepees, and we move around depending on the season. Before the white man came, we had no horses and used dogs as pack animals. But we learned to ride easily and quickly. We are excellent horsemen. Imagine how good it feels to cover ground on such a fine animal." Miss Nolan looked out at her new tribe. Cricket listened like these were the instructions she would need to survive a great storm. Miss Nolan said, "There always has to be a love story. Otherwise what's the point? Imagine a young brave, setting out to scout for a new pasture for the animals. Imagine he sees a small encampment of settlers with their wagons and their log cabins. Imagine he sees a beautiful girl out hanging wet dresses on a line. She is pale and red-haired and she must be from so very far away. Imagine the instant they look at each other and a tap of electricity hits them both in the heart. He goes back to his people, she goes back to hers and they can never, ever touch each other because they will make each other sick with foreign diseases and their families would have them hung and scalped, and despite how much they love each other, they would be miserable their entire lives." The children were dumbstruck.

"But . . ." said a girl with pigtails.

"But," Miss Nolan said. "But. They can write letters and they do. They write letters and they leave them under a particular rock. It gets so that touching the rock feels like touching the other person. It gets so that the letters and the rock are the only thing keeping the brave and the frontier girl alive." Cricket wanted to know everything that every letter said and she could feel for absolute certain that a lot of what was contained therein would be very unsuitable for her young eyes and this made her want it yet more. All the answers to all the questions of every adolescent and preadolescent must be contained in those letters.

"Your homework," Miss Nolan said, "is to write a letter as if you were the frontier girl or the young brave."

"Except we don't know . . ." one of the football-playing boys said.

"Hush. The human condition is universal. Just put yourself in their shoes. Put yourself in their moccasins."

Outside the covered windows, the trampled lawn collected maple leaves one by one from the big climbing tree. But inside, it was the West, it was all emptiness, and the troop of Indians made fire, ate beef jerky that they said was rabbit, learned to whittle sticks into sharp spears to be used later for the hunt. They were braves and they were girl-braves. No one wanted to be a squaw except Muffy Tapscott who had torn out her ribboned ponytail and was already braiding her hair. At the end of the day, each boy and girl who had been good — and they were all good because this was serious, this was the reason to live the rest of the week, the rest of the school year — got to choose a feather from Miss Nolan's leather satchel.

Like yesterday, there were no parents at home after school. Cricket stood in the living room, so quiet, and remembered her father, two days earlier. How he had taken the telephone from its cradle, sat on the stairs leading to the basement and closed the door. No light through the crack; Father was talking in the pitch dark.

"Just us, alone?" he had asked, and Cricket had heard because she was crouched on the floor, her ear against the cold wood. There had been another noise — the same ocean heard in shells, in cupped secret-telling hands. Then there had been a long silence, and the conversation had turned to hurricane season. "I'm a good sailor," Edgar said. Already, they had come to L and it was only September. Lisa. Next it would be a boy's name beginning with M. Cricket knew this because she and her brothers had always played a game of naming hurricanes. Bets were placed in July. Each child got an A-to-Z and if they guessed right, Father promised to buy them any toy. Each year the children said, "Any toy?" And Father said most seriously, "Any toy, sweetlings. Any toy you can find." They discussed this after lights-out in the freedom of the night. "Is a submarine a toy? Is an airplane? A horse is something you play with." But none of them had ever won. There were too many names.

Cricket, ear to the door, had listened to the ocean in the wood. Her father had said, "They can manage without me. One parent is enough for now." He had waited for the person on the other end to talk. "Kids this smart can handle themselves if they have to. They could use more space to roam." Cricket had agreed about space. There was less air in this house than they needed and it was either too hot or too cold, and she was tired of having to ask first about everything.

Before she had tried to explain her parents' absence away, but remembering the overheard conversation, now Cricket thought that Father could be someplace where hurricanes were a concern and that Mother might not be with him, though she certainly wasn't here. What Cricket knew was that no one was in charge. Her brothers were eating crackers at the kitchen table and playing checkers. They had unbuttoned their white school shirts and their little-boy chests were all rib and sinew. There was no mark of their parents' departure on the air, no ghost of them. The silence was clean. At least until the red rotary phone began to ring and all three of them looked up. The boys ran to answer but Cricket yelled at them. "Wait!!" she said. She was sure that if it was known that they were alone, uncared for, they would be taken to an orphanage. Cricket imagined a dogcatcher's van filled with sickly children. She explained to her brothers the danger they were in and they all stood there over the ringing phone like it was the most dangerous thing in the house. "You must promise never to answer," she said. Finally, the thing quieted.

Needing to admit that they may have been abandoned for good, Cricket led a search around the house for clues. They looked in every room and every room was neat and unlived in. Then they looked in drawers. The same things were missing that had been missing the day before: clothes, not just

Mother's. Things had been taken from each of their drawers. James was missing his overalls and two sweaters, Will was missing a handknit scarf that he always folded at the top of his underwear drawer and Cricket was without a stack of days-of-the-week underwear that had been there before her parents had vanished. This had led the boys to believe their parents would be back for them, that they had organized all the details of a trip and forgotten just one thing: their children. To be helpful and prepared, they each packed a duffel with all the necessaries for a number of different climate possibilities. They had grown up with the good counsel of dressing in layers and they applied this to the new, parentless state. Cricket was not as quick to believe that their being left here was a mere oversight, that, two days into whatever their parents were doing, neither of them had realized that the three smaller members of the family were not in the backseat or the ship's cabin or the sleeper car. She played along, though, because she did not want to alarm the young boys. That's what a caretaker did — faked okayness. Cricket tucked tights into her bag, light sweaters and heavy, scarves and matching double-soft cashmere gloves that she had always been too afraid of ruining to wear.

When they had packed and placed their bags by the front door, they bundled themselves on the living room sofa in front of the big windows where they could watch the path for rescuers. "Tell us about orphanages," the little ones said, and Cricket lowered her voice to its most serious octave. "In orphanages," she said, "there is a very old woman with a stick and everything is horribly clean. All day, the children, whose heads have been shaved because they all have lice, scrub the floors with bleach. They eat pig slop once a day and all night they are woken up each hour when the very old woman comes to stand next to each child's bed and whispers into her ear, 'You have no parents at all.' "

They had spent all their lives washing up, cleaning up, being quiet at parties, saying *please* and *thank you* and smiling when some old woman on the street touched them on the head. Now they were free of all of that, free but alone and in who knows what kind of danger. Cricket felt hungry and lawless and she went to the freezer for ice cream. Without discussion the children stood around the tub with spoons, scooping huge bites of chocolate, vanilla, strawberry into their mouths. They were lonesome and unstoppable.

Earlier that same day, Edgar woke up in Glory's house and put on his jeans, fastened his big brass belt buckle and looked in the mirror. He did not look like a person capable of destruction — he was just a thirty-two-year-old man, the first grey hairs, the first lines, a few days of beard and hair that his mother would say was much too long. What should he have done? Gone home, promised away his future? There it was again, the burn in his chest, fury. *Not yet,* he thought, *she should suffer for this.*

Freedom, first thing, was a foreign kitchen and too little for breakfast. Edgar had never cared about food the way his wife did. He wanted the utility, she wanted to discuss the butter and the spice. Without her, he could eat a small piece of bread and get on with things. Glory woke up and she slunk over to him in no clothes at all — she had thick brown hair between her legs, under her arms, on her head, and all that pale skin. She looked at him, this new man in her kitchen with tea and bread. Thank goodness for John with his carefully tuned gauge for unwantedness. He might have been good at other things, but scarcity seemed to be his most valuable skill. John had left a note. *Go-*

ing to Mother's, and his signature, and nothing else. Glory knew all the elbows and S curves of the highway that led to that cottage on the cuff of a peninsula so far north it was snowbound from September to May. She could tell that John had packed almost nothing, probably not even wanting his wife's handprints with him in this ache. What he did bring she imagined he had washed first in a Laundromat in an industrial washer with very hot water and too much soap. As if he could be free of every last of her skin cells. The residue. The scrim of his wife.

In situations of distressed marriage, the usual first step for the woman was to clean out all the closets and redo things. Have a guy in about new wallpaper, do something with the floors (everyone was carpeting these days, plushly, but Glory still preferred wood). She had money and no one to disagree. She could have bought the huge round lamps that had become popular, a set of white tulip chairs, covered a ceiling in mirrors. If John had been the one to stay, the walls would already have been scaled with paint-color cards. To Glory, the house was a shell, her current favorite item inside of which was Edgar. He had bought a toothbrush and left it in the cup. He had pajamas there. That was it. The house, if it was paying any attention, might not have noticed a difference. A woman and a man. A certain amount of warmth emitted from them.

"Let me make you some eggs," Glory said.

"Nothing for me," he said. "Just you." There was kissing, and since she was naked, there was more. Edgar could not get used to a morning with no children around. It was both more fun and less — anything could happen on the floor, on the table, but with all possibilities available at all times, Edgar found it difficult to know when and where. For now the answer was always and here. It was exhausting and Edgar was used up.

Glory smoked a joint and ate fruit after. Strawberries. She began to cook eggs even though no one wanted them. Edgar was enjoying the slip into someone else's life. His existence was momentarily unencumbered. He had locked the door on his own house, leaving on the heels of his wedding-dressed wife — that was a puzzle he still had not solved — whom he knew would be able to care for the children for a few weeks. In order to walk out of his own life, Edgar had driven less than two miles where a beautiful woman had laid out curried

213

chicken salad on a plate. In those two miles, the whole world had changed.

The eggs that Edgar had not wanted needed salt but he let it be. This was a small point, and simple, and it was almost pleasurable to stand beside a bad cook and kiss her without suggesting any changes. Breakfast would be over soon whether he enjoyed it or not. The woman would be warmer if he asked no questions.

The sea, that fathomless beauty, stood waiting for them. They could almost hear the wash of it.

Who was this person with whom Edgar was about to sail away? She was all yes, all open door. She seemed less woman than invention.

Glory's money came from textiles and because she was a girl it never occurred to anyone that she would play any role except to inherit and spend. She was always putting some African through medical school, sending a check to a repressed ethnic minority in the Russian Caucasus, funding the election campaign of a native son who might have won if trees had votes instead of people. Glory had taken peyote in a hogan in the Sangre de Cristo Mountains. She had slept in a school bus at a music festival in

Santa Cruz beside a lover who was wearing nothing but an Indian headdress and a pair of tube socks. She had nearly died of malaria while counting the last surviving members of a species of miniature bat in Brazil.

The world's idea for a young woman of a certain class was to show her wealth only in her own form: hair, nails, clothes. Otherwise, modesty was the way. Shush yourself down to the quiet only one man at a time can hear. Become a kind of silence that the man has to get so close to notice, close enough to feel like no one's ever heard this particular whisper, and probably they haven't. This violet-scented whisper is your girl, she's never been anything until now. Watch her bloom before you.

Not Glory.

It was her husband who was the whimper. He was an apology, his entire being begging for forgiveness for the space he occupied on earth. The air he did not deserve to breathe, the soggy elastic of his skin uncomfortable in anything but temperate shade. They were matchmade by their parents who looked only at the numbers. Grades, height, account balances, companies owned by their fathers (rubber, shipping). Love was not discussed at any point. Glory wore the hideous tulle of her ancestors for the cere-

215

mony but she snuck out to change into a crocheted dress and flower crown before dinner and once she had been seen, it was too late to force her back into the gown. She got drunk. She told old women that they looked old and young women that they weren't hiding their flaws as well as they thought they were.

Glory's mother, at the sight of her daughter's unraveling, retreated to the bathroom where she ate three skinless chicken breasts while she cried, sure that Glory would ruin both of their lives. Her mother carried, like a beloved pet, a fat slice of cake into the car when the awful night was over. Her husband said, "Is it possible that I've never seen you eat dessert before?" He seemed excited. He pinched her thigh. "Get a little meat on those bones." At a red light, Glory's mother took a glob of frosting and applied it like lipstick, then kissed him hard with a lot of tongue. A car pulled up behind them and she did not stop when the horn began to blow, did not stop when the other driver screeched around them. She only let up when her husband began to pull over and tried to find his way through the clasps of her dress. "What are you doing?" she asked.

"What do you mean?"

"Don't be crude. We're on the street, Donald. Get your eyes on the road." And she sat back in her seat as if she had never sugared her lips, never sugared his. She unrolled the window and threw the cake onto the street where it would be accepted with gratitude by a feral cat drowsy with unborn kittens.

Glory's mother was never the same. Her only daughter had swiftly managed to undo all the social upkeep of her whole house-wifely career. Glory's mother spoke to her father only when others were around and at those times she feigned a happy marriage so well that Glory's father went slowly crazy, believing and then disbelieving his own life in intermittent waves that left him seasick. He took up model airplanes, then real airplanes, then ballooning and, since money for him was plentiful, he built a hangar behind the summerhouse on the Vineyard and set to work on a life-size papier-mâché hot air balloon made from dollar bills. He gained a following over the years of similarly lonely men who would come from other cit-ies and other states to discuss the mechan-ics and weight-bearing principles, the mix of flour and water. He meant to send the balloon up, knowing it would not last long, once the fire was lit. Knowing it would probably land in the sea where the saltwater would work as a solvent until the whole mass sank, soggy, to the bottom.

Glory's mother, in fate's usual torture, wanted what she did not want. She found a joint in Glory's underwear drawer and smoked it to punish her daughter, fully expecting the evil drug to require her heroic rescue by a truckful of firemen breathing one after the other into her lungs, begging her to come to. She imagined the phone calls: emergency room to husband, husband to daughter, and what she saw in her mind was not a string of words and information flowing through those wires, but guilt, thirsty and bright as a weed. The surprise: she smoked and she felt good. She wanted to take her clothes off so she did. A bath sounded nice, and she took half an hour to make a peanut butter sandwich first, which she had never before realized was a perfect object, and she brought it upstairs to the bath and ate it and tasted it and ate it and tasted it and when she got thirsty she lowered her head into the bath and drank. Whatever her body was made of was exactly what it was supposed to be made of. On the same night, on the other side of town, Glory was also high in the bathtub only she had wine and slices of cold cantaloupe. It was the closest mother and daughter would ever be and they did not even know the moment had occurred.

After Glory's wedding, she had to make decisions about the marital contract. She would consummate, because who knew, maybe the pallid skin concealed a workhorse of a lover (it did not); she would do some cooking because she liked to; she would certainly do her own cleaning because she did not believe in hiring poor people to get on their hands and knees for the sake of her hardwood (this decision meant that the house was always covered in a film of grey, as it turned out that Glory, who'd had a maid all her life, did not realize how long it took to dust a five-bedroom house); otherwise, John and Glory were two planets in the same orbit. They slept near but not close, ate the same thing for dinner but only one of them was enjoying the meal at a time. Glory liked the couscous and tabouli, John the sugared ham steaks.

They did both like to travel, so they went places with sand, hot springs, huts, natives in bright clothes, and they smoked weed and liked each other better. It was almost friendly. They ate mangos, they ate fried ants. Glory overpaid for things she did not even like, thinking of it as a donation, where John haggled hard for things he dearly wanted. They wore embroidered shirts and leather sandals, but John always changed into his loafers for the flight home. It felt like waking up from a good dream. She had understood the locals, she felt. She had seen, really seen, their baskets and their beadwork. She imagined disassembling her world and replacing it with something real.

By evening the boat was coming down from its dry dock and Edgar had made a list of needed supplies. Provisions, he called them. Water and beans and first aid and vegetables and suchlike. This was happier than Glory had seen him in the few days she had known him, his head over a list, checking. He fogged his glasses with his breath and polished them. Everything was a blur of faded color until he replaced the lenses over his eyes.

Glory packed layers as instructed but she only took real care with the most underneath of these. Much lace was considered. She packed jean shorts and thin T-shirts and sundresses and a poncho. Mexico, she said to herself, and the word was all X, a spot marked.

Edgar intended to go home for clothes. He drove there, sat in the car out front and looked at the house, so familiar, so un-. He let the engine run, his hand on the key, about to turn it off. He needed a few more shirts and a better sweater, his slicker. He could have used the right pairs of shoes. The trouble, of course, was the wife who lived in that house. He thought of Fern on the bow of his boat, pole and line dangling. Occasionally, she had caught a tiny fish, big-eyed with surprise in the strange air. In the pictures, she was always smiling, her hair in a bandana. Glory was untested, possibly sick on the water, but Edgar wanted the trip enough that he was willing to risk her suffering. Edgar needed a good thing. He needed to go east, away from whatever fate awaited him. He needed the salt.

The lightless windows made him almost, almost sneak inside. Five minutes and he could be out again. It was not that he worried about being caught and stopped — he had already made the decision to wriggle free — but that some residue of the house, of the family, would stick to him and he would be unable to wash it off. He did not want their smell or their tears or their questions to join him on his journey.

Instead, Edgar went to the department store to buy everything new. The whole place was sweet with perfume and women reaching out to him with flowered bottles they swore his love would love. They had pale pink lips and sprayed-stiff hairdos. They could not know what journey he was preparing for but he resisted looking them in the eye anyway. Shoes, jacket, slicker, sweater, shirts, he kept repeating to himself as he navigated the sea of pretties.

"Think how good she will smell," they said to him. "Later and so very, very close."

They drove through Boston to the harbor and found the boat, one of several Edgar's father kept there (they didn't want to go all the way to the Vineyard where Edgar's own boat was dry-docked for the winter). Edgar was fast with the lines. Glory had no place to stand, in the way no matter where she went. Eventually, she sat down cross-legged on the dock and watched her new man thread and pull. Glory read the boat's name in dark blue: *Ever Land.* "So you're not the only one in your family who doesn't want to grow up," she said. Edgar reached high and then ducked under the boom. He found himself a little angry with her for looking so right in the fancy harbor.

"You should know that I don't really believe in money," Edgar said. The yacht, the freshly bought clothes, the southerly escape, counted as evidence against his argument and Edgar knew this.

"You don't believe that it exists or you don't believe that it matters?" She said this like he was a highschooler in his first Philosophy class. He was quiet. He thought about his father, who was probably also standing on a dock, half-wet ropes in his hands. He would be dressed in whatever you were supposed to be dressed in that season, linens probably, and crisp white canvas shoes, while back inside the yacht club, Edgar's mother would be midway through a story she was good at telling about the time the sleigh-horses lost the road in the snow and they spent Christmas Eve out in the woods while the maids waited, worried sick, the shine of a roast goose cooling on the table.

"In Chicago? A horse-drawn sleigh?" the astonished listener would ask.

"It's an antique. From Lapland. We have a *lot* of land," she would say, aiming for maximum jealousy. The people might have been all right, but the lives were deplorable. The spending, the charity events, the art collection, the jewelry. He thought of his future, the twin possibilities of struggle and riches.

"I don't believe it matters," he said. He had always wanted this to be true; now his life had offered him a chance to test it.

"That's the most obvious thing in the

world, sweetheart. But I don't know anyone dumb or brave enough to give it up." She stood to kiss him but they both remembered in time that they were in public and nothing was safe yet. They had to wait for the open ocean to touch in daylight.

Even though Edgar's family had once been poor, poverty for Edgar was impossible to imagine. Money was both disgusting and ever-present. He hated it but he did not know how to live without it. The puritanical New Englanders around him in Cambridge were just as rich but spent very little, watched the accumulating numbers in the bank account. They saved, drove older cars, wore their clothes for twenty years, the children only seeing the spoils of their family's wealth when someone died. To them, Edgar probably looked frivolous, garish, but Edgar would have explained his purchases differently — he thought of spending as getting rid of money. The things he acquired had been secondary. He had an expensive English car, but look at those thousands of dollars he had spread out into the winds. He had managed to turn his money back into metal, back into mineral. And anyway, he hated expensive things so owning them was a kind of punishment. To him, his parents were the frivolous ones —

not only owning but enjoying their spoils. He disbelieved in everything they loved. Edgar's intentions were entirely different from his parents', though to someone on the outside, his life was nearly indistinguishable from theirs.

Like many of Edgar's things, the sailboat that he and Glory would run away in had been custom-built by his father. It was wooden and her hull was painted bright red. She was built exactly like the boat of a famous seaman and family hero who had sailed alone around the world. She was thirty-six feet long, fourteen feet wide, four feet deep in the hold and weighed nine tons. These dimensions were known by everyone in the family, as important as everyone's own height and weight. The deck was Georgia pine and the mast New Hampshire spruce.

Edgar's father had thought of himself as a counterpart to the famous captain, the same spirit, only he had to stay home and have a job. The ship was a lien on his future, a holding place for the yearlong voyages he planned once he could pass the business on. Edgar's mother was a fine sailor herself, kept pretty even in a gale, always found a way to have a proper supper on the table, and when they came into port, she was always the one to tell the tale so that the men with their cold gin laughed hardest. They were different from the other rich people in this way. They showed up at resorts, but they did so on their own airplane, flown the long way around, or by sea on their own vessel with no crew, or they rode horses for six days over the mountains first. The privilege of money, as Edgar's parents saw it, was that you could get yourself into the great wild beauty — the thousand-meter-deep sea, the wide open West, an island inhabited mostly by dangerous animals, and feel alive and real — and then come over the crest of the hill and have someone meet you with a silver tray containing fresh fruit, aged scotch, a cold towel for your hands, and show you to a seat with a perfect view from which to tell the story of your adventure.

Edgar's father would have been proud of his son and happy enough about the voyage to keep the affair a secret. Edgar had not told his father that he was sailing south exactly because his father would have slapped him on the back and offered advice about whether to take the Intracoastal or stay farther offshore for speed. But Edgar wanted to believe that this was a different kind of trip. He wanted to believe that this was not a holiday, though in fact he had made every decision exactly the way his parents would have. It made Edgar feel better that he would be very dirty soon, that his hair would be crisp, his clothes thick with salt with little freshwater to spare for cleaning.

For Glory, Cuba would have been ideal, revolution-wise. The island was shorthand for everything she believed in and she could almost picture Edgar wearing black, a beard coming along nicely, all worldly possessions relinquished. Glory would be tougher than most of the men and more serious. But she could tell Edgar was not as brave as she and so had eased down to Mexico. She did not realize that even this was too much to ask. To Glory, Edgar had said, "When we get there, we'll drink tequila and dance on a deserted beach and be so far away from home," though the story was a lie. He expected that Glory really could live without anything except good lingerie, and she would have happily died for a cause. Edgar believed in the same things, he did. He shared the fantasy about being tan and possessionless, though he had never lived without.

The thought of possessions brought the

thought of Fern, sitting alone at the table, hating and worrying about Edgar. She did not know where he was. No one did. He decided that he would go up to the harbormaster and call the house one more time before he sailed so that his family did not think he was dead. Only in the dimmest, smallest corner of himself did Edgar realize that Fern might not be there when he came back. Guilt snaked through him again, a hot zag. But he thought about his book, the life he had lived while writing it. The person he had grown into. His mind. No, he thought. I should be worth more to my wife than the house and the furniture. She is the unfaithful one.

The actual course Edgar had charted was to Bermuda. Bermuda, where he had been six times with his parents. Alluring and easy and safe Bermuda. Famous for powder sand and crisp shorts, every lawn ready for a game of croquet. Bermuda, where he had sat at the waves' edge at age ten, memorized the feel of the warm wash and the pale pink sand in his leg hair and the sound of his mother's voice in the distance, pausing when she took a sip of cold wine. Edgar wanted that again for the same reason everyone did — it was beautiful and comfortable. He would order freshly grilled lobster. He imagined a little hotel that looked like nothing on the outside, looked local and regular but inside someone had thought about comforts and there would be a wedge of balcony with a view of the sea, and a good place for Glory to stretch out her fine legs. This was not the journey the pair had discussed. Glory's ending included a darker-skinned overthrow of an unjust government, nothing to eat but beans and plantains, maybe a beer when it was earned. She would learn to sleep in a hammock with a gun across her belly. Glory could not sail, though, and Edgar was the one with the charts. It would occur to him only later that the woman who would have loved this trip most in the world was Fern. She would have loved the small quarters of the boat, the length of the day with nothing to do but talk and fish and eat and swim, the way it would feel to spot land finally, to come ashore, to shower and eat, their bodies still tossing in remembered waves.

He broke the news to Glory over spaghetti on deck, the boat still tied to the pilings, after he had tried the house again and let the phone ring ten times before hanging up. He explained, trying to convince himself as much as Glory, that Bermuda was a good stopover, partway. He explained the possibility that the island was at the brink of declaring independence from the British crown, though he had no actual reason to believe this. He said you never knew with these things, they could happen so quickly. One small incident and a new country could be born, a new flag flying glorious over the electric turquoise water. They might get lucky and be there for the moment itself, Edgar said, trying. He imagined his ideal scenario — a quiet revolution of a few thousand people on a beautiful island, the friendly natives celebrating with rum by sundown, the defeated colonizer setting sail for the homeshore with a hold full of lobsters and limes.

Glory said, "Huh."

Edgar said, "Picture pirates. Picture a prison camp where unfaithful citizens were sent to starve until they pledged allegiance to the crown. Hurricanes are a constant risk."

"Yes, I am still a little worried about that." Of course she should have been worried. Of course this was not the time to embark in an easterly direction by pleasure boat with a crew of two.

Edgar had no reasonable response.

"We'll be fine," Glory said, for him. They needed this now. Their landward lives were already upturned and they could not go back, gently ask their families to play normal for six months while the jailbirds waited for better weather conditions.

The *Ever Land* rocked slightly, and Glory felt lopsided but not sick. There was no longer a solid world beneath them.

1968

Fern had put gathers of daisies by the bed in preparation for her husband's return from the cold north. She wrapped up the baby and set off for the bus station to wait. Outside it was early morning, dewy and anxious.

Fern did not know what she would say to her husband. What she would report from days of walking without purpose, of her slow evenings sitting at the window with a bowl of cooling soup, watching the insects take over the skies. She had cooked a certain number of eggs, thrown away the rotting vegetables, dug a hole for an oak seedling that she never planted. That her daughter did not seem like enough of an accomplishment would strike her as sad only later.

The strangest thing was when that mythic person, that impossible, imagined soul was supposed to step off of an oil-sweated, slack-muscled bus. Fern stood there, shoes on and dress pressed, the baby in white linen, and the bus pulled in and sighed, and the engine settled into a worried rumble. Boys in uniforms held their hats to their chests, stooped in the doorway and then unfurled. There they were: just bodies. The same size as when they left.

As Fern waited for her particular counterpart to emerge, she studied the other boys for scars on their necks. She imagined their wives and girlfriends undressing them for the first time, touring the hash marks of war, running their fingers over those oversmooth patches where feeling-skin had been erased. Those were just the physical reminders — what of the heart's tissue?

And just like that, the last off the bus, Edgar stooped, stepped and stood up straight. His smile was a white heat. He put his bag down and scooped Fern up. That warm chest, that warm breath and she felt very small. "It's you," he said.

They knelt together at Ruth's side, each of them taking one of her small fists. Edgar did not move or breathe. The moment was a sheet of ice, thin and perfect and Fern wanted badly not to crack it. "You are already so big," he said to the baby he did not know.

"Isn't she beautiful?"

A cricket landed on the baby's chest, green and an inch long.

"Hello, Cricket," he said. Edgar would never call his daughter anything else. Soon, neither would anyone.

The other couples began to retreat, arm in arm, hand in hand, to their cars. They rumbled home to lunches already prepared, to houses scrubbed for the occasion. These boys had survived the war; some of them would also survive coming home from it.

There had been a third phone call to the General, this one made while Edgar's father drank a bottle and a half of champagne himself and watched the news — dozens of soldiers had died that day in a raid a few miles from the blue glare of the South China Sea. Behind the newscaster in the mud there was a hand and wrist, the familiar green cuff, but no arm was attached. Hugh had not been calling for another favor but to offer thanks for what his son had avoided. The General had a son who was studying business, who would soon graduate from college. He said this to Hugh and, again, they chatted a friendly circle. After they hung up, Hugh called his secretary and told her to schedule an interview with the young businessman and the General nominated

Edgar for a medal of bravery. It had become a reflex, the doing of favors.

Both sets of parents came to see Edgar and watch the ceremony in which he would receive the medal he had not earned, only a few hours after he had come home. Edgar had gone on early to line up while Fern and the parents stood around in the yard drinking lemonade. Fern's mother wore a black lace dress from the 1920s that had belonged to her great-aunt and had been mended by the same tailor fifty times. Her hair was short and grey and her face free of makeup. Paul wore pale linen and a thin striped tie and a fedora. On the way, Evelyn had snapped at him for buying a new suit.

"I've had this for five years," he had said.

"Exactly. There are perfectly good things in the attic."

If Edgar's parents, on the other hand, could have worn clothes sewn from money itself they would have. Everything they had on was the most expensive version available: Mary wore a silk shift minidress with palm fronds printed in dark green, white stockings to cover her varicose veins and a mink stole even though it was summer, and yellow heels that had been made for her very feet by an ancient Italian cobbler whose hands had cupped the heels of every movie star to set foot in Rome. Hugh's suit had cost as much as any of the war-widows would receive as compensation for their husband's lives.

"Maybe Cricket will grow up to be an artist, like you," Mary said to Evelyn. She swished her lemonade, took a big sip.

"Maybe. As long as she can avoid having children of her own."

"Mother," Fern said.

Evelyn apologized but she did not see the statement as unfair: unless one bought her way out of it, motherhood was a small room with high walls and no door.

"How's Ben?" Mary asked.

"They're trying to figure out what's wrong," Evelyn said.

"What's wrong is that you sent him to war and are now frying his brain," said Fern.

Evelyn looked at her daughter and narrowed her eyes. "He didn't go to war, dear. He went to *Indiana.* People have survived much worse things."

Outside the stadium there were at least a hundred protesters. They had signs with skulls wearing Uncle Sam hats and signs with flowers that read *War Is Not Healthy for Children or Other Living Things.* They were young but not much younger than Fern,

236

who felt all wrong in her tailored dress with her fresh, clean baby in the pram. To them she looked like the enemy. Maybe she was.

The family sat in the high bleachers of the football stadium and fanned themselves. Cricket screamed and Fern bounced her, whispered in her ear, promised her anything in the world. The brass band played so loud that Fern covered the baby's ears and the instruments caught the sun and made her temporarily blind. Cricket settled, as if she was finally satisfied that the world could make its own noise.

Down below, the boys sweated in their wool uniforms. All the commanding officers, the Generals, the top brass, their foreheads beading and their lapels as flat as cadavers, looked stoic but proud. They announced the names of the heroes, and the boys climbed the stage stairs in their over-polished shoes and accepted, graciously, the honors. There were three soldiers in a row on crutches, each missing their right leg, as if they had been grouped by loss. Another was missing an arm. Four were in wheelchairs, two were wearing eye patches.

When it was Edgar's turn, he walked on stage on his intact legs and stood board-straight while his name was read, his two good arms at his sides. He had lost nothing more than a few months of his life and gained no more than sadness.

Like everyone else, Fern and Edgar and Cricket and their parents went out for lunch after the ceremony. They slid into a booth in the diner, and Fern felt better the moment she was pressed up against her husband. His new medal was bright and sharp-edged.

"Are you okay?" she whispered into his ear.

"I'm ready for this day to be over," he said back.

She smiled and took his hand. "Me too."

All the other couples looked like they were having a day to remember. Edgar felt as if this celebration was designed to distract them from the question of who they would be after they had done whatever they did. His parents ate fried chicken and mashed potatoes with plenty of gravy while Fern's parents ate plain dinner rolls with a thin smear of butter. All the town's old women had been up all night baking pies and cakes, which were served to the overfull couples and their squalling babies. "Apple pie without cheese is like a hug without a squeeze," the waitress said, so each piece came out with bubbling orange on top, and there was vanilla ice cream on the side too because, why not, they had earned it.

"I'm going to be in the car," Paul said after a cup of black coffee. "My head."

Evelyn asked the waitress for some ice and when it arrived, she took out a hand-sewn bag from her purse and filled it with cubes. "That's so nice, Mother," Fern said.

"It's a mess because I made it. I'm no seamstress." But this bag of ice was the warmest thing Fern had ever seen her mother create. She imagined her parents behind the closed bedroom door, him blind with pain, her lying beside, holding the cold to his forehead while she read an art magazine. Fern almost thanked her mother for giving her this gentle image. She knew she would come back to it.

Before the parents left, Edgar's mother brought out a bag of gifts: a tiny silver spoon with a gem in the handle, a watch for Edgar, a tennis bracelet for Fern, all in pale blue boxes. The other families were spending more than they could afford on lunch while her mother-in-law insisted on clasping to Fern's wrist a slither of cold diamonds.

Finally, the family of three went home and Fern gave the baby milk at the kitchen table while Edgar had a glass of whisky. He was home, finally home. Fern opened the windows now that it was cooling off outside. Cicadas started to saw, and the stars came out. Cricket went to sleep, and Fern came and poured herself a drink too, sat down with her husband. Fern and Edgar fell into each other, hands in hair, hands on skin, eyes open for a glance to check if this was true and real, then closed again. Fern felt like a weed growing crazily over Edgar's body, vining him up, suffocating him. She felt green and vital, her arms thick and ropey. They swapped air, breathing the hot wind of the other, lightheaded and oxygen deprived.

Fern's skin was still prickly from lack of touch. She was used to the feel of her own hands washing with soap, shaving, holding the arch of her foot while she trimmed her toenails. Edgar's touch was so soft on her belly it almost hurt. When he slipped her dress over her head, she saw her body and it looked like something undone. Her skin was loose where it had stretched and shimmered with lines.

Edgar said, "God, look at how beautiful you are."

"What?" she blurted out, truly shocked. Couldn't he see how incomplete she was? He traced a line from the top of her fore-

240

head, over the jump of her nose, lips, chin and right down the middle of her. Fern would not have been surprised if he had split her right in half. He told her, "I've been wearing six layers of clothing for months."

"Then let's see it," she said, and together they took his clothes off, buttons and undershirts and zippers and shorts and socks until he was nakeder than she. He looked down at himself. He really was pale. Moonlit.

"I remember," she told him, and she did. Fern palmed his chest, his neck, his arms. She felt the topography of his back, pressed her fingers into the riverbed of his spine.

At the other houses, the boys took out special frames for their medals and measured to make sure they were hanging perfectly straight. Their pride would never be big enough to spend.

The wives, meanwhile, what of them? They had no commemorative anything to hang on their walls. No one acknowledged the thousands of times they'd swept the floors, the window trim they had repainted themselves, perched on ladders, their hair tied back in a kerchief and something quiet on the radio. Their babies were supposed to

241

be the prize. The reupholstered sofa and chair sets, the matching rug, the place for everything and everything in its place. That was supposed to have been enough.

Edgar poured himself another drink. He fogged his glasses and cleaned them on a washcloth. He looked out the living room window at the sloppy world, so grey. The baby woke and nursed. "Cricket," Edgar said, offering his pinky for her to grasp. He wanted to see his own face in hers and almost could, but then she looked creaturely again. "You are my daughter," he said, and neither of them was convinced.

To Fern he said, "I want to keep writing. These things take a long time but I think I can do it. It feels good to get this stuff down." He felt a separateness from his surroundings. Like he carried his own slightly poisonous atmosphere.

"Sure," she said. She was glad he wanted to write — he was smart and big-of-heart and she wanted the world to have his thoughts — yet she wished he wanted only her. They had already missed so much of each other. She would have her own work, she told herself: the house would need to be cleaned, the wash would need to be hung on the line; the baby, the baby. Edgar, drink-

242

ing his drink, looked like an unfinished drawing of himself. He was home but he was not necessarily whole. Fern had suffered corrosion too. Loneliness did that to a person. She would continue to find rust from this year's hard weather. And life put holes in things, Fern knew.

"Did the protestors say anything to you today?" he asked.

"Protestors?" she lied.

"I spit on one of them because I wanted him to spit on me," Edgar said. "Because I deserved it. He didn't, though. He was too polite." Edgar took his glasses off and cleaned them on his shirt.

"Did anyone see you do it?"

"No. I was at the back of the line. I apologized after. I felt so stupid. He looked like he was about to cry."

"I'm glad you want to keep writing," she said. "I'd love to read it someday."

Cricket, on Edgar's lap, made a noise like a caught bird. All three of them fell asleep on the couch, ice still whining in their cocktail glasses.

Edgar played on the floor with Cricket who had acquired the words *pulp, fish* and *want.* She said *butter, dog, hello-hello, enough.* She woke screaming for no good reason and

Fern held her in the rocking chair, so tired, hating and loving the warm knot of a girl. Edgar went into his study and thwacked at the typewriter. All he had was the need to articulate his own wrongness, his existence thanks to the profound suffering of others.

He read books about coal miners who died deep underground, the earth caving in around them. He read books about manufacturing and pollution and wage-slavery. He read about workers who lost limbs to the heavy equipment and were fired for being useless. He read about the children of those men who stopped going to school so they could earn money. He read books about the cotton that had earned Fern's family their fortune and the dark hands that had picked that cotton, the dark breasts that had wet-nursed Fern's ancestors from babies into children, the dark bodies that had driven the white bodies in wide, comfortable cars through the green ache of the South, fields bursting with soft, white money. She knew and Edgar knew that eventually one of her relatives had become a famous abolitionist, that the story went in the right direction. She also knew and so did Edgar that while the family had embraced new values, the dollars they carried with them were old and plenty dirty.

He came home and watched the news. American forces burned Vietnamese villages. An offensive began in a city on the edge of the South China Sea that would last for weeks.

They did not know yet that Ben would die a few weeks later when the doctors attempted to perform a partial lobotomy, as if they could simply remove the troubled part of him. Slice and eliminate. That, in what would turn out to be the last moments of his life, he would sit in the dawn light preparing for the operation and jot down a note to Fern: *Thanks for the sweets.* Over all their years on earth together, all the ways she had betrayed him and cared for him, this was the tiny kindness that had risen to the top of his memory. She would lock the note in a metal box along with a sprig of Cricket's hair and a photo of her and Edgar the summer they had fallen in love. Of all the objects in the world, these were the only three she could not risk losing. Fern would blame her parents always for Ben's death. Her parents, who had not been able to leave her brother alone, who had continued to write checks to the doctors who promised that money equaled treatment equaled health. Her father would never recover from the twin loss of his son's body and his daughter's heart, and her mother, though heartbroken in her own way, would appear to continue her calm, cold walk through life. Evelyn would think of Fern's anger towards her as one gift she could actually give to her daughter: she would take the blame.

Fern, young and sleepless, had once sat on the bottom step and listened to her mother and a group of friends in the kitchen, teacups and spoons tinking. The conversation had gone from tennis to golf to shoes, and then it had grown a little later, and they were drinking, and one woman said, "I was driving today, and I couldn't hear anything because the boys were screaming at each other. I thought about driving off the bridge. I thought about how quiet it would be underwater." Fern's mother had confirmed: normal. To think of killing your littles, to think of dropping them from great heights, to think of the gentle or terrible demise.

The Tennessee house, after Ben's death, had a new temperature. Cricket toddled around tugging at curtains and pressing anything that looked like a button while Fern washed the dishes and swept the floor. The motions were a memory in her muscles. All of it felt bloodless now.

Edgar closed his eyes but could not fall asleep. He saw the white sheet of the north, the sky sparking green and purple. He saw Runner at the door that dawn, walking steadily out. He had no idea where Runner had ended up. He might have died in the cold. He might have been eaten by wolves. He might have walked all the way to the edge of the ice to the place where the cold grey sea began. Edgar imagined him undressing there and jumping in. He imagined that the cold would have been violent, impossible for Runner to fight.

Or maybe he had gone to town, gotten a job. Maybe he lived in a house just like Edgar did. Maybe he was warm and happy. Maybe he was grateful.

On the third day after Ben died, Edgar convinced Fern to leave the house. They went to a department store where all of them, pretending there was such a thing as comfort, bought things. They chose two matching oak dressers, new plates, water glasses, wine glasses, juice glasses, champagne glasses, whisky glasses. Edgar bought a wooden rack for his nice shoes, and then he bought nice shoes to put on it.

Edgar bought and bought and bought and it had the desired effect: he hated shopping, he hated owning, he hated money, and each transaction hurt him. He wanted this surface hurt, this material hurt, which was a cut, a sting, a bruise. Fern usually liked new things, pretty things. She liked surface comfort and material comfort but today she was grief-battered and everything made her sorry: silverware, hats, eyeglasses, the chime of the perfume girls' voices.

Cricket wilted at her mother's feet, sat on the floor playing with a stuffed giraffe. She was too small to understand what it meant to die, but she seemed to know that she needed to be easy to love, that her parents would not find her otherwise.

On the third night after Ben died, Fern and Edgar and Cricket lay there in the big bed and Fern thought, *This is what it feels like to be married today.* Because the feeling was utterly different from being married the day before, the year before, the day they had made those vows. There had been a short stretch at the beginning when being married was a recognizable state — eggs were cooked, walks were taken, parties were attended, and in the dark, their bodies were two ropes, knotted and loosed, knotted and loosed.

Fern felt the shape of Edgar's legs against

248

the back of her own. The scratch of them, the temperature. She could feel his heart beating inside his chest, tapping out its music. "Tell me something about when you were away," she finally said.

He thought for a moment. "By the end I got so used to cold so that I hardly even felt it."

Fern knew that this was a prayer for her. A wish that she would learn to adapt to the new weather in her heart.

"On the night I was walking back home from calling you, I saw a huge figure approaching. The ice was blue that night and this creature lumbered out. My gun was in my backpack, unloaded. I didn't know if it was a person or an animal. And then the figure got closer and I realized that it was a polar bear. A huge white bear and he was coming straight towards me. He glowed in the moonlight and his eyes were completely black. I didn't know if I should run or play dead. It was so beautiful and so terrifying and I couldn't turn away. It felt like this was what I had been waiting for all that time. Like whatever he did to me was what I deserved."

Fern knew that her husband must not have been eaten because here he lay. But her breath was caught in her throat. She squeezed Edgar's hand.

"The bear came right up to me and stood there, and I could smell the sea on his breath. It felt like he had a question he wanted me to answer. I put my hands up in surrender and waited to be eaten or carried away. I told him that I had a baby, as if he could understand or care. He just looked at me and looked at me. I knew I was cold by watching the snow gather on his body. He scratched at the ground by my feet and then he stood up on his back legs, towering over me, and then he turned and lumbered away again."

Fern could smell the sea and oil on that bear.

"I feel like he understood. Like Cricket saved me."

There it was: that thick, slippery scar tissue Fern had known she would find on her husband. "I believe you," Fern said. "I believe you that it was beautiful."

1976

Math was math and Cricket did not care which passengers would arrive first if two trains left Pittsburgh at 10:14 a.m. and 11:51 a.m. respectively, one going forty miles per hour and one going sixty-six. "Whichever one does," she said. "Call the station and find out." The math teacher did not appreciate this kind of attitude and she had a special look she gave to say so. It was all eyebrows — her whole face withdrew behind their shadow. The teacher said, "How are we ever supposed to get out of this recession if we have citizens like you?" Cricket scribbled on her paper and tried to seem like a person who cared about numeric facts. After a while she raised her hand and asked to go to the bathroom.

Cricket soaped her hands and wrists and rinsed until her skin squeaked. Her fingers were bright pink from the hot water. She looked in the mirror, checked her chin to inspect the progress of a bruise she did not remember getting. It was not better and not worse than it had been in the morning. Then the lights went off. Cricket held her breath. It was black-dark in the bathroom — she could see absolutely nothing. She imagined a knife murderer standing in one of the stalls. And she thought she could hear breathing, now that she listened, but she could not tell where it was coming from. The space around her seemed vast and instinct made her stretch her arms wide, feel around in the air for a boundary. She found the wall and began to follow it towards the door. She wanted not to make noise but her body had weight and when she placed her feet, no matter how carefully, there was a sound. She imagined a trapdoor, a secret way out, a hiding place. The wall was cold and black. The air was warm and black. Her breath was hot and black.

Which is when someone came in close, body and arms, arms that slid around her waist. Lips were a surprise. Lips and tongue. It was only a short moment but it felt like a long one, that mouth hot and wet and her own against it and the arms keeping her. Cricket wrestled away, ducked under and out, and she ran from the room into the hallway, whitelit. Her eyes did not want to adjust. The floor was cleaned to a shine. Cricket could not see her face in the floor but she could see the reflection of her small form, the slight blue of her dress, black nicks of shoes on her feet. The reflection was fast moving, poured across the floor like liquid.

Cricket did not turn to see if anyone came out of the bathroom, and she did not hear a second pair of footsteps. The school looked just as it had — plain and organized and sad.

Cricket huddled at her desk in the safety of a set of fractions. Her insides were turning.

"Cricket, please," the math teacher said. "This is not so horrible as you think." The woman stood over her, turtleneck and shin-length skirt and large wire-rimmed glasses. Cricket tried to quiet her shaking feet and hands. The math teacher was certainly not going to be the person she went to. It was not the story the older girls told about kissing. Yet: her lips felt warmer from the kiss, her first. This had been a soft kiss, violent because it was uninvited, because Cricket did not know who was on the other end, but gentle. Here were three-fourths plus one-fifth, one of one kind and one of another, and what did it equal? She tried to recall the details: the person was taller than she and did not have a kid smell. The person had a smooth face. The person was confident. It was a woman, she thought, which was embarrassing and awful and also not.

The math teacher came to stand above Cricket and waited until her pencil began to manipulate numbers on the page. Cricket's hand attended to the integers and their additions and divisions, but her head was still in the dark of the girls' bathroom. Cricket did not think she had been kissed by either of the Hancock brothers who were the sweethearts of other girls' emergent fantasies, nor Adam or Stuart, the nerdy boys who might someday have wanted to be on the other end of her mouth. The person she imagined, whose lips had been on hers? Miss Nolan. Kind Miss Nolan, smart Miss Nolan. Too tall to match face-to-face, but maybe she had knelt on the cool tiles? Cricket imagined wrapping her arms around the woman's waist, the cinch of her skirt, the tuck of her blouse, the long waves of dark hair. She would rest her head on Miss Nolan's chest, listen for the beating heart. This story unmade the fear almost completely — the moment, which in fact had been terrifying, changed to a gift if Cricket told it the right way.

When math was over and Miss Nolan came back, she smelled like the outdoors. Her hair had been wind-tossed and her cheeks were pink. Cricket tried to meet her eye, to show recognition for what they had shared, because by now, Cricket was sure it had been her teacher in the dark. By now, no other pair of lips seemed possible. She knew it was inappropriate, and perhaps Miss Nolan was embarrassed. She would get fired if anyone knew. But love was unwieldy. Cricket already understood that.

When it was time to journal, Cricket started a love letter. *Dear Beautiful,* she wrote.

Dear Brown Eyes. I sit at the foot of the mesa as I write this under the blue skies. In the sand there is always silence. Human life can easily be forgotten. If you are quiet you will notice that there are animals burrowing into the sand and into the trees and cactus. Forget your own self and you will discover so much more. The Gods of the Skies and the Earth and the Water are always watching us and they know that I love you. I love you, Lady of the Crescent Moon with the ebony hair. I will bury a shard of turquoise in the sand two paces from the cliff's edge, near the place where the cactus breaks through the earth. You will know the place because the lizard nests there in the first rains of the season. When you find the blue stone, then it is time for us to wed. I will be waiting, dreaming of your blood red lips.

Cricket had little to draw on but cartoons of the West. She wished she knew what it actually looked like. And all she knew about Indians was what Miss Nolan had told them already, plus whatever images of half-clothed Natives adorned common kitchen products: butter, baking soda, honey.

Before the end of the day, Miss Nolan gathered her flock in a circle and crinkled her red fire paper, and without being asked, all the children tied their leather strips around their heads. Miss Nolan said, "The buffalo supplied nearly all the needs of the Plains Indians. They were meat and their hides were made into clothing and teepees. The buffalo went away in winter but as soon as it started to thaw, the Indians put their ears to the ground to listen for the stampeding hooves." Miss Nolan handed out sheets of paper, the edges of which she had burned so they looked old and mysterious. There were little pots of ink and feathers to dip.

The children laid their paper out on books and they drew buffalo, which they had never seen in real life. Miss Nolan described the big shoulders, the curly mane, the horns, the wide, square head. The children's drawings looked like cows, like dogs. They drew smoke coming from the animals' nostrils because that seemed fierce.

Miss Nolan said, "Imagine that we are the tribe of the young brave, gathered for the hunt. It is windy and still cold, even though the worst of winter has gone. While we walk, the men explain that we will trap the herd by surrounding them and closing in with our sharp spears. The men explain that it will be hard and it could take all day and all night and all day again and we will not be able to sleep or eat. The buffalo could easily kill us by trampling. The young brave tries to find the strength of the ancestors in himself and tries to feel confident and sure of his feet and arms. We set out at dawn. The sound of the hooves is like a gathering storm, and the young brave wants to run away but he cannot. He has to follow the rest of us and get ever closer. He thinks of his sweetheart, who is in a house, a log house, in a settlement. She has a kettle of water on and a fire and bread dough rising on the table. She is wearing a dress with a hoop in the skirt. She is writing him a letter, right that very minute, describing the very ways in which she loves him.

"Slowly, we close in around the herd, a half-circle of bodies wearing leather and feathers. On the other side is a cliff. We press the herd on across the grasses. The noses of the buffalo are wet and their eyes are dark and afraid. They are so much bigger than us but the trap is working."

Miss Nolan looked at the children who looked back at her from their inky drawings, and they wanted to say that they knew what it felt like to be both the dumb animal following along and the cruel human, pressing. They knew, and neither feeling was good.

"We come to the cliff and we spread out to make an opening for the animals, a doorway to their death. We keep walking, moving the herd onward, onward, until the first beasts fall. We howl then, a celebratory call and we thank the gods, and we beat at our chests. The huge animals continue to fall, thunderous, crashing against the cliff walls, making the exact sound you would expect from an animal falling a hundred feet through the air. The dust rises up around us and they die. Or they break their legs, in which case we kill them with arrows."

258

The children, by this point, were not drawing. They had expected the heroes to slay one animal, one dignified, beautiful animal and perform a sacred ritual of thanks over its body. Mass murder had not been on the children's minds. Miss Nolan either did not notice or did not care. She described the way the young brave killed those buffalo that remained alive, the way the group set about skinning. The sound of skin and muscle separating. The way the blood pooled. The way the brave thought of his love and the moccasins he would make for her out of this bloody skin. The way the flies began to gather, loud as a storm, and the blood smelled sweet and the animals were still warm, even as they were cut apart.

The men thanked the animals because Indians are grateful, everyone knows that. "No part left to rot, every organ used for something: water sacks, thread." Cricket tried to draw this scene, an animal gutted, heat rising, a man and a boy and a girl kneeling there, giving thanks. She wanted Miss Nolan to see that she was not afraid of what must be done. She was brave beyond her years, beyond her race. In this tribe, she wanted to be chosen as a leader, to be taken into her teacher's teepee where the fire would be especially warm, where the skin was painted beautifully and the fur mat on the floor was soft. Miss Nolan did not look at Cricket any more than she looked at the other children. She was fair, and Cricket admired this, though she was jealous of the care her teacher gave to anyone else. She reminded herself that no one else was kissed today. How resourceful, Cricket thought, to use the dark that way. To make a wilderness out of a school bathroom.

Miss Nolan said, "Right there at the bottom of the cliff, we Indians feast on the fresh meat. We especially love the liver, which we eat raw immediately. The young brave slops it up with his hands. It is still warm from being in the animal's body."

One boy, at this, fainted into his drawing. Miss Nolan did not seem surprised or worried, but she crawled over, lowered her head to his and stroked his hair. She whispered something into his ear that no one else could hear and everyone was envious. When he woke up after a moment, he looked peaceful. He said, "I dreamed of the prairie," and Miss Nolan kissed him on the palm of his hand.

A loud bell rang, which made the children jump, but it was only the bell that signaled the end of the school day. The places where they lived — the maple-lined streets, the

260

crossing guards and sets of fractions, the after-school snacks — fell down on them like a rainstorm. They were not blood soaked on the plains. They had not killed anything on this day. Some of the children were grateful and could not wait to leap into their mothers' station wagons. "Your homework over the weekend," Miss Nolan said, "is to list as many uses as you can think of for a dead buffalo." She told the children about how the skulls could be used for sleds, the manure for fire, the skin of bulls for moccasins, the thin skins of calves would be used to keep warm the yet thinner skins of Indian babies, hooves were melted and used to make glue.

Cricket, who did not have a mother yesterday and did not know if she would have one today, was in no hurry to go back to her life. She lingered behind, tried to think of questions about her homework — what did the Indians use for a needle? How did they keep warm in the winter? What sorts of rituals did they perform when a person died? Miss Nolan answered in a teacherly way, as if the two of them had not shared something, as if they were not bound together for all of time.

Miss Nolan's information about Indians

came from three sources and three sources alone, two of which she had purchased at a roadside attraction on a childhood roadtrip to the Grand Canyon. One was a coloring book of the Navajo, featuring pictures with titles like "An Initiation Ceremony Means a Mud Bath," "A Medicine Man Doing a Sandpainting for a Curing Ceremony," and "Grandfather Tells Interesting Stories." In every picture, the people wore silver belts and leather moccasin boots and turquoise necklaces. In every picture, the backdrop was a mesa, a cactus, a horse in the distance. The second source was hardcover, textbook size and written by a white Floridian. Its jacket promised information about some of the "most colorful" tribes. It contained chapters on "Plains Indian Braves," "Women's Work" and "The Best Dressed Indians." Miss Nolan had packed and shelved these books in all six of the suburban houses her family had inhabited. She had never been out West again, but it seemed to her an obviously better, richer place than the Atlantic seaboard.

The third and most important source of Miss Nolan's information was her imagination.

While her father sold knives door-to-door and her mother ran a cake shop, Miss

Nolan, who was then only called Anna, revised the family history. Her teacher had assigned a family tree and Anna drew hers on archival paper that included, at its bottommost branch, a fake name: Helen Fighting Water. Anna was nine years old. She wrote an essay for class about this long-ago relation from Montana and how she had lived in a teepee and tanned the hides of buffalo with the mashed brains and internal organs of the animals and how she had fallen in love with a white trapper who was kind and respectful of her culture and how, for a time, they had lived with the tribe instead of in town, but then there came a terrible winter and half the Indians died and the trapper convinced his bride to move with him into a cabin near a doctor and better sources of food and water and heat. They raised sixteen children, Anna wrote, and each of them was smart and kind. When Anna's parents looked at her assignment they said, "That's nice, sweetheart," because they did not know or care where they had come from. Because where they had come from — West Virginia, North Carolina — was poor and probably dirty and most of the relations had had too many children and died of the flu and it was not a story they had wished to drag with them. They had enough to drag with the house and the daughter and the three-legged dog she had insisted on adopting. They had enough to drag with a marriage, two station wagons, alternating Christmases in the nursing homes where their parents lived, a few good days on the shore in summer, maybe a trip to Florida sometime when it was too cold to breathe in New Jersey. If they wanted to get someplace better, the less they took with them, the easier the passage.

Anna fell in love four times in her life. First with the relative who did not exist, second with a mute boy in third grade who drew pictures for her of castles with moats thick with dragons, third with a college professor who taught her about endangered species, and fourth with the man she eventually married. He was a doctoral student in Post-Colonial Literature. He was proud of his beard and his Mustang and the time he had spent in Senegal, Peru, Burma. He collected antique glass bottles, which he lined on his windowsill above the place where he and Anna lay naked while he told her that he knew it was ironic that he was a white man studying the danger of the white man studying the brown man. Because the truth was both absent and boring and because she could sense this man's hunger for an exotic story, Anna told him that she was descended from a Salish brown-skinned woman who had, ten hours into a forty-hour labor in the coldest winter in a hundred years, walked to the rural Montana hospital in snowshoes. The lie worked. The man fell in love with Anna for her stolen stories. When she went to school to become a teacher, she got good grades because of her stolen stories. Without them, Miss Nolan might not even exist.

When Cricket went to get the boys at the end of the day, she was told by their teacher that they had painted their faces with ketchup and mustard, trying to look like the Indians Cricket had told them about. Because the boys were not in a Social Studies unit about the American West, they had gotten into some trouble for this, but they seemed happy about it. The teacher asked Cricket about their mother, and when she could have a little chat with her about the behavior of the boys. She said the phrase, "Nip this Savage thing in the bud," a phrase with which Cricket was unfamiliar.

"My mother is away. We have a sitter. I'll be sure to relay the message."

The question, as they walked, was whether anyone would be at the house. A mother, a father, a dog.

Cricket would not tell her mother about the kiss, whether she was home when they arrived or not. She might want to confess to *a* mother, someone else's, one she imagined to be beautiful and always baking, but not her own. Still, it would have been nice to have someone to avoid telling, someone to hate a little bit over the course of an evening, from pot roast to homework to dessert to television.

The boys Indian-danced home, or did a dance they had invented that they thought of as Indian. They patted their mouths. Cricket was fairly sure this was inaccurate but they were her pair, and she was in charge of loving them and it was sunny out and they had been indoors all day.

Cricket and the boys unlocked the big red door, put the mail on the small table where the mail was meant to be put.

"Hello?" she called, hopeful. The house made whatever sound a house made, which was not the same sound a waiting parent made.

Evening thickened and the children let the feeling of unrest gather at their feet. They let worry in, a rising tide, ankles, knees, thighs. They swam in it and what struck them was that it felt kind of good. Something noteworthy was happening to them. They were in a situation. You could become an orphan at any moment. You could be motherless, fatherless, alone with nothing but your brothers and sister and your wits. The seconds and minutes meant something, suddenly. How long would they survive on the food left over in the house? How long until someone picked them up and took them to an orphanage? They imagined this place — rows of cots and angry old women and a kindly, powerless man who swept the fallen hairs and dust from below them. The brothers took an inventory of the cupboards. Crackers, cereal, soup. The refrigerator: cheese, eggs, milk, butter. There was a huge freezer in the basement, and though they knew that much ice cream was inside, it was dark and very far and the steps creaked and the light was a bare bulb with a string that snuck up on the back of your neck.

They sat down at their familiar kitchen table and everything around them felt new and strange and they each took a spoon and ate one soup can cold, gathered around it like it was a source of heat. The room sounded different now that they knew for sure they were orphans. So many more noises than any of them had noticed before: the refrigerator working to keep cold, the

clock tracking time, time that felt quite endless. Without a mother, there was no sup-
pertime, there was no bedtime. No one
would make them brush up and wash up
and kneel down to pray. They could, if they
wanted, become nocturnal, walk the streets
at night with the skunks and raccoons, get
into trash and trouble and shine flashlight
bulbs into the downstairs windows of every
house, examine the leftovers from the day.
Probably there were unlocked doors, and
Cricket imagined slipping inside, rearranging other people's books, eating their
food, reading the letters on the kitchen
table, living a whole life in their house while
they slept so that the house would have two
families: day family and night.

She thought then of efficiency, which was
a word her third-grade teacher had often
used. The old woman had valued this thing
above other things, commented on how well
or badly the world was managing at it.

Once, Cricket had taken note of the
concept and decided to leave her bookbag
in the car, so she would not have to remember it in the morning. But the next day the
teacher had sent home a note: *Cricket did
not do her homework.* She had explained to
her father the reason, that she was being as
efficient as possible, and her father had both

patted her and scolded her and Cricket had not known whether she was smart or dumb. That night she had decided to sleep in her clothes so that she would not have to get dressed in the morning, and when she had woken up, she had begun to think up a system. She called it Efficient Life. The main idea was to do each type of thing all at the same time rather than switching around: eat all the butter for the year at once, all the peas, all the rice, all the toast. One week is egg week and you eat eggs until you can't stand to anymore. Then it's time for bread. School should be twenty-four hours a day for however many weeks and then you take a long break. One month you do nothing but swim. One month you do nothing but dig.

Her own empty house now made her think of the downstairs of all the houses quiet and empty at night while the families slept upstairs, and she thought of the poor, whom she had only ever seen once, on Thanksgiving years ago when her mother had taken them all to the soup kitchen where they had tied kerchiefs around their heads and sawed at turkey carcasses for two hours until their palms had been blistered and their clothes meaty. The poor had come by in a line like a dirty river and the volunteers put a slop of cranberry next to a slop of stuffing on their white, white plates, and the poor had looked grateful, but not as grateful as Cricket thought they might have. She had looked forward to this day, to being charitable, but now the poor had just walked on down the line and sometimes even turned down one offering or another.

No gravy for me.

I can't stand sweet potatoes.

Stuffing looks like it's already been digested.

"Beggars can't be choosers," Cricket had said to one old woman with teeth like chinks of pearl in her head. Her father had said it to her at many dinners before while she rearranged the peas on her plate.

Mother had smacked her on the cheek. "They aren't beggars," she had said. Cricket had apologized but she was confused. Weren't they, though?

Anyway, now she had an idea that the poor could live in the downstairs of the houses while the other people slept upstairs. The owners would never even notice. The poor would have to get used to being awake at night, but that seemed like a small enough task. Father would be proud.

The three orphans ate their soup without

slurping, even though no one was there to notice. They were still very hungry afterward and ate bread and butter, but they did not enjoy it because these were their reserves and they were being depleted.

They went to the living room and turned on the television. The newsman in his maroon jacket and fat tie came on to tell them that Mao Tse-tung was dead and five white journalists were killed in rioting in Cape Town and it was flooding in Mississippi. They showed a picture of a house floating away and another of a lot of men in overalls building a wall out of bags of sand. *M-I-S-S-I-S-S-I-P-P-I,* all the children said in their heads. They wished their state had a little song you sang every time you thought of it.

How long had it been? Cricket looked at the watch she had been given for her tenth birthday. One hour. One more small hour, of one more small day. There was so much time left to fill. It was a darkness, dragging at the children. If only Maggie was there, they thought. Mother and Father, yes, maybe, but Maggie, for sure. No one should have to be an orphan and dogless too. Cricket imagined gathering around the warm, furry body, petting and handfulling the extra folds of skin. The heat of her. The encouraging repetition of her breathing.

The children lay down in a huddle on the floor. They felt very tired. The house sounds ticked along, as if it were not a small lonesome island. The children fell asleep in the dusking dark, alone on the earth.

The trouble with Chicago had always been history and now it was the future too. The whole point of Fern's endeavor was *away*, not *home*. The city approached on the horizon, skyscrapers looking out over the wind-howled flatness of the prairies and lake. Fern had sprouted here; all the strange fruit bearing up across her life was planted in this land. Outside the car the corn should have been a city itself, stalking and spawning and smelling the way it did, but it was fall and someone had just razed it for the winter. Miles of chopped-down, miles of spiny want.

"This portion of the trip is not helping your mood," Mac said.

"I grew up over that way. And Edgar's parents are probably switching out the wicker furniture and summer décor accents for a lot of gourds and leaf garlands. No doubt there is one last pitcher of fresh lemonade on the counter and a cleaning staff of ten."

"We should confront this, get it out of your head."

"We should keep driving."

But, Mac reasoned, they were hungry and the food would be so much better here. All through pizza and soda Mac nibbed at Fern about her family, about coming up against the past so she could move on. He had once read a book on the subject. It was a question of killing off your demons by facing them down.

"It sounds dramatic," Fern said.

"This is serious. You'll never be free. Let's start with Edgar. What does he do for a living?"

"He hasn't had to earn a living."

"Oh?"

"Steel. It's the family business. Only Edgar doesn't believe in it. It's complicated."

"He doesn't believe in what?"

"Industry. Making money on the backs of poor people who work in factories and mines and get paid hardly anything. Money in general." She waited for Mac to scoff but he didn't. "That doesn't sound stupid to you? Hating money? Hating one's good fortune?"

"Of course not. We all need enough of the stuff and sometimes there's fun to be had, but it's not exactly a new idea, that money doesn't buy happiness."

"Except everyone secretly believes that it would for *them*. Everyone wants a chance to try."

"And you? Do you hate money?"

"Not as much as Edgar does. I hate that other people don't have enough but if I was going to fight for something it might be for other people's lives to be more like mine than mine to be more like theirs. I wish money didn't exist but that doesn't mean I want to be hungry and cold."

"What about your parents?"

"They just died. Last winter."

"Both of them? I'm sorry."

"Both of them." She did not elaborate on the unusual double death. "And they turned out to have spent everything. My childhood home will be sold to pay the taxes. Which is why I think we have to move back here and why Edgar might have to become a steel man, which is why he kissed Glory Jefferson and why he thought I was going to screw John Jefferson and why I'm in this car with you."

The giant let this list hang in the air. "Wow. Okay. Do you have siblings?"

She did not say that in addition to escaping and punishing her husband, the other reason she was in this car was that the giant reminded her of her brother. Fern pictured Ben, tender and strange, always more inclined to speak with birds than people. She thought of the shadow of him behind her in high school while she laughed with the pretty girls and boys. She thought of him in the expensive, ivy-crawled institution, looking more like a university than a mental hospital. If Fern ever wanted to make herself cry, she thought of Ben alone in that room, the quiet pressing him flat to the bed after a day of electroshock treatments.

"I had a brother. He was not as big as you but he was big and possibly crazy but it wasn't his fault and they killed him by trying to save him and you can't fix it. Can we be finished?"

"That all sounds so difficult." He paused. "I think you should see the house," he said finally.

"If I agree to stand in front of the house where my parents died, will you stop questioning me?"

In the last years, Fern's mother's hips had started to click and ache. Evelyn's knees had hurt. Her body had been out to get her all along, but aging had been the grand finale. At the country club the young women had all been smooth-skinned and tan in

275

precisely the same way. They were beautiful for the purpose of enjoyment by men and envy by women while Evelyn had become invisible — someone to be politely moved aside.

At the country club Evelyn had stopped a much younger woman, her skin luminous with tennis sweat. "I'd like to sculpt you," she had said to the girl whose name was almost definitely either Sue or Betty, like all the others. "You're so young and enchanting. Would you mind?"

The girl pinked up and smiled and said, "I have actually done some modeling. For catalogues."

A few days later the Sue or Betty — Evelyn never bothered to sort out which — had arrived at the studio with her hair curled and her lips stung red. She had sat on the stool. Evelyn had taken out her clay and worked it into a twelve-inch person-shape quickly. "You know what would be really beautiful," she had said, "is a nude. That's the real art form."

The girl had hesitated. Her outfit had been carefully chosen and it seemed a shame to lose it. Like everyone with a near-perfect body, she had had a catalogue of the tiniest faults.

"It'll be tasteful. Legs crossed. I won't be

276

specific about your nipples." Evelyn had known that the gracious thing would have been to go outside to give the girl privacy to prepare herself — it was a smaller humiliation to be seen naked than to be seen undressing. Which is exactly why Evelyn had stayed and also why, once her subject had been bare, Evelyn had opened a window to let the cool air in. It had also been why she worked slowly, worrying curves she had known she would fix later, as the girl's skin had puckered and she had struggled to sit still. The sculpture would never come to much. It had not been meant to. The real purpose of art had been to give beauty back its discomfort. To remind this girl that her body had ways of harming her.

In the club, Fern's father had tried to tell the stories of his ancestors and his wife's ancestors but the young men had no idea when their relatives came to this fine land. The future was the thing, they said. "Time to look ahead, old man," they had said. They had talked openly about money, earned and spent. They had talked about cars and boats and dance clubs, and they had talked about women. Not ladies, but women, and their parts and the things the young men had done to them, or wanted to. Fern's father sometimes faked headaches even when he

277

had none.

Ben — his life, his death — had shadowed Evelyn and Paul always. Evelyn had known that she had not cared for him well. She had thought of the call from the hospital, reporting his death as if it had been just the next in a series of developments they had been monitoring: *Patient exhibits schizophrenic behavior; patient does not respond to electric-shock treatments; patient undergoes prefrontal lobotomy; patient experiences death.*

The body had been sent by car so that Ben could be buried in the family plot. Fern and Edgar and Cricket had flown in and taken a taxi straight to the cemetery. Evelyn had asked Edgar to carry the bronze cast of a sculpture she had made of Ben when he was four, old enough for his parents to know that he was unusual but too young to realize how much it would matter. In this bronze Ben was hugging a small dog and the dog was licking his cheek. The statue made Fern endlessly sad. The companion Ben would have wanted forever was Fern. They had been born together and he wanted to live together and die together. Here he was, dead, with only a metal dog to love him.

After that, Evelyn had spent money to

have the entire garden in the country torn out and replanted with something less soft than English roses. The roof had had to be replaced. The basement had flooded. Fern's father had made large donations to libraries and zoos that he did not tell his wife about. Paul had given and given, each sum larger than the last. It had not occurred to him that he would one day reach the bottom of a reserve that had always seemed utterly endless. Giving money had been the only way anyone thanked him anymore.

Evelyn had gone to the doctor and said, "I'm so old all of a sudden." As she had said it she realized that she had not known very many truly old women.

"Are you ready for your prescription? I don't want to rush you, but I recommend having it around earlier rather than later. One never knows how these things will progress."

"My prescription?"

"For when your body is no longer able to house you properly. For when you are ready to move on."

She had remembered learning in school that women lived longer than men and thinking, *Not here.* Even as a girl, Evelyn had been aware that women died politely. Almost always in bed, having bathed and

279

tidied up, called the children and grandchildren to say goodnight. Lucky men died
of heart attacks, usually while playing a
beloved sport. It was considered a good way
to go. Racket in hand, having just sent into
the sky a gorgeous, sailing volley. Unlucky
men wound up in a home where someone
mashed their green beans and helped them
with their diapers. But well-bred women
never died in public and they were almost
never so decrepit that they had to be sent
away. Now she understood why.

"What is it?" Evelyn had asked.

"Just sleeping pills. Strong sleeping pills.
I'll give you more than enough. I think
you'll feel better having them around."

Paul had given money to the National As-
sociation of American Thoroughbreds, the
Lakeshore Beautification Campaign, The
Poor.

By Christmas, Evelyn had made a plan.
She had thought of her daughter in her nice
house with her nice husband and children.
Fern had turned out as expected. She could
take care of herself. Evelyn thought of her
son and hoped that whatever kingdom had
taken him in could care for him better than
she had. Evelyn thought of Paul, his headaches, and decided easily that they would
need to go together. She had not told her

husband the plan. She hoped the pills would be sufficient for them both. She bathed, encouraged her husband to bathe. Though the maid would not be there until morning, she hung up a tag on the bedroom door that they had received on an African safari decades ago: *Resting,* it said.

"The doctor gave me something that he said would make us sleep better than we have in our whole lives," she said to her husband. "Shall we?"

He reached out his same old hand and she had poured eight pills in. "This is a lot of pills," he said.

"It's the regular dosage, apparently."

"Cheers."

Evelyn leaned over and kissed him on the mouth. It had been a long time. Their lips had felt different together than they used to, but hardly.

Fern had gone home alone to bury her parents, flown in and out the same day and seen only the cemetery. She had been sure the men and women of the North Shore were disgusted with her decision not to hold a proper funeral with all the fixings, but she had not cared. She had cared about seeing the boxes that held the bodies. She had cared about watching them as they descended into the earth beside her brother.

After that, she had eaten something in the airport and gone home.

Mac followed Fern's directions to her old house. There had been much new development since she had last been back. Big houses, uglier by a thousand degrees than their predecessors. Fern said, just as her mother would have, "It's wretched what they've done." White columns had replaced brick, old trees were cut, lawns were unearthly green, vibrating with color much too late in the season. She figured the interiors would have been filled with flash and bright colors, mirrors, shiny white plastic. Fern felt old. She had not expected to miss what had come before so much. She had not expected to be a skeptic about the way things were going, the future outlook.

And then came the old wooden fence, the familiar driveway, and they turned down it and the old house was the same cream color with blue trim, the same stone geese sculpted by Fern's mother out front, the same pink geraniums in the window boxes.

They parked and stood outside looking at the house. Fern had planned to take a moment, maybe walk the perimeter, but now she went to the door and knocked. Of course it went unanswered. Of course it was locked. But there were so many entrances and Fern knew all of them. They tried the screened porch, the kitchen, the garage. At the maid's entrance the doorknob turned easily and they stood in the laundry room where there was still a load of whites hanging on a drying rack.

The house, awaiting the legal process, was exactly as her parents had left it, exactly as they had died in it.

Fern stood in the living room and smelled the wood of it, the fibrous old-age rugs. Mac pulled out a huge leather-bound edition of *The Pilgrim's Progress.* The pages were half dust. The room was breathing, was what it felt like, and Fern had to sit down on the floor because the chairs were all too familiar. All those same books, all those same pictures, the fireplace and the nooks beside it for reading. Her grandfather had built the house for a happy family, the children tucked away with books and the mothers and fathers on the porches with their sketchpads and tall glasses of iced tea. Outside: bees, butterflies, a constant parade of roses in the garden, dripping fountains. It had been a true dream, sometimes. Fern running through the wildflowers and grasses; supper on the porch by candlelight; lying on the dew-grass at night while the stars poured down.

Fern thought of her brother. Ben, inside alone with a gardening catalogue, a pair of scissors and a roll of tape, rearranging the plants so they were grouped by family, rather than alphabet. "Lily, lily, lily," he said, pressing garlic beside onion beside a picture of a massive white bloom, like an outstretched hand. The floor around him was covered in bits of paper like so many snowflakes. Ben, making better sense of things. He had been safe in this house and should never have been made to leave it.

Mac stayed downstairs but Fern went up the creaking stairs. Her parents' door was closed. There was a hang-tag on the knob and Fern remembered the trip it had come from. They had all gone on safari when she was ten, had watched the beating heart of a water buffalo slow down while a lion untangled the ropes of its muscles with her teeth. Fern had been able to smell the blood. It was sweet in her nose and the lion looked right at her while she ate the buffalo's living leg.

"It's beautiful, isn't it?" Evelyn had said. "The cycle of life."

Ben had had to turn around. He was watching the clouds change. "Tell me when it's over," he had said. Fern watched, trying to prove strength to her mother.

Fern, standing at the doorway to the room where she knew her parents had died, had to choose to enter or walk away. She knew the bodies had been buried but she was still afraid that she would find some leftovers of them lying in bed. Bones or blood. She had to tell herself to stop being crazy but crazy was what she felt as she let herself in, knelt at the edge of the bed, which was empty, of course it was empty, and tried to hear them or smell them or sense the residue of their death in the room.

The rug was warm; the sun must already have passed through.

Surrounding Fern were the trappings of a good life. The house was stately and big, the lawn rolling, miles of prairie with trails through the wildflowers. Hardwood furnishings, a silk rug, crystal chandelier, a closetful of dresses and suits. Here were the belongings with no one to belong to, so many objects sitting dumbly where they had been placed. It seemed almost obscene to Fern, this huge remainder, when the lives themselves had ended.

Fern opened the bedside table drawer and found a handful of pens, a tube of lip balm and four index cards with her father's shaky script. On each was a name: Evelyn Westwood, Paul Westwood, Ben Westwood, Fern Keating. There was nothing else written. Fern imagined her father lying on this bed, his brain liquid with pain, trying to remember the names of his family members. She imagined him holding her card as if the mere fact of her could calm him. She wished she had offered more, anything more.

The lawyer had mailed Fern the note her mother had left in an embossed envelope with her name on it.

Dear Fern,
   This is the kindest thing we could possibly do for you. Being old is terrible. Think of this as a gift to all of us.
                    Love always, Mother

On the table was a glass with a white mineral ring at the bottom, the evidence of dried liquid. Was the fact that the glass remained untouched a question of politeness? The rule was not to clear a person's place until she told you she was finished. None of the people who had passed through this room wanted to be the one to clean up a deadwoman's cup. Before she left, Fern took the glass to her lips. Lipsalt on the rim, hers and her mother's.

The dock where Edgar and Glory were still tied off was busy with pleasure boaters hauling huge coolers of drinks and snacks out for a day on the water. The women wore kerchiefs and sunhats and minidresses and the men had long fringy hair and no shirts. They would fish, drunken and uncareful, and grill whatever they caught on deck. Edgar wanted to be rid of them so he and Glory skipped breakfast and untied the lines that held them to land. They left the harbor on a port tack then swung past a ferry sounding her long, sad horn. Edgar's pulse was quick and strong. The shore was green and tangled from a summer of growing. Beach plums were dying on the branch, and Glory, looking through the binoculars, could see their dusty purple shapes. The wind was steady and they both put on their jackets, but it was sunny and clear. The boat threw water off her prow in long ribbons of white foam. Rainbows were cast in the water-light. "See?" Edgar said out loud. "See how good it is?" Glory smiled at him, a boy in the middle of a favorite game. She did see. They were out, away, and the wind pushed them farther. Edgar could feel Boston getting smaller and if he traveled far enough away, the whole idea of Chicago, he hoped, would turn to a speck. Glory went belowdecks to make toast, learned to spread her feet wide for balance, hold on to something with one hand while the other worked. She liked that everything was just so — the jars fit the shelf perfectly. There were three plates, two cups. They had plenty of food and water stored deeper, but what was in front of Glory was the precise amount needed. There should be a word for this happiness, she thought. The happiness of nothing extra.

To Glory, the route was just *out to sea*. Edgar hitched the lanyards as they passed a small island. The Island of Tragedies, it was called. Edgar knew that they would pass above the Nantucket Shoals, Powell Canyon, Picket Seamount and the Hudson Fan. He knew that two hundred million years before, the Atlantic Ocean had just begun to form. Hot plumes of magma had pushed upwards and volcanoes were made. Mountains rose from the seafloor, and the steam-heat seeped through and warmed the water and forests began to grow, corals and fans. All that made food for the animals — lobsters and fish and brittlestars. Thousands and thousands of feet of water separated the sand and sediment and rock bottom from the mirror-surface. But the water was thick with life — microbes and krill and amoebas and shrimp and sharks and tuna and whales and lobsters and dolphins and halibut and turtles.

Two hundred years before, in this spot, a trading vessel bound for America had been making good time. It was a Sunday and the crew had been preparing to bring up the nets to see what they would have for dinner. The cook had his hands in a basin of grey washwater. And then a wave had appeared, a huge wave, alone on the surface of an otherwise still sea. Like an obedient dog, the ship had rolled over. Her crew had been underwater before they knew they were in danger. She had sunk slowly, air caught in the hold. The sea was featureless except for the mast, which stuck up like a knife-stab. The captain's body came to rest on the foredeck. A hundred years later divers had found his bronze watch in a tangle of seaweeds. The steel hands were still set to the time of the wave: nineteen minutes before twelve.

The sloop floated above the distant bottom like a star.

By late afternoon they were crossing into waters Edgar had never sailed before. This was the part he had wanted. Out beyond. They were headed southeast at eight knots and the water peeled out from below them and the wind was strong and steady.

"How do you feel?" Edgar asked.

"I feel wobbly."

"The sickness goes away after a while. We could swim. That helps."

Edgar let the mainsail down and made it fast. The sloop slowed and slopped, rocking now instead of skimming.

With tethers to their waists, they dove overboard. The water was warm at the surface and cold just below, and they kicked hard against waves that had appeared small when they were aboard but now seemed big. Glory lost sight of Edgar and spun, looking for him in the vast blue. She thought: shark. She thought: dead. Her only hope without him was to send a distress signal and wait to be rescued. She realized that she should ask more questions about what to do in a series of what-ifs. She thought of being dragged from a rotting ship, half dead, even though it only would have taken a few hours for a rescue boat to find her. Edgar appeared beneath her and lifted her up; she kissed him on the salty mouth. They kicked together, ran to keep above the surface. They laughed hard, knowing this was the best it would get. It was never a mistake to swim.

Back aboard, they lay naked on deck and let the sun warm them. Glory rolled a joint and they passed it back and forth and then she lit a cigarette and Edgar took a drag. He didn't like the taste but it felt good in his lungs, the heat. He coughed when he exhaled. The salt dried on their skin and shone. Cold to warm, wet to dry. "Bermuda," Glory kept saying, trying to get used to it. Edgar drank beer, Glory said that word — everyone aboard had a way of making the time pass. The *Ever Land* slapped at the water, and the halyards clanged the mast. Such specific sounds and so few. Edgar thought that people would be different in a world with fewer sounds. When Glory touched him on the back of the neck he jerked away, wanting less rather than more. Finally, there was so little.

"Remember the night of the party when we met? Was that really your mother?" he asked.

"Oh, God. I think I'm so different from her and then there we were on the same vacation, trying to get drunk at the same party. I spend so much energy trying to be unlike my mother but then she responds by turning into me. It's like she's trying to

291

prove to me that no matter what we do, we become the people we were always going to become."

"Does that mean you were always meant to wear a fringe vest?" Edgar teased.

Glory laughed. "I'm sure she looked in the mirror twenty times before she left the house and felt great every time."

"My parents are even more embarrassing than yours," he said. "Mine are gluttons. They own everything a person could ever purchase."

"Did they grow up with money?"

"No. Maybe that's it. Maybe they're trying to use it all before someone realizes the money doesn't belong to them."

The immigrants in Edgar's family had crossed these same waters on a boat from Ireland, an old thing, the boards fat with seawater. The immigrant relatives had thought about waves as landward things, rolling onto the beach and rocks. That the whole ocean rolled was a surprise. Most of the earth was covered by water, and the water was in turmoil.

After three weeks at sea, four miles from the Cape Cod shore, from their promised home, and in the middle of the night, the ship had quietly and unceremoniously sunk. The passengers' deaths were dreams they dreamed or dreams they woke into — by the time they understood that they were beneath there was no such thing as above.

The currents gathered the bodies and distributed them on a single beach along with driftwood. One woman and one man still had air in their lungs and their hearts had not stopped and the blood moved. They woke up slowly and coughed. They had never met but they already knew the story: God only needed one of each, but from them, a whole race could be carried forward.

The immigrants worked in carpentry. They moved from Hope Street to Prospect Street to Promise Street.

When Edgar's father told the family story, the turning point was always exactly the same. Great-grandfather Joseph, Chicago, 1871. He was poor and his people had always been poor. He lived alone in a building that stood only because it seemed used to standing.

Joseph sold metal parts and pieces from a shop next to the dirty river. One morning he sat out back with a donut and coffee and watched the affected water pass when he spotted something upstream in the slow current. *A hand?* he thought. *Wait, a hand?* It was grey and dead, fingers curled softly, the glint of a ring. The river slinked. Joseph squinted and the hand got closer. He wanted it to transform into anything else. No, no, just an old shoe, just a piece of packaging. The closer it got, the more hand-like it became. Joseph ran inside and pulled a long rod out. He held one end and reached.

He flipped the hand. The ring winked in the sun. A diamond. Joseph reached out, breath stopped, and he held the hand with a greasy rag. The ring did not come off easily. Joseph wiggled it back and forth, back and forth, but it stuck at the knuckle. By then, his heart had claimed the ring; the ring was already his.

Joseph spit on the ring finger and eased the sparkler over the knuckle. He threw the rag and the hand into the river. Joseph tried the ring on his pinky. *Welcome, fortune,* he thought. *Come on now and love me.* He turned to the side and threw up.

That night was hot and windy. His eyes began to burn. He smelled smoke. He coughed. Joseph's lungs dragged him to the door.

One by one, the people of the city ran towards and then into the lake. The water was night-cold and it took Joseph's breath away when he stumbled in. The wooden buildings, bright with fire, showed their skeletons before they fell.

Next to Joseph in the lake, there was a young woman.

"What comes after?" Joseph asked her.

The woman stared at the fire. She took Joseph's hand. She was crying and she did not look at him. He did not ask her whom she had left behind and she did not ask him. Metal would replace wood. Huge factories would be built, trains clanking across the country, so much need for metal.

Joseph felt the ring in his pocket. Without asking, he broke the handhold, slipped the ring onto the woman's finger.

Silver fish began to soar over Edgar and Glory, arcing across their view. "Flying fish," Edgar said. The sea was putting on a good show. There were dozens of fish, silver as ice. Glory did not know such things were real. The fins on the fish were spread wide like wings and they seemed to be jumping for no reason except fun. When the sky was fishless, Glory sat up and found three bodies flopping on deck. "Dinner," she said, and went below to get a bucket for the fish to swim in until it was time to eat them. Edgar loved her for seeing the beauty of the fish in midair and for seeing the food in the ones on deck. A woman walking naked across the deck of a ship with a bucket full of fish was the best thing a man could ever hope to see. The sun was strong and they sweated, adding their own salt to the seawater dried on their skin. They ate strawberries and drank freshwater that was still shade-cool.

The journey had been worth it already. Any other life seemed foolish. Edgar would gladly have lived this day a thousand times more. Edgar thought about Fern and he felt kindness towards her. If he could have, he would have told her that it was not the other woman so much as the other life, the other Edgar. If he could have extracted Fern from the particulars of their marriage — their parents, their house, their losses, their years, he thought he would have been just as happy to have her body instead of Glory's on this deck — happier even.

Edgar and Glory felt far away, but in fact, on the big chart, the boat was bobbing just offshore. It was deep water and very blue, and though the sailors could not see land, they were well within their nation's borders.

After a nap Edgar raised the sheet and they rolled over the small waves. A pod of dolphins finned the surface and surfed the wake. Their grey brightened the water. Glory said, "Are we lucky or are there always so many animals out?" Edgar thought it was both. Glory hung her legs over, her graceful legs, and laughed with the sprinting dolphins who came in close to play.

"They say dolphins are the spirits of dead sailors," Edgar said.

"That's cheery."

"It's supposed to be a nice thought."

"I like them better as fish."

Above the wreckage, Glory and Edgar set up the charcoal grill on deck and charred the flying fish, which were sweet and bony. They ate apple slices and drank cold gin from a bottle Glory had dropped overboard with a rope around its neck.

Sunset filled the entire sky. Fire at all the edges. There was no wind, not even enough to shake the sails. "Doldrums," Glory said. "Isn't that something bad?"

"Nothing else to do now," Edgar said, and she started to unbutton his shirt, but he held her hand. He did not want to break the surface of this perfect moment. He said, "Let's not."

"What do you mean?" she hissed. Why else were they there?

"I just want to be quiet. I just want to listen." Glory rolled her eyes and poured another drink. She found a joint and fumbled for her lighter.

They slept on deck under a sky ferocious with stars. Edgar looked up at all the universe and he felt what people always feel: the sudden truth that he was a speck. He was an air-breather with only a few feet of deckspace and two triangles of fabric keeping him from fathoms and fathoms of water. He had chosen this. He had needed to walk out of his life for a time, even to walk out of himself. The experience he wanted was to be nowhere, no future, no history. Not the father of a girl whose pockets were always full of stones and feathers or two boys who were born a minute apart and stayed that close. Not the husband of a woman who had seen the shards of his sadness. Edgar wanted to be reduced to his own small self. The water rocked the hull. Edgar felt pleasure, which was what he wanted to feel. He took his glasses off and rested them on his chest. He was nearly blind without them, everything reduced to a smear of color. At his wish, the world quietly erased itself.

1970

Fern was never sure where Edgar had gotten the magic mushrooms. He had taken the car someplace, been gone all day, showed up later at their little house on the Army base with the first smile of its kind she had seen on him in a year. He said, "I want to do something together. Don't freak out." When Cricket had been bathed and read to and her warm, three-year-old head had been kissed by both of her parents, Fern and Edgar each chewed two small mushrooms that tasted half-rotten and metallic and stuck in their teeth, and thirty minutes later the room took on a purple-green hue and Edgar started singing a song from a musical he had seen as a child and had not thought of since and Fern sat on the floor with an apple for an hour without taking a bite.

He said, "Did it really happen that we put a man on the moon?" and Fern said, "I think so. We watched it." Later they went outside and said, "Outside!" like they had never really been there before, and they hadn't, not this way, not with the grass this sharp and the leaves on the trees so individual and the sky — the sky! — dark and rich and flush with stars because they were on a tiny planet currently facing away from the sun and the universe actually might have been endless — endless! — and here they were, two bodies, maybe three hundred pounds of human between them, and they were both alive and they had made a child who was beautifully asleep. "I miss your brother," Edgar said. It was a risk to bring this up and they rarely did but tonight Fern felt alive enough to talk about the dead. "Thank you for loving him," she said. "I miss him too, but I'm glad he's free of it all. He didn't need to live in that place." She looked at Edgar and his skin shimmered with color. "I do not forgive my mother," Fern said. "I feel sorry for her, but I don't forgive her." Edgar nodded. They stood at the fenceline and looked up into the peach tree that was about to explode into blossom any day and they held hands — hands! — and they did not let go even when dawn flushed them with so much light that they felt overexposed.

■ ■ ■ ■

The next day they took turns playing with Cricket, eyes sandy and burning, drinking glass after glass of water while the other slept. It felt good to be thankful.

That afternoon in the mail there was a letter for Fern. "Radcliffe?" Edgar asked, reading the address in the top left corner.

"Oh," said Fern. There had been a fight, like a dozen others they had had in the year after Ben had died. Edgar had just received a postcard from Runner in Alaska who said he had married the Inupiat librarian and they were living off the land near Nome and that he had just killed his first seal. Edgar had said, "People are living communally and growing their own food and hunting or fighting for civil rights and we're sitting here on an Army base in fucking Tennessee," and she had said, "You were the one who insisted on this life. We have a three-year-old. I don't know how to be a mother on a commune," and he had said, "You know, women don't have to be only mothers anymore. Don't you want more for your daughter?" Fern had shut herself in the bathroom, furious. He was right and he was terrible. That night she had sent away for an application

301

to Radcliffe because it was the best college she knew of and she thought she would never get in, thus proving to Edgar, to her mother, that she was nothing but a housewife. In the months while she had waited for the answer, the possibility that she could be accepted was a thin but bright crack. She had counseled herself not to want it, but she had.

Fern took the envelope. *We are pleased to offer you a place in the incoming class,* the letter read. "Oh," she said again. She expected Edgar to be angry that she had sent the application without talking to him but instead he grabbed the letter and whooped. "This is amazing! This is exactly what we need!"

She wanted to be a mother and a wife but maybe she could also be her own self, separate from the needs of others. This possibility kicked at her from the inside. Just like that? Send one stack of pages to Cambridge and a door to yourself opens?

With the mushrooms still a vague fizz in their veins, Edgar and Fern hugged. "I'm proud of you," he said. "I'll finish my book, you'll study, Cricket will grow up near the ocean."

Out there on the edge of the country, new soil was a promise.

■ ■ ■ ■

They had rented a cottage to begin with and when they drove onto their new street they found big trees and beautiful old houses all freshly painted and all the children in the yards were clean and white. They also found that Edgar's mother was already in residence in a fancy hotel nearby. Road weary, the family sat at the table while Mary, wearing a red pantsuit with a huge collar, her hair trimmed into a new blond bob, served martinis. She said, "The good news is that I have already done a lot of research on houses."

"Houses?" Edgar asked.

"I know you don't care about these things, Edgar, so Ferny and I will take care of it."

Over the next weeks, Edgar took Cricket to watch the Red Sox lose three games, to the museum where they stayed all morning in the ancient art collection and discussed philosophy with the sculpted heads of Roman noblemen. Another day he took her to the harbor so she could learn the names of different sailboats. "Gaff-rig, cat-boat, Herreshoff," she said in her little voice.

Mary and Fern spent every day with a real estate agent who wore pink from head to toe every time they saw her. She drove them all over Cambridge in her big bronze sedan, which sighed over every bump. They drove along the edge of the Charles, sparkling blue and dotted with boats, the Boston skyline on the other side. They went to neighborhoods made of brick and neighborhoods filled with Victorians, neighborhoods around Harvard Square where they stopped for lunch in a sandwich shop filled with students with round glasses and long hair and jeans and leather jackets. They did not go to the neighborhoods where Irish people lived, where black people lived. The agent offered an edited version of the city.

Mary fell for a huge brick colonial with white trim and columns holding up the porch. It had six bedrooms, four baths, inlaid floors, three fireplaces and a garden thick with roses. "You can't fake an old lawn," the agent said, tapping her pink pump on the grass. "The younger stuff simply isn't as dense."

Edgar would hate it, Fern knew, but she liked it. It was beautiful — the big brass knocker, the long path to the door, the porch-swing. Mary was buying and Fern could let her mother-in-law take the fall for the choice. She had spent the last years in a box of a house on a base in the South where she was too unlike anyone else to have even one friend — a little comfort did not seem unearned.

To Fern, Mary explained that she would need at least four sofas and eight armchairs. All-new appliances. Fifteen good Persian carpets minimum, six chandeliers. "Teak is best for outdoors," she said. "Inside I would recommend something warm."

Fern said, "Edgar is going to hate this house. You know that, right?"

"The poor baby," Mary said, frowning an exaggerated frown. "I wonder how he'll ever survive such a sacrifice."

Edgar did hate the house and he also didn't care. He was thinking about his book and about sailing and about starting over.

The first night in the house, Fern sat up in bed in the blue hours and tore the blanket off. Her heart was racing. She jumped up, looked on the floor, under the bed, in the closet. "Where is he?" she yelled. "Edgar, where is he?" Edgar woke up and ran to his wife. "Where is Ben?" she said. "Where the hell is Ben?"

Edgar pinched her earlobe to wake her up. "Ferny, Fern. Ben isn't here. We're in Cambridge in our new house. It's 1970." He did not say the word *dead*.

Fern sat down on the floor of their big empty house and shook hard enough that Edgar felt it in the floorboards. He held on to her hands but said nothing. He had learned this from her brother: sometimes the only comfort is the fact of another person. Not a dam, but a surface to wash across.

Fern did not know that her father also woke sometimes and went looking for Ben. She did not know that her mother dreamed about him three nights a week, that in each dream, Evelyn and Ben were running side by side and they were lost and tired and it was on the brink of twilight and they had to keep going until they found the path home. Fern did not know that in her mother's dream Evelyn held Ben's hand, coaxed him gently forward, spoke to him the whole, hopeless way.

In the morning, the family went to the pet store and Cricket picked out a sloppy Lab that she named Flower. The dog and the girl followed each other around, each revering the other more. Before bed Fern went to pull Cricket's blankets up and found them curled together like they were part of the same litter, legs and tail, fur and skin. She could almost feel her brother's warm kid-back against her belly, the way they had folded together at bedtime after their day-long separation.

Summer's torch fizzled down quickly. Fern suffered over clothes for an hour in the morning of her first classes. Everything she put on made her look too old to be a college student but too young to be a mother. She settled on a pleated skirt and blouse and oxfords not because she felt good in the outfit but because it was time to go. She dropped Cricket off with a sitter around the corner and drove to campus. Her first two classes were Modernism and Introduction to Sociology. Both professors were ancient men in ancient suits who could hardly hear and Fern was years older than the other girls, all in minis or bell-bottom jeans, their hair long and pooling behind them in the chairs. Fern's hand hurt from taking notes and she felt incomplete away from Cricket, but also good, she noted. It also felt good. Since high school, Fern had been oriented towards another person. This was the first time in her adult life that her efforts were her own. She did not have to drag a child to the bathroom every hour. She did not have to carry snacks. To sit still in a chair and listen for a full hour and a half was luxury. She almost cried, to think that she might actually belong there.

Edgar rented a studio near campus in which to work on his book. It was small and run down and he loved it. He leaned out the window onto the fire escape and watched the students with their big hair and big glasses and he smoked cigarettes and read Tolstoy and worked to get the specter of a novel to emerge out of him.

At night Edgar knelt on the floor and put his ear to Cricket's chest. Fern could not hear what he heard, but she knew what it sounded like because she did this too.

"How was writing?" she asked.

"Hard," he said. "Today was hard. I think I figured something out about the structure though. How was school?"

"It was good. Everyone is so young," she said.

Edgar was twenty-six years old. He still did not want to run a steel company. He still did not want his only contribution to the world to be suffering on one side and profit on the other with a thin column of vacations between. Edgar still did not want to turn into his father. Everyone would have to continue to wait for him to grow out of his own mind.

Edgar brought his lips down to Fern's and

held them there while a spark passed between them.

Fern recognized the symptoms immediately:
she was so tired that her legs felt leaded;
she was starving yet no food seemed edible.
She called her doctor but already knew what
the test would say: for the second time, she
was not alone in her body.

The leaves changed to red by mid-
September and it snowed a week later. It
was as if the earth had been wobbled off
her axis, as if the memory of however many
tens of thousands of years of summer, fall,
winter, spring had been undone. Fern fell
asleep in class and woke up to the professor
saying to her, "Missy? I'm terribly sorry to
bore you." She bent her head, stared hard
at her notebook, which was blank except for
the time and date of Cricket's next dentist
appointment. She could feel the snickers
and the glances of the other students like
pinpricks. They were scholars; Fern was a
mother.

She stood in the line of girls waiting to
talk to him after class. The other girls all
had questions about selfhood and the public
sphere. She heard a tall black girl with big
eyes say the words *the offmodern condition,*
and suddenly Fern, pregnant and tired and

nauseated Fern, understood clearly that she had been mistaken: there was no place for her here.

"I'm so sorry," she said to the professor, whose nose hair quivered with each breath he let out. "It's not an excuse, but I'm pregnant."

"Congratulations," the professor said. For a moment, she thought he might have meant it. Perhaps he saw kinship in their shared adulthood — a person might get tired of looking out at a sea of nineteen-year-olds. But no. "Good for you," he said, with a skip of mockery to his voice, "you've achieved the biological imperative. But here at Radcliffe we have other projects. You can stay in the class provided you stay awake in it, despite your condition."

The neighbor was watering the hacked-back stubs of rosebushes out front. "Tell me again where you all have come from?" the woman asked when Fern got out of the car. Fern just wanted to get inside and hate the professor while eating ice cream and sitting in a warm bath. "We lived in the South but we're from Chicago. The North Shore," said Fern. Fern knew that this fact, which had been so heavy to carry on the base, would keep her afloat on the sunlit surface of this particular social sea. They were wealthy with other wealthies, all of them having had the same upbringing, the same training, the same assumed values. This was not the whole of it, though — she did not care which wife was at the top of the pyramid, which wives were working their way up and which wives had slipped lower having made the wrong dish for a party, having gotten too drunk, been too honest. The woman sprayed her hose over a new tangle of Princess Graces and Polar Stars and Black Magics. "If you need anything . . ." she said, but her back was already turned.

That night Edgar put Cricket to bed and came downstairs humming. He had written two thousand words, some of them good. He was reading James Baldwin and wanted Fern to read it too so they could talk about it. He got a drying rag and began to work on the pile of dishes she had amassed in the rack.

"If you want me to say something about 'the off-modern condition,' then forget it," she said.

"What's wrong with you?" he asked.

"I'm dropping out of school," she told him. "I'm having a baby — what's the point of pretending I'm a serious student?"

Edgar went to the freezer and took out a

pint of vanilla ice cream. He got two spoons and patted the counter. They hoisted themselves up and ate big scoops.

She told him about the professor and Edgar said, "Don't drop out. Take a semester off. Take a year off."

"Do you think it's lonelier to be a foreigner around people who obviously don't understand you or to be among people who seem just like you but whom you don't like?"

He kissed her on the neck. "Both," he said.

"Maybe we should go far away."

"I was as far away as a person can be and it didn't help."

Edgar would convince Fern not to drop out and give the professor the satisfaction. She would finish the semester with Bs, but she would not reenroll in the spring.

A few weeks later they would learn that Fern was carrying twins, and though twins ran in her family and this set was nothing more than genetics, it would feel to Fern like a direct apology from whatever god had made Ben and taken him again. Replacement plus addition. Fern was afraid and she was hopeful — here was a chance for a twin-pair to be broken up; here was a chance for a twin-pair to remain whole. It made her miss Ben too much. How good it would have felt to sit on a sofa next to her brother, both of them grown, a baby on each of their laps. She imagined the photograph of that day, how they would both smile the particular smile of a twin holding a twin and how she would have pinned the picture beside her vanity so that she could look at it every single day.

Fern remembered when she had first bought a razor and how she had sneaked off with it, embarrassment and excitement humming in her, and how, when she had come out of the steam and wrapped herself in towels Ben had been sitting on the sink and his face was thin and sorry and they both knew that the years when they were the same had just ended. Maybe they will both be boys or girls, Fern thought, rubbing her belly. Maybe they will always be each other's mirrors.

At night, Fern dreamed about the end of the world, only the dreams were cheerful. It was the end of the world and she had a nice bow and arrow and was an extremely good shot. It was the end of the world and everyone played softball all the time.

The twins kicked her hard from the inside. So many little feet.

All through the fall, winter and spring, Edgar sat at his desk and he tried to explain to the white space of the page what it meant to be a son and a father. He tried to explain to the white page what it meant to have so much and yet to feel mostly the emptiness of desire, unfillable. He tried to explain that there was no life without want. He thought that if he could get these thoughts to make sense in language he himself might make sense in the world. Edgar was trying to write himself a way to exist.

Some days the magic trick almost worked. He got a few sentences that felt true, a scene of a boy in a limousine in a poor neighborhood, a scene of a young man in a bar in Kentucky feeling more companionship with the miners than he had with his own parents, except the miners died from their jobs and he was safe, a scene of a new father and his baby who was filled with a midnight-sadness that she could not explain and he could not discern, both of them weeping by dawn. Other days he reread his pages and saw there the whine of privilege, a character fooled by the sound of his own voice. Edgar wondered whether he even deserved to tell a story. Because of his father's money, because of the men who earned pennies in the mines, pennies in the mills, he could sit at this slab of wood and write. His clothes were paid for by their effort, his glasses, his lunch. He did not know what it felt like to work close to the edge of survival. Maybe severe lack brought clarity — the skin-bone monk at the top of the mountain, having given up everything but his mind. Edgar was supremely lucky, but luck was a lonely place.

He turned on the radio and listened to the news of the war that had continued even after he himself had been sent home. The American position had grown weaker and weaker. Forty boys had died that day. Edgar thought of the unknown person whose job it now was to write to their mothers and fathers. He put his pen down and went walking. It was warm outside after having been cold for so long. The trees were tipped with buds.

In the windows of all the stores were objects made to shine and beckon, to distract. Edgar went inside a shop and felt the cold porcelain of a set of nested white and green mixing bowls. He weighed the bowls in his hands. "Shopping for someone special?" a pretty young salesgirl in a long flowered dress asked. The promise of this transaction was so simple — an object, a certain price and everyone left smiling.

"My wife," he said.

"Is she a cook?"

"Not really," he admitted.

"Can I show you something? It's brand-new. We haven't even put it out yet." The girl touched Edgar's elbow, led him to a locked case where she pulled out a box. Within: a gold chain with a deep locket. "It's meant to hold a lock of hair. It's old-fashioned and I think it's so romantic."

Edgar opened the latch. "It's beautiful," he said.

"I could cut the hair for you," she said, her thin fingers miming a pair of scissors, closing. It was not something Edgar knew how to say no to. It was expensive, this locket, etched gold with a ruby in one corner. This was a gift his mother would have congratulated him for. The girl took out a pair of scissors from behind the register and pulled a curl at the back of Edgar's head. "Hold still," she said. He could feel her breath on his skin. She cut.

The day after the incident with the professor, Fern, seeking comfort, had ordered a desk from a famous modern designer in Sweden. She had not asked Edgar because the price was absurd and the shipping costs even more. It took months to arrive. She had received postcards letting her know of its progress, as if the desk was a friend who greatly anticipated this visit: *Hello from Denmark; Love from London.* The desk had traveled all through her pregnancy, as if it was following the same gestational calendar.

There had been a long break between mailings while the desk had sailed across the ocean. Fern had thought of it, crated up in the belly of a ship, rocking against the waves. Her own belly had grown enormous. She could hardly fit in the car anymore and baths were impossible, half of her sticking up out of the water. Then the correspondence resumed: *I'm here in New York.* Then, days before her due-date, two men knocked on the door, tall men with thick blond eyebrows and matching blue worksuits.

"We have come with your desk," the first man said. The dog barked at him.

"Flower, shush," Fern said.

The men had suitcases and another bag full of tools. The crate was on wheels, and they brought it in. The two men looked tired and thirsty, so Fern waddled into the kitchen and offered juice in juice glasses and slices of cheese and crackers on a plate. "Sit down a minute," she said, "before you begin unpacking it."

"Thank you. It was a long journey." They had to fold themselves up carefully to fit at the table.

"Where are you coming from?" she asked, thinking of a shipping hub in a nearby city.

"Stockholm," they said, surprised. "We traveled, with the desk."

"You traveled with the desk from Stockholm?" The shipping costs made a new kind of sense.

"An American would do wrong setup."

Fern looked at the clock. She was glad that Cricket was at preschool. Edgar would be home in a few hours and she wanted very badly for him not to walk in and discover that his wife had bought a completely unnecessary piece of furniture from across the world, and accidentally ordered two blond men along with it. "Shall we get to work then?" she asked. Another thing: she had begun to feel contractions. They were mild enough if she breathed right.

The Swedes looked too big for the house, for the chairs. She imagined that where they lived, everything must be much larger. Larger table, larger chairs, larger juice glasses, larger wives.

"It's a big desk?" she asked.

"It is a Swedish desk," said one of the men, revealing his yellow teeth. "It is right size."

"So," she said, trying to make conversation but not wanting anyone to get talking too long. Her body cinched up. She could feel the babies pressing down. The dog circled her as though she knew what was going on.

"We began the first day much early," the yellow-toothed man explained. "Travel by train." He smiled, waiting to see if she understood him. "That day was a cold day. How do you say this weather, like rain but not rain?"

"Fog?" she asked.

"Fog?" he asked back.

"Fog," she said to confirm, and he repeated the word again.

For such big men, they took surprisingly small sips of their juice. Fern said, "I'm sorry, I think I am in labor."

"For the baby?" said one.

The other Swede continued the previous conversation. "The last herring, we ate in the train. After, only bread and butter and meat from a can."

"You have some herring?" the yellow-toothed man asked.

"No, I'm sorry. I don't have any herring. Only meat from a can. Very old meat from a can," Fern said, hoping to discourage them from wanting anything else to eat. She breathed through a wave of what was now definite pain. The two men watched her patiently. One went over to the crate, knocked on it.

"I should call my husband," Fern said but when she dialed Edgar's studio number it just rang and rang.

"We can help," said yellow tooth.

Fern watched the clock, had to kneel while the pain peaked. She remembered this pain now — how could she have forgotten it? She also remembered that it went on and on, and figured that she had many hours to go. Flower whined with her. When Fern was back in her chair the first man said, "London was nice city. Having bad weather, but having good time." Did the men have return tickets? Fern wondered.

"There are many dark people here in America," one Swede said. "Do you feel fear of them?"

"Of the dark people? The black people?" Fern stumbled. "No, no, we like them." It came out sounding wrong, as if they were a kind of animal some people thought of as pests and others found sweet.

"But not in this neighborhood," the second man said.

"No," she said, "not so much in this neighborhood." Pain and shame peaked at the same time.

Finally, finally, yellow tooth stood up and stretched. He gave the small chair a dirty look. Fern wanted to defend it — we Americans can fit in chairs that size. We are not being cheap. He came to stand beside her and wiped her forehead, which was sweating. "You have a cloth? I can make it cold for you." He wet a red gingham dishtowel in the sink, squeezed it in his big hand and draped it over Fern's forehead. The contractions were closer together but she could not keep track of the time and survive at the same time. She kept expecting Edgar to walk through the door and drive her to the hospital.

The two blonds began to unfasten the nails in the crate, pulling at them with the back of a hammer. Boards fell away. It was like excavating a tomb. Musty, woodsy smell came out when they opened the door panel and the inside of the crate was so dark. The bigger man reached inside and pulled at a handle. Inside was a ramble of wool blankets.

Tape was cut and the two blonds pulled the blankets off, revealing the desk. Just a desk. It was rectangular and sleek and the wood was rich and marbled like meat. But it was only wood, not some precious material. It seemed now like a very strange thing to do — spend money to have some nailed-together boards brought from the other side of the ocean, complete with two handlers. And there was no assembly. All the Swedes had to do was take it out of the crate and run a soft rag over it to remove the shipping dust.

When Fern was between waves, yellow tooth pulled one of the kitchen chairs over to the desk and said, "Sit down."

The desk was big. It was technically too big. Fern felt like a little girl sitting at it. She thought of her father at his big desk in his big study, a fat novel in front of him and a red pen.

Fern dialed Edgar again and again he did not answer. She finally called her doctor and he could hear in her voice that she was very far along. "Why didn't you call earlier? I'm coming over."

"You are?" she asked. "Don't I have hours to go?" Only poor people and hippies had babies at home. Fern wanted the hospital. She wanted the drugs.

"I don't think we have time to move you."

While Fern rocked on her hands and knees, sat back up and rocked again, the Swedes drank coffee and found and ate cans of tuna fish to which they added a smear of butter. Fern, in a lucid moment, said, "Is that customary? Is it always done that way?"

"Never," said one. "It has never been done that way."

It was so hot in the house. Fern said, "I have to push now," as much to herself as the Swedes. The dog paced.

"We understand," said the yellow-toothed man. "You must lie down. Don't worry, we understand what to do."

The doctor would arrive just after the two boys had been safely delivered into the hands of the yellow-toothed man, wrapped in blankets by the other Swede and placed on Fern's chest on their sides so their lungs could drain. The Swedes had waited until the cords stopped pulsing and then cut them with kitchen shears. One man had given Fern ice chips to suck on. The doctor said, "Oh, hello." He had not expected this particular kind of company. The towels the Swedes had put under Fern were soaked with blood and fluid. "Thank you," he said. They had done exactly what they were supposed to do. The babies, two boys, were scrunched but beautiful, one slightly larger than the other, and Fern was fine. Everyone was absolutely fine.

While the doctor put fresh towels under Fern and tended to her and Fern tried to figure out how to hold both babies at the same time, the Swedes began to cinch up the laces on their boots. They smoothed their shirts.

"We have to go back now," they said.

Fern told them to make themselves a bag with the rest of the tuna fish and some bread and a thermos of coffee. They stood at the doorway, looking east towards the hills, towards the train, towards the many miles. "You are all right?" they asked.

"Thank you for taking care of me," she said. "I'm sorry you had to do that."

"It was a luck," yellow tooth said.

"Miracle of life," the other told her. She had forgotten the desk completely. In the sunlight the Swedes had such tender, pink skin.

When Edgar came home he found that his family had nearly doubled. The doctor was there and Fern was lying on the bed covered by a blanket. "You gave birth," Edgar said. "I missed it again."

"Two boys," Fern said, her whole body still flushed. "Come closer."

"Are they all right?" he asked.

"They're perfectly healthy," the doctor said.

Edgar felt the weight of the locket against his leg. It made him feel stupid, this small, purchased beauty, when Fern had brought forth two lives in the space of an afternoon.

She grabbed his hands and pulled him onto the bed. "When Cricket comes home from school, we'll be complete. This is our family." Fern wanted to freeze them on this first day as a whole family before time got to work on them. The babies were tinier than tiny. They wanted to be pressed together, like two halves of a circle. Fern recognized this because she had felt it twice — first with Ben and then with Edgar. It was as if the idea of a single body did not exist — only in joining did either of them come true.

As if the family had tipped over the edge of a waterfall, time sped up. The twins were healthy and happy and neither of them was overquiet or odd. They were regular babies and then regular kids. Everywhere they went people said to Fern, "I guess triplets would be harder," and "You certainly have your hands full," and Fern smiled and nodded. The twins learned to crawl, to walk, to beg. She put them to sleep in their own beds but by morning one had always migrated over to be close to the other. Cricket learned to put on her own shoes, to pour a glass of milk. She learned to read. She learned to scold, to congratulate and to console. Time doubled, tripled. Edgar went to his study and read and wrote. Some days the story unwound and some days it tangled. Some days he came home feeling like a writer and some days he wanted nothing more than to give it up. Edgar felt the magnetic pull of misery less strongly than he ever had before. He was too busy trying to articulate the complicated fact of his own privilege to hate it the way he always had.

Edgar's parents sent gifts, Fern's parents sent short letters detailing the repairs that had been required on the house, the sculptures that had sold, the number of headache-free days Paul had had each month. Fern replied with news of the children, news of the summerhouse they had purchased on the island, the sailboat to go with it. She had to give her parents something because she was their daughter, but she wanted their reach to be shallow, surface-level, since everything they had touched before had been left aching.

Fern bought furniture and clothes and art and then spent time taking care of those objects. Edgar teased her for the purchases and then forgot about them. When the twins were two years old, she enrolled in one class — Archaeology — and imagined digging up bones of ancient people on the banks of the Nile, in the deserts of Syria, the mountains of Central Asia. At dinner she explained the methods to Edgar and the children: the way the area of a dig must be marked off in squares with flags and pegs. "The earth is like a layer cake," she explained. "The deeper you go, the older the soil. It's your first information about how old your find is." Fern promised that they could conduct a dig at their summerhouse. She imagined wearing a bandana and sitting on the ground, brushing away the dirt from an Indian femur with a toothbrush. The children imagined bigger beasts: mammoths, pterodactyls.

Fern liked taking the class but she was afraid of a full schedule and afraid of failing again and afraid of being told just how small she was. "I have three children to raise," she said when Edgar pressed her. "My mother had two nannies to help her. One of the kids is always waking up in the middle of the night. Everyone is always hungry. I'm doing all I can." She kept picturing that professor and his nose hair and the humiliation that had bloomed in her. Learning to be a mother of three was hard enough and she had not slept a full night in all these years and no one gave grades for it and there was no end-of-the-year party or vacation and school sounded lonely and surrounded with teenagers and tests she did not have time to study for, old professors looking at her like she was already overripe.

"When they're bigger," she said, trying to smile. Edgar let it be. He did not want to tell his wife that he thought she could amount to more, though he did, because he loved her and because she was smart and because he was blind to so much of the work she did in their home, the invisible structure she built to support five lives.

Six cats were adopted and six cats were hit by cars or eaten by wild animals. Flower did not come home one night and Cricket quit eating for two days. The dog was replaced by a beagle, which could not be housebroken and was soon given away and replaced by a golden retriever whose blind enthusiasm even Cricket did not have the strength to match. Later there was a turtle, a rat and a series of fish. Maggie appeared on the doorstep and the children immediately made her family.

The house was all noise and then quiet, noise and quiet. Edgar's parents came to visit with ever-larger gifts. In Chicago, the world's tallest skyscraper was built using

Edgar's father's steel. Fern's parents sent a letter saying that the First Lady had purchased one of Evelyn's sculptures to put in the White House garden and she had gone to see it settled, reported a long conversation at dinner with the wife of the Spanish Ambassador about the difference between American aphids and European ones. Fern replied with basic facts about the children — Cricket was growing a garden and could cook her own eggs and was reading books about fragile young British women, the twins were obsessed with building great block towers and crashing them down. In every conversation with her parents, Ben was a dark maw that would not close. Fern knew blame had no purpose but she hoarded it all the same.

The children always needed Fern to be a different kind of mother than she had been the week before. They exhausted her and she longed for a break and then she missed them acutely the moment they were out of sight — that was the truth of motherhood. Birthdays accumulated under everyone. Each year Edgar said, "Would you consider finishing your degree?" and each year she said, "Later."

The rest of the world came into Fern and Edgar's house on television: the Ohio

National Guard shot unarmed students at Kent State, the Weather Underground bombed the US capital, abortion became legal. The first American space station was launched into orbit, people all across the country lined up in their cars to fill up during a gas shortage. The President resigned in scandal. The daughter of a rich newspaperman was kidnapped. North Vietnamese troops encircled Saigon. The last American soldiers were lifted by helicopter to an aircraft carrier in the South China Sea. Nearby, the Cambodian dictator forcibly emptied his capital city and began killing thousands of people, but the world was war-weary and it would be a long time before anyone intervened.

A serial killer began and completed a spree. The economy was slow, inflation was high, people were stabbed and robbed in the subways in New York. There were gays in the streets and performance artists and cocaine; the music changed again and men grew long sideburns and everyone young was always taking their clothes off.

Edgar had a chapter of his novel published. Then on a winter Saturday, he sat at the kitchen table and held a thick stack of typed pages in his hands. They were heavy and felt warm. Almost like a living thing.

Edgar looked at the title page: *LUCKY by Edgar Keating.* He found a large envelope, sealed the manuscript inside, wrote the name and address of an agent, and kissed the flap. Fern and the children were outside stomping snow into paths and chasing each other. Edgar was too nervous to say where he was going. "I'm taking the dog out," he said. His whole body felt electrified. It would have been easy to talk himself out of mailing the package: the potential embarrassment, the concern that he had wasted his time, that he would have to find something else to do with his life. The day was deeply grey. A snowplow had created dirty piles on the sidewalk. It was not as bitter as it had been and Edgar was without gloves for the first time in weeks. On a busy corner he saw a thin man his own age wearing pressed plaid pants and jacket, a nice wool coat and sneakers. It took him a minute, but then Edgar knew. "Runner?" he said to the man.

"Holy shit, brother!" the man said. He had huge sideburns and curly hair that resisted the side-part it had been forced into. Edgar did not feel as grown up as Runner looked. Runner, whose wild and unapologetic life Edgar had sometimes wished for, a shadow of which formed the story in his novel.

The summary: he was there to close out his mother's estate. He still lived in Alaska and was still married to the librarian but they had moved off the commune. "All we wanted was a real fucking toilet," Runner said, "and we ended up with a big house, a couple of trucks, three kids and two law degrees."

"You're an attorney?" Edgar asked.

"I know. But I'm on the right side." He told Edgar how he and his wife were working for the American Indian Movement. "There's so much fucked-up shit in the past that it's hard to know where to start," he said. "Broken treaties, stolen objects, stolen land, stolen children, forced boarding schools, systematic rape. Mass murder. I could go on." He looked Edgar up and down. "You seem happy," he said.

Edgar squeezed the package in his hand. "Thanks. I am."

Runner wrote down his address. He offered the guest room. He said, "We see the northern lights in winter and there's almost no night in summertime. Come find me when you get tired of the city. I'll take you salmon fishing. Bring the family."

Runner, true to his name, held his briefcase up to his chest and jogged off. Edgar watched him until he turned the corner. For the first time, Edgar did not feel like he was living the worse life. Even the hippies were buying houses and having babies. They had all grown up.

Two weeks later the agent called with the news that Edgar's novel would be published.

A few weeks after that Fern's parents died.

Spring came, the roses bloomed, Fern dreamed about Ben. She talked to him in her head. Edgar waited impatiently for notes from his editor. Fern once again did not register for classes for the fall.

Fern thought of a hundred things she might have said to her parents about Ben, about herself, about being a woman, a mother, about love. She might have told her father that she didn't blame him. She might have told her mother that she understood that it had not been fair for her either. Mostly though, their death was a quietness in Fern instead of an explosion. That her parents were no longer behind her on the path did not feel like an event; she had been walking away from them for a long time. Summer came again and the family packed for the island. They sailed, they swam. They plotted out a square of the cliff to dig up and followed the protocol Fern had learned in school — the grid, the logbook, the careful use of tools. Cricket discovered an arrowhead and toothbrushed it out of the soil and they found dozens of quahog shells with dark purple lips.

One afternoon Fern watched Will and James, the side-by-side of them, at work on a puzzle. She brought lemonade over and said, "You are so lucky to have each other. I hope you know that." They did not even look up. They were years away from the treachery of adolescence, from the time they would turn to look for love elsewhere. She wanted them to always have each other, to never outgrow this perfect pairing. She imagined a corresponding set of girls for wives and a house big enough for everyone and one next door for Cricket — Cricket who did not have the luck to be a twin but also did not stand to lose her match.

The whole family went fishing and cooked chowder and sang sea songs on the lawn in the evening, slapping mosquitos under a sky that flashed with a coming lightning storm.

Then came August. Then came the call from the lawyer. The known world shook them off.

1976

Fern had not noticed at first that the giant preferred to stay in the car when she paid for their motel rooms. "Mr. and Mrs.," she always said, peering over the ledger to see the name. She was another woman, otherwise betrothed. She remembered the early days of her and Edgar, of walking around with her new last name like it was jewelry. This new version of herself would have a short life — a few weeks, sea to shining sea. Fern wanted to know if hunger was churning up in Edgar's belly, hunger for her. Absence was the last tool she had and she had no way to see if it was working.

They had traveled over a thousand miles now, had eaten and slept, eaten and slept and the trip had developed its own life. The rooms were all cheap and often a little dirty and Fern found that she didn't mind. She still startled sometimes when she looked in the backseat and saw three empty spots instead of three children and when, for a moment, she allowed herself to think of the distance between them and the speed with which she was driving farther away she had the feeling of having climbed to a high mountain where the air was thin. Fern was breaking a physical law, unbinding herself from the lives she had created. This feeling of airlessness also brought a high. She was a person responsible for no one else.

Fern hummed along to the pop station to songs she somehow knew even though was sure she had never heard them before. That was the genetics of this music — a virus, caught upon contact. "You can feel autumn in the air," she said.

"Time to head south anyway," said Mac. As they cloverleafed onto US 55 south-bound they both laughed and simultane-ously reached to crank the volume button to celebrate. It was that easy to solve the cold. The signs switched from Des Moines, Lincoln, Cheyenne to St. Louis, Jackson, New Orleans. The roadside was deep green and overgrown sooner than they would have expected. Vines worked their way across the land, tangling.

Fern thought of her ancestors, early set-tlers of this big country. They had spread out, moved a little farther west, seeded the

Kentucky hills with their good name. They bought plantations bursting with cotton and they bought bodies with darker hands to gather the white bursts off the branch. Money accumulated. The houses grew bigger, and the purebred Americans owned ever more stable-hands, maids, nannies, ever more darker hands to tend the fields. Their wives were more beautiful with each generation, bound into shape by corsets made from the bones of whales.

The sons of the sons of the sons took over their fathers' plantations, ran for government under their fathers' trusted names. But soon when some of the young men came home they had a harder time watching the darker hands in the fields knowing that the people, the men and women — whole bodies, selves, the sons of sons could now admit were attached to the hands — were a line item in their lists of holdings. This many acres, this many bushels, this many males, this many females.

One son freed his father's slaves while his father was in the hospital with pneumonia. The boy's father, who might otherwise have recovered, died surrounded by white-capped nurses who had no remedy for anger or shame. The boy's mother hanged herself in the parlor. When he found her, he cut her down with a pair of silver scissors and lay beside her on the floor until evening, fireflies sketching lines across the dark.

To their friends and children both, generations to come told the story of the abolitionist over the story of his father, proud of the relatives who had fought on the side of right. They did not speak of the fact that in order for a family to free their slaves they must first have owned them. They did not stop spending the money that had been earned with the help of bodies, bought and sold. It was that money that furnished every single thing in their good American lives.

After lunch, Fern and Mac walked a small town's main streets. He could not help himself from imagining for a moment that a woman like Fern could fall in love with him and how they would move in, buy a little farmhouse, get the garden going, bake pies in its kitchen. No one would know about their lives before this. He was not falling in love with Fern — he knew that she belonged to someone and he was unreasonably huge and they each had real lives to which they would return. Mac still let himself have the fantasy. He had been alive long enough to know that this was one of the safer pleasures.

She said, "I like that little blue house with the picket fence."

"It's cute. I'd never even fit in the door."

"What size is your house at home?"

"It's a two-bedroom apartment down-town. But the ceilings are high and I paid a lot of money to have everything redone with big doors and tall counters."

"And here I am this small woman in a huge house."

"You know goldfish grow relative to the size of their habitat?"

"Maybe we should switch," Fern said. "Make our habitats relative to the size of our bodies. Edgar would love to live in a two-bedroom apartment, even if he couldn't reach the sinks."

Next to the Laundromat was a pink slice of a building with a purple sign that said *Astrology, Spices, Travel Arrangements, Notary Public.* There was a bell, and Mac walked right up and rang it. Fern hung back, but the door opened and there stood a middle-aged black man in a tight T-shirt advertising a team called the Bay City Char-gers.

"How can I help you?" he asked. He looked the giant up and down, as if he was trying to see the step the man must be standing on. The man said, "Tarot, tea

leaves, palm reading, astrology. Every reading gets a free cup of tea or a beer." He
looked like a Little League dad, not like a
seer.

All the lamps had purple scarves hung
over them and there were piles of cigarettes
in ashtrays all over and a stack of magazines
at the top of which was a glossy for teens
with a blond cover model. On the wall was
a picture of a topless black Madonna nursing her baby and the room smelled of
cardamom. Fern realized that the only other
time she had been inside the home of a
black person was in Kentucky. She wondered what had become of the miner's wife.
That house had not surprised her — here,
nothing was as she would have expected.

"Who's up first?" the man asked. He sat
them at a table. Mac gave him his birthday,
the place, the time. The man put on a pair
of reading glasses and thumbed through
some papers and said, "In ten years' time,
you'll find a home you don't want to leave.
You won't struggle for money. You need to
eat more fats. If we were in India, I would
tell you to light a candle and send it down
the Ganges."

"Have you been there?" Fern asked.

"We were hippies. When we were younger.
Now we're adults with kids and a mort-

gage," the man said, seeing a question in Fern's eyes. She looked down at her feet.

The giant softened his voice. "And love?" he asked.

"Yes," the man said. "Absolutely. The best kind."

Then the man traced his soft, brown finger across Fern's pale palm lines and made small noises of recognition. *Do not tell me the bad news,* she thought. *Do not show me to my horrible self.* Because there were her children again, real and actual and far, and her life that she had walked out of. There was her husband whose happiness she had tried to trade for material comfort. There was her twin brother whom she had failed to protect. Due south was coal country and below that the Army base. To the east was the town where Ben had jumped out the window and to the north was the ivied building where he had spent the rest of his life. Fern felt as though she was standing in the center of her entire life, all those points of departure. If one thing had changed along the way, who knows who they would have become. If the mine had not collapsed, if Ben had not been drafted, if Edgar had been sent to the jungle instead of the ice. Would they have been happier or sadder or wiser or gentler or better or less afraid people? Would she have had to run away?

She closed her eyes. "You'll have three children," the man said. "Two boys and one girl." She felt the presence of them so strongly that she snapped her eyes open, sure she would see them standing in the room.

She tore her hand away.

Fern heard rain in her ears and could not say anything, and the two men looked at her and then she was on the floor and they were offering her water and she saw in their faces that the storm was her own. Everyone else was dead dry.

They sat in the car, but Mac did not start the engine. "I'm sorry. I can take you home."

Fern took a moment to answer. Her mouth was dry. "Do you remember being a teenager? Everyone feels so sorry for you and you can't be saved." Fern was dizzy still and she could not get out of a dream she had had of being lined up with all the other teenagers on stage in her high school auditorium. The fourteen-year-olds stood there, arms at their awkward sides, their faces broken out with pimples, their forms raggedy and disproportionate.

The giant said, "I grew two feet in the fall of eighth grade. They had to get a teacher's desk for me to sit at. Pretty soon even that didn't work. Everyone else just had bad hair and skin, but I turned into a mutant."

"Cricket is nine. She still seems like a kid, but in a second she'll fall down the waterfall. She'll be a woman and probably a wife and a mother. I'm afraid for my boys to grow up and stop being alike. My brother didn't survive that. The days are so long, but then it's over."

"At least you were there to watch your children grow up. I don't know what my son looks like. I can't even imagine the thousands of versions of him that I've missed."

"Thank you for helping me in there. I don't know what happened."

"We've done too much too fast."

Life seemed improbable. All the turns of fate it had taken for Fern to be the mother of three particular children and the wife of one particular man. How furiously she loved them and how heavy it was to carry that quantity of love, how perilous to care for those delicate bodies in the spinning world.

Fern told Mac a story: in ninth grade at a party the boys proposed to the girls that they "do it." The other girls all turned

343

quickly away, but Fern, because she wanted to seem brave, said, "I'll do it." She did not know what *it* meant, not exactly. She understood which parts were involved and the general idea, but the mechanics were foreign. Frederick Dawson drew the lucky card and led the way down into the basement where an old bed was stored. They both took off their pants but not their underwear. Frederick was no better informed than Fern. She lay down first and he lay down on top of her, still as a fallen tree. They stayed for several moments exchanging nothing more than air. He shook slightly with nerves. As they ascended the stairs, Frederick seemed to fill with confidence, like a balloon inflated. He told the other teenagers, "We did it." And Fern assumed they had. At school the next day everyone said, "Frederick did it with Fern," and when Fern went home that afternoon her mother was weeping on the sofa in the front hall. "You're ruined," she said to her daughter.

To Mac, Fern said, "I didn't realize until my wedding night that nothing had happened. I remember feeling so much more ashamed for how little I knew than I ever had for the indiscretion."

"Did Edgar know the rumors?"

"I'm sure he did. Maybe part of what

344

made me fall in love with him was that he forgave me for something without ever bringing it up." She paused. "I wonder if my parents would have let me marry Edgar if not for that story. I'm sure they were already talking with other, better families before. Without Frederick Dawson my whole life might have been different."

Mac leaned against the doorframe. His silence was always warm, an invitation rather than a wall.

Fern said, "My parents and my twin brother are dead and my husband and I have each done a terrible thing to the other and when I think about my children I feel like I've left body parts behind."

"We can be back tomorrow if we drive all night."

"We have to find your son."

"I have to. You don't have to."

The giant's big head touched the top of the car and static electricity pulled his hair upward. "I don't have any real friends," Fern said. She thought of the black miner and his wife, the other women on base, the crisp, perfect Cambridge neighbors. Everyone had either been too different or too similar. Fern and Edgar had lost them because they were poor or hated them because they were rich. She thought of Ben, to whom she wished she had been more loyal. He might have been all right if he had stayed near her. "You are my friend," Fern said. "I'm coming with you to find your son. We're already halfway."

"Thank you," Mac said.

"Two conditions: I don't want to go to Kentucky or Tennessee and I need to use the phone."

Fern stood outside the movie theater and dialed, collect, her own number. Each ring seemed longer than the ring before it. "Hello?" she kept practicing. But no one was there to answer. They're all fine, she told herself. They're probably out drinking a milkshake. She pictured James and Will building a tower designed especially so that it could be collapsed while Cricket strung a series of tiny glass beads on a silk thread. They were probably having the best time, now that boring old Mother was gone.

Mac was standing at the car when she returned, his face bright, and he was holding a bucket of movie theater popcorn. "Come on," he said, laughing.

They sailed through the day. They ate the buttered kernels and watched the world in front of them open up. It was so quiet, just the sound of the wheels on the road, the wind. They did not talk or listen to music.

346

They just drove and ate and watched the world appear and pass. The road turned and new scenery revealed itself. A raccoon lumbered out of the way and fled into the bushes.

"The first time I came to the South was when I visited my great-grandmother here as a kid. My parents sent me alone on the train," Fern said.

"What was she like?"

"My great-grandmother? Tiny and terrifying. She washed her face with old-fashioned laundry powder and then put petroleum jelly on after. For a week we were driven around to museums and parks by Mr. Collins, her chauffeur, who was very dark-skinned and never spoke. 'Why won't he say hello to me?' I remember asking. Great-grandmother was angry. She said, 'Talking is not his job. I keep him because he knows how to be quiet.' She looked at me and must have seen that I was upset. 'Don't worry, I doubt he's dangerous,' she said. 'Not all black men are.' "

"Were your parents like that too?" Mac asked.

"They knew Great-grandmother was racist and they would have told you they disagreed. But my father also forbade our cook from using garlic or onions because he

347

thought it was too Italian and therefore low-class."

Mac knew what it meant to live as an outsider. He was a minority of one, and not part of a group anyone was fighting for.

"Minds are hard to change," he said.

She thought of the palm reader, her own expectations. "Yes," she said.

Fern took his hand. It was buttery. This was not an answer or a question. Outside the window, anything green overgrew itself.

"If you could go anywhere?" she asked.

"India," he said. "For the elephants."

The bucket of popcorn was generous, meant to occupy two sets of hands through two hours of horrors and delights, and Fern and Mac went back and forth between eating and twisting their fingers back up together. They never got tired that day and they never rested. "Tell me more of your story," Fern said, and he began.

Mac met his future wife during a high school summer when they had nothing to do all day. The teenagers all gathered in the park under a shade tree and fanned themselves with fat leaves or books or their own sticky hands. It was too hot to think or act. The girls put their heads on the laps of the boys until they could not stand the extra heat. They whined like puppies.

Claire was not a pretty girl, but she was a girl. Her sister brought her into the group, otherwise she never would have been tolerated. Little sisters could come if they were worshipful enough. Giants could come if they brought treats.

Claire took the giant's cold drink, held it until her palms hurt. Her hair was unsmooth and unfixed. Mac knew that he had earned no right to be choosy. It was within this conciliatory fog, the day too bright to ask questions that Mac and Claire first kissed. His lips were fat as fingers on her little mouth, and she was salty and grassy-tasting.

The month passed. Behind the widest trees, the not-very-pretty girl with a not-very-pretty bow in her hair on his huge lap; in her parents' house, in the basement, both of them shirtless on the concrete, which was almost, almost cool.

She said, "I don't deserve you," and Mac thought that maybe she was right, maybe he was just one notch better than she, wrongly sized but good-looking otherwise. He was thankful, so thankful not to be the less loved party, to have a hold on the ropes keeping his heart in.

"You are so good to me," he said, and that

part was true.

Claire braved the oven and baked blondies for her giant. She delivered them to his door in an antique tin with a red ribbon around it. Mac's mother answered. She brought the girl in and asked her to kneel down at her altar so that they might pray together. Claire would hear the story, as all visitors had, and she would say, "Wow," because she was polite and wanted the mother of her love to approve of her. Every teenage girl has within her a lurking gene to make the parents think of her as a daughter, no matter if she loves the boy or hates him, expects to marry him or leaves him by midnight.

When it was time for Claire to leave, the giant ducked under the doorjamb to kiss her. Mac's mother was standing there when he closed the door, her face pink. "Oh, oh," she squealed. "She's just perfect. And she's not too good for you." It was the same thought Mac himself had had, but hearing it did not feel good.

"Yes, she's very nice. And not very pretty." He tried to celebrate this fact with a smile.

"You'll ask her, then?" Mac's mother asked.

"For?"

350

"For her hand, you idiot. No one ever expected this. No one ever thought it was possible."

He knew it was true. That night, he looked in the mirror, which was really three mirrors that he had nailed to the wall in a tall line so that he could see his whole self at once. He looked good when he stood alone. His belly was flat and his arms were muscled and his neck had a mannish character to it. Good proportions, good hair. The trouble came when a normal-size body stood beside him.

The proposal took place under the original kissing tree. He drew a ring out of his pocket, the ring his great-great-grandmother had worn. The size of his palm did nothing to make the tiny diamond look bigger, but Claire wrapped her arms around as much of Mac as she could and pressed her face into his chest and wept, saying over and over again, "Yes, darling, yes, darling, yes, take me as your loving wife."

Mac's mother took over the planning of the event without asking for opinions. She took the girl shopping for a dress and insisted upon the one with the widest, most dramatic skirt. She wanted bows, fat white bows on the chairs, and she wanted red roses on every surface.

Meanwhile, the temperature dropped slowly. Fall changed the air from half-water back to all air, and everyone felt as if they had just woken up. September passed, but the change grew noticeable in October, when Claire began to look different. Her hair seemed soothed by the new weather, her skin was not rashy any longer. Her eyes looked clearer. Mac said, "You look so nice," before they went into the school building.

November, and she was prettier still. She started smoking. Had she grown taller? Mac wondered. Her legs were very long and lustrous, and somehow tanned, despite the season. She wore skirts that were tight in the waist and silk blouses, shoes with a small heel, lipstick.

The other boys started to congratulate the giant on his good work. How did he know, they wondered, that the barely-okay girl was about to get so beautiful? Mac, though, grew more and more uneasy. He was notching down, his inferiority to his fiancée increasing by the day.

Mac and Claire did soon stand in a church presided over by one of the city's many Father O'Briens and make their lifelong promises. They ruined the sheets in the hotel room, took a weekend up north and

352

walked in the woods after the season's first snow.

Six months after his wedding, Mac visited his mother. He passed her slumped on her chair, seemingly asleep, carried the bags of groceries he had brought to the kitchen and unpacked them. He poured the beans and flour and sugar into the correct jars on the shelf. He cleaned the last of the butter from the dish and placed a new stick there. He rearranged the fruit in the drawer and took out the piece of greening cheese. How quiet it was. How nice to be in his mother's house without her telling him what to do.

He sat in the living room opposite his mother for half an hour, waiting for her to wake. Finally, he grew worried that she would upset her bedtime if she continued to sleep. He got close and began to sense a wrongness. Her knee beneath his hand was cold. The giant picked his mother up and held her like a child, and she was nearly that small in his arms.

Claire came to him a few days later with a piece of paper in her hand. Condition: pregnancy. A doctor had signed it at the bottom. As if she was trying to get out of school, out of work. An excuse to stay in bed. "How dare you trap me like this?" she said. She had a faceful of makeup on, and a plaid skirt he had not seen her wear before. She looked like someone trying to turn famous.

He had had a plan, to raise children without worrying about raising giants. An easy sperm donation. No one had to know. He had not expected her to get pregnant so easily. Mac looked at her fair belly, in which resided a tangle of cells. He wanted to kneel down and press his ear to that wall of skin, listen for deformations. "Can they tell if it's normal?" he asked.

"It's a sin not to have the baby," she said. "But if it's a giant, you can keep it; if it's normal, it's mine."

"But we're married. I assume that means we'll raise our children together."

"Look," said Claire. "When we met, you were the best I was going to get. Now I think I have a chance at a better life."

Claire then produced a second set of papers from her purse. They were legal-size and covered in writing. This time, the signature at the bottom was his mother's. "Little squirrel," Claire said. There was a number at the bottom with a dollar sign preceding it.

"She played the lottery every week for twenty years," Mac said, "but I didn't know she had won anything." The number seemed impossible: $927,000.13. Claire explained that her half of the money would support her for the rest of her life if she was careful.

"You're already leaving me?" he asked.

"Now I'm pretty *and* I have money in the bank. I have to look out for my future."

"And our baby's future?"

"Your baby or my baby, not ours." Claire said, "If the baby is yours, you'll have to make your own nursery. I wouldn't recommend buying the smallest sized clothes, either."

He went to a store full of pinks and blues and felt larger than he had ever felt in his life among the tiny objects. Shoes that he could have worn on his fingers, miniature hats, pants no more than a few inches long. There were little tables and little chairs and little toilets and little fake telephones. The giant crouched down and picked up a pair of socks from a low shelf. For a doll? he wondered. And he put them in his basket because he wanted to rescue them.

The salesgirls avoided him at first, but got braver the longer he stayed. "I just need the very basics," he said. He did not explain that there was only a fifty-fifty chance of him getting to be a father after all. The brunette said, "Bathtub, towel, christening dress, pram, crib."

"I can do that," he said.

"I wasn't done. Sheets, bassinet, spit-up rags, diapers, pins, wipes, rash cream, books, mobile, teddy bear, pants, dresses, shirts, pajamas, socks, hats, blankets for summer, blankets for winter, first aid kit, gauze for the umbilical cord, bottles, bottle brush, soft spoons, plastic plates, high chair, rubber ducky, a book about colors, a book about seasons, a book about Mommy and Daddy."

"Stop," said Mac.

He bought everything she said he should and it felt like insurance. Here was this room, all ready, drawing the baby towards it.

The day came when Claire stopped in the middle of painting her fingernails and said, "Get over here," and she slapped Mac hard across the face. "Are you kidding me? It already hurts this much and I'm just getting going. What have you done to me?" Her belly was massive, much bigger than average, and Mac pretended to be neutral, but he thought the win was his.

The doctor stood between her legs and received the head, the shoulders, the body. He declared, "A boy!" and Mac and Claire both yelled, "How big?" before he could even congratulate them.

"It's perfect. He's perfect. Not a bone too large."

The doctor wiped his brow as if he had been the one to labor the creature out. The baby looked to Mac like a human heart, purple and beating, and when Mac went to reach for him, Claire pushed his hand away. "We made a deal," she said. "Giant baby: yours; normal baby: mine."

"I wasn't always giant," he said, but she was not listening.

She let him hold the baby that night, and he was as light as a kitten. He was still belly-rounded and yet to unfurl.

When Claire fell asleep, he whispered things: "I am your father and I love you no matter how far away you get." Again and again: "I am your father and you are my son. My son, my son, my son."

Mac never got rid of the baby's things. He did find other uses for them — pots and pans in the crib, his own clothes in the dresser, laundry in the small bathtub. He always felt that his boy, who Claire named Matthew, lived there with him a little bit.

Years passed with no news of the pair. He did not know where they were. Each year, on Matthew's birthday, Mac baked a small yellow cake, frosted it and sunk the correct plus-one-to-grow-on number of candles.

Each year, he put one slice of the cake in the freezer for Matthew to eat when he finally came home. The rest, he forked into his big red mouth.

And then, thirteen years later, a pink envelope arrived, marked *Palm Springs, USA.* Within it were these sentences: *It's your wife here. I preferred the baby and little kid years. The boy is getting too large.* An address followed.

Fern thought about the story. She thought about the way the poles change and draw people close, push them away. "Would she have left you if your mother hadn't turned out to have money?"

"I doubt it. Being good-looking is a help, but she still would have been an eighteen-year-old divorced mother. I doubt she would have trusted her chances without the bank account. A person can afford to be brave when money is on the table."

"Did she remarry?"

"I don't know anything except this address. Not one single thing."

"What about your half of the money?" Fern asked.

"It's in a savings account. The things I want are not for sale."

Fern knew he meant love. She knew he

meant family. Everything she was driving at high speed away from. She thought about the giant's job at the bank, him sitting there in his security guard outfit with a dog-eared book and a half-eaten sandwich. It was the kind of job she would have expected someone to quit if his mother had saved almost a million dollars playing the lottery. She asked if he had considered it.

"I like working. A reason for being."

The good ladies and gentlemen where Fern came from would have scorned people like these: a woman like Mac's mother, an immigrant, all those cheap red roses, the Catholicism, lace doilies on each surface, a too-big man who took pleasure from his unprestigious day job. "It's funny that of the two of us, you're the rich one," Fern said.

He winked at her. "Tables turn, eh? Better be nice to me."

Now it was truly hot. All the way south, and the air was nearly swimmable. They passed a series of hand-painted signs advertising something called the Regal Reptile Ranch and Menagerie. The sign read *Over 20 Gators Plus 7-Foot Anaconda Cottonmouth Tegu Coachwhips Beaded Lizards Fox Snake Rat Snake Cobra.*

They stopped for gas. Fern went inside the service station to pay. She added red licorice, a pack of Pall Malls and a bottle of Coke, and held the cold glass to her forehead. The man behind the counter was too handsome to work in a service station. He had long hair and a mustache, and he was wearing blue coveralls stained with grease. Minus the outfit, he belonged at an expensive party near the blue light of the swimming pool, all the girls topless or better.

"Well," he said. "Am I glad you walked in. Have you come far?"

"Boston," she said. Where were they now, anyway? Louisiana, someplace with no plants she could name, a completely different kind of forest out the window all morning. "Are you from nearby?"

"Marquette," he said. He hit the buttons on his register, left off the candy. "That's for you, from me," he said. He was a beautiful boy with a suntan that probably never faded, no winter to speak of in this part of the country. A man needed to own a good wool coat to be trusted. A man needed to be able to go outside in the pink of a snowy morning and scrape what was iced, shovel what was blanketed.

The bell clinked and the giant walked in. He went towards the *Ice Cold Drinks* sign, opened the chest and let out a cloud of cold.

"Holy shit," the handsome boy said, in a

whisper. He leaned in to Fern, and they were kiss-close. "What a freak," he whispered. His breath was stale-smoky and she noticed a freckle on his lower lip.

"Him?" she said. "He's my *husband.*" Discomfort tangled that pretty face and it was the best thing she had felt all week. It was good to cause pain to someone who deserved it.

When Fern was in high school, one of her friends' fathers had a long, public affair with a bank teller not more than two years older than his daughter. The girl's mother drank, wrecked her Cadillac, became a point of gossip and ridicule. Fern remembered wondering why the wife didn't simply turn love off, like a spigot. Her husband was a bad person, cruel and unforgivable, and it seemed like it should have been so easy to walk away.

In the car Fern opened the pack of cigarettes. "I felt like smoking," she said. She lit, coughed, inhaled again.

"Give me one of those," he said, and she lit a cigarette for him too.

Fern flicked ash out her window. "I don't love Edgar less than before the kiss," Fern said. "I should. I know what other women would think of me. I'm still angry with him and I still want to hurt him and I still don't know if I'll forgive it, and I still don't know if he'll ever forgive me, but even taken together those feelings are nothing compared to how much else has gathered over our years together." It might still drown you, but love got deeper with time.

The giant put his cigarette out in the ashtray. "That tasted too good," he said. "Don't let me smoke too much."

They paralleled the railroad tracks for the next few hours, and then a train chuffed alongside them at nearly the same speed and Fern could see the dining car in which a single man in a cowboy hat sat reading a newspaper while three cheap-suited servers stood in wait. Fern could almost hear the coffee cup rattle on his saucer.

Mac slowed suddenly and gasped, and when Fern turned back to see, it was not a stopped car or a deer he braked for, but a flock of butterflies, hundreds of orange wings, tinking into the windshield. Some caught in the wipers, some hit and spun off. Mac put his arm out across Fern to hold her in while the car lurched to a stop. He jumped out, and then stood there for a long time, mute, looking up at the colored sky.

Fern was hit by the heat as she picked the dead flyers off the windshield. Their bodies were warm and their gorgeous wings nearly dissolved at her touch. Most she tossed onto the roadside. One, still half-beating, she dropped and quietly crushed under her shoe. She hoped Mac did not see. Maggie the dog came back to her.

"I need to use the phone again," Fern said. "At the next place."

An hour later she stood at a payphone that was almost too hot to hold in her hand and deposited a handful of quarters. This time she did not call her own house. The secretary at the vet answered and Fern said, "Don't kill my dog. I don't want you to put Maggie to sleep."

The boys had been given a teepee for Christmas last year, which Cricket realized with a sweep of joy that woke her up at dawn and jigged her blood. She did not bother the sleeping boys before she ran into the basement and found it, dusty and toppled, next to a box of abandoned stuffed animals and a rusted lawn mower. She carried the poles out to the lawn first and had to stand on a chair to attach the fabric. She was good at this, which did not surprise her. The teepee was not big, but Cricket figured if they curled up they could all three lie down inside.

It smelled like motor oil and there were

inelegant pictures of deer and arrows, but through the hole in the middle were the three crossed poles and beyond them the blue sky, and those things were true beyond this backyard, beyond their neighborhood, beyond the parentlessness. Wherever their mother and father were, the sky also was, and Maggie was under it too. Cricket went into the house and dragged her boys out of bed saying, "Come see, come see the home I've made for us." They were as pleased as she was, and immediately they all went gathering blankets to make a rug, pillows for comfort, the stash of canned goods, suitcases with clothes. They tried to make a fire by rubbing sticks together but could not even get a spark or tinder so they brought matches and a newspaper with a cover story about a Mafioso who'd donated thousands to charity on the same day he had killed three people. They burned it. The man's face, red from the Florida sun, went black and ashed. The children were filled with celebration. They were native to this backyard and it was morning-cold and the sun was coming over the lip of the roof and they were eating breakfast out of a can. The boys, in unison, said, "Let's never go to school ever again." Cricket knew what they meant and here they were with no adult supervision and no one to make them behave. The trouble was that she wanted to go to school. She wanted to see Miss Nolan, she wanted to go to the bathroom, turn the lights off and find out what would happen.

"Lucky for you, it's Saturday," she said. Cricket turned on the hose and they wetted the shirts they had worn the day before and sponged themselves down. Their skin puckered in the cold water. Their scalps ached when Cricket doused them.

The children ranged around the yard gathering wood. They wore their headbands and painted slashes of color under their eyes with their mother's lipstick. They discussed new names: Wind-feather, said James. Deer-paw, said Will. Cricket already had an Indian name, they agreed. She was the lucky one, born better.

In another version of their house and yard before anything had been built there, before there was such a thing as the city, a non-imaginary Native family had lived in this same spot. When the ships began to arrive from the Old World, these people were the first to make contact. An anthropologist had gathered the family together and drawn pictures of them with their long braids, their leather clothes, their New World faces. The anthropologist told the Indians that they were beautiful savages, so much closer to nature. To him, their beauty was like that of the tiger, the peacock. The anthropologist's painting traveled with him like a treasure until America was America. It was presented, along with a portfolio of others like it, to the young country's President as a gift, but he refused to hang them. "The Indians are an obstacle to expansion," he said, "and nothing more."

By then, the tribe that had covered the land around the bay had mostly died off. First, from foreign fever, next from foreign slaughter. A few members remained, adopted some of the new religion, went to the new schools, most lost their language. Their descendants still lived nearby, though Cricket never thought of Boston as a place where Indians could be. The whole idea of them was too storybook, too long-distance. People like that, she thought, needed the huge expanse of a western desert. People like that could not live in this kind of density. Where there would have been fishermen out in a canoe at night, stirring the phosphorescent sea with their oars, Cricket thought only of lean men running long, dry distances to catch up to a herd of antelope. Where there would have been roundhouses made of birch bark, Cricket only imagined teepees.

Of course she knew the story of the first Thanksgiving with its benign savages and needy settlers, and had made the construction paper pilgrim hats and Indian feather headbands each year at school, had even visited the site where the colonists came ashore, but the story was so diluted by the modern city that she could not hold on to it. If the ghosts of that long-ago family still circled this backyard, Cricket did not sense them. If their Massachusetts descendants lived in the neighborhood, some strain of that old blood in one of the brick houses, she would have been sorry to know it. She would have been sorry to know that her version was an invention, the truth infected with hundreds of years of tragedy.

After breakfast, the children, in their plaid pants and T-shirts and headbands, took to the neighborhood but did so under cover of hedges, hid behind parked cars. Likely, they were seen but written off as kids at play. Their *Lost Dog* posters were still up and the corners were sagging. They missed Maggie more and not less than ever. They needed her. Cricket asked the same question she had been asking every few hours: When should we assume no one is coming back? The answer had been recalculated each time and pushed farther back. At first she had told herself not to worry until bedtime. The next day she had decided her parents would be home by the time school let out. Then it was the next morning. Now she was giving the world the rest of the weekend to return to sense-making.

The three braves sneaked into the backyard belonging to the boys' friend Tommy because Will remembered a raspberry bush there. Tommy's parents were unfashionably in love for their stage of marriage. The children would not have been able to articulate the problem, but they picked up on their parents' discomfort around the couple. By that time, husband-and-wifedom should be transactional, functional, domestic duties divided up, a weekly date to the movies, monthly love-making in a completely darkened room after each partner had showered. Without anyone having explained it, the other couples all understood this. Tommy Smith was an only child to boot, which made all the sex the adults knew his parents were having utterly indulgent, producing no concrete result. Enjoyment was not the work of the upper class. To prove that they

368

were worthy of their wealth, they had all silently agreed to remain in the upper margins of unhappiness. Some had fun in private, in secret, but the volume was kept low in public. No one deserved fortune and joy both.

Cricket and the boys crouched, feathers in their hair and leather strips around their foreheads, looking into the Smiths' kitchen window where a pile of dishes sat in the sink and the woman of the house, in cutoff shorts and a blouse, cut a fat slice of butter for her bread. She was reading a paperback. They imagined that she was listening to the radio, something jazzy with a throaty singer who certainly dressed in sequins. And then, as if scripted, Mr. Smith walked into the room with his long hair wet, wearing nothing but a towel, which he dropped. Cricket wanted to cover her brothers' eyes but did not manage it in time.

"Don't look," she said, looking.

"Sure," they said back, looking. There was a lot of smashedmouth kissing before the locked pair fumbled away and left a buzz in the children's ears. Tommy, poor Tommy, the boys thought. Was he hiding out in his room? Had he been sent away to a wretched aunt for the morning so that his parents could be alone and awful? This proved it:

civilization was no good. The boys wanted the big grassy plains more than ever. Animals and meat, tribes and fire. Cricket, if she had been alone and unwatched, would have climbed dangerously high in the big maple in order to peer through the upstairs window. In her life, she had never seen love happen this way and she wanted it not to end. She wanted, someday, to be on the inside of that kiss.

"Come on," Will said. "That was disgusting."

"Yes," said Cricket because they would never trust her again if she said how she really felt.

At the next house a man sat at a big wooden desk with reading glasses and a stack of bills. The thick brown carpet had vacuum marks in it. The walls were painted beige and were undecorated. The hand on the grandfather clock ticked along. Nothing mattered in there, the children were sure of it. This was every Saturday and would continue to be, and the weather did not matter and the happenings of the world did not matter. Adults worked hard to shave down the inconvenient and difficult edges — love smoothed over, war and death sanded out — until all that remained was a midline. A routine. Cricket was old enough to know that she was meant to inherit this same equator, to resist the pull of her own north and south. She was meant to find a good-enough life and settle into its quiet.

Cricket, surprising herself, backed up, picked up a big rock and threw it through the window. Her brothers looked at her in shock and reverence. They would never not love her, no matter what she did for the rest of her life. This was why she was their leader. In the long second that followed, the man looked up and the kids ducked down, and then they ran as fast as a herd of deer, ducking and dodging and taking cover. Maybe he had seen them, their backs, just a flash. Maybe they would be caught and dragged to the police. Regret arrived reflexively, then subsided.

In the park, the three hid behind an ancient maple. A small dog pooped in the dead grass and its owner looked the other way. No one seemed to be hunting them. What was actually in front of them were well-kept Victorian houses, rutless sidewalks, streets with yellow dividing lines. What they saw: elk, buffalo, a ring of mountains dark as a bruise, snow already dusting their tops. They could smell their campfire, they could smell the bears that lived nearby, their oily hides. The wish was to run, fast and unyielding, and they climbed out of the tree and took off, crossing their city as outsiders until their lungs burst and their eyes watered and they collapsed in their own backyard, a heap. Other days had mattered, other days had been good, but these three children were in no way untrue, this day. They were absolutely themselves.

They ventured back inside and gathered more supplies. A pot, more beans, bread and butter. Butter, they knew, was probably not a Plains Indian truth, but they liked it and also they felt they should learn to be resourceful, use what they could find. If the Plains Indians had come upon butter, however that might have happened, the children were sure they would not have left it to rot.

The night was harder than the day, but the children stayed warm with nearness. The children lay on their mats in the teepee and Cricket gathered her brothers close and told them one of Miss Nolan's stories, finding that she could put on the teacher's voice, replicate her cadence and her language as if the story held some of the woman itself.

"Some Indians," she started, "believed that the mountains where they lived were the center of the earth. It was an island and they were floating on it, suspended by four cords from the sky. Before there was an earth, everyone lived in the sky and it was crowded. One day, a beetle dove down into the water, and he burrowed into the mud and lifted an island up on his back. The beating of a buzzard's wings made the mountains and valleys, and the plants and animals came down from the sky. A man hunted and skinned the animals and washed them in the river. A boy-child sprang from the bloody river, and the man brought him back to the woman who had always wanted a son even though that idea hadn't existed until right that minute. The boy was wild and they could not tame him. His hair was snaky and tangled and he wanted to eat only raw meat and never to wash. He ran off for days at a time and his parents did not know where he was. He could climb trees like a bear, and he could burrow like a rabbit. His parents were so proud of him, and they missed him when he was gone, but they did not try to change him because they were wise and knew that loving this boy meant being hurt by him. Two more boys soon joined the first.

"One day, the brothers watched as their mother rubbed her belly and corn spilled out into a basket, and then she rubbed her armpits and beans poured forth. The boys snickered and snorted and turned away. A mother shouldn't keep having a body after her children are born. The boys began to sharpen their sticks, because this was a witch, and it was their duty to do away with her. She knew it, the mother, before she even saw them making spears. Her skin knew it. When your child is going to kill you, the blood in your body has a different feel.

"When the troop came at her in the early morning with their spear-points, she looked at their eyes, which were the color of turquoise because they were made of that stone, that's where the stone comes from, and the mother said, 'After you're done, drag my body in eight circles around the house. Where my blood spills, corn and beans will grow.' Even then she wanted to take care of them. Even then, she was a mother.

"The boys took the woman by the hand and walked her outside where the day was white with sun. They laid her down, made a small pillow for her head from corn husks, and she was proud of them and thankful. They raised their stakes gleefully. They believed in the rightness of their motions. They had never felt more loved, and they never would. They felt the resistance of their

374

mother's body under the sharp wood, and they pressed against it. It was hot and the blood was free and thick.

"It was hard work, killing the only woman in the world with pine spears, and it only got hotter as they worked. By the time she was gone and the boys put their spears down, they could not believe how quiet it was, they could not believe how quickly the flies came. They were too tired to drag the body of their mother around the house in eight circles and went around only twice. They found shade and they lay in it, spread out so as not to touch each other, so as not to get into the heat of another brother, and they slept for three days straight."

Her brothers fell asleep to this story, but Cricket was sleepless. She knew they had not killed their parents — a thing like that is something you don't have a question about. Being abandoned felt like being abandoned. It was plain and sad and she would almost rather have been at fault.

In the morning there was a dead fawn in the backyard.

The animal had cooled and looked sleepish and peaceful. She showed no visible wounds, and the children felt that they would have been able to tell if she had died afraid. Fear was a mark you did not lose.

"Sweet fawn, poor fawn," they chanted. All of them had thought about dying in the days since they had been abandoned. There was no one to protect them from any of the many dangers of the world: poison, robbers, floods, hurricanes, famines, disease. This small animal felt like a sign of what was to come. The fawn might have lived a few days alone in the wooded corners of the city, finding food and shelter. It might have been her will that went first, or perhaps she had simply grown too hungry. Maybe she had watched the children and decided to trust them but came a few feet short of their tent. Cricket wished she had not slept so soundly. She should have heard the fawn and coaxed it close with sugar water. She would have nursed it back to health.

The children kept waiting for the fawn's mother to appear at the fenceline. Mothers, in general, seemed to be scarce.

Cricket thought of her homework assignment about the buffalo. She thought of all the things a resourceful person could make out of a dead animal. She looked at the hooves and tried to see small cups. She looked at the two stubs of horns, still fuzzy, and tried to see something that could be carved into jewelry. She wanted to bring these things to Miss Nolan. Cricket went inside and found a sharp knife. She knelt beside the spotted fawn and willed her hand to make a cut at the spine's ridge. It was harder than she would have thought and there was blood right away. The boys were shocked into stillness. The fawn jerked under Cricket's knife and the skin separated as she went, but when she tried to peel it from the body, Will threw up and Cricket was grateful for a reason to stop. She wished she could uncut the cut. Now the fawn was dead and undone too.

"We at least have to thank her for her service," she said. "We at least have to bury her."

Cricket carried the body to the edge of the yard and settled it in the ferns. While Cricket took her clothes off and washed the blood from her own skin, which she could not help but imagine now as a sliceable surface, the boys ran madly around the yard picking flowers. They invoked whatever gods and saints and angels they could remember from their lessons. Michael, Jesus, Christopher, Moses, Odin, Poseidon. They chanted while they put their good, young bodies to work. They added dirt until the fawn was a hill and then decorated the hill with flowers.

"The soil here will be very rich," Cricket said. She was still naked and the boys decided to take their clothes off too. The ceremony immediately felt more important.

"We should grow corn and beans," said Will, thinking of Cricket's story. Inside they ravaged the cabinets, hunting for plantables. The children had no time for neatness. This was a ceremony. Nothing was more important than this. They found popcorn in one jar and Will poured it into the waiting hands of his sister like it was precious gold. All over the floor, beads of corn tinked and escaped under the lip of the sink, behind the chairs, beneath the table. The children walked outside with their cupped hands, slowly, slowly, transporting a little bit of life out to the dead. They poured the seeds over the fawn and pressed them into her soil.

"Grow," they said. "Grow, grow."

When Edgar awoke on deck he reached for his glasses, but they were not on his chest where he had put them. He sat up. His glasses were not anywhere around him. He looked at the ocean and knew. He imagined his glasses slipping silently into the sea. "Shit," he said. "Shit, shit." The world, without his bottle-thick lenses, was all smudge and smear. Glory woke up and looked at him. "Morning, handsome," she said.

"I lost my glasses," he told her.

"Do you have a spare pair?"

Edgar had never lost his glasses. The only time they were not on his face they were on the bedside table, safe. Edgar shook his head.

He got up, not wanting to admit how compromised he was. He cooked oatmeal but his eyes made things harder. He had to put his face directly over the drawer to find a big spoon. His feet were hungry for the old paths of his familiar house.

Glory sat down at the table, the slip of a silk robe hardly bothering to cover her.

She had plenty of pretty, even if Edgar could hardly see it. He was ashamed to tell her how blind he was. As if this woman would have to watch him turn decrepit and old right now, today. Their trip was a moment plucked out of real life, a moment in which two young-enough bodies tried to pretend that the future and the past did not exist, that there was nothing else but pleasure on the surface of the earth. Edgar did not speak during breakfast. Glory was a blur of skin, hair, the dark holes of eyes. Finally he said, "I really can't see."

"Shitty," she said. "Do you want to

smoke?" she said, taking a little green bud out of her metal cigarette case.

It was not the first thought, but it was not the last either, the thought that God had done this, taken the world away as punishment. Edgar did not say this out loud in case Glory was already thinking it. She worried something around her neck, the vague shape of her hand at her collarbone. He leaned close to see it: a gold cross on a chain. It was as if it had grown on Glory's skin, seeded by uncertainty.

"Have you always had that?" Edgar asked.

"It was a gift from my husband or my father, I can't remember which," she said.

Men, landbound and restless for her return. Edgar wished it would go away again, leave them symbol-less and quiet.

"You don't *believe,* do you?"

"It's just jewelry," she said, lighting a match.

Edgar did not want Glory so close to him. She smelled like dried sweat and her breath was smoke-stale. "Maybe I should take a nap," he told her. He went below and curled in his bunk, which smelled of wet wool. It was dark and warm and too small and he tried to sleep but couldn't. Edgar picked at a knot in the wood.

Fern came into his head. Her fingers,

which had cooled him out of so many fevers. She who knew to bring hot lemon-water first, then cold juice, then a pot of boiling water with torn mint leaves and a towel for him to drape over his head to catch the steam. She who brought saltwater to gargle, lozenges to suck, pillows with fresh cases. She whom he had loved hardest when things were worst and when they were best.

Once, when Cricket was sick with a cough, Fern had gone into her room to help her back to sleep and come back to bed weeping. Edgar had panicked, sure that something was very wrong with his daughter.

"She's okay," Fern had said. "She's going to be okay." Somewhere in Africa people were dying of an incurable contagious disease and Fern admitted to Edgar that she had understood, holding her feverish girl in her arms, that she would take care of her daughter even if it meant that she herself would get sick and die. "And there's no question. Just none," she had said.

Edgar had not known if he would sacrifice himself. He felt terrible that he might hope to live beyond. He also thought that before the children were born Fern would have crawled in beside a sick Edgar and held a frozen washcloth on his forehead, prepared to die a few days after he did. Edgar remembered getting sick when the boys were two, a bad flu, and Fern had stood at the doorway, blown him a kiss. She had no longer been able to afford to infect herself. She had paid for every comfort — cold watermelon, cashmere socks, good books — and had delivered them on a tray, then scrubbed her hands and arms up to the elbow. Every part of her had been in his room except her body.

And his own mother? He tried to remember being cared for by her, but Mary took care of details and not people. For a party, she would sacrifice her own health and sanity. For sickness, she sent a nurse.

When Edgar's cousin had died of a stroke at twenty-eight, Mary never once went to the hospital, but she did seek out every friend he had ever made, every girl he had ever kissed, every teacher and coach, and when they all gathered for the funeral she had filled the room with fifty bouquets of white roses, platters and platters of roast turkey, pastas, sweating piles of vegetables, little mushroom pastries that waiters passed incessantly around, forcing everyone to take another and another. There were mashed potatoes and macaroni and cheese and a cream soup that was pale, mint green and went entirely uneaten. There were vegetable salads and fruit salads and seven different kinds of bread and pats of cold butter molded to look like daisies.

Edgar's mother had set the roomful of people to the work of closure, that untrue moment. She watched the boy's parents, her brother and sister-in-law, to see if the cure was working. Edgar's mother's makeup was right all day, no streaks, no smudges. The guests ate and ate and all of them cried when people stood to remember the dead boy. All except Mary. And in the morning, his mother had baked a breakfast cake, poured fresh juice from a frosted pitcher and sat down beneath the hum of a violin concerto to scrub clean the silver that had touched the lips of the grieving.

Edgar opened his eyes to the unfocus of the world and closed them again. Opened, closed. "I am basically blind," he said. He had never thought this before, his eyesight so fixable in the modern world. He couldn't see detail in anything more than a few inches from his face, and he was in the middle of the ocean. Edgar's heart sped up and he did not have enough air and he wanted to sit but couldn't in the tight space of the bunk. He jumped out, clambered upstairs and, dizzy, lay down on the deck of his boat.

The boat rocked. Beneath him was everything — the depths and depths, the cold blue a mile down and thousands of miles across. He could have rolled quietly off the *Ever Land,* let his body take water in, sunk or floated, and the sea would have made no sound. The birds would not have changed their pattern. Above him was the vast expanse of pale sky, the entire universe, now just a blue light. Land seemed very, very far away. His form was so small that it might as well not even have existed. Edgar, never seasick in his life, was seasick now. He reached his hands out and grabbed at the wood and what he wanted to find there was grass, leaves, soil. Fern — the earthen thing he wanted to find was Fern. "What have I done?" he said to the blue above and the blue below. There were things he wanted to see again: Cricket performing a dance in the living room, the boys trenching on the beach. All those elements he had gone seeking, all that wide-open, but what he needed was the landscape of his own life. What he felt could not be described as missing — one person wishing to be nearer to another. Instead, Edgar, sea-tossed and gripping the wooden deck with his fingertips to keep from throwing up — understood that his body, his self, was not individual but shared, that to put too much distance between himself and his wife, his children, was to disassemble something whole. He was sightless now, and what would go next if he stayed away? He was just a body, a million tiny mechanisms, any of which could go wrong. Water slapped at the hull of the tiny craft. Edgar could hear Glory washing dishes in the cabin. He imagined full black and then soundlessness too.

Edgar would have done anything to hold Fern's hands over his closed eyes. Just for the feel of her particular palms. He knelt and then stood and that's when darkness fell over him.

The next thing Edgar knew he was in the water and Glory was throwing the life preserver in and diving in after him and he was fine, spitting but fine, and he took the ring but pushed the woman away. "Don't fucking push me, you asshole, you fucking asshole. Were you trying to *drown* yourself? What the fuck is this? I come out here for a few weeks of fun and you won't even fuck me anymore and then I have to save your life? I don't know how to fucking sail. What the fuck am I supposed to do if you die?"

Edgar said, "I didn't mean to. I think I fell." He was pale.

385

"Oh," she said. "I'm sorry, but fuck."

"It's time to turn back," Edgar said, holding on to the ring. He was still dizzy and he still couldn't see and he still felt cored out.

"Which shore are we closer to?" she asked. "I'm sure they have optometrists in Bermuda."

"We're about halfway. But I want to go home."

Glory would have preferred to keep sailing east. Her skin was thirsty for the pale blue water they had been traveling towards. An unreached island was a special kind of disappointment. "Fine. Can you do it?" It was the question they had both been asking themselves. They were surrounded by many miles of water and the only sailor on board was hardly sighted.

"You'll have to help," Edgar said.

They swam to the ladder and pulled themselves up. Glory settled Edgar in a deck chair with water and a sliced apple and bread and butter. He breathed in and he breathed out, and none of it made it less scary to be nearly blind. She smoked. Edgar and Glory floated. They were anchored, unmoving, and far.

Edgar began to unfasten and untie. Glory listened to his instructions and did as he asked. He could sail, sailing was known in his body, and he could still see colors and vague shapes, but he felt better knowing that there was one good set of eyes on board. They were a quiet and unaffectionate team. He had wanted sun and distance and she had wanted the knots two bodies can make of each other. Disability was a third party. How quickly the pull could weaken.

Though the view was the same, it felt entirely different to travel in the opposite direction. Bermuda receded. The powder sand, the gin-clear water, the tiny satellite islands believed to hold both pirate treasure and the ghosts of the crew that had been killed to haunt that treasure. There was no fantasy ahead of Edgar and Glory. The only unknown was the future, the damage they had done to their own lives.

Edgar did not realize it, but his parents were also sailing, and not far away. Hugh and Mary had wanted the same thing Edgar did: away. Theirs was a weekend excursion. At the moment that Edgar and Glory turned towards home, Mary was squeezing limes to put into their cocktails. She was marinating the meat they would grill. Hugh was reading a magazine article about the upcoming elections and smoking a cigar.

He looked up every few minutes to survey the horizon, to admire the taut mainsail, sweeping them outward.

The two boats might have crossed paths if Edgar and Glory had continued on, if the wind had pushed them a few degrees southwest, if they had caught up to a particular current that a school of striped bass was also riding, if Mary had insisted on an after-lunch swim. It could have happened that Edgar and his parents would have found themselves in the exact same spot on the Atlantic Ocean. Edgar would either have had to explain Glory or hide her, both of which would have made something go flat in him. He would have seen his shirtless father, his neck just beginning to show the sunburn that would keep him awake all night, his legs shimmering with dry salt just as Edgar's legs were, his hands ready to tie or release or tighten a rope just as Edgar's hands were, and maybe seeing that would have felt like proof of the thought that had entered Edgar's mind — that he could take over his father's life. That it was worth it. He had written his book just like he had said he wanted to and he knew that it was good enough to be published and maybe those things were enough. Maybe the doing was what mattered. He had people to care for. He had a lived life and maybe that was bigger than the imagined one, bigger than the one he led in his head.

And maybe watching his mother come up from below and holler with joy at the sight of her son like a mirage would have had the same effect on Edgar that his faded eyesight did: a skeletal want for his wife, for the person who loved him like that. The tack-sharp feeling that he was at sea with the wrong woman, that there was a story without his family but not a life.

But the two boats grew farther apart instead of nearer. None of them would ever know that they had brushed so close.

Edgar knew there would be a storm before the clouds or the wind or the rain. The air changed. The water hummed. Edgar kept the sheet tight, trying to make time before they couldn't anymore. Maybe they would die out there, he thought. Maybe that was the design of this trip — to quietly extinguish them, the dangerous flames of them, in the saltsea. Hero or villain or slave, the lungs fill with water, the body falls deeper, the fish come. On another day there might have been a small part of Edgar that wanted this. To fall not to the small, suburban unhappiness of a particular decade, a particular generation, but to nature.

The storm battered. Glory, finally, got sick. She didn't want or not want; she couldn't. She said, "This is the worst feeling I have ever felt," hung, like laundry, over the edge, a rope around her waist so the whole of her did not pour overboard. Edgar never would have found her again in all this seafoam.

"This is not a terrible storm," he said. "It will be over in a few hours." She looked at him with contempt.

"Who are you?" she asked. "I hate you."

"Do you want to smoke?" he asked.

"I want to die," she said.

Edgar knew they had to ride the storm out. There was no way to flee. To be tossed was their job.

They went belowdecks when Glory could. The cabin was dark and musky and Edgar was aware of the press of that small space. Right then floating and tossing, he was a husband, he was a father, he was a son. He felt the distance, the terrible miles and miles he had gone. His life was too far. Even the horizon was unclear.

When the storm died down, Glory reported that there were two silver fish swimming in the caught water. "We should eat them," he said. Glory netted and Edgar held them down on deck while she bashed. He could help bail, but first he would heat the grill and they would eat. That, at least. He remembered playing by the river as a boy, catching frogs. One spring, there were babies, weightless but sticky in the hand. Edgar, once, needing to know the feeling, crushed one of the tiny creatures in his fist. It went so easily. Not even the bones held.

"I'm sorry," he said to Glory, who was washing her face, running freshwater through her hair.

"Some days I do believe in God. I want to," she said.

"You want someone powerful who can release you," he said, understanding perfectly.

"Maybe that's who He will turn out to be. Or else the other kind."

They grilled the fish and there was even a lemon. When cut, the fragrance was so earthly, so terrestrial, it made Edgar ache. It was the kindest feeling, this homesickness, this desire for the very thing that actually belonged to him. It was good to be a land creature in love with the land.

"Are you getting used to not being able to see?" Glory asked. She rubbed her hands together to warm them, and reached out to Edgar's face.

"Not at all."

"Luckily there's nothing actually wrong."

"Sure." He paused. "Tell me something about yourself. Tell me something you have done that you like," he said. As if they'd only just met, as if they had not already saved and ruined each other's lives.

"In junior high school, I tried out for the cheerleading team. I had these bangs. I was not well-liked. The only reason anyone was nice to me was because my parents were unspeakably rich. I thought, what if? I made up a routine and practiced in my room. I can't imagine what it looked like, I actually cannot imagine. I was not chosen. I'm sort of proud of myself for doing that. For being so oblivious as to think I might make it."

"You could have been good."

"I was not good."

There was a pause. "Will he take you back?" Edgar asked.

They had nothing to offer each other after this journey was over. Neither of them, Edgar realized, had ever thought so.

"He'll take me back and he'll forgive me eventually. That will probably be my project for a while." This was Edgar's first leaving but not Glory's. Like an experienced doctor, she knew what wounds to expect from this particular kind of explosion. She knew how to sew them closed and keep them clean, how to pour tonic over. She also knew that the scars were worse, and permanent.

Glory smoked and imagined that John had felt it the moment the sloop on which his beloved sailed had turned back towards the homeshore. She pictured him sweeping his mother's floor and kissing her on the forehead and getting into his car. As Glory made her way, so did John. The forests, which they had driven through together dozens of times, were maple, oak. He would listen to cello concertos and leave the windows open when he went into the diner for a tuna sandwich and a coffee. He too would know what work was ahead — the understanding that would come quickly and the understanding that would never come.

John would be at home when Glory arrived. He would be sitting in his armchair not reading, not watching television, just waiting. She would look at him and he would be just as boring as ever, but he would be hers.

"Do you want to go to Mexico?" she would ask. "On anything other than a boat?"

Both of them were still packed from their journeys so all they would have to do was turn off the lights and lock the door behind them. On the airplane, Glory would take

John's hand and put her head on his shoulder while they waited to rise.

Edgar slept on deck that night and let Glory have the berth. Her sympathy and touch would have cost him something. A well man could wake up in another woman's bed, but a helpless man was too sad to. The tug towards home was as strong as a thick line, woven through his ribs and tied tight. He thought of the sights he had to look forward to: the twins at nineteen years old, their faces longer, a shadow of beard on their cheeks, about to turn into the people they would always be. He thought of Cricket at thirty, married to someone of her own choosing. He thought of Fern. He wanted his wife to see him get old and for him to know all the versions of her face. That night, lying on the deck of the *Ever Land,* Edgar looked up at the dark. Above him, the blurred scuff of the Milky Way.

"Land ho," Glory said in the morning. Edgar looked out but the shape was inexact. He squinted, and it did not come clear.

"Do you have glasses at your house? Do you need a ride?"

"No. I'll take a taxi. You should go home."

"It was fun. At least it started out being fun," Glory said.

"Should we say goodbye here?" Edgar asked, wanting some space in which to seal this opening they had made. The water churned below them. Their arms around each other were cool and they did not hold long.

For Edgar, the city in which he lived, the coastline that he had sailed towards for the last several years of his life, disappeared the closer they got.

Later that night Fern and Mac stopped alongside the big river, muddy and roping inside its banks. *M-I-S-S-I-S-S-I-P-P-I,* she said in her head. They looked out at it and tried to hear the water there, but it was too slow, too constant. There were ghosts of white shorebirds on the bank of a small island, and some in the air, and the trees were so thick with leaves they looked trunk-less. Fern and Mac were standing on a hill above the water and there was a path down to it and many small footprints. Fern wanted the children who left them to have been carrying homemade fishing poles, wearing half-crushed hats, chewing a piece of hay in the sides of their mouths. There should be places that stay the same. Museum-of-life places, preserved for remembering.

Fern was tired from a long drive and her

body still vibrated from the car and it was a warm night, and the birds and the water and the clouded night. Fern let herself fall into the generous pillar of the giant. She rested her head back and let it settle against the top of his belly. She could hear the process within: air and liquid, moving through.

It was more than they had touched since their wedding. Fern's skin was still used to Edgar only. It made her want to go home. The craving for the twins' weight in her lap came at her fast. Fern thought of a feverish Cricket asleep, her face red and the dreams making the pale pulse of her eyelids go, the way Fern had knelt at the bedside and put her head down against the child to try to absorb some heat, for both of their sakes. Fern remembered bringing Cricket an apple to eat when she was finally hungry. She had taken a few bites and left it on the bed when she fell asleep. Fern had picked it up and bitten the uneaten half and what she had tasted, strongly, was not the fruit's flesh but the taste of her daughter's palmsweat. Soon, the child would be up again, and running, and hungry and doing something sweet or dangerous that Fern would have to put a stop to. But Fern had kept that fever day like a gem.

In that want for her real family, she leaned against Mac, and the giant put his big arms around her and they watched the river, which was a moving body, yet also so still.

Their heartbeats changed pace. Something new came to the surface. Fern felt a kindness flare up in her. She felt the gift that her body might be. Both of them were at a deficit. Charity made her warm, and she turned then, and she looked up into Mac's face, which the moon was whitening, and he looked back at her, the big black eyes, the bright teeth. He was her friend and she told herself that she could give him that missing thing, though later she would be able to admit that what she really wanted was the wound. She wanted it for herself for what she had done wrong and she wanted it for Edgar. Fern closed her eyes, and stood on tip-toes and waited to be kissed.

Fern half expected the scene around them to change, to take notice: birds lifting from the trees, the clouds breaking for a moment. She was winning something, is how it felt. She was the victor. Her tongue and his tongue, his cheeks a scrabble on hers. They had earned this honeymoon, finally, by the famous river, deep in the moss and muck of this country, far away from everything that was true about their past and everything that was not.

All the way to the hotel, she leaned into him, and his chest heaved a little too much, and she wanted more of that. More longing, more pain from it.

The only hotel was called the Locust Tree and it was half-fallen. The sign was neon, blinking to say that there were rooms to let. Fern went inside as always, and the lobby was a tiny room with a counter with a full ashtray and a small bell, like a church-bell, which Fern picked up and shook so that the tongue clanged.

A very fat, very old man came in. He had a few strands of hair, combed over, and a pair of large square wire-rimmed glasses. He said, "Cheapest room is six dollars." It was too little and it made Fern nervous. She was used to being better taken care of than that. After the rat room, they had avoided the worst places.

"What's the most expensive room?" she asked. It was one of the things she liked about traveling with someone who hid in the car — she could overspend and no one had to know.

"Ten. That one's got a closet."

"Nothing more than that?"

"I'll take your money, young girl," the

man said. He coughed into his hands then, hard and long and when he pulled them away, he cupped within them a small, golden ball of mucus, which he held as carefully as a robin's egg. He showed it to Fern, the slippery jewel, the dug-up treasure. "You're not a nurse, are you?" he asked.

"Ten. We'll take it," she said. "There are two of us." She wrote the last name in the greasy book and counted her money. The fat man continued to examine his hands, and to smile, and he yelled his thanks after Fern.

There was a cockroach on the bathroom floor, and nothing was whole. The headboard veneer was molting, the blanket was losing its fill, the mattress was concave. The water in the toilet was mineral yellow. Who knows how long it had been stagnant, what kinds of small creatures were growing within.

Mac and Fern fell into the pits of the bed. Fern removed the giant's clothes and he covered himself with the blanket. Batting fell out, banked up on the floor like fake snow. He begged for her, and unrolled her pants. The bed sank below them. They did not worry about their noises in such an establishment. *Let them hear us,* they both thought. Fern imagined the fat man and his bad lungs. It hurt a little bit, the giant's size.

The old question was still unanswered: Did it feel good? There was pleasure, definitely, in a job well done. A man on his back, the covers kicked off, sweating with his eyes closed and thankful.

After, Fern had the urge to walk to the bathroom so he could admire her from behind. Ridiculous, the thought — she was not that young, and when she had been, she would have been careful to keep covered up in the light. She felt small next to the giant, was that it? But she did not get up and walk, covered or bare, because she remembered the roach and the dirty toilet. *I just had sex with a giant,* she thought.

Mac asked for a cigarette, which they split, and after he fell too quickly asleep. He did not pull her into his chest, or trace her collarbone, or spread her hair across the pillow. Somewhere, these ideas had been seeded in her brain. She was the gift and the giver. Thanks ought to have been next.

The room grew more disgusting the later it got. The bugs were audible on the tile, and worse, inaudible on the carpet. Fern checked the chain lock on the door and it fell off into her hand. She dressed and lay back down on the farthest edge of the bed, away from the canyon Mac's body made, and Fern waited, eyes closed, for the infestation.

1966

The first time Fern and Edgar had touched
was at her Junior Dance. He was back from
college and had agreed, as a favor to his
mother, to take a neighbor girl who was as
uninterested in Edgar as he was in her. Fern
was in a sleeveless dress, the color of a vague
star. She had spread butter on her shoulders, just a thin slick of it because it made
her skin bright. It was not an idea she had
learned in a magazine or from a friend, but
something she had thought of that eager
night before, while she tried to seed her
dreams with the smell of a boy's cheek
against hers. Her mother would not have
approved, would probably have issued a
warning about some rabid dog that would
be attracted to her scent. At the country
club? Fern would have asked. A rabid dog?
So she kept it to herself. Her hair she
twisted up, the points of pins poking into
her scalp when she turned her head.

The night would be good, that was decided, voted upon. All the mothers had worked hard to ensure it. The mothers remembered falling in love as if it were a sudden amusement ride drop. Hands in the air, wind burning their eyeballs, down. All of it made Fern feel prematurely sad for her older self: she did not like the idea that this was the best part of her life. Could it really be that tight skin and blond hair defined the potential for happiness? Or was it just that when you got older, everyone started to die around you?

Fern, buttered shoulders and doubts, went to the dance on her own, having turned down all the invitations for dates from boys she did not want to feel obliged to kiss. It was not so different from any day at school, except for dresses. Boys hunched and punched, girls pattered and giggled and pointed. The boys' suits fit them sadly and seemed to be standing on their own, a little distance between fabric and skin. Inside the suits, the boys looked like boys. Scrawny and a little butchered by the process of growing as quickly as they were. The girls, at least some of them, managed the disguise. The girls seemed to want it more too. This was the prize of womanhood: looking angelic in a gown and someone asked you to dance and everyone in the room noticed you. The prize of manhood came slowly and later: earn something, put it away, buy yourself a car, flirt with the child's teacher, get a raise. Fern wondered where these two axes crossed — what single moment in the life of a man and woman, their lives joined forever, felt exactly the same amount of great to them both?

Edgar was there in handsome glasses with thick lenses. His date was with her friends and Edgar talked to the younger brother of a classmate. Fern appeared at the punch-bowl and Edgar stopped short. They had seen each other plenty of times at school, said congenial hellos, but never more than that. She saw him see her. He looked less dumbed by the slow music and intention of romance than some of the other boys. She caught his eye, and as practiced, looked demurely away. It was all that was needed and he came over, raised her gloved hand and kissed it. She regretted the gloves, regretted the missed opportunity to have lips on her skin. They danced, parted, drank punch separately, danced again. So many rules followed by all the young ladies and gentlemen. Somewhere along the way, between being swaddled, nannied babies, they had been infused with the knowledge of how to behave and could not help mimicking their mothers and fathers. Fern wondered if it was cellular — would an adopted daughter from some faraway, charity-deserving country wake up at seventeen knowing how to spear an olive and spit the pit into her napkin without anyone seeing it?

Along the edges of the room, the non-dancing tried to appear unafraid. The popular girls and boys looked away. One of the important skills of being socialized seemed to be the ability to overlook other people's unhappiness. Maybe the awkward ones would be pretty in college, or after, and if not, maybe they would be very successful, and if not that either, then they would be very giving, they would take care of the sick or the young or the old.

At the moment when Fern and Edgar had danced themselves into a corner, a huge wind slammed into the building and rattled the panes. They separated, the music stopped. The wind shrieked and pawed at the windows. The lights went out, girls screamed and huddled, boys just huddled. The teachers tried to act calm. Edgar looked at Fern and saw her hair shine in a flash of lightning. His hand gentled around her waist. In her ear he said, "It's dark now," and she knew just what he meant and turned to kiss him. It was the richest kind of darkness, the falling-into kind, and down they went, and they were holding on.

1976

Monday came and Cricket fell into its arms. There was a time by which all three must be dressed and human, having eaten bread and butter, having cleaned the tribe-paint from their faces so they looked like nice little white children. She watched the colors run from her brothers' wet cheeks like blood and silt. They were giving up their orphaned selves and acting like all the other parented boys with alive dogs and selves that had not recently come up bruised.

Cricket made sure shoes were tightly tied. She brushed her hair and styled it in the youngest way she knew how — two braids tied with navy blue ribbons — wanting not to be grown today. If she could look like a child maybe someone would take care of her. These were small illusions — the three little orphans would go unnoticed. The decision had to be made about whether to go inside again and get fresh clothes or if they should wear last week's uniforms. It was hard to be near the old version of life because it made it obvious how far away they had drifted. Once, their mother had worried for a week over a decision about the upholstery for the new sofa and whether red sent the wrong message. Once, their father had paged the many subscribed-to but rarely read magazines while drinking weak coffee in the rocker by the window. Maggie had slept there, and there and there. The house was full of ghosts. Cricket went in alone and fast, gathered what she needed and ran back out to the safety of the yard.

This morning, they did not bother to light a fire in order to warm their bread. The need for ritual had not quieted, but it had thickened. It was the only medicine and they were worried about using it up. Cricket held the hose while her brothers drank. They looked at the fawn's hill, the now wilted petals, the demonstration of their love looking smaller the next day. There would be no one here to keep watch. No one to befriend the mother if she came.

When it was time, the boys waited at the gate in their blue-and-whites, little ties hanging around their necks, and Cricket checked their cheeks and hair to make sure they would pass. She slipped the latch and out they went onto the sidewalk with their bookbags and their finished homework as if they were the same as all the other kids, alarm-clock grumpy, cheeks pillow-creased. Cricket still stepped over the cracks like she had always done, and she still noticed the difference between smells as they passed houses — bacon, woodfire, cold brick. The boys were slack. Their bags seemed too heavy, but as they came closer, as other children appeared like wild game on the horizon, the boys stood taller. Cricket could see them get their boyness back, remember that there were balls to kick and sticks to swing and girls to tease. She could see the blood return. They would be scratched up and happy by the end of the day, beaten back into their bodies by wind and the speed of their own legs, running towards base.

Cricket herself doubted that she would be so easily restored. Her head felt heavy, her brain. But it was a good sight, the flapping red and white of the flag and the gathered mass of young bodies, supervised. She knew her brothers would shuck her off when they got there, assert their independence, so before it was too late, she grabbed their hands, one in each of hers, and she squeezed tight. She wanted to cause enough pain to last them.

The classroom smelled like melted crayons. The fourth graders yowled and bittered at being back, stuffed their backpacks into cubbies, found their seats. No one except Cricket noticed that there was no Miss Nolan at the front of the room. They did sense a lack of balance: the room was a boat on which all the passengers were astern. The chatter continued, weekends were remembered, the near-loss of a softball team against the dreaded Somerville Pirates was recounted. Some kids had been taken back to the beach for the weekend, which was almost cruel, giving them summer in such a tiny sliver. They started to sense that someone, by now, ought to be forcing them into quiet. Someone ought to be civilizing them. *Ladies and gentlemen,* they were always being called when they were at their scrappiest, as if the name alone could cure them.

"Where is Miss Nolan?" the girls asked.

"This is excellent!" the boys yelled. "No teacher! Guys! No teacher!"

"Is she all right?" the girls asked.

The room hummed. Cricket wanted not to cry in front of friends and enemies, but she had already been abandoned enough this week. It was her. She was repellent to grown-ups. Wherever she went, the person taking care of her evaporated. She got up and went, as calmly as she could fake it, out the door and down the hall. In the other classrooms the children were quiet at their desks, following instructions from an adult with a lesson plan.

Someone else was standing in the stall next to Cricket, someone with big feet. Someone who was crying too. Cricket knew the shoes. They were the shoes of her beloved. She said, "Can I come over?" and wriggled under the wall. Miss Nolan looked at her like Cricket was a puppy and she sat down on the lidded toilet and Cricket crawled up into her teacher's lap. Miss Nolan received Cricket like she had been expecting her, like this had always been the plan. They held on tight. They soaked each other's shoulders.

"My mother died," Miss Nolan said. "I shouldn't be here."

Cricket thought of an early snow on the Great Plains, a small woman out gathering berries, lost in the whiteout. She thought of a gathered flock of mourners in the teepee, a good fire, food available but uneaten, the wind through the seams. "How?" she asked. "What happened?"

"A car accident on the expressway."

"The expressway?" Cricket tried to add the long strip of pavement, the rushing cars, toll plazas, to her idea of the plains. "I didn't know they had those."

Miss Nolan looked the girl over, swiped a tear away from each of their cheeks. "In New Jersey? Of course they do."

New Jersey was a brick and it hit Cricket hard. She said, "You aren't an Indian." She felt terribly stupid and terribly small. No one was from Montana, no one was from Oklahoma. They were all city kids. They were all part of the same tidy, boring tribe.

Miss Nolan kissed Cricket on the forehead. "You are sweet and good," she said.

Cricket wanted to ask about the lip-kiss last week, but she could not risk another loss. "Of course I knew that," she said, reinhabiting maturity. "I'm sorry about your mother. I actually kind of understand because my parents are gone too. They've been gone since Wednesday. We're orphans now."

Miss Nolan tried to conceal her panic. The girl looked clean and fed but probably in shock. Cricket did not see the effort it took for her teacher to keep a steady voice as she asked a lot of practical questions. Hospitals: not called due to fear of orphanage. Police: not called due to fear of orphanage. Relatives: not called due to fear of orphanage. Food: eaten. Sleep: slept. Safety: managed.

"You'll be so disappointed in me but a fawn died in our yard, and I tried to skin it but I couldn't. I'm sorry. I really tried. We buried her," Cricket said, wanting to prove that they were good survivors, that they could take care of something else even when they themselves were broken.

"I didn't expect you to know how to skin a *deer*. You poor ducklings," the good teacher said, and Cricket had never felt so grateful or stupid in her life. "You should have told me what was going on. We'll find them. I'm sure they're all right." Miss Nolan was relieved to have a situation to manage, to turn, for a moment, away from the ink-bloom of her mother's death.

"They could be not all right," Cricket said. She had allowed the possibility that her parents had left on purpose for a trip or to start a new life and the possibility that they had gotten lost or hurt, but to say out loud the fact that they could be dead carved her out.

"I'm going to help you," Miss Nolan said. "You are being taken care of." The woman took Cricket close and hugged her and it was this touch that Cricket understood she

413

needed, not a hot-mouth kiss, not the kind of close that she would look for later but the kind she needed now, had always needed: her small head against someone's chest, a heartbeat dull but steady beneath the bones.

They were still a long day's drive from Mac's son. Neither of them knew what to say about what they had done together. Fern had not realized that the desert was so big. Cows in the distance, horses sometimes, once a herd of elk, their wide racks up against the sky. "They look fake," Fern said. "They look too much like elk to be elk."

"You make no sense," Mac told her. The animals lowered their necks towards the ground.

"There's nothing to eat here," Fern said. The ground was brittle with sage.

"They spend their lives looking for food," Mac said. "They have to search all the time to get enough."

Even the sky was greenish and dry. Low mountains were a stripe between pale and pale.

Sex had been a mistake, of course, but Mac had also meant to make it. He had never expected Fern to love him in a realer world. He had taken advantage of her

distance, of her strained marriage. He knew
that escape, at this point, was starting to
wear at Fern like a blister. The generous
thing would have been to brush her off, to
hold her hand and talk about the river, go
for ice cream, keep things safe. He was not
sorry, though. He too deserved to be
touched. He wanted it, even if it would cost
them both. And anyway, he told himself,
her husband had surely slept with the other
woman by now, and it would be fairer for
Fern to come home with her own secret.

Fern, on her side of the car, was afraid of
the wreckage a body could cause. Edgar's
body, her body, Glory's, the giant's. She was
afraid that she would never be able to stop
causing damage, now that she had started.

They drove through mesquite and red
dust. The sky was bluer at the edges and
then purpled with rainclouds. They watched
for an hour as the storm came towards
them. The diagonal lines of rain, darkening
the ground beneath. It was dry, dry, dry
until the smell of the air changed and the
windshield turned milky with rain. Fern
looked at her companion, the bigness of his
face and chest. They had come all this way
together, and the rain and the butterflies
and all that new air in her bloodstream. She
did not know if she should hold his hand

415

and pretend to love him. They stopped and got out this time, and the rainwater was warm and the air was warm and it all smelled plant-bitter and grateful.

In all this space it felt safe to admit that a marriage, her marriage, could end. She imagined it this way: her on the sidewalk in front of the big house, mounds of belongings beside her. She would have chosen things to bring with her into the next life. The huge Swedish desk, a blond dresser. The headboard, which she knew was the very thing you were meant to get rid of in a divorce — keep the silver, but relieve yourself of the bed on which your marriage succeeded and failed. The past years belonged to her, even if the future did not.

Her parents, though dead, would be nonetheless ashamed.

She told Mac about going to the institution after Ben died. How in his room she had found children's books, the same ones they had read in the nooks by the fireplace when they were small. In the bottom corners there were grease stains from fingers, turning. It was a sour-smelling room, and the walls were soft blue, the color a sane person would choose for a crazy one. There was a small television, and a box of letters from Fern, which she took but did not read, not ever. She remembered writing them about the hugeness of motherhood, what it was like to live after your heart had been born out into the world and was at risk every second of every day. How Cricket liked to ride her bike too fast and play with animals, sharp-toothed dogs, possibly rabid, their mouths foaming while the child petted them and loved them and curled up against them. Little lion-tamer, ready to put her head into the mouths of beasts.

"I should have stopped them from performing the lobotomy," Fern said.

"It wasn't your job."

"That's why I always stood to the side. But my mother should not have been in charge and my father was too sick to be. Ben should never even have gone to basic training. I wish Edgar and I had brought him with us." She looked out at the desert, swooshing past. "I thought when you fell in love with someone you had to give your whole self over to them. I wish I had known that there was enough of me to share. I wish I hadn't left my brother behind." A vulture stood over the remains of something unrecognizable. "This might be a weird thing to say considering what happened last night, but when I first saw you I thought you were Ben."

Mac was glad that he could think of his big form at the end of the aisle as a gift. Not a gift for himself, but nice all the same.

Fern reached out and put her hand on Mac's leg.

He knew she wanted him to be an ax, swung against the wall to see if the house would stand. It wouldn't, he thought, if she was lucky. Not the house. But what was inside might.

"I'm not what you're looking for," he said, without turning towards her.

"What am I looking for?" Fern thought about the day with Ben after they had begun to cook his brain with electricity and drugs when he had shown her her own reflected face in her patent leather shoe. The answer was too easy. Love, home, herself — what else did people go searching for?

A herd of cows stood in the middle of the road ahead of them. Some of the cows had lain down. Some were looking, slack-eyed, at the cars. All were chewing. Mac slowed and stopped. The earth was pale, bleached by the sun. The plants were spiny and un-welcoming and the horizon was a long way off. The pickup truck in front of them veered off the road through the cactus and scrub until it had passed the herd. It would take an hour for the air to clear of its dust.

Fern got out. She walked over to the cows and could smell them as she approached. Hay and urine and mud and shit. From the car they seemed stupid, from up close they seemed big. "Cows!" she said. "Shoo!" Flies, like a thick black aura, rose off the animals and resettled.

From the other direction came an old red van. It stopped and out stepped two young women with lots of eyeliner and shaggy hair and big sunglasses. They smelled of smoke and one of them was holding a kitten. They looked to Fern like they had just woken up after a long decade in California.

"Cows in the road," Fern said. The girls looked bored. "They don't seem to want to move."

"Have you been to Houston?" one of the girls asked. "Her brother lives there. He's cool. We're going to become airline stewardesses. In the sky you don't have to deal with this kind of shit."

One cow let the weight of her body fall back with a deep groan — Fern knew it was a she because her teats rested in front of her, engorged.

Mac got out but stayed close to the car. It's what her brother would have done too. How afraid a person could be, how big and how afraid. She stood close to him as she would have with Ben.

Thunder clapped. From where? — the sky was clean. The cows stood and ran awkwardly into the desert. Hooves rang hard against the dirt. Dust rose out and up, and it glinted.

"Mica," Mac said, without Fern asking. They were standing in a glittering fog.

Mac went into a restaurant and Fern stood at the payphone in the shade, leaned against the stucco wall. She would ask the question even if there was no answer. She wanted to make noise occur in her own home, to create the specific sound of the phones in the big living room and the kitchen, like a pair of birds calling to each other. She dialed collect and held the phone away from her ear so that she could imagine that she was hearing the real ringing in the real house, the real life. Not this faraway tone in the hotel telephone.

And then: "Hello?" It was Edgar's voice.

The taxi drove to Edgar's house the same way he would have gone, the way his hands knew and his feet knew, drawing back at the reds and pressing down at the greens. Stop signs and straightaways all mapped in Edgar's reflexes.

He had had the keys in his pocket all this time. The house smelled its old smell. It was empty, was all. He thought of the agreement made all those long agos, sickness and health. He had not considered that Fern might be anywhere but in this house when he returned. Edgar walked around, looking. Though his vision was weak he could tell that the house was a mess, especially the kitchen, and something was in the backyard, that, upon closer examination turned out to be the boys' teepee with bean cans strewn all around. Edgar had never known Fern to live with a mess like this, even for a day. Upstairs, he found her note on his dresser. He had to hold it two inches from his face to see it. "No," he said to himself. His hands began to shake. He imagined his children kidnapped, jailed, dead.

He called the school. "Are my children there?" he asked, finding no way to sound like anything but a horrible father.

"You don't know if your children are in school?" the secretary asked.

"I've been away. Can you just tell me please?" She took the names.

She put the phone down and he heard her clomp across the room and yell to someone. Moments passed before she came back on the line. "All present," she said. He cried when he hung up and thought about going to get them early just to have their little bodies in his arms, but he was half blind and dirty and he did not want to fumble into the school and try to explain.

He called the eye doctor to ask for new glasses. He was nervous, apologetic. "It's no trouble, Mr. Keating. We'll have a brand-new pair for you tomorrow afternoon," the singsong receptionist said. Two lenses cut to the right thickness and Edgar would get the world back.

His hands would not still. He needed to move around.

Edgar took out the almost forty watches in the case on the dresser beneath which Fern's note had been tucked. They were gifts from his father. Time had always felt as if it was collecting against him, but now it seemed like the only true treasure.

He looked at the jewelry his parents had sent Fern. Some of the pieces had never been worn: a diamond brooch in the shape of a stag, a pair of emerald earrings that would have dusted her shoulders.

Edgar leaned into his wife's closet and remembered only a few of the clothes. He should have paid closer attention. He found the blue dress she had worn when they first danced and again on the night he had tried to give Fern away to John Jefferson. He put his face into it. The silk was stiff and almost cold. He remembered the feel of her body inside and the promise of it. That was a day to keep, exactly as it had been lived then.

He looked for the red dress he had bought for her and when he could not find it he guessed that Fern had already thrown it away, which was what he wanted to do too.

Here was the accumulation of years and things. The needlepoint cover his grand-mother had made for the rocking chair with a picture of a sailboat and his name. The good table linens he and Fern never ever used because they were too nice.

Edgar, his fingers shaking, picked up the phone beside the bed and dialed his parents. No one answered. What he needed to say was not meant to be left on a machine, but he was half grateful for the gift of a blank tape instead of a person and he told himself that he had no idea where they were or how long it would be before they came home. "Mom," he said, "Dad." The air was static. "I'm ready to take over the business. I don't know if you'll still want me. Thank you for everything." He waited for an answer he knew was not coming. "I hope you're hav-ing fun wherever you are." There was more to say: that he still wanted his children to be seen for who they were instead of what they had, that he wanted them to know what it felt like to earn their own way, that he was glad he had written the novel he had, that he was sorry it would go unread. But Edgar could say those things later. He had time now. The click of the phone in the cradle marked the end of years of waiting to make this decision. It was not the ending he had imagined it would be.

The telephone rang, the exact ring it had always rung. It would be his father full of congratulations.

"Hello?" he said.

"Hello?"

"Fern?"

She had the same question he did.

"Ferny," he said. "Where are you? I love you. I miss you and I love you. I think the children have been living in the backyard." He sounded relieved. He sounded like another version of himself.

"Did you say the children have been living in the backyard?"

"I'm sorry I left," he said. "I wish I had never left."

"But you didn't leave. *I* left." There was no answer. "You left too. Oh my God."

"I called the school and they're all there. There's a teepee in the backyard and a lot of bean cans. I think they are all right. I went sailing. I was sailing to Bermuda but now I'm home. I lost my glasses. You were right about everything."

Too many things required an explanation. "I'm in California with a man, but I don't love him and I never did."

"Are you leaving me?"

She imagined their life disassembled. No wealth, the remaining family disowning them when the novel was published. Again, she imagined standing on the curb surrounded by belongings, but this time Edgar was with her and the children. They would get an apartment or a small house. They would have less of everything, but they would need less too.

"I'm ready to take over the company," he said.

"What about your book?" she asked.

"It's my job to support you."

"It's your job to love me."

When she hung up the phone, Fern thought of her mother's decision to give half the pills to her father. Fern had always assumed this was done because her mother did not think Paul could make it alone. But maybe it had simply been impossible to imagine crossing whatever it was she was about to cross without her person.

When Fern met Mac, he had eaten his eggs and bacon and ordered a second round of toast. He said, "I got you a muffin, and look." A piece of cream pie was sitting on the table, leaning slightly to one side. "No charge," he said. He was smiling.

Five days ago already felt ancient. The miles they had covered made the days seem bigger. At home, a loop between the house, school and the grocery store took a whole day. Fern and the giant had crossed mountain ranges, threaded mesas, traced a river bend for bend.

"I need to go home. Edgar tried to sail to Bermuda. My children were orphaned."

The vinyl of the seat was red, and it stuck to Fern's thighs. She peeled a leg up and sat on her hand. The waitress freshened Mac's coffee cup, and recommended the ham to Fern. She was wearing a white jumpsuit under her apron and she had redrawn her eyebrows with black pencil. The pot of black coffee was the same shape as her hair. "It's good today. Sometimes it isn't, but today it's good ham." Fern did not want to be hungry. She hated to need anything on a day like this, hated to be reminded of her mortal skin and bones, the nonnegotiables.

"Just some cereal with milk," she said.

"I don't recommend that today," the waitress said. "It's not what I'm recommending." She patted the puff of hair on her forehead that she probably thought of as bangs.

"Then I guess I'll have the ham. And toast, if you think the toast today is all right."

There was brewing disaster in the grey of the waitress's eyes. A bad storm, high winds. There was a crease in her fake eyebrows. "Toast is toast."

Mac said, "Are the kids okay?"

"They must have been terrified. Their family splintered and they were all that was left."

The ham arrived, a fat pink slap. Fern asked the waitress for an ashtray. She buttered the toast, which was already soaked in the stuff, and she spread strawberry jam on it. She cut the ham into the shape of a heart, putting the scraps on the table. It was foamy under her knife, lost water as she cut. And this was a good ham day.

Fern had stood below maple trees while James climbed the branches, waiting to catch him; she had held Cricket's cold-puckered body in the ocean and tried not to imagine her going under and being lost to a wave; she had watched Will sled down a street and hit the tree at the bottom, had run to him sure that she would find a pool of blood. Every tenth word out of her mouth for nine years had been one of caution. It was as if she had not completely let her breath out since Cricket was born. And yet they had survived on their own for five days. They had gotten themselves to school. They had eaten. Cricket, amazing and brave Cricket, Fern thought. Maybe she did not need to be so afraid. Maybe none of them did.

Mac carved the last imperfection from her ham heart. "There," he said, trying to cheer her. "A masterpiece."

A few hours away waited a valley of palms up against a mountain range, where it was warm all year and everyone wore white shorts and stayed outside and let their skin turn brown. Even in old age people moved to this valley to get too much sun. The giant's son was there and so was the airport from which Fern could fly home.

Mac worried that his boy would be leather-skinned and reptilian, no good for snow. He was worried that the boy would become pallid and malnourished if he could not eat citrus picked directly from trees in the yard, fragrant and intoxicating with their blossoms.

Fern and Mac drove, and the desert was drier and drier still. The earth felt like a bone, brittle, tired out. What grew was scrabble and cactus. Even the mountains were brown.

"It's not a smart plan," Mac said. There must have been bugs in the air because there were yellow splashes on the windshield.

"What's not?"

"I'm nobody's father."

Fern knew this feeling. The disbelonging, the nonmatch. Except that she was sure the giant would be ever tender and patient. He and the boy would talk the whole drive home, those long black stripes through the country, and all the pie. They would swim in the hotel pools and sit outside after, their skin chlorinated and warming back up. They would stop to see the snakepits and dinosaur skeletons, admire the neon signs, the roadside of their great country. The hours would be enough to become familiar to one another. What they each liked to eat. What they did to get ready for bed. Behaviors while dreaming.

Fern was sure that by the time they hit colder weather, they would be related. Maybe not father and son yet, but family.

She said, "There is every kind of father."

There were actual tumbleweeds, tumbling. As if the West had been ordered up and delivered.

They passed the Wigwam Motel, six concrete teepees scattered along the highway. There was a neon sign in the shape of a woman in a bathing cap, diving.

"We should stop for gas," Mac said. Fern knew he was stalling, but she also understood why. On every day after this one, he would have to reconquer a small heart. He would have to persuade him that algebra was important, that the essay deserved writing. Friends would need to be made, played with, dropped back off at their better houses.

With sudden breathlessness, Mac said, "Do you think she warned him?"

Fern knew what he was asking, but she pretended she did not.

"Does he know what I look like?"

She wanted to tell him that it would not matter. That the boy would not notice, used to being smaller than everyone, anyway. It could be true. But she remembered her children once. "Mother, we saw a midget.

Not just a small man but a real midget."
They crouched low to demonstrate the size.
Children knew how to do certain things
without having been taught. Climbing.
Meanness.

"He was absolutely tiny," the one had said.

"Tinier than tiny," added the other.

"And his voice was strange."

In the car Fern said to Mac, "Your son is
going to think you are marvelous."

They stopped at the service station and
Fern went inside to pay. There was a thin
old woman at the register, her hair long and
black with grey strands. Maybe she was
Indian. Maybe not. Fern only knew what
cartoon Indians looked like. On the rack
next to the counter was a tray of arrowheads
carved from obsidian. They looked like the
one Cricket had found on their dig on the
island. Fern thought of her children in the
teepee in the backyard of their Cambridge
house. Resourceful little creatures. She did
not know the story yet, but she was proud
of them. She bought three arrowheads and
put them in her pocket.

"You seen the dinosaur bones?" the
woman with the long hair asked.

"No," said Fern.

"They're real old. You ought to go. White

431

people always like to see real living Indians and real dead dinosaur bones."

Fern reported the detour to Mac and they took the dirt roads like the woman told them to. Dust kicked up. It looked like they were headed into nowhere and they were. Then, a hand-painted sign on plywood: *Dinosaur Fossil, 1.2 Miles.*

In the bush-scrub, there was a hill and as they approached they saw a near-perfect skeleton. As if the great animal had only recently lain down there for a rest. Fern had seen them in museums, these bones, and understood that such creatures had existed, but it was different to see it here in the dirt and bush, unmined. She knelt down at the skull and carefully brushed sand off the snout. The wide openness, the amount of space, made more sense when populated with huge animals.

"Plesiosaur," Mac said. "You can tell because of the little fin bones."

"How do you know that?"

"I was a five-year-old boy and a *giant.* All I thought about for years was dinosaurs."

"Did you say fins?" She looked at the endless dry land. They both pictured water covering the desert, land as ocean floor, mountains as islands. The entire world, utterly changed.

There were flies and ants and a stink bug. A crow landed, pecked, took off. "It's nice to feel small for once," the giant said.

For Fern it was good to kneel in the dirt, her hands uncovering something.

She said, "Can I tell you a secret? I took a figure drawing class last year. I didn't tell anyone because Edgar had been nagging me to go back to school and it felt like he was as disappointed in me as my mother had been. I didn't want him to win."

"What was it like?"

"The first day of figure drawing the teacher said, 'Leave if you are afraid of nudity.' No one had left. At the second meeting there had been four fewer people in the room. The teacher had said, 'Good, I'm glad they left. There's no room in art for fear.' "

One day, Fern said, the students had walked into the room and there was a black man on the platform. He was tall and muscular and very dark, his hair short and neat. Fern had been taken aback by her own discomfort. Most of the women kept their eyes locked on their papers. "At one point the man looked right at me and we just stared at each other for maybe three seconds. A hundred years ago there were plenty of times when a black man stood naked in front of a room of dressed whites because he was *for sale.* People in my family were in those rooms. I didn't deserve to look at this man, but he did deserve to be seen."

"There are some things that can't be righted," Mac said. "It's good to name them."

She took a deep breath. "I'm sort of relieved that that money is gone. We'll find a better way to earn our living." There were so many questions for her at home — money, love, lies, three children who had been abandoned for nearly a week. She looked out at the desert where there was so much room in which to get lost. She wanted something to press up against. She wanted her own confines.

"What about the steel company?"

"No." It had been hanging in the back of her mind, the image of Edgar calling his editor to say that he had to retract the book. The image of him at a huge oval table in the teetering tip of a skyscraper and a dozen investors who wanted to know how he had cut production costs. "I think I'd rather live with nothing." She could have used another shirt and pants, but otherwise what she had in her suitcase was sufficient. She wanted her people and she wanted water and wind. Enough — just enough.

Fern took the giant's hand.

"I like you," she said.

He did not squeeze her hand, but he let it sit there in his big palm, salt-wet on this hot day. He said, "We came a long way."

"I hope I didn't hurt you."

He smiled his big smile. "I knew you were trouble from the moment I married you." He looked down at her. "I like you too, Fern. I think you're going to have a really good life. You are not only a rich housewife."

"Not anymore. I'll need to get a job." She was joking but she was also serious.

"Life is effortful," said Mac. "That's the way it's supposed to be. It's good to have work to do."

Fern thought of hiding in the tall grass outside her mother's prairie studio to watch her work. Evelyn was a different woman with clay than she was with people — it was as if the rest of her body was only there to support the existence of her hands. She thought of Edgar, up late all those years at the typewriter, his fingers banging out a reason for his being. She thought of Ben in the earth, the misunderstood parts long since rotted away. So many bones in the ground.

This dinosaur skeleton was a body plus time. They all were. The question was what they wanted to do and who they wanted to love in the years when muscle and skin still covered them.

Fern walked with Mac up to the house where the boy lived because it was a nice thing to do and she could not think of the giant standing at the door alone, his too-big finger finding the bell. She could not think of him waiting alone for someone to let him in.

The house was split-level, brown on the outside, gravel instead of grass. A group of tall green-brown cacti kept watch. There were bird holes — even in those spiny stalks, a home.

A woman opened the door, short and blond and overtan. She said, "It's my old man," and laughed hard. She punched him in the stomach, which was nearly eye-level and Fern thought of them as husband and wife, trying to consummate. She would have been lost in it all. Those rigid, manic little arms, looking for purchase on his hills. Poor girl. Poor boy.

"Lovely home," Fern said. It was not. There was almost no furniture and the windows were covered in heavy curtains. The organ-pink carpet could not possibly have been an intentional color. This was the kind of house you holed up in after the murder, the body buried in some dry wash nearby.

"I have cold coffee or I have gin," the lady said.

"Just some water for me," Fern said.

"No water. Sorry."

The air conditioner was on so high Fern could feel her pores closing to keep the heat in. Mac rubbed his arms.

"Nothing then?" Claire asked.

They sat on the couch and Mac asked after her months and years. She answered him like a daughter swatting away her father's concerns. "Doing great! I love living here! It's warm all year! We have a pool! Desert people are nicer than city people! My guy's name is Dale and he's a real sweetheart!"

"And the boy?" he asked finally, after he had waited long enough for her to bring him up.

"He's fine," she said. "He'll be fine. Doesn't talk much, but he's lost some of the weight."

From a cracked door down the hall, Fern caught sight of a pair of eyes high off the ground.

"I'm parched," Claire said. "Neither of you wants any coffee at all? It's nice and

437

cold. I made it up this morning."

Fern wanted to ask for a blanket or a scarf instead. Claire left the room and she nudged Mac, motioned to the hallway and the cracked door.

Mac, without a pause, knelt on the floor like someone trying to befriend a cat. He put his hands out towards the eyes, peering. He scooted closer, his palms up. "Hey there," he loud-whispered. "Hello, hello."

Fern wanted to kneel too, to beckon, but she was no one's mother here. She was no one's aunt or step-. It did not seem right to promise friendship this close to the end. So she sat there in the freezing dark room and watched the giant try to make himself small, watched him shuffle across the dirty floor towards his son, his hands empty but open. She had to pace to survive the thirst for her own children.

The boy came through the door. The mother tinked ice into a glass in the kitchen and said something about golf. The boy, seeing his father, knelt down too and, on the pink carpet, under a painting of a Jesus so pale he was nearly translucent, the two looked each other over. They did not say a word. They did not shake hands. They just looked.

■ ■ ■ ■

The boy was hungry, frantically hungry. Sitting on the hotel bed, he ate a whole chicken and a loaf of white bread and a bag of individually wrapped chocolates. He seemed more dog, more stray, than boy. But he said his pleases and thank-yous, and his fingers were delicate, carefully working the meat off a bone without getting dirty.

Fern and Mac sat in the pink paisley chairs by the window watching. "More?" they asked, handing him bread.

Before they'd left, his mother had given him a packed suitcase and an extra pair of sneakers. "You can't imagine how fast he goes through these things," she had said. "How he does it, that's beyond me." She had stood on her tip-toes and flicked him on the nose with her thumb. "Honey pot," she had said. "Don't get any bigger." She had opened her wallet and taken out a scroll of paper on which was written several columns of numbers. "If you want to measure him, you can," she said to the giant. "But I guess you don't care one way or the other. He's not getting any smaller, so he's yours now." The boy had bent down low and given his mother a hug. She had been

439

lost in his frame. "How did I raise up something like you?" she had asked. "Something so sweet." The twang in her voice was unconvincing. She wore it like heels she did not know how to walk in.

The boy brushed his teeth for fifteen minutes, making tiny circles over each tooth, studying himself in the mirror. From behind he looked like a man. Fern wanted him to be all right. She wanted to hug him. She wanted the son of him, and her the pretend mother. She had not meant to actually do it. She had meant to admire from the other end of the room. There she was, next thing, squeezing him hard, her head on his wingbone, no stopping now. He was softly sweated in the day's shirt, and all the heat she had hoped for. Fern could hear the boy's breath inside his body, inside the papery folds of his lungs, inside the rattle of bones. She could hear his heart too, gathering and sending back. It seemed fast to her.

The boy, gentle or afraid, did not move. They stayed there, and Fern did not know how to let go.

Mac, on the other side of the room, also waited. Everyone needed everything. The woman needed to hug the boy and imagine her brother, her sons, her daughter; the boy needed to be hugged but then to be freed.

440

Mac would have liked someone to come up from behind and wrap her arms around him, and to mean it, beyond the dare she had made for herself, beyond the attempt at revenge. If only he could meet a huge woman, he thought. In a huge house, with a huge car, and so much land for them to drive on, and herds of only the largest animals: elephants and giraffes, the stamp of rhinoceros feet in the mud after a rain. They would put off going to town for supplies, put off relativity. You can't be too big unless someone else is small. Mac looked at his son. He looked like he still had growing to do. He would get bigger every day with chicken and bread and pie and steak and all the things for sale in restaurants and grocery stores across the great land. They would order four meals for two people, and Mac would watch his boy eating. A match, finally. More and more a match by the day.

There was Fern, at his son's back, and neither one his.

Mac said, "There's dessert. There could be. Does anyone want pie?"

Outside: wind, sirens.

That night, the boy slept hard in one bed and Fern and Mac, fully clothed, shared the other. They passed a cigarette back and forth. The room echoed with Matthew's rattling breath. He hardly even shifted in his young sleep. The giant hugged Fern. There is such a thing as love in this room, he wanted to say. We are capable. Even though we feel too tired or too big or too old or too young or too quiet or too loud or too formed or too unformed.

"What do you think will happen when you get home?" Mac whispered.

"I don't know. It has never been easy to be a wife or a mother or a woman or a man or a child," she said. "But we are each other's family." He understood this. In the bed nearby was a stranger, but it was also a son.

Things could go all different ways and this was one of them: two drivers, on the other side of the country about to head home. The next day, a father and son would get into the car to begin another kind of family. A wife would get on a plane and go home to the family that she belonged to.

Miss Nolan took Cricket down to the office where the secretary said, "Your father just called to see if you were in school. Are you getting into trouble, young lady?"

"Is he home? Did he say if he was home?"

"He said he had been away."

442

Cricket did not wait for more information or to explain herself or to ask for permission. She ran to the boys' classroom and grabbed their hands and together they sprinted the ten blocks to their house. Miss Nolan did not chase them and she did not allow the secretary to call the principal. "They're all right," she said. "Let them go."

The air hurt the children's lungs and they did not slow down.

They found Edgar standing in the light of the refrigerator. The house was clean. It looked the way it used to before the children were alone. They fell on him like prey. He sat down on the floor and they crawled onto him and they smelled like the outdoors. He kissed them five thousand times, it felt like, and it was not nearly enough. "Are you okay?" he asked. "Are you all okay?"

They said, "We buried a fawn and lived in the yard and we didn't know if you were ever coming back and where is Mother and we're hungry for something other than beans and we're sorry if we did something to make you go away and is Maggie here too and we don't want to be orphans and where have you been and please stay."

"I'm staying," Edgar said. "I'm staying, I'm staying. Mother is coming home too. And the vet called and Maggie is there.

Weren't you answering the phone?"

"We were afraid of orphanages," Cricket said.

"What if it had been Mother or me?"

"Take us to get Maggie," the boys shouted.

"I can't drive right now. I lost my glasses and I can't really see." Edgar looked at Cricket hard, and in the blur, she was herself. "Do you remember once when I sent your mother flowers and they came in a vase full of marbles that you thought were treasure and for months you always had a marble in your hand, even when you went to bed?"

Cricket did not remember but that did not matter because someone else did. She was not the only one carrying the story of her life. That's what she needed her parents to be, more than caregivers: keepers of the selves she had grown out of.

"I missed you so much," he said. "I'm sorry if it sounds stupid to say."

"Not stupid," she told him.

"We could walk to the vet if you want."

"We want," the boys said.

The children would be angry later, but now it was too good to be home and not alone. For the rest of the afternoon and evening they all moved as a clump. Edgar needed Cricket to read the labels on everything and the children needed to be close to the person whose job it was to care for them. Together they went down into the basement and found pork chops in the big freezer and together they cooked them in the pan with onion and white wine and together they steamed frozen peas and together they buttered them and together they walked to pick up the dog who licked and jumped and yelped with the fevered joy they all felt and together, children, father and dog all went to sleep on Fern and Edgar's bed, legs over legs, arms over arms, faces pressed into the soft pillows. The burden of Edgar's family was beautiful. Heavy and beautiful.

1976

The airplane took a few hours to cover what had taken five days in the car. Beneath Fern passed the desert, ridges of dinosaur remains in the hillside, cows, weather. The earth looked painted — red jags of canyons rimmed with gold. An hour later the earth was covered in trees. From this high up, time too felt condensed: in those green swaths was coal, steel, money. In those green swaths her people had owned other people; black boys had been hung from the trees; her people had freed their slaves, fought for the freeing of all slaves; her people had moved north, and as privilege allowed them, the memory of what they had done receded; Fern had lived on that same soil on a base where American bodies were taught to kill Vietnamese bodies; the black boys and brown boys went to the jungle and some of the white boys did too. Her twin was down there someplace in the thick green swath, buried in a box. But that was only his bones, and by now those hardly felt true: he was here, always here. Life and love had separated Fern and Ben, but they could not be unjoined.

The clouds had thickened beneath the plane and Fern could not see that they flew right over the sharp jut of the Chicago skyline. Above the prairie where Evelyn had failed at motherhood, a job she had never asked for, and succeeded at art, the job she was meant to do; above the porch swing where her father had rocked through the last headache of his life, through the dazzle of the aura, the beat of pain and the feeling of near weightlessness hours later when he finally opened his eyes, released; above the spot at the base of the stone angel where Ben had sat on the morning before he went away for basic training, wings blocking the wind and a view of the grass grown summer-tall; above the wooded lanes where Edgar's parents' house was empty after the summer season, where Mary and Hugh would return over Christmas, the whole landscape trans-formed by a heavy snowfall, where they would drink hot toddies and let go, for the last time, of the idea of the son they had meant to have. Fern was high above that life, those lives — would always be — and

447

asleep by then, her head on a balled-up sweater. Outside, ice had formed on the window and the sky was white and jagged with light.

Fern stood outside her own house. From a distance it looked like a replica. A model of a gracious family home on a nighttime street, the light from within unnaturally warm. Figures inside. A man, sitting at the table, and his children moving around him, bringing dishes. There was no wife in the scene yet. A wife could be upstairs with a headache. Maybe her husband would go to her after he ate, bring her a plate on a tray, a folded napkin, a fork and knife and a glass of water. Maybe he would sit with her while she ate, rub her feet, keep his voice low. A wife could be out for the evening with a friend taking Italian lessons and drinking wine after, pretending to be in Tuscany, in a sundress, in summer. A wife could be in the kitchen taking a pie out of the oven. A wife could be at school, studying the particulars of a dinosaur knuckle. A wife could be at work.

Fern stood on the street. She smoked two cigarettes in a row and then crushed the rest of the pack under foot and put it back in her bag. With her she carried a suitcase within which were pieces of clothing that belonged to the family inside. They were ironed and neatly folded. She also had her own roadworn clothes, dirty and familiar and full of the big country's dust and grit. Plains dirt and swamp water, desert. She was whole, which she had not understood before. She wanted those others in her arms — when they were it would not be completion but addition. Each of them entire.

Fern waited to go inside. It was such a beautiful family and she wanted to hold the picture still.

The man stood up from the table after a while, and he was unsteady. The eldest child went to him, gave him her wrist to hold and walked him through the house. Though he was being led, this man did not look lost — maybe he never was.

Fern and Edgar, awake late that night, would begin to sort through their things to see what they could sell for money. Fern would walk him through the house, describing the offerings. "What about the oak bookshelf? It's the one piece of furniture we kept from Tennessee." They went to the kitchen. "I think your mother gave us this crystal bowl. We've never used it. Here is the cutting board with our wedding date on it, and the candlesticks. These ivory-handled scissors — careful, here is the safe end — belonged to someone in one of our families, but I don't remember who." Edgar could see if he held the objects close enough. In doing so, he looked ancient.

In the yellow kitchen light, she handed him the tiny silver spoon his parents had sent when Cricket was a baby. Edgar pressed his thumb into the cool curve. He remembered that little mouth mashing at a banana, taking one more step towards humanness. On the handle was a small ruby. James's spoon had a sapphire and Will's an emerald. Edgar had hated these gifts for their grotesque indulgence: Shouldn't the babies have been treasure enough?

"I still think my parents were wrong about the objects, the things. But they were right about time. They were right about pleasure. We should go to the Caribbean with them. Before we have to sell the summerhouse we should stay for the year even if we never leave the bedroom with the woodstove in it."

Fern thought of their own big country, the way her pulse had changed the moment she was outside the range of home. "Are you afraid of losing your parents when your book comes out?"

450

He was quiet for a long time. "It might not be worth it to publish the book," he said. He was afraid that Fern would be angry — all those years she had taken care of their life so that he could write his novel. "They are my parents."

"You spent so long." It was the last thing she expected him to give up.

"There are more stories," he said. "There is other work to do."

He opened a drawer and put his hand inside tentatively, unsure what it contained. It was full of collars. Together, they remembered each one. Rosie and Rufus, both hit by cars; Marty, given away when he could not be housebroken; Lucy, sweet, droopeyed Lucy, the only one to get old before she died; Tex, Bessie, Flower.

"Maggie did not get lost," he said, offering her a chance to explain.

Fern told him that she had thought Maggie had been miserable, aged. "Bad hips, bad eyes. I wanted to save her from that."

"Bad eyes," he repeated.

Edgar looked older too. His hair had the first grey in it and his eyebrows were longer. "Can I do something?" Fern asked.

Edgar expected to feel her lips on his. He waited for it. His breath changed. They would kiss eventually, but she did not feel

451

ready to give it yet. Instead, she put her hand on his cheek and said, "Careful. Don't move." She took something out of the drawer and he heard the high whine of a pair of small scissors, closing over his eyebrow. She blew on his forehead to clear the trimmed hairs and did the other side.

"I thought I could solve everything difficult by loving you," Fern said.

"I thought I could solve everything difficult by trying to understand it." They were both half right.

From the back of her closet, Fern produced the small box in which she kept the things she had always been most afraid to lose: locks of her children's hair, her brother's last note to her, a photo of her and Edgar on the night they had first danced. He touched them. That was all she wanted from him — to take what mattered to her into his hands.

The things that Edgar wanted to keep, Fern taped a note to. *Edgar,* the notes said. All over the house, his name. The bookshelf was Edgar, the glass vase — Fern was surprised by the things he cared about, by the resting places for his nostalgia. The bedside table was Edgar, the coatrack, the crystal bowl, two old milk-crates that they had stored magazines in. The collars.

"We can throw them away," Fern said.

"You don't want them?"

Fern did not. It was safe to be less loveable now. "The animals are for the children. You all are the ones I'm here to take care of. And myself."

She took a few steps away from him, let him stand there alone in the house in which they had lived, one of the many attempts they had made at their marriage. She watched her husband, her love, nearly sightless. He looked like a headless flower, just a stem. She forgave him and did not yet. She was more his and less than she had been. Ahead of them were years of pulling closer and years of pushing away and years of pulling closer again. The children would grow up and maybe they would talk every day or maybe years would pass between calls. Will and James would become two men and lead two lives and yet they would always be twins. That was what it was to love someone across the duration, for the entirety.

"Fern?" Edgar asked. She had backed far enough away that he couldn't see her.

She did not answer him right away. She went to the light switch and flicked it off so that the two of them were standing in the same darkness. She let him ask the question again, until she could tell that it hurt him to

453

say her name, so badly did he want her on the other end of it.

ACKNOWLEDGMENTS

My boundless, heartswollen, jumping-up-and-down thanks to:

My teachers, who are never not with me when I write: Michelle Latiolais, Ron Carlson, Geoffrey Wolff, Christine Schutt, Brad Watson, Amy Gerstler, Doug Anderson and Jackie Levering-Sullivan.

My editor, Sarah McGrath, whose insights opened this novel up. Thank you for taking such ridiculously good care of my work.

PJ Mark, who is always exactly the person I want on the other end of a draft (and a question and a joke and an idea, etc., etc.) and to Marya Spence for smarts and welcome.

Matt Sumell, Michael Andreason, Marisa Matarazzo: mighty indeed.

Elliot Holt for being a gatherer of writers, just when I most needed it.

Everyone at Riverhead, especially: Claire McGinnis and Katie Freeman (!!), Geoff

Kloske, Danya Kukafka, Kate Stark, Jynne Martin, and Glory Plata.

Glenn Schaeffer, the International Center for Writing and Translation at UC Irvine, the Squaw Valley Community of Writers, the Tin House Writers' Conference, the Bread Loaf Writers' Conference, the Sewanee Writers' Conference for generous and much appreciated support.

Jon Davis and the faculty and students at Institute of American Indian Arts for infusing my year with wisdom, humor, stories and conversations about stories.

Several books were especially helpful in the writing of this novel: *Sailing Alone Around the World* by Joshua Slocum, *Class: A Guide Through the American Status System* by Paul Fussell and *Old Money* by Nelson W. Aldrich, Jr.

The Ragdale Foundation, for continuing to be a place where art is made.

My unimaginably great family: my parents for forever-faith, my dear sister, my amazing in-laws, my uncles and aunts and cousins and cousin-lets.

My friends, especially the lifelong variety: Melissa McNeely, Phoebe Waldendziak, Kari Hennigan, Byron Thayer, Ashby Lankford, Lauren Coleman and Margaux Sanchez.

Teo: for every mega-good thing you do every day forever, whoa.

Clay: for providing gorgeous, unflagging gusto.

Prairie: you were my inside companion while I finished this book and I feel sure that you made magic happen. This one is for and because of you, Miss Lemon Pie.

ABOUT THE AUTHOR

Ramona Ausubel is a graduate of the MFA program at the University of California, Irvine. She is the author of the novel *No One Is Here Except All of Us* and the short story collection *A Guide to Being Born*. Her work has been published in *The New Yorker, One Story, The Paris Review Daily, Best American Fantasy,* and elsewhere, and has received special mentions in *The Best American Short Stories* and *The Best American Nonrequired Reading.* She has been longlisted for The Frank O'Connor Short Story Prize, and a finalist for the New York Public Library Young Lions award and the Pushcart Prize.